INTO THE CAULDRON

LEE JACKSON

Severn River Publishing
www.SevernRiverPublishing.com

ISBN: 978-1-64875-597-2 (Paperback)

ALSO BY LEE JACKSON

The After Dunkirk Series

After Dunkirk

Eagles Over Britain

Turning the Storm

The Giant Awakens

Riding the Tempest

Driving the Tide

Into the Cauldron

Storming the Reich

The Reluctant Assassin Series

The Reluctant Assassin

Rasputin's Legacy

Vortex: Berlin

Fahrenheit Kuwait

Target: New York

Never miss a new release! Sign up to receive exclusive updates from author Lee Jackson.

severnriverbooks.com

Dedicated to the Memory of
Christine Granville
née
Maria Krystyna Janina Skarbeck of Poland
codenamed: "Pauline"
Her warmth and friendliness encouraged many.
Her courage and intrepidness saved countless thousands.
In the annals of heroes and heroines, she ranks at the top as
"Churchill's favorite spy."
The debt we owe for the freedom we enjoy can never be repaid,
As it is also owed to
Every Resistance member who fought the Nazis in WWII.

PROLOGUE

June 6, 1944
Sark, Guernsey Bailiwick, Channel Islands

Through her front window, Dame Marian Littlefield watched the German doctor and the *Wehrmacht* staff officer accompanying him approach the *Seigneurie*, her ancestral home, which also served as her official seat of government. The island, a British possession, remained the oldest feudal system in the western world, with her family having administered there as benevolent rulers for the past two hundred years.

Sark had been occupied by the Germans since the outset of hostilities in 1940. Marian had implored the residents to remain on the island to preserve its culture, steadfast in the belief that Great Britain would prevail. Every one of them had stayed, including some who had considered accepting Prime Minister Winston Churchill's offer to evacuate them. Since then, the entire population had suffered under the German regime's occupation that regimented their lives, imposed curfews, strung barbed wire along the coastline and around their fields, restricted their fishermen, reduced food and ordinary supplies necessary to live, and in every way obliterated the islanders' customary quality of life. The people's suffering evolved into Marian's sense of guilt for convincing them to stay.

They continued to support her for the way she held against German officialdom, and her obstinacy garnered her a measure of German respect. Owing to the Guernsey Bailiwick's status as the only British soil that the Germans occupied and thus its propaganda value, Berlin was careful in its handling of the islands, including Sark, and of Marian and her family members. She exploited that caution on behalf of her people, whom she considered to be friends.

She had just finished her breakfast of fried mashed potatoes and ersatz coffee, less than satisfying but the most readily available current sources of early morning sustenance, when the doctor and his escort appeared. She went immediately into her library, and listened as her two white poodles barked their alarm. Moments later, her housekeeper escorted the two men into the book-lined room.

Marian was aware that the escort, a *Wehrmacht* officer, was sent along to spy on the doctor. Since the beginning of the occupation, she had known a series of German army doctors who administered to the island's ill and infirm, and all of them had been nice men, dedicated to their practice. Each had, on occasion, dropped pieces of information pertinent to the war that she might find useful. Each time one did so, he required the officer-escort to leave the room, ostensibly out of concern for patient privacy, so that the doctor could discuss confidential matters with Dame Marian.

This morning, as soon as the two were shown into the library, the doctor dismissed his escort. Waiting until the door was closed, he indicated the need for quiet with a finger to his mouth, then took Marian's elbow and nudged her to the farthest corner. "I have news," he whispered. "The Allies invaded France at Normandy." His eyes widened for emphasis. "This morning."

Before Marian could act startled or thank him, he said loudly enough to be heard at least in muffled tones beyond the door, "About this patient, Mrs. —"

Marian smiled obliquely. She had heard the news earlier over the BBC on a radio she kept hidden in her storage room at the back of the mansion, under threat of death.

June 11, 1944
Guam, Mariana Islands

In his earlier years, US Navy radioman George Tweed never would have thought that the most beautiful sound he would hear in his life was that of American bombers flying over Guam's northwest coast. He had been eating breakfast deep inside a fissure among the cliffs, where he had taken refuge to avoid capture by Japanese troops, when the air resounded with the deep-throated roar of many engines flying above the clouds on this gray morning.

He rushed to his lookout. The planes' steady drone sent a comforting thrill through him such that he had to steady himself to keep from falling down the three-hundred-foot cliff onto the wave-drenched rocks below. Then a break in the overcast sky revealed the aircraft, and in that moment, long silvery tubes dropped from their bellies. The sun glinted from the bombs' skins as they fell and then faded from view below the clouds, plunging into Agaña Harbor a few miles to the southwest. Moments later, their explosions rolled across the waters, muted by thick foliage along the coastline.

As the sounds of the aircraft faded, Tweed leaned against the cliff wall and breathed deeply. *Perhaps rescue will come. All I have to do is stay alive.*

1

June 12, 1944
Bréville-les-Monts, France

British Army Lieutenant Colonel Paul Littlefield watched in dismay as a distant battle unfolded. Artillery carrier rounds streaked across the night sky and released flares, which then descended on tiny parachutes, illuminating the battlefield in ghostly light. They were joined by their invisible high-explosive companions hissing to their targets, falling on them with thunderous impact. The ground trembled. Small arms popped and crackled, and machine guns spit out tracers amid their rhythmic cacophony. The skirmish was going terribly awry.

Paul stood in the churchyard of Saint-Pierre de Bréville-les-Monts less than two miles from where the firefight raged in the fields southwest of and belonging to Château Saint-Côme. Not even forty-eight hours earlier, another disastrous battle had taken place in the same locale. Germans occupying a position in a tree line east of the château had presented a potentially major threat to the Allied beachhead's northeastern perimeter. The British 12th Parachute Battalion of the 6th Airborne Division had been sent in to clean them out.

Having fought across North Africa, the battalion was combat-hardened.

However, its strength had been reduced by casualties to only a hundred and fifty men by successive charges against a German shore battery at Merville that had threatened the landing at Sword Beach. Finally occupying that objective after fierce two-day fighting, the battalion moved on and arrived at the château in Bréville two days ago.

There, they learned the hard way that they must adopt new tactics. They started across a field in line abreast as they had done in the African deserts, only to be mowed down by German machine guns positioned behind hedgerows.

Hedgerows had proven to be a major obstacle across the Normandy front. For centuries, farmers there had fenced in their fields by piling rocks along their properties' boundaries. They overlaid the rocks with a thick layer of dirt, the resulting formation rising to roughly five feet, crowned with hedges and trees. The resulting quilt-like tapestry of verdant fields enclosed by thick foliage dominated the forty-mile front and proved deadly to the attacking infantry and armor forces.

For armor units, the greatest danger occurred when they attempted to break through the hedgerows. In doing so, they encountered the unyielding stone bases, and the tanks' fronts rose into the air, exposing their vulnerable bellies. German anti-tank weapons made swift work of them.

For infantry, the threat came from German machine guns positioned at the corners of the fields, opposite the direction of the attacking forces, and ensconced in thick foliage. The fire they delivered, accompanied by small-arms spread out behind thick cover between them, was murderous.

A further disadvantage of attacking through the hedgerows was that the enemy knew the terrain and had been digging in for weeks. Even Allied air supremacy, gained in fierce dogfights over Great Britain, North Africa, Italy, and already a hundred miles deep over France, had proven to be of minor effect over Normandy because the Nazi fortifications had been reinforced with concrete and steel, and because the sunken roads and lanes between the fields were covered by thick tree canopies, thereby obscuring targets.

The challenge presented by the hedgerows, called "*bocages*," was not entirely unexpected. The army had trained for them in similar terrain in Ireland. However, the stony bases under the soil had been unanticipated as had the full-grown trees obscuring them. Advancing by inches rather than miles in "bocage country" had thus become a major and deadly frustration across the front.

Paul hardly believed that six days had passed since he led two troops of French commandos ashore at Sword Beach on D-Day. Officially, he was their commander, but he had full faith and confidence in *Capitaine* Philippe Kieffer of General Charles de Gaulle's Free French army. The Allies had flipped the army in Algeria away from the Vichy-French regime, which owed its allegiance to Nazi Germany.

Despite his formal position as commander of the French commando battalion, Paul's role had been largely that of liaison. Because of his combat experience and French language proficiency, he had been recruited for the position by Brigadier Simon Fraser, 15th Lord Fraser of Lovat, commander of the 1st Special Service Brigade under the British 6th Airborne Division. Given the importance of the Normandy landing, Lovat had insisted on at least a mid-grade officer with a combat-experienced officer who was fluent in French to command the French commandos during the landing and initial actions immediately thereafter. However, the French captain, Kieffer, had proven himself capable and had, in fact, been the officer who had conceived, organized, and led the French commandos.

Kieffer had subordinated himself and his troops to British command willingly for the chance to fight for France on his home soil, and he was the first man onshore. His troops needed no urging. Intent on re-taking their homeland from the German invaders, they had set about their mission swiftly and competently. Facing light resistance, within an hour of landing, they were in position to support British paratroopers in securing a bridge, codenamed "Pegasus," south of the village of Ouistreham astride the Orne River on the road to Caen.

Capturing Caen had been a main Allied objective on D-Day. Situated along the Orne ten miles inland from Sword Beach, the city was a major intersection for road and railway traffic and was within striking distance of the German border, four hundred miles due east. The overall plan had been to secure a beachhead along the Normandy coast from Ouistreham in the east to Grandcamp-Maisy in the west, and then to charge inland to expand the perimeter and seize Caen and Saint-Lô, two towns with major crossroads within a short distance of Normandy's coast. However, both remained in German hands. The plan had been thwarted by the bocage.

The Germans had put up stiff resistance, but initially, their forces had been deployed in other areas in reaction to Allied deception operations intended to draw enemy units away from Normandy's beaches and the amphibious landing. On D-Day+1, the *Wehrmacht* mounted a major counterattack along the Allies' southern perimeter. It had been repulsed, but the bocage slowed Allied forward movement to a crawl.

Brigadier Lovat's No. 4 Commando, after meeting its assigned D-Day objectives, had been seconded to the 12th Parachute Battalion and set up defensive positions at Ranville, a village adjacent to Bréville, on the east side of the river. There, because *Capitaine* Kieffer had demonstrated his combat effectiveness and required only an interpreter/liaison of lesser rank, Paul had relinquished command to him and joined Lovat's operations staff.

German artillery salvos had preceded vicious German counterattacks at both villages, and they continued for two days. They were repulsed each time. This morning, those against Ranville had subsided, but they continued at Bréville.

Lovat had gone to Bréville to observe the fighting and to see how he might support his neighboring commander. He had taken members of his staff with him, including Paul.

A 51st (Highlanders) Division field artillery section had set up in a field behind the church. The reports from their guns were loud and their reverberations shook the ground. Flames burst from their muzzles, lighting up the ground around them.

Paul had wondered about the wisdom of observing from a position forward of the guns. A short round could eliminate the entire command group. However, the position in front of the church provided the best vantage for observing the battle, and Lovat deemed the risk to be small. So, Paul swallowed his angst and followed along.

For a moment, Paul reflected on a similar scene he had experienced as he prepared to attack a village at the base of Monte Cassino in Italy. He shook his head in disbelief. *That was only six months ago.*

A fragment of a memory entered his mind. It was the same one that had flashed before his eyes back then. It was a frequent memory now, one he wished he could erase even while he cherished it, of a little girl, her body still warm, her terrified face untouched but for the tears that were still wet on her cheeks. Clutching a dust-covered teddy bear, she was alone in her home, which had just been demolished by exploding artillery. Apparently, a shock wave had snuffed out her life.

Paul had wished then, and he wished now, that he could have held and protected her and seen her eyes and lips flash a bright smile. Instead, he had carried her to her grave in a non-descript, remote hamlet. Now he wondered whose homes would be destroyed by guns tonight, which children would lie lifeless when the terrible projectiles exploded, and how many more innocents this war would consume.

He wandered away from where Lovat stood with the other staff members. By the light of a waning half-moon, the worn stone structure of the little ancient church braced pale against the night sky. In the field behind the building, the artillery batteries, lined up in a row, launched salvo after salvo. Paul watched, fascinated by the yellow flames shooting from the barrels of each gun, the rising smoke, and the thunderous noise as the rounds arced over the battlefield.

A change in sound caught his attention. A hiss turned into a whistle and grew louder. An improbable short round was heading straight toward the church.

Suddenly, those Paul loved and held most dear flashed through his mind: his mother and stepfather, Marian and Stephen; his siblings, Claire, Lance, and Jeremy. An image of Ryan Northbridge seemed to materialize too, the woman he adored who had been snatched away, shot down while ferrying a bomber to its forward position. Now, the vision of her appeared almost real enough to touch.

His chest caught. He whirled about and called out a warning. An instant later, he heard a thunderous clap, saw billowing smoke all around, and for a brief moment, he felt himself being thrown through the air by a shock wave.

2

June 13, 1944
Villers-Bocage, France

British Second Lieutenant Derek Horton quelled terror rising from his gut into his throat and tingling along his arms and legs. At the other end of this tiny village, a Tiger tank maneuvered around a corner. It took no pains to hide its presence behind standing rubble of ruined homes. Instead, its powerful 88 mm cannon rotated slowly to the left.

Inside the locked-down war monster's turret, Horton knew, a set of eyes belonging to a seasoned veteran searched for a new target. And Horton's tank squatted in the middle of the next intersection with nothing to hide it from the Tiger.

His Firefly, a modified Sherman M4 with a 76.2 mm gun, was more of a match for the Tiger than a regular Sherman M4, which had proven all but ineffective against the German behemoths in head-to-head firefights. The Germans had developed the Tiger in response to the Soviet T-34, giving up speed and maneuverability in exchange for thicker armor, greater firepower, and more reliability. An advanced tread design allowed the Tigers to travel over rougher ground with a smoother ride, but they tended to bog down in mud and snow due to their added weight. Once damaged by natural elements, repairing them in a field setting was untenable. Hence, Soviet commanders planned attacks against Tiger units during the coldest and wettest times of any day.

But this was neither the Soviet Union nor a cold or wet day.

The last week had been a blur to Horton. After landing at Arromanches on D-Day, surviving the landing at Jig Green sector of Gold Beach, the murderous ground-level machine gun fire, and the race to the dubious shelter of a sea wall, he had then led his platoon of Sherwood Rangers Yeomanry back across the beach to retrieve their Fireflies. On re-grouping, he had learned to his dismay that his platoon commander had "bought the farm" during the first moments of the landing, and that he, Horton, now led the platoon.

This was the second such instance in less than a year, the previous one having occurred at Anzio. He relished neither the added responsibility nor the cause of his promotion, the loss of his immediate superior. After the latter occurrence, he had been elevated in the field to his current junior officer rank.

Despite the scale of early casualties, the objectives of the British 5th Division landing on Gold Beach had remained the same: secure a beachhead, capture Arromanches to the west, press in the same direction to establish contact with American forces at Omaha Beach, take Bayeux to the north, and link up with the Canadian forces at Juno Beach on the eastern flank.

The Sherwood Rangers' mission was to support the 1st Hampshires in capturing German headquarters at Le Hamel Surrain, which controlled the coastal weaponry in their sector, including four 150 mm guns at Longues-sur-Mer. Difficulties at the outset, including landing too far from shore and west of the intended spot, had resulted in many Hampshire casualties from drownings and withering enemy machine gun fire.

The Sherwoods had also encountered trouble. Their tanks arrived separately, late, farther down the beach than intended, and in the opposite direction from the Hampshires. Nevertheless, the Sherwoods and Hampshires had coalesced on the sand within the shadows of the enemy guns and traversed the length of Jig Green Gold for two and a half miles under blistering fire to knock out and capture the gun position at Longues-sur-

Mer. They took several prisoners, finding that most of them were men in their forties or older who were in shock, not only at the mass of men, ships, and machines streaming to the shore they occupied, but also that it was happening at all.

The Sherwoods and Hampshires delivered their prisoners to a guard detail established for the purpose, continued along the beach, and cut inland. Heading south, they circled to take Le Hamel from its rear. Meanwhile, other units at Gold linked up with the Canadians on the left and the Americans on the right. By 19:00 hours, the beachhead had been secured all along Normandy. Expansion of the perimeter and a build-up of supplies and reinforcements began and, in the Gold sector, preparations went into place for an assault on Bayeux.

Then the next day, a French civilian with a message made his way to the beach and was swiftly escorted to British headquarters. The *Wehrmacht* had vacated Bayeux, he told the astonished commanders, and the Allies could enter unopposed.

Word spread quickly of the joyous reception of Allied troops into the first French city to be liberated. As the convoys rumbled through the town and the defensive positions abandoned by the *Wehrmacht*, women and children lined the streets and showered the troops with flowers, kisses, and many bottle of Calvados, the local brandy.

The Allies had been frustrated in not seizing Bayeux and Caen on the first day of the invasion. Both cities were important crossroads for moving troops and supplies across northern France to liberate the country and threaten Germany. Now, with Bayeux under Allied control, General Bernard Montgomery, then the Allied ground commanding general in France, decided to attack Caen from two sides in a pincer.

An unexpected quiet fell over the Allied front south of Bayeux, even as British and Canadian divisions continued fierce combat on the left flank, and as the US First Army under General Omar Bradley fought to liberate Cherbourg within the Cotentin Peninsula on the right. Controlling ports, major roads, and railways was key to winning, and seizing Cherbourg, Bayeux, and Caen would ensure clear avenues over a major section of northern France.

Horton and his tank crews had settled in to enjoy a few days of relative tranquility. His thoughts wandered to Chantal Boulier, the French girl who had stolen his heart. "Bloody hell, she knocked my socks off," he muttered to himself, and chuckled. He had met her when she was fourteen, then a scared little girl escaping to Marseille with her older sister, Amélie, from the German onslaught at Dunkirk.

Only three and a half years older than Chantal, Horton had seen her in Marseille. Because his mother was French and took pains to make sure that her son spoke the language fluently, after his escape to England, he had been inserted back into France by MI-9 to support a French Resistance organization, codenamed "Alliance," in helping downed airmen and escaped POWs evade recapture. Chantal and Amélie had been taken under the wing of Madame Madeleine Fourcade, who had founded and led the group. Alliance's reach had grown countrywide.

Chantal's infatuation with Horton was immediate and intense. In contrast, Horton viewed Chantal as a little sister and was therefore annoyed and embarrassed by her attentions. He had tolerated them because the sisters' mother had died several years earlier and, at the war's start, they had lost their father and home during German operations at Dunkirk.

Chantal had since grown into a beautiful young woman. Petite, with auburn hair and honey-colored eyes, she looked like Amélie's twin, regardless of six years between them. Both had become fierce Resistance operatives, even having been trained in spycraft in England. Chantal's affection for Horton had not diminished over the years, and when he saw her again after a separation of several months, she kissed him.

He remembered the warmth that shot through him. Her kiss had been passionate and spontaneous. Horton had not expected it, and he had pulled away. Chantal persisted, however, and Horton succumbed.

She had cried as they parted ways after Christmas in London. That was six months ago. He was then heading into combat in Italy, and she was going back to France to work for Fourcade's Alliance.

Horton had landed at Anzio and fought up Italy's mountainous spine. Then he had been transferred to the Sherwood Rangers for the invasion at Normandy and landed at Arromanches.

For a fleeting moment as he slogged through the surf and machine gun fire at Gold Beach, he had wondered where in France Chantal might be.

Now, as he sat enjoying rest at Le Hamel, thoughts of her diverted his mind from horrors he had seen, the responsibilities he carried as a lieutenant with men to lead, and days ahead of more combat. As he imagined her eyes gazing into his, his chest suddenly swelled and constricted involuntarily, and he laughed quietly at himself. "Blimey, you fool," he muttered. "That little girl you couldn't stand to be around now has you by the nose." He sniffed. "One day, I'm going to marry her—if she'll have me."

His platoon sergeant approached him. "Who're you talking to?"

"Just m'self," he replied, and laughed. "I do that when I need an intelligent conversation."

"Well don't talk to yourself too long," the sergeant jibed. "We've got another mission. The first sergeant sent me to find you. You need to be in a briefing in fifteen minutes." He grinned. "See how much fun it is to be a platoon commander?"

Horton groaned. "I didn't ask for this. All right. Get the men ready. I'll brief as soon as I get back."

The mission had arisen quickly from an Ultra-level intelligence report just received at General Montgomery's 21st Army headquarters and distributed hastily. It provided details on a major counterattack against Allied forces extending across the Normandy perimeter from Caen to Bayeux. In the sector that included the latter city, the main enemy force would be the *Wehrmacht's* elite Lehr *Panzer* Division, a *Waffen SS* unit. It would include a particularly notorious *Waffen SS* Tiger company led by an officer, Michael Wittman, whose name had become legendary on both sides of the war. He was credited with having personally killed one hundred and seventeen tanks on the eastern front in the Soviet Union during Operation Barbarossa and during battles at the Kursk salient during Operation Citadel.

Immediately after the invasion began at Normandy, intelligence reports filtered down of massive transfers of German reinforcements to Normandy's coastline. The troop movements had stepped up as Allied elements pressed inland and fighting intensified at Caen and around Cherbourg.

Now the disposition of the new enemy units threatening Normandy became clear. The 21st *Panzer* Division and the 12th *SS* Division would attack at Lebisey in the northeast and Cambes to the west of Caen, respectively. The Lehr Division would simultaneously strike northwest through Villers-Bocage to retake Bayeux.

Michael Wittman was believed to be headed toward Villers-Bocage.

The Sherwood Rangers were ordered to defend there.

Again in a support role, the Sherwood Rangers, including Horton's tanks, followed the British 7th Armored Division to meet and expel enemy forces at the town.

The "Desert Rats," as the division was known for its successes in North Africa, was a highly respected unit. However, the tactics that had proven so effective at El Alamein, Medenine, and in the campaign to take Tunis had been modified in Italy where the tanks were largely confined to roads. Now, on encountering sunken lanes bounded by hedgerows that provided little visibility across bocage country, the division needed, once again, to change its maneuver schemes and to do so on the fly as it pushed to meet the Lehr Division and Michael Wittman's company.

From a mile north in the neighboring hamlet of Villy-Bocage, Horton watched as the Desert Rats rolled along hedgerow-lined lanes in a convoy of one hundred and thirty-eight tanks and armored vehicles. Ordinarily, he would expect Allied aircraft to saturate the area with bombs and that fighters would be circling to strafe enemy convoys. However, the nature of the bocage country had become plain. Enemy positions could not be spotted from the air, and their movements were difficult to detect. It was a defender's dream and an attacker's nightmare, each small field constituting a killing field.

Villers-Bocage, set at the top of a high ridge on a main road, provided a rare vantage for viewing the surrounding countryside. From there, Horton glimpsed reflections of the sun on 7th Division vehicles at infrequent breaks among the foliage as the convoy climbed the hill into the town.

Time passed. Reports from Villers-Bocage indicated that the 7th Division had found it empty of German troops. They had spread to both ends and the breadth of the town with no contact. As had happened in Bayeux, townspeople came onto the streets and met their liberators with flowers and Calvados.

Then, the unmistakable sounds of Tiger tanks' 88 mm guns broke the calm. In quick succession, they fired from the 7th Division's flanks, their explosive rounds piercing the Shermans' armored sides and setting off their ammunition.

Men tumbled out of the stricken vehicles. Radio reports poured in. Within fifteen minutes, fourteen tanks and fifteen other British armored vehicles had been destroyed, and an unknown number of Allied soldiers had been killed or wounded. Receiving orders to move in, Sherwood Rangers shoved their Sherman Fireflies into gear and headed quickly to Villers-Bocage.

Rocking in his commander's cupola from the uneven rhythm of his tank as it rumbled past close-in hedgerows and headed uphill, Horton watched grimly. When he neared the crest, he spotted a break wide enough to allow passage through the forbidding embankment. It was on the opposite side of the road from which the Germans had fired and had been the site of a gate, now long gone and overgrown. "Take that right," he ordered Mikey, the driver, "through that hole in the hedge. Don't stop. Once inside, hug the trees on the uphill side closest to the village."

Whirling in his cupola, he signaled the tank behind him to follow and radioed his entire platoon of four to do likewise. When all were safely within the enclosed field, and he had ascertained that no threat existed from within its boundaries, he ordered them to spread apart close to the trees, with their guns pointing in the direction of enemy fire.

Behind them, British infantry units had arrived, sought shelter in the same field, and spread out to assess the situation. Meanwhile inside the town, the battle raged, and the roar of tank engines among the two-story stone buildings reverberated as their commanders sought advantage.

Horton leaped from his turret and met his platoon sergeant. Both men panted from exertion. "I'm going forward on foot to take a look," Horton said, and then waited and listened to the battle sounds. "I don't think the jerries have very many tanks here yet. We heard a huge number of shots at the outset, but those could have been good gun teams reloading and firing rapidly. If Wittman's here, that's what I'd expect from his men. I think they were already here and caught the 7th by surprise. Send a couple of scouts to our right to see if there's a way to skirt the town and come in from their flank. I'll be back in a few minutes."

Removing his sidearm from its holster and gripping it in his hand, he crept ahead, mindful of the cover provided by the bocage to his front and left. Then he entered the tree line and inched his way forward until he could see clearly into the town.

The destruction already wrought caused him to suck in his breath. Sherman M4s had plowed into stone buildings, bringing down upper floors on top of them. Their main guns protruded into the sky at odd angles. Smoke rose from most of them, their hulks blackened with soot, and pools of blood mixed with ashes. Wounded men cried out for aid. Corpses lay sprawled among the rubble.

The Germans had also paid a price. At least two Tiger tanks that Horton saw were bumped against buildings, their hulls blackened, smoking, with rounds of ammunition still cooking off. Their dead and wounded lay close by.

Firing from the opposite side of town had waned. Horton withdrew and headed back to his tank. There, he met once again with his platoon sergeant. "There's another gate at the opposite end of this field closest to the town," the sergeant said. "There must be similar openings in all these fields or they'd be useless."

"All right then, let's get some infantry chaps to scout out a route to the other end of town. I spotted two Tigers destroyed on the main street, so at least some of them have moved in. Trouble is, we don't know how many they had to start with or how many are left, so we'll just take out as many as we can." He glanced at his tank with its 76.2 mm barrel. Although the main gun was smaller than the Tiger's, it could kill or disable a Tiger, provided that it fired first.

Horton sent one of his tank commanders to liaise with the nearest infantry leader. Then he and the platoon sergeant devised a plan.

3

A squad of infantrymen scouted ahead of Horton's platoon as it made its way to the south end of Villers-Bocage, opposite where the Desert Rats had entered. He paused behind a building before entering the main street while his three other tanks continued to the eastern side of the town. The infantrymen remained in the fields.

Horton keyed his mic. "Let me know when you're in position."

"Roger. Out," his platoon sergeant replied.

The battle had died to intermittent firefights, mostly with small arms and machine guns and occasional blasts of tanks' main guns—those of the Tigers being several decibels louder than those of the Shermans. Horton maneuvered forward so he could see down the main street. The damage was incomprehensible, particularly given that the battle had commenced little more than an hour ago. Rubble and blackened vehicles lay all about, as did dead bodies.

Gripped by the sense of playing cat-and-mouse, Horton waited. At present, no active tank from either friend or foe appeared on the street other than his own.

Several minutes elapsed, and then the platoon sergeant called. "In position."

"Roger." Horton directed Mikey to drive down the main street to the first intersection, turn east, and halt there. Then he directed the gunner, Matt, to keep the cannon pointed down the main street.

When that had been accomplished, Horton fired several bursts from his machine gun into the air. Not seeing or hearing evidence of the effect he wanted, he ordered Matt to fire a round straight into one of the wrecked Tiger tanks.

Minutes passed. Monitoring his radio, Horton listened to a disturbing message. The German unit that ambushed the 7th Division was, indeed, Michael Wittman's. It had come to Villers-Bocage ahead of the Lehr *Panzer* Division's main body. However, the rest of the division was approaching from the south and expected to arrive soon, time indeterminate. The good news was that Wittman had arrived with only six Tigers rather than his normal complement of thirteen—and two were dead.

Horton's buttocks tightened. He fired another burst and directed the gunner to take another shot at the destroyed Tiger. Then he waited.

From down the street he heard the roar of a powerful engine that did not belong to a Sherman. The sound grew louder, and the ground trembled. Then the long barrel of an 88 mm gun and the front of a Tiger appeared. Its commander stood in its cupola directing its movement and scanning up the main street.

Horton kept a close eye on the Tiger. Then, as the *panzer* proceeded cautiously into the far intersection, now on his left, its turret began rotating toward the Firefly, accompanied by the high-pitched sound of its electrical motor.

"Mikey, inch toward the edge of town, but stay in sight of that Tiger. I'll let you know when to bolt and run."

He had studied the German tank and knew of its speed and maneuverability tradeoffs for heavier armor and greater firepower. He wondered if his foe had equally studied the Sherman and its variations. Compared to tanks in current use, the Sherman, a medium tank, had relatively light armor, and its short-barreled 75 mm main gun had considerably less piercing power than the Tiger's 88 mm cannon. The Sherman had compensated for its lighter armor with the simplicity of its design, which made it reliable, fast, maneuverable, repairable on the road, and deployable in large numbers.

The Shermans' advantages, however, were of little use in Villers-Bocage, as Horton now witnessed. One hundred and thirty-eight armored vehicles, most of them Sherman M4s, had been ambushed by a numerically much smaller unit. He wondered how many on each side remained in the fight.

As Horton intentionally allowed the Firefly to be spotted by the enemy tank commander, he gambled that he could exploit a vulnerability of the Tiger. The big tank's turret turned slowly, needing a full minute to rotate three hundred and sixty degrees. That meant fifteen seconds for each ninety degrees.

Like any tank, the treads on a Tiger were vulnerable. A hit on them could disable the vehicle. Likewise, a projectile striking at the seam between the turret and the lower hull could disable its traverse capability, rendering the main gun almost useless.

Horton had no illusions regarding the danger. A direct hit from the Tiger could kill or cripple Horton's Firefly. A reverse outcome was less likely. The Firefly's direct hit on the Tiger might bounce off with minimal damage.

Horton watched the Tiger's main gun rotate while Mikey inched forward, careful to stay outside of the line of fire.

The enemy tank turned onto the main street, effectively speeding up its cannon's turn toward Horton and his crew.

Mikey accelerated.

When the Tiger's gun was about to acquire the Firefly in its line of fire, Horton shouted, "Floor it, Mikey. Keep going past the edge of town. Then turn hard right."

Mikey needed no urging, and the Firefly rumbled along at top speed.

The corner of a building now stood between the two tanks, screening the Firefly's flight. The Tiger's engine roared louder as it also accelerated.

Horton's tank passed the last structures on the town's eastern edge. Another one on the right was nothing more than a single stone wall of a destroyed building standing at a right angle to the street. "Hold up here," he called to Mikey. Then he turned around in his cupola to watch.

The Tiger once again came into view. Its turret had rotated fully to its left. As the tank completed its turn, the turret began traversing to the right, but was still too far left to score a hit on the Firefly.

"Go!" Horton called into his mic.

Mikey pressed the accelerator and completed a right turn.

"Do a U-turn, and pull back alongside that stone wall. Stay back far enough so the gun barrel doesn't show and leave enough clearance to the left so we can point the gun that way." He called to the gunner. "Matt, are you ready?"

"Cocked and loaded."

"Good. Point the gun due west."

When both maneuvers had been completed, Horton scrutinized the wall. It provided good concealment, but given the force of an 88 mm round, it was not much for cover. He searched its side, and found what he was looking for—a chink through which he could observe the Tiger.

He checked his .50 Cal M2 machine gun mounted on the turret. It was ready.

Climbing onto the rim of his cupola, he stood upright. He was too far from the wall to use it for support, but he needed a clear view. Balance was precarious. He squinted to peer through the hole.

The enemy tank had accelerated and advanced half the distance separating them, and it continued rotating its gun to its right.

It was locked down. The tank commander had closed his hatch.

Horton watched until the gun was near the Tiger's five o'clock position. Then he dropped into the cupola and grabbed his mic. "Matt, fire as soon as that Tiger crosses your reticle. Aim for the seam."

He glanced to his tank's front. This would be a rough ride, with rubble and uneven ground to cross. Hopefully, the rest of his plan would work. Otherwise...

"Mash it, Mikey. Go straight ahead, and don't stop."

Sweat streamed down his face. The thought flashed through his mind that this maneuver had risked the lives of his crew as well as his own. Images of home and Chantal flitted by.

He grabbed the .50 Cal handles and wheeled it in the direction of the Tiger.

His Firefly roared across the street.

The Tiger bore down from mere yards away.

In the hull, Matt held his breath, his eye pressed to the rubber gunsight, the view magnified behind the crosshairs. He elevated the gun to the approximate height of the Tiger's seam.

The end of the wall flashed by, and the Tiger's huge hulk appeared. Its enormous right track with huge sprockets passed in front of him, and then its monstrous cannon aimed slightly above and to the right of him.

Matt pressed his trigger.

Above him, Horton thumbed the .50 Cal machine gun, aiming at the commander's hatch. Tracers screamed out of the muzzle. He shot two short bursts, sufficient to keep the tank commander buttoned up.

The Firefly buckled as Matt's armor-piercing round shot out of the cannon.

Horton heard Matt's shot strike the enemy's hull but could not see where it hit. He heard his own bullets ricochet from the vertical sides of the Tiger's turret and saw the small pockmarks they left behind.

Flame shot from the Tiger's muzzle. A trail of smoke hissed across the rear of Horton's tank. As he had anticipated, the enemy cannon had been ready to fire, but it was aimed too far to the right and too high to shoot effectively when the Firefly crossed the German gunner's sights.

The Firefly sped to the other side of the street and passed the corner building that now provided cover. Horton took a breath as he contemplated the Tiger's slow rotation to re-acquire its target. *I hope Matt hit that seam!*

A new thought struck him. *How far away is the rest of the Lehr Division?*

He turned to look back. The Tiger had moved forward, and its gun swept slowly toward Horton and his crew as the tank pivoted to pursue.

Fifteen seconds passed, then twenty.

The Tiger needed a few more seconds to put the fleeing Firefly in its reticles.

Two almost simultaneous blasts erupted. Horton dared not breathe. Seconds later, he heard two more.

Then, over his radio, he heard his platoon sergeant. "Mission accomplished. Two shots to the seam of the turret. Two shots to the track. Tiger disabled. Turret inoperable. One crew member escaped, running for cover on foot. No other signs of life."

Moments later a huge explosion split the air. "That's the Tiger's ammo cooking off," the platoon sergeant called.

Horton exhaled. "Roger," he radioed back. "I just received word to break contact and head to camp. We're regrouping. The Lehr Division is closing in."

He called down to Mikey on the intercom, "Slow down and reverse course."

4

June 14, 1944
Bayeux, France

Almost too exhausted to move, Horton left a hastily called company commander's meeting and returned to the bivouac area on the edge of Bayeux where the Sherwoods had set up after yesterday's battle at Villers-Bocage. The enemy Lehr Division had counterattacked, as expected, and had driven the Desert Rats and the Sherwoods out. Then the favor had been returned, and the Germans were routed. Both sides then vacated the town, leaving it desolate.

During the commander's meeting, much had been made of Horton's successful tactics that had taken out the Tiger. Word had gone round that the destroyed Tiger had been carrying Michael Wittman, but no one could say for sure.

"But I didn't gather you here just to say that," the Sherwood commander said. He held up his palm and grimaced. "The reason I called you together is that General Charles de Gaulle will be visiting here today. This was the first major French city to be liberated, and he intends to make a statement."

Amid groans quelled by a stern look, he continued, "There's nothing for you to do other than look presentable and station your men along the way, particularly at major street intersections."

Walking back to his platoon area, numb with fatigue, Horton hardly believed that he might encounter the stoic general whom most French citizens idolized. It was Charles de Gaulle who had escaped to Britain. Even before the Germans had secured their hold on France, he had broadcast to his fellow citizens over the BBC a message of hope and defiance, and he had issued a challenge to all French people to rise up, resist, and take back their country.

Horton well remembered times in Marseille when he had huddled in hidden rooms or remote barns with members of the Resistance, Chantal included, to listen to the general's broadcasts on radios forbidden by the Nazi regime.

Was that really four years ago? Horton marveled at the fleeting passage of time. Back then, the notion of evicting the Germans had seemed impossible, and yet here he was, in France, with the British Army, and fighting to do just that. And today, the embodiment of that scratchy, distant radio voice would walk freely among his own people.

Hours later, townspeople filled the streets carrying with them celebratory flowers and bottles of Calvados. They showered the soldiers with gratitude, but their excitement now centered on seeing their homegrown hero, the man who had inspired them to fight on and never surrender, and they jockeyed for the best viewing positions.

Horton saw the general for only a few seconds, finally putting a face to the previously disconnected voice. Stoic and dignified, de Gaulle walked at a measured pace, glancing and waving in all directions. He stopped to shake hands with people as children scampered around him, and he allowed himself only small smiles that seemed to emerge despite his attempts to repress them.

As he passed by, Horton thought of his own French mother and how proud she would be to know her son was there. And he thought of Chantal, Amélie, the Littlefields, and all the men and women who had fought alongside him to bring about this day. He scanned across the exuberant faces. He had seen sorrow and grief on other faces in other places as the war progressed. Yesterday's devastation at Villers-Bocage stood in stark relief against today's happy occasion. Glancing down the street for another glimpse of the general, he saw the tall figure disappear around a street corner.

Horton started back to his tent. *On with the war.*

Bletchley Park, England

"That was a good call regarding the counterattack in Normandy," Commander Edward Travis told Claire Littlefield. She was sitting in her accustomed seat before his desk in his office where he presided over Britain's top-secret decoding facility. "Your section's *Wehrmacht* intercepts were accurate and timely. We got word out to our field commanders immediately, and so we were ready to meet the German counterattack, particularly by that chap, Michael Wittman.

"Technically, the battle at Villers-Bocage was a defeat for us, but both sides vacated the village. And I must say, if not for that lieutenant—" He looked down at his notes. "Horton, his name is—"

Startled, Claire interrupted. "Excuse me, sir. Did you say Horton?"

Travis glanced at his notes again. "Yes, yes. Derek Horton." He read on in silence, and then, with his eyes still fixed on his papers, he said, "He had recently been elevated in the field to lieutenant from staff sergeant." He looked up. "Do you know him? He's credited with disabling Wittman's Tiger. Both sides ended up withdrawing from the village, but without his actions, it would have been a rout." He drew a deep breath. "Some heads will roll over this calamity. Of that, I am sure."

Claire suddenly found her heart beating faster with a long-forgotten sense of thrill, despite the accompanying bad news. "I do know Derek Horton if he's the same man. I suppose there could be others. The one I knew was a staff sergeant. The last I heard, he was in Italy. He's like a brother to me."

"If it's him, you can be glad to know that he's alive and well—"

"And still in the thick of fighting," Claire murmured disconsolately.

"Yes, well there is that." Travis arched his brows. "Although we fought the Germans to a standstill in Villers-Bocage, the fact is our initial force outnumbered theirs by nine to one. That should have been an easy victory, but instead, we lost over fifty-five armored vehicles not to mention the men and equipment. Granted, the full Lehr *Panzer* Division showed up later, but we also had the Sherwood Rangers there." He shook his head discontentedly. "Nevertheless, once again, your section's intelligence paid off, or things would have been worse—we could have lost Bayeux. Please extend my congratulations to your colleagues."

"Thank you, sir."

Before the war began, the organization at Bletchley had developed the capacity to decrypt German radio communications as fast as they had been transmitted. That ability was one of the country's greatest war secrets, and employees at Bletchley were sworn to silence regarding their work. A breach was punishable by death. Claire now oversaw three sections of decoders and analysts. "Bring me up to date across the European Theater."

"The situation in Italy remains roughly the same," Claire began. "The Germans are committed to defend there. They're fiercely shielding the Gothic line north of Rome under orders to fight to the last bullet. They see that if we break into the Po Valley, we could either go northeast to attack through Yugoslavia and threaten Germany's eastern border, or go west and join those forces with our armies in France. Neither option is attractive to them, and they're buying time to complete development of their advanced 'super weapons.'"

Travis grunted. "Well, we've stopped their designs on an atomic bomb for the moment. As far as we know, that leaves only their V-1s and V-2s. Anything new on those weapons?"

Claire shook her head. "My teams know to listen for anything about them, but the only information we have is what you provided. My sense is that they are never discussed outside of closed rooms. Recall that MI-6 only learned of them from a spy who had worked at the German headquarters in Paris."

"Yes, well, we've been expecting them for a while," Travis said, "and I imagine that Hitler will be more anxious to deploy them now that the Allies have planted a permanent beachhead on French soil. Let's hope our air forces and our air raid wardens are prepared to deal with them. Anything else new I'm not aware of?"

Claire scrunched her brow. "Perhaps, sir, there's an interesting situation developing in Germany's intelligence service. The head of the *Abwehr* reported to Hitler that thirty divisions threaten the German western flank in addition to our forces in Normandy. The thing is that those thirty divisions don't exist. From all I can gather—and this conclusion comes from our analysis, not from a clear statement out of *Abwehr* channels—the report was generated to coax Hitler to transfer more forces to that area. General Jodl is not convinced that the Atlantic Wall is strong enough to stave off an Allied invasion of northwestern France. Hence his apparently deliberate deception of the *führer*."

Travis almost laughed out loud. "You don't say? Add that to General Patton's imaginary forces in southern England, and that's quite a ghost force." He paused, his expression indicating a question forming in his mind. "What's the latest on how the *Wehrmacht's* divisions are positioned?"

Claire shuffled through her notes. "They have two hundred and six of them facing the Red Army on the eastern front, twenty-four in the Balkans, twenty in northern Italy, and fifty in France."

"How do the ones in France look now?"

Claire consulted her notes. "When I last briefed you on the German dispositions, the *Wehrmacht* had twenty divisions covering the beaches on either side of the Franco-Spanish border; ten were inland from the Cotentin Peninsula in western France, and the remaining ten covered the coast in northwestern France through Belgium and the Netherlands." Claire glanced down again. "They've since spread half of them somewhat evenly along the Atlantic Wall from southern France, through Belgium, and the Netherlands. The rest are along the southern coast and the Italian border."

"That's about half a million men throughout France." Travis arched his brows. "Which leaves less than a hundred thousand to defend on the Mediterranean coast."

"But much of the armor in the south has been pulled and sent north to reinforce around Caen," Claire interjected. "I see why Jodl is concerned. He still thinks we'll invade France north of Calais, and he doesn't have nearly enough troops there. And that's where he's placed the thirty divisions he conjured up for us."

Travis chuckled, almost chortling. "And now, having put those ghost divisions on Hitler's map, he can hardly take them back. Hitler will be anticipating a second landing there for months, far away from Normandy or the south of France, and he'll keep those real units in place to defend against an invasion that will never come."

Claire repressed a gleeful impulse. Nevertheless, she smiled. "Yes, sir, and there's another aspect to their dispositions—they've not only stripped their best units in southern France to reinforce around Normandy, but the units they've left to defend the southern coast are underequipped, poorly trained reserve units. The only armored reserve capable of defending anywhere on the Mediterranean coast is the 11th *Panzer* Division, and it would need to travel four hundred and fifty miles to get there. Otherwise, they have no strategic reserve in the area.

"For a week, Colonel General Balskowitz, the commander in the region, has begged Berlin to send the 11th *Panzers* to him, and he's gone so far as to alert that division's commander to be ready to roll within two hours of notice. He's convinced that the southern invasion will come in the vicinity of Marseille and Toulon.

"The German High Command, on the other hand, believes the next landing will be at Biscay. That perception is likely dictated by Hitler.

"On top of that, many of the *Wehrmacht's* soldiers in the south are conscripts from countries they had previously conquered: Czechs, Poles, Russians, Yugoslavs—"

Travis mulled over that tidbit. "It won't be a cakewalk," he mused out loud, "but they're overestimating our true strength in the north, and their defenses along the southern coast appear weak. That will cause them to take defensive actions that will benefit us. I like that."

He leaned back in his chair, very pleased with what he had heard. "I'll need to report this up the chain straight away. Anything else?"

"No, sir. I think that's all for the time being."

A concerned smile crossed Travis' face. "Now tell me, how are your brothers getting along. The last I heard, one was in Colditz POW camp, one was in Italy, and one was in France."

Claire withdrew slightly and bit her lip. "I appreciate your concern, sir. That was Paul in Italy, but I believe he was transferred and probably landed at Normandy. I've not heard from him in many weeks."

"I'm sorry to hear that, but maybe no news is still good news. What about the other two?"

Claire let out a sardonic laugh. "We received news that Lance had escaped yet again from Colditz, but we've got no other word about him. I remind myself that he was the most adventurous of my siblings. He's probably figured out a way to survive."

A sudden thought crossed her mind. "It's through Lance that we became acquainted with Derek Horton, the young sergeant—or lieutenant now—we spoke of earlier. The two escaped from Dunkirk together."

"My, my, those young soldiers do get around."

"As do most in our military these days."

"Of course you're right. Now what about Jeremy? As I recall, he's the youngest of the Littlefields."

Claire tossed her head in resignation. "He's somewhere in France. That's all I know. God help us, I hope he's not near Normandy, but I suppose anywhere over there now puts him in peril."

Travis regarded her compassionately. "You have an extraordinary family, Miss Littlefield. Your own contributions are remarkable. The country is in your debt."

"As it is to you and all who defend her, sir, but thank you for saying that." She scanned her notes quickly. "There's one more thing I should bring to your attention. Are you familiar with a high plateau in southeastern France called the Vercors?"

With a blank expression on his face, Travis shook his head.

"It's catching a lot of German High Command attention lately," Claire said. "Apparently, the area has been left to its own devices for most of the war because of its mountainous topography. But elements there have raided *Wehrmacht* facilities, and when the Germans sent a patrol to retaliate, they were attacked and sent packing by the local Resistance."

"Bully for the Resistance," Travis interjected. "*Vive la France*."

"Yes, well, unfortunately, the story did not end there. The *Wehrmacht* sent in reinforced patrols, demolished three villages, and massacred the residents."

Travis sighed. "The senseless bloodshed."

Claire continued, "The Germans see that the area could present a strategic threat to them. It's a rather large area protected by a ring of mountains, and could host a large military base capable of striking at the Germans' rear and flanks in almost any direction."

"Hmmm. Sounds interesting. It'd be good to know what we're doing to exploit its position."

"That's beyond my purview, sir."

"Of course it is." Travis paused in thought. "Keep an eye on the situation, and let me know what comes up." He rose to his feet. "Now, before you go, I must ask, how are your parents?"

"They're alive as of my last correspondence a while back." Claire stood and started for the door as she replied. "How well they are is another matter. The Nazis have stopped Red Cross messages from Sark. The same for Father. As far as I know, he's still in the detainment camp at Tittmoning Castle in Germany."

"I trust they'll be fine," Travis said unconvincingly as he escorted her out.

Stony Stratford, England

Claire arrived at her home twenty minutes from Bletchley Park by bus to a happy welcome from Timmy, an orphaned child whom her brother Jeremy had rescued from a shipwreck. Jeremy had been granted temporary guardianship of the boy pending discovery of blood relatives, and he in turn had left Timmy in Claire's care while he fought in the war.

"Gigi!" Timmy greeted her with wide-open arms, running to her when she arrived at the garden path leading to her front door. Elsie, the nanny, watched in amusement as the two made their way toward the house. She had been with Claire and Timmy since shortly after the child's arrival and was now considered a family member. Without her, Claire could not have coped with raising Timmy while continuing her responsibilities at Bletchley, first as a cryptologist, then an intelligence analyst, and then being promoted into a supervisory capacity to oversee the messages being decoded and the conclusions derived from their analyses.

Timmy led her to the back garden where she pushed him on a swing until Elsie announced that dinner was ready. A month ago, Elsie had moved into the spare bedroom, to which she retired for the day shortly after the three had eaten dinner. Then, as darkness settled in, Claire read Timmy a bedtime story and tucked him into bed.

Alone in her own room, Claire sat in front of her vanity and stared at her reflection. Constant fatigue and lack of exercise had taken their toll. Her skin, previously toned by activity in the sun, now looked puffy and pale.

She tried her smile. People had often commented that it was brilliant, but now small lines appeared at the corners of her mouth as they did across her forehead and at the edges of her eyelids. Such changes were expected with age, she told herself, but she wondered how much more was brought on by the stress of the war and her job.

Claire's colleagues respected her as something of a legend for pulling off several intelligence coups. Chief among them was to locate a spy in the German headquarters that was planning the invasion of Great Britain. The spy proved invaluable in providing information enabling the Allies to take countermeasures that prompted the Germans to cancel the invasion. Additionally, she had devised a way to use German communications to pinpoint the location of the battleship *Bismarck*, thus allowing British warships to move in for the kill.

She glanced again at her face in the mirror. Her hair, matching the dirty-blond color and hue of her brothers, still fell in thick locks to her shoulders, but months had gone by since she had enjoyed a proper trimming.

She stood and twisted one way and then the other, examining her figure. Her clothes still fit, but they hung loose in some places and were tight in others, and many of her dresses and skirts were worn. *Will men still find me attractive after the war?*

She chuckled at the thought. Men had been so far from her mind since

Timmy had entered her life. Her main fear now was that one of Timmy's bona fide relatives would appear and take him away or, for that matter, that Jeremy might do the same when the war was over. He had legal custody, and he doted on Timmy.

She laughed at herself. *I'll end up a spinster sharing an apartment with Elsie.*

Quiet, loyal, reliable Elsie loved Timmy as dearly as Claire did. *What will I do when life returns to normal? Will that ever happen?*

The Battle of the Atlantic had waned, and life had improved appreciably in the United Kingdom. Food and its varieties were more plentiful, and most nights, people slept peacefully without being bombed. But worrying about loved ones fighting overseas never left anyone feeling peaceful.

She thought of life before the war, when she had been a pianist in the London Symphony Orchestra. Music had been her passion, and she had been recruited to Bletchley on the basis of her musical abilities. As it happened, skilled musicians made superior decoders—the disciplines were similar. Her fluency in English, French, and German added to her value, and her superior analytical skills were soon recognized.

She sighed, feeling a sudden longing to be playing the piano again in the symphony hall. She imagined the thrill of running her fingers up and down the keyboard, in concert with other orchestral instruments to produce magnificent, majestic music.

A strange sound interrupted her reverie, one she had never heard before. It was a buzzing sound, faint, yet as she listened, it increased in volume until she realized that it was produced by multiple sources. The buzzing reminded her of the sound of German bombers over London during the *blitz*, and it engendered a sense of dread. Whatever was making the noise seemed to be coming from above.

Claire whirled from her mirror and rushed through the house and out her front door. There, she looked up into the night sky. It was moonlit against myriad stars, and yet, as she watched, she saw many dark blotches scattered about the heavens. They were definitely the source of the buzzing sounds. But these objects flying through the sky were small—too small to be bombers, yet too bulky to be fighters.

As she watched, she noticed that the sounds emanating from individual shadows suddenly ended as the propulsion system of one after another of these strange aircraft shut down. They were followed by a whooshing noise as they plunged to earth.

Claire's mind flitted to her conversation with Commander Travis earlier that afternoon. The German V-1s and V-2s! She had heard of them only peripherally and had no knowledge of if, when, or where they would be deployed. German security concerning them had effectively blacked out any word of them.

Claire raced back into the house shouting, "Elsie, wake up! Go to the cellar. Hurry. We're under attack!" Then she headed for Timmy's room as many explosions broke in the distance.

5

Same Day, June 14, 1944
The Vercors Massif, France

British Army Captain Jeremy Littlefield awoke numbly to air-raid sirens wailing over Grenoble in the valley far below his position near Saint-Nizier-du-Moucherotte. He and a group of French commandos he had joined temporarily had camped a short distance from Saint-Nizier, at Charvet Hill, overlooking a winding road. Three days earlier, they had fought together through a skirmish against German troops until sunset. The enemy had then unexpectedly broken contact and retreated into the valley.

Now instantly alert, Jeremy clambered to his feet while reaching for his Lee-Enfield rifle. Around him, the French soldiers, also roused by the siren's mournful wail, scrambled, grabbed their weapons, and stared down into the valley. Grenoble lay in the shadows of mountains to its east, seemingly asleep but for the piercing warning.

Dawn broke against a crystal-clear sky over a thin mist deep in the valley, and the sun's fingers spread an orange glow across the horizon and reached into a blue canopy. It should have been a day to enjoy, but as

Jeremy absorbed his surroundings, he heard the ominous, throaty growls of approaching aircraft.

Next to him, the commandos' leader, Chief Sergeant Abel Chabal, called to his men, "Spread out and take cover. Only shoot if necessary. Remember, we're low on ammunition."

The sky brightened, the roar of engines elevated, and then Jeremy spotted the aircraft, at first as a group of horizontal blots floating toward them against the sky, and then, as the wings caught the sun's rays, as gleaming shards of silver against the valley's haze. The soldiers ducked into prepared positions and pointed their rifles toward them.

"They're American!" one of the men shouted excitedly. "Look at the markings under the wings. They're American! Finally, our support is coming."

The commandos emerged from their positions, cheering and waving as the formation swept overhead and flew toward Méaudre, a hamlet six miles to the southeast. It circled once, the pilots obviously checking their bearings and confirming their drop zone, and then flew back over Méaudre where they released a number of cylinders via parachute.

The men at Saint-Nizier watched, their faces at first hopeful and then turning to uncertainty, as the canopies floated to the ground. "That's not nearly enough, and the Germans won't let this drop go unanswered," Abel growled. "I hope more is coming, or our Allies just struck a match over the Vercors."

Jeremy regarded him grim-faced, but did not respond. A week has passed since the Allied armies had landed at Normandy, five hundred miles to the northwest. In conjunction with that operation, Resistance organizations across France had been ordered by the Free French headquarters in Algiers to activate and mobilize in anticipation of a supporting amphibious landing along France's southern coast in Provence.

The Vercors was a natural fortress with a high plateau protected by a ring of mountain ranges. The military command there had been ordered to execute Operation Montagnard, which envisioned operating the Vercors as a vast, behind-enemy-lines base from which to attack German positions in almost every direction. Succeeding at that required a *Maquis* force of six thousand fighters, which the local Resistance organization had assembled.

However, less than half of the force had rifles, and most of the fighters were untrained volunteers who had escaped a Nazi forced-labor program into the mountains where they lived off the land.

Operation Montagnard also required a regiment of airborne troops, heavy weapons, and anti-aircraft guns to be delivered into the Vercors, and construction of a runway at one of its major towns, Vassieux, thirty miles southwest. Already, Major Huet, the Free French military commander in the Vercors, had divided the area into military districts and appointed commanders in each one. Supported by his immediate superior, Colonel Descour, he had impressed upon Algiers that the situation was critical, that without the promised support, the operation would fail and the population of the Vercors would be massacred.

Three days ago, on the same day as the skirmish at Saint-Nizier, Huet had received a message from the Free French headquarters informing him that Operation Montagnard and the Vercors had been activated prematurely and that the volunteers should stand down. Huet was infuriated. He had been ordered to activate his forces over his objection that it was too soon and that the Germans would most certainly retaliate. The response from Algiers was an admission that Huet had been right. Enraged, Huet fired off a response stating that the blood of innocents spilled on the Vercors would be on the hands of the Free French senior commanders. By implication, he included General Charles de Gaulle.

Assurances were forwarded from Algiers that the support was forthcoming and that weather had caused delays in delivery and communications. However, days passed, no support appeared, and more ominously, no date had been set for the planned southern invasion of France on which the success of Montagnard rested.

Jeremy and Abel shared Huet and Descour's very real concerns. Already, prior to Normandy, *Wehrmacht* troops had raided the Vercors at Échevis, Vassieux, and Les Barraques, setting homes on fire with women and children inside, razing farms, slaughtering livestock, destroying crops, and executing men accused of being terrorists.

"Finally, something," Jeremy breathed while watching the parachutes float to the ground. His dirty-blond hair needed cutting and was unkempt, and he needed a shave. Although he had always been athletic, now his body was lean and hard from combat, and his gaze deliberate and constantly searching, a habit gained from having survived, both as a commando and as a fighter pilot.

"If that's all there is, we're in trouble," Abel growled from beneath his iconic beret, without which he was rarely seen. Lanky, and known for his humor and discipline, he had a rare rapport with his men that allowed him to mix as one of them or command them without hesitation and know that his orders would be carried out.

"Maybe more will come," Jeremy said. They conversed in French since Jeremy was fluent in the language and the only one among them whose native language was English.

"Maybe." Abel turned his gaze to the valley and Grenoble lying silently below. The sirens had ceased. "We'll know soon enough." He gestured toward the city. "And we'll hear the German response within hours. They won't let this pass."

He glanced at the crest of a tall mountain south of them, the Moucherotte. The tricolors of the French flag, modified by a blue Cross of Lorraine on its white section, flew proudly. On Abel's arrival just before the skirmish three days ago, he had ordered the banner placed high on the mountain where it could be seen by all in the valley, including at *Wehrmacht* headquarters. "That will jam up Karl's throat," he had murmured, referring to General Karl Pflaumm, commander of the German 157th Reserve Division in Grenoble. The Vercors fell within the general's operations area, and it had been a constant irritant to him.

Reflecting on that action and the Allied air delivery of materiel to the Vercors, the first instance of such direct support, Abel now muttered, "He'll come in force now."

A runner approached. "Orders from Captain Beauregard," he said, panting. "You are to defend on the left side of Charvet Hill. Major Huet is sending reinforcements out to defend on the right, and another unit up the Moucherotte."

Abel nodded tiredly and gestured toward Méaudre. "Is anything else coming?"

The soldier shrugged, shaking his head disconsolately. "I haven't heard of any."

While Abel prepared his troops, Jeremy, codenamed Labrador, hiked the distance to Saint-Nizier to meet with Major Huet. Jeremy was at the Vercors as an agent of Prime Minister Churchill's Special Operations Executive, the SOE, detailed to liaise between the headquarters in London and the Vercors' Resistance group. His immediate boss, Major Francis Cammaerts, codenamed Roger, advised Resistance commanders across a much larger area that included the Vercors. Roger's responsibilities included several networks amounting to nearly twenty thousand fighters, nearly a third of all Resistance members.

Jeremy had been brought to the Vercors to be Roger's deputy and to be prepared to step in should something happen to him. However, events moved rapidly in the few weeks after Jeremy's arrival and leading up to D-Day at Normandy. Operation Montagnard had launched in Roger's absence, and thus Jeremy had found himself operating on a level he had not anticipated so soon, making decisions, recommending actions, communicating directly with London, and taking part in ground combat.

His prime responsibilities had been to advise on military matters, keep communications open between the Vercors and London, provide intelligence on enemy activity, and keep a supply line open to the Resistance. Support for Operation Montagnard had been promised by both the London SOE and the Free French headquarters in Algiers, but until this morning, none had arrived, and the drops over Méaudre were disappointing.

Major Huet, a trim, serious officer of demonstrated competence, met Jeremy at the door of the villa below Saint-Nizier where he had set up his temporary headquarters for the duration of the fighting there. He shook his head as Jeremy mounted the stairs onto the porch. "It's no good," he said. "We've already had reports from Méaudre." He scoffed. "The Allies sent us 8 mm Hotchkiss machine guns left over from the last great war, and they weren't packed well, so a lot were damaged. Even if they were good, we received only a fraction of what we need and hardly any ammunition."

He put his hands on his hips and stared down into the valley. "I've studied the whole area from General Pflaumm's viewpoint and considered his assets. He will start the assault today, here at Saint-Nizier. I feel it. In his shoes, that's what I would do.

"He feels pressure coming east from the Normandy landings, he sees the value of the Vercors as a military base in the German rear, and he knows he can't let it fall into Allied hands. His window to attack is narrowing, so he'll do it now. He's coming, and we don't have nearly the manpower or weapons to stop him."

"I'll send another message to London—"

"Go ahead," Huet said grimly, "but I'm not optimistic that they'll respond adequately. Without massive reinforcements immediately"—he swung his face around and thrust his chin out angrily—"and I mean now, we're doomed. We can do nothing without heavy weapons and air support. The residents of this town will suffer horribly tonight. By morning, Saint-Nizier will smolder, and General Pflaumm will mount sustained operations in force across the rest of the Vercors for as long as it takes."

Jeremy regarded the major with mixed compassion and awe. Despite the French officer's anger, Huet remained calm. "Go ahead and send your message. You'd think we could at least get a bombing run on Pflaumm's headquarters at Grenoble."

"Yes, sir, and after I send the message, what would you have me do. I have no current orders. I'm at your disposal."

Huet glanced at Jeremy and allowed a small smile. "You're a good man, Labrador. I hope we both make it through this war. Take your pick of defensive positions. We need all the firepower we can muster."

"Then I'd like to return to Chief Sergeant Chabal's unit on Charvet Hill."

Huet nodded and once again allowed a smile, this one grim. "Of course. You two have become close friends. He speaks well of you. He'll need you. Charvet Hill is the most critical position. If the Germans break through there..." His voice trailed off.

An hour later, after Jeremy had sent an encoded message, he walked back onto the villa's front porch. Huet was still there, joined by Captain Beauregard. Together, they observed a friendly convoy of trucks and cars entering the town from the south along the road to Villard, bringing in food and reinforcements. The vehicles created a cacophony of motor sounds and clouds of dust, but despite the imminent danger, spirits remained high, particularly when fighters looked up at the Moucherotte and saw Abel's flag billowing in the wind.

Captain Beauregard, Abel's commander, was a young, big officer who seemed to always smile, even under the direst circumstances. Abel's commandos aside, most of Beauregard's men were civilian volunteers whom he had been required to train in the most fundamental concepts of military discipline and tactics, but he had been wise enough to understand that they had not chosen military careers. Hence, despite their willingness to learn, and although they accepted regimentation, they did not embrace it. In his own words, Beauregard took the approach of "keeping one foot in both military and civilian camps."

The two officers stood at the edge of the veranda in the shade of its roof observing the hurried activity in the town. Jeremy joined them. "I'll be leaving now, sir, back to Charvet Hill."

"Visit with us a while," Huet said. "We have time. General Pflaumm's artillery will announce the start of his attack, but his ground troops will take hours to climb the mountain roads."

He grimaced. "The operation at Normandy coincided with my arrival here, and that was a little over a week ago. All we've had time for is this grim business. I'm curious about you. You're British, but you've thrown yourself into this fight fervently. You speak French fluently, but your accent is a bit peculiar."

Jeremy chuckled. "I'm *Sercquiais*, from Sark—"

"Ah, yes, one of those little British islands off the western coast of Normandy."

"That's it, sir. We all speak French there as well as English."

"That's commendable. I fear for your people, though. They must be suffering awfully under German occupation."

Jeremy frowned. "I'm sure they are, but getting news from there is difficult. My mother does her best to keep things going and to get news out through German censorship, but then again, I'm over here—" He bit his lip and left the sentence unfinished. "I don't dwell on the situation."

"But you fight so hard for France—"

"As does Roger," Jeremy interrupted stoutly. "We all have our reasons, and we have a common enemy." He let out a long breath. "I was saved by a French family at Dunkirk at great risk to themselves. The father was eventually killed. He might still be alive but for—" His lips quivered and he looked away. "We grew close," he continued in a hollow voice. "I'm engaged to marry one of his daughters, Amélie. Her sister, Chantal, is with the Resistance in Normandy at a place called Saint-Laurent-sur-Mer—"

"Ah, I know the place. It's near Arromanches, where the Allies are building a large port out of nothing. Amazing, really."

He searched Jeremy's face. "So, you are in love with a French girl."

Jeremy flushed red, and he nodded. "We haven't had much time to be together. We met in the war, and it's been going on as long as I've known her—four years now. And she won't marry me until it's over."

"Smart girl. Do you have other brothers and sisters?"

Jeremy sighed deeply. "Two brothers and a sister, all in the war." He gave a short summary of his family and their current situations as he knew them, and then stopped suddenly, staring stonily at the ground. "I've just broken all security protocols."

"We all have our weak moments," Huet said kindly. "Your secrets are safe with me. I don't expect to live through the coming onslaught." He sighed. "You have an amazing family. I see where your dedication comes from."

Beauregard had listened quietly. Now he broke in. "Jeremy flew fighters in the Battle of Britain and nightfighters in the *blitz*. And he was one of the commandos on the raid at Saint-Nazaire."

Huet stood back to regard Jeremy with increased admiration. "You had mentioned that to me, Captain Beauregard. I had forgotten. Labrador, that raid all but secured the Battle in the Atlantic for the Allies. Without the drydock at Saint-Nazaire to service the big battleships, the *Kriegsmarine*'s warships became useless."

The three men remained quiet, observing the town's preparations for battle. Then Jeremy said, "What about you, Major Huet? I know some of the captain's background, but I know nothing about your history."

Huet shook his head slightly and pursed his lips. "There's not much to tell, really." He let out a small laugh. "By rights, maybe we should trade places."

"I don't think so, sir. From what I've seen, you've handled your command very competently."

"You're kind to say so." He rubbed his chin. "Let's see, what can I tell you? I'm married and have six children. Before the war, I was a laborer, a roofer, and then a fireman. That last job kept me out of the army and the war. I became part of it only two years ago when I joined the Resistance. I'm as surprised as anyone to be a major in de Gaulle's secret army."

Jeremy regarded him with new respect. "You've done remarkably well, particularly under the circumstances."

"Not well enough to save us." Huet glanced somberly at the mixed throng of *maquisards*, soldiers, and villagers hurrying about their business and then turned to gaze across the valley and the purple-hued peaks surrounding them. "My family used to come here on summer vacations every year. I know the Vercors well. It's such a beautiful place with its lofty mountains, its wide plateaus, and rich earth." He paused as he continued to survey the town's urgent activity. Then he sniffed and straightened his shoulders. "Well, let's get on with things. We have a country to save."

Grenoble, France

At dusk, General Pflaumm responded to the Allied air drop. His big guns opened up from the base of the mountains, firing forty heavy artillery rounds within a matter of minutes. Houses caught fire and buildings were demolished—but remarkably, there were no casualties, civilian or otherwise.

Jeremy recognized the hand of Major Huet moving men, women, and children to cover, doing his best to protect the few residents who had refused to evacuate and save them from the travails of war. But his efforts were futile concerning the town itself. The picturesque, pre-war ski resort nestled on a small plateau at the precipice of a wide break in the walls of the majestic Alpine peaks was reduced to rubble.

Now, Pflaumm's ground assault would begin in force.

June 16, 1944
Villard-en-Vercors, France

Jeremy trudged southward through Villard, with Abel by his side. Behind them were the twenty-six remaining commandos out of an original force of thirty men. Ahead of them, scores of *maquisards* tramped through the village, their heads down, shoulders drooping, and spirits low. Behind the commandos, hundreds more Resistance fighters slogged along, their faces registering a sense of defeat and despair.

Surprisingly, the villagers of Villard welcomed the somber procession as a band of conquering heroes, cheering the fighters on, thanking them for their protection, and showering them with food, wine, embraces, and kisses. The men accepted the gestures glumly and continued their dismal trek. Not even the bright sun, blue sky, or majestic peaks lifted their moods.

Soon after the artillery barrage had commenced at Saint-Nizier, the German infantry soldiers began their ascent of the mountainside. This time, however, rather than just sending convoys up the narrow, winding roads, General Pflaumm had deployed highly trained mountain troops on a more arduous but direct climb on the left and right wings of his attack force. They had moved swiftly through dusk up the steep slopes, and before 21:00 hours, while Huet's attention was focused on enemy forces moving on the roads, the Germans on the flanks attacked before their presence was detected.

Seeing that the tide of battle was against him and that keeping his men in the current fight would lead to encirclement and useless slaughter, Huet ordered a withdrawal to the next defensive line. A few subordinate leaders, including Abel, ignored his order. For two hours, his men fought, holding the approaching enemy at bay until they were about to be surrounded by more Germans pouring onto the plateau.

With Jeremy at his side, Abel pulled his men into a circle. "We're going to break out of here toward Saint-Nizier," he said. "*Les boches* won't expect it. Don't be afraid, and don't turn back. We'll be going between the units circling to our front on each side of us, so they won't shoot for fear of hitting each other. When I give the word, start running, and don't stop."

They gathered under the night sky, and Abel pointed out the route. Then, with little warning, he shouted, "Let's go! Move! Run!" and he took the lead, running and zig-zagging across an open field, headed south.

Jeremy ran close to him, and as Abel had predicted, the firing at them stopped.

"Faster, you idiots," Abel shouted, and he increased his pace.

Jeremy ran harder than he ever had before, and behind him and to his left and right, the French commandos raced over the field, tripping along its plowed furrows.

Then came the pounding, rhythmic sound of machine guns. The commandos had run past the point where German fire was fratricidal, and the enemy now fired indiscriminately, their red tracers blazing through the night.

Jeremy's lungs heaved, he gasped for more oxygen, but he dared not slow down or stop, changing direction every few steps. A forest line grew large in front of him, but with every step, it seemed more impossible to reach, and he struggled to even greater effort. Then suddenly, he was inside the tree line, within its welcoming shadows, and he sprawled behind a thick trunk. He lay there panting, but only seconds later, he heard Abel bellowing, "Let's go. No time for sleep. We have a ten-mile trek ahead of us, through Lans and beyond Villard."

They passed through Saint-Nizier, now a demolished wreck, its homes and shops in ruins, with only a few upright walls standing in ghostly silhouette against the sky. Then, when they had withdrawn down the road a few hundred yards, they heard the crackle of fire and, turning, watched in horror and shame as massive flames leaped against the dark sky, devouring the beloved small town.

All night they marched, joining with the rest of Huet's command in the northeast sector of the Vercors. Just after dawn, villagers lined both sides of the road, shouting encouragement and cheering the fighters on. The first residents appeared at Lans, and the closer the procession came to Villard, the larger the crowds grew.

As the fighters proceeded through Villard, their spirits were initially lifted by the buoyant crowds, but then they heard shouted celebrations of the "great victory" of nearly a week earlier when the French fighters had held the German probe back and the enemy had broken contact. Obviously, the more recent news of Saint-Nizier's destruction had not reached the villagers, and the fighters tramping through had no desire to enlighten them.

The procession continued south with a dismal reality registered on many faces: the Vercors *Maquis* had been routed. The *Wehrmacht* would move onto the plateau in force. Soon.

6

June 17, 1944
Saint-Martin-en-Vercors, France

Jeremy listened closely to a discussion between Major Huet and Eugène Chavant. The latter, commonly referred to as *le Patron*, was the recognized civilian leader of the Vercors. A former restaurateur from Grenoble, he had fled into the Vercors at the start of the war and quickly won the hearts and loyalty of its residents. Approaching six feet in height with thick white hair and a heavy mustache, he was an indomitable figure.

The three sat at a table in Chavant's makeshift headquarters in the café of the Hôtel Breyton. In times past, villagers and interested parties had congregated around such discussions, but with the battle now joined and concern that spies might infiltrate, only principals and cleared persons, including Jeremy, were allowed in the room. Huet had established his own headquarters upstairs on the third floor. Outside, villagers clustered about to pass along rumors, hear wisps of real news, or catch a glimpse of the leaders responsible for the Vercors' defense.

"I see no sense in trying to re-take Saint-Nizier," Huet said angrily. "We lost fifty men in that fight. The Germans pulled back, but they left an occupying force and set up a *Gestapo* office in Villard. They didn't raze the village or punish the residents, I suppose, because no resistance was met there.

"Our fighters are willing to go back to Saint-Nizier, and we could hold the Germans at bay if we had the weapons, but we have the whole Vercors to defend. The break in the mountain wall into the valley is wide there, and General Pflaumm is not nearly done. And then there's this." He held out a poster.

Chavant took it and read. Then he looked up grimly.

"We sent two spies into the valley," Huet continued. "Two girls. The Groll cousins, Gaby and Jaqueline—"

Chavant reacted in astonishment. "I know them. They're very young."

Huet nodded. "Eighteen years old, each. But they came to me to offer their services. They convinced me that because they are so young, no one would suspect them. They rode their bicycles down and made sure to smile and wave at German soldiers along the way. We had them meet with a contact in Grenoble who gave them good information on troop dispositions and numbers, and they picked that up."

"May I see it?" Jeremy broke in, pointing to the poster.

Chavant handed it to him, and Jeremy scanned it. It informed that, per Article 10 of the Franco-German Armistice, any Frenchman who resisted German troops by force of arms would, upon capture, be treated as a terrorist and immediately executed.

"Pflaumm's troops are already forming into battle groups all around the Vercors' periphery," Huet went on. "Did you hear about what happened at Barcelonnette?"

Chavant nodded.

"I heard that something happened there," Jeremy said, "but I don't know what."

Huet snorted in disgust. "Barcelonnette is a town roughly one hundred miles southeast of the Vercors' southern rim in the Ubaye Valley. The day before the Normandy landings, the residents proclaimed themselves to be a free republic and, right in front of their city hall, they flew the French flag with the Cross of Lorraine stitched on the white center panel."

He closed his eyes and shook his head. "Another Nazi massacre. Two days ago, General Pflaumm's troops stormed into the town in tanks and armored cars. Within hours if not minutes, one hundred and fifty *maquisard* defenders were gunned down and the newborn republic died." He let out a long breath. "But for our mountain walls and the fighters blocking the passes, that would already have been our fate."

All were quiet for a time, and then Huet resumed. "The only resources we have are our fighters and about twenty percent of the small arms we need. People forget that we had only one rifle between two men before the Normandy invasion. Since then, forty-five hundred more *maquisards* have joined us, but most didn't bring weapons with them. Most of them are untrained, and time is growing shorter. Our best course of action is to continue to block our eight main mountain passes, use our time for training, and keep pressing London and Algiers for support."

Chavant glanced at Jeremy and sighed heavily. "Reluctantly, I agree. We have to protect those major passes and keep watch over the hundreds of small paths across the mountain crests. We're stretched thin."

"We'll do our part and keep you informed," Jeremy said.

"Another concern is mounting," Huet went on. "We're seeing increased activity at the airfield at Chabeuil outside our southwestern rim. The *Luftwaffe* is bringing in more bombers and fighter planes. They'll start their main offensive with an air assault, and Chabeuil is only five minutes' flight time from Vassieux. If we don't get air support and the weapons and ammunition we need, including anti-aircraft guns, we have little chance of defending the Vercors effectively."

An orderly entered the room, approached Major Huet, and handed him a message. It was from General Koenig, in London, the Commander-in-Chief of *les Forces françaises de l'intérieur*, also known as the Free French, the Secret Army, or the FFI. It was the army that General Charles de Gaulle had organized and included the troops in North Africa that had been coopted from the Vichy-French government.

Huet read the note and looked up quickly, his eyebrows arched. "And the news just keeps getting better," he scoffed, and read it again, out loud. "'Be advised that all Allied air resources are committed to other areas. Unarmed Resistance members and civilians should avoid assembling near German units.'"

The major almost jeered. "Koenig described exactly the situation in the

Vercors, except that we have no choice in the matter. *Wehrmacht* units will move into our unarmed areas regardless—" His tone elevated to exasperation. "Aided by our lack of air support and anti-aircraft guns."

"Our support will come," Chavant proclaimed unconvincingly, "you'll see. And soon. De Gaulle would not have activated Montagnard if he did not intend to send troops immediately. They've had weather problems to contend with. Those officers I met with in Algiers understood our support needs and the military advantage the Vercors offers. Operation Montagnard is important to the southern invasion's success.

"Meanwhile, we'll train and man the passes, as you ordered. We've been asked to hold out for three weeks."

Huet's face jerked up. "Two weeks of that's gone by," he spat out, "without a hint of when we'll see our promised support." He grunted. "No coordination either for dates or locations. Nothing."

Bletchley Park, England

"Sir, some activity is taking place that I think you'll want to know about," Claire told Commander Travis. "It's at that place in southeastern France, the Vercors, I mentioned in our last conversation."

"Yes, yes. I remember. What's going on there?"

"Perhaps nothing, but it's causing such concern in Berlin that it's worth watching."

"What's the situation?"

Once again, Claire scanned her notes. "This place is on a high plateau. You might have heard of a town at the northeast end, Saint-Nizier. It was a popular ski area before the war."

"Yes, I have heard of it."

"Well the Germans just overran it and burned it to the ground."

Travis looked perplexed. "That seems odd. What strategic value could it possibly have? It must be on the opposite side of the mountain range from the Rhône Valley where the Allies intend to push through France to the German border."

"Yes, sir, but from the communications we've intercepted, it appears that Saint-Nizier sets in a wide break in the mountain wall that allows entry into an area that's given the Germans some grief since they occupied southern France."

"How so?"

Claire withdrew a map from her folder and handed it over. She had outlined the periphery of the Vercors in dark ink. "You can see the entire area there," she said. "It's about forty-eight miles long and eighteen miles wide. In the northern section, it's dominated by high mountains, and in the south, it's a wide plateau. The north and south are divided by a huge gorge."

Travis peered at the map closely. "And the whole area is encircled by a ring of mountain ridges and peaks?"

"Yes, sir. And there are only eight major passes into the Vercors' interior. The Germans have left the people there alone for the most part until recent months, but apparently a big operation is building to seize it and subdue it by force."

Again, the commander looked perplexed. "Why now? I'd think the *Wehrmacht* would be concentrating its attention on the invasion in Normandy."

"I think a culmination of factors is at play. When the Germans occupied southern France and began taking the young men to work in their arms factories in Germany, thousands fled to the mountainous areas across France, including the Vercors. They call themselves *maquisards* because they live off the land. Before D-Day, Berlin estimates that they numbered about four thousand in the Vercors."

"I'm familiar with the *maquisards*. You've briefed me on them before. They've organized into groups called *Maquis*."

"Yes, sir, that's them. Before D-Day, some elements at the Vercors raided German facilities in a valley and killed a German officer in an ambush at one of their mountain passes. In retaliation, the Germans mounted raids into at least three villages, which they burned to the ground. In their reports, the Germans don't mention civilian casualties, but their orders left little doubt about what was to be done with locals."

Travis grimaced. "I see. And what's been done there since D-Day?"

"I'll get to that, but first, you asked why the *Wehrmacht* would commit resources to subdue the Vercors now when it faces a growing Allied presence in France. Of course, their generals are worried about the threat of a southern invasion thrusting north and joining with our armies moving east out of Normandy to catch them in a pincer. The Vercors is located inland from the Mediterranean." She explained the significant geographical and topographical advantages of the Vercors to the Allies.

Travis looked up at her, round-eyed. "Are we exploiting them?"

Claire pursed her lips and shook her head. "Not that I've heard, but you'd have more insight into that than I would."

"Hmm. And I've heard nothing of the sort." He sat a moment contemplating while studying the map more closely. "What prompted the specific attack on Saint-Nizier? Between the town and the main plateau are numerous mountains. If the Germans wanted to prevent Allied possession of the area, I'd have thought they would take the plateau first."

"It was a punitive raid. The German 157th Reserve Division is headquartered at Grenoble, which lies below Saint-Nizier. Its commander, General Pflaumm, had been probing all the entries into the Vercors. Five days after D-Day, which was three days before the raid on the town, the Germans sent a probe up the main road there. It was effectively stopped—"

"So the Resistance does have some good fighters?"

"Apparently, sir." Claire then explained about the huge French flag with the Resistance symbol that flew from the mountain over Grenoble. "It can be seen by everyone in the valley, including General Pflaumm at his headquarters.

"I imagine that it buoyed the people, particularly coming as it did on the heels of the Normandy invasion. It probably infuriated the general who saw that he not only had to contend with the notion of an enemy base in his backyard but also an aroused population. His orders from Berlin were to use all measures to squelch the matter.

"From what I gather, he is doing just that. He's being deliberate in assembling ground forces for entry at various points of the Vercors and gathering *Luftwaffe* assets for an air strike. His obvious intention is to hit in a coordinated attack in force. If he does that, the people of the Vercors have no chance without Allied support."

Travis listened intently and drummed his fingers on his desk as he absorbed what Claire had told him. “They must be tying up a lot of German resources,” he said at last. “Those are forces that won’t be brought against our men fighting to break out of Normandy.” He chuckled. “Just like the ones being pinned down by the ghost divisions provided by General Jodl.”

Startled at the apparent disregard for the atrocities the Germans must be committing on the Vercors population, Claire stared at him. “I hadn’t thought of the situation like that. I feel for the people there. They’re likely to meet overwhelming force, and from what I gather, the residents in those three villages were massacred. If the Germans—"

“Yes, that is regrettable,” Travis said. “I don’t know enough about the situation, but from what you’ve told me, the residents on that plateau seem stout enough to handle what comes their way in the near term. I’ll pass the information on to MI-6 and designate it as a high priority.”

7

Eleven days earlier, June 6, 1944, D-Day
Camp Griffiss, Bushy Park, United Kingdom

General Dwight "Ike" Eisenhower, Supreme Allied Commander—Europe, studied the signal he had just received from General Sir Henry Wilson, Supreme Allied Commander—Mediterranean. The message informed that, having secured operations sufficiently in the Italian campaign, Wilson was prepared to commit forces and materiel to the southern invasion of France and would start planning the transfers immediately. The last line of the message read, "The target date at which I am aiming is 15 August."

Eisenhower glanced at a calendar on his wall. "Two months away," he murmured to himself. His face remained impassive as he considered his dilemma. He knew that the Brits were not keen on the southern invasion of France. From their view, the Allies in northern Italy should seize the Po Valley, skirt south of Austria, and veer eastward into Yugoslavia and up through Hungary to attack Germany from the east. Doing so, they believed, would force Adolf Hitler to transfer divisions from Normandy, thus relieving pressure on the Allies there.

Further, the move would prevent the Soviet Union from expanding its control of the Balkans. Unbeknownst to the Nazis, Stalin was only two weeks out from launching Operation Bagration, intended to push across eastern Europe simultaneously with the thrust through France. The race to Berlin would then commence in earnest from opposite directions.

However, as opposing visions of postwar Europe emerged, tensions mounted among the Big Three leaders: Secretary Joseph Stalin, President Franklin Roosevelt, and Prime Minister Winston Churchill. Jostling for post-war geopolitical advantage had begun.

The American joint chiefs were dubious of the British plan, preferring to thrust north from Provence on the French Mediterranean coast to support and then join with Allied armies crossing France from the west for a direct thrust into Germany. From their view, the British plan would stretch forces thin while the American plan would mass for a killing assault into the heart of Hitler's Third *Reich*.

Eisenhower walked from his office to the operations room and viewed the situation map. He saw that Pegasus Bridge had been captured on his left flank, troops had landed on all five beaches—Sword, Juno, Gold, Omaha and Utah—and the 101st Airborne Division had secured Sainte-Mère-Église on his right flank. A rumor floated around the headquarters that, as one paratrooper had come down over a church, his parachute caught on the steeple, and he hung very still for hours while fighting raged below. Eisenhower heard the rumor without immediately accepting its credence.

An orderly crossed the operations room and posted new information. The general was pleased to see that Arromanches had been secured, the town where the first and largest of two ports was to be built within days by tugging in huge sections of floatable moorings. Allied engineers would join the sections to form docks extending into the sea and capable of servicing large ships carrying thousands of troops and tons of supplies.

Without such ability in the early days of Operation Overlord, the invasion would flounder. The two major port cities, Cherbourg and Le Havre, separated by over one hundred miles, were heavily defended; and of the two, only Cherbourg was within the zone of the landing beaches.

A key objective was taking Caen. It was a major intersection for rail and highway traffic located a few miles inland on the left flank. Securing that junction would provide a route along France's northern border for a thrust into Germany. It would be much shorter than a trek across France from Cherbourg or from the south along the Mediterranean coast. However, such a push into Germany would need massive support from the Allied armies entering France from the west.

Eisenhower rubbed his chin as he contemplated the map. An aide brought him a cup of coffee. The general thanked him, but otherwise continued studying in silence. Outlined were the countries within his area of operations, including the United Kingdom, France, Norway, Denmark, Holland, Belgium, Germany, and Italy. Also sketched in were the Soviet Union and the countries that Stalin intended to invade in pursuit of the Nazis. Among them were Poland, Czechoslovakia, and the Balkans, stretching south to but not including Greece.

Greece and Yugoslavia had turned into points of contention between the Allies. Both Roosevelt and Churchill, on one side of the issue, were adamant that post-war Greece should remain within western spheres of influence. Stalin appeared to be posturing to extend his hegemony into Eastern Europe. To prevent squabbling among the national leaders while troops were still in combat, the descriptor "spheres of influence" was strenuously avoided.

Studying the map, Eisenhower understood Churchill's concerns regarding Stalin's intentions. Clearly, if the Allies did not advance through Yugoslavia and Hungary, those countries would likely fall under Soviet influence. However, the general's orders, approved by both Roosevelt and Churchill and issued by the Allied Combined Chiefs of Staff, left him no room to consider political factors. His directive was simple but clear: "You will enter the continent of Europe and, in conjunction with the other Allied Nations, undertake operations aimed at the heart of Germany and the destruction of her Armed Forces."

He had held steadfastly to that mandate in planning and, on this day, executing Operation Overlord. As troops were landing on Normandy's beaches through monstrous waves, gale force winds, rain, and murderous artillery and machinegun fire, he had to decide whether to order General Wilson to plan and execute Operation Dragoon, the amphibious landing in the south of France, or to release him to continue north through Yugoslavia as Wilson's prime minister urged.

The decision was Eisenhower's alone. Authority had been delegated to him.

He saw merit in Churchill's proposed concept for operations in the Balkans. Certainly, the prime minister had been a master in previous maneuvers to goad Nazi leaders to move divisions all over the European continent to the Allies' advantage. First in Norway, Churchill's commando raids had compelled the *Wehrmacht* to place several divisions there permanently, keeping them out of combat in North Africa.

Later, the commando raid at Saint-Nazaire had turned the tide for the Allies in the Battle of the Atlantic and obliged Hitler to expend huge resources and commit massive numbers of troops to build and defend the Atlantic Wall. Another of the prime minister's gambits was to outfit a cadaver in a Royal Marine uniform with the rank of major. The dead body was left with several secret documents to be discovered by the enemy. The documents ostensibly showed Allied plans for invading Sardinia and the eastern Adriatic coast, rather than Sicily. That ruse had caused enemy divisions on the latter island to be transferred away, effectively clearing Sicily's beaches for an almost unopposed amphibious landing.

Further, an intelligence operation in Brazil had prompted that country's leader not only to desert the Nazis but also to provide ports and ships along his coast to support the Allied invasion of North Africa and commit troops to combat. Churchill had accomplished this particular maneuver without firing a shot. The success of these and other deception operations exceeded expectations and proved Churchill's canny ability to tie up enemy resources.

As Eisenhower perused the map, he saw the advantages Churchill had pointed out of going up through Yugoslavia. That country would be liberated, and its people could probably be counted on to fight alongside the Allies to invade Germany from the east. Doing so would no doubt cause Hitler to divert divisions from the western front.

Eisenhower also saw the disadvantages of a Balkan campaign. Most significant, it would split the Allies' main effort and dilute their combat power on both axes. Moreover, the Allies could not count on winning every battle. If the *Wehrmacht* stood firm, then it could use the principle of interior lines to redirect divisions to more critical locations within areas under its own control.

Another disadvantage was logistics. Operation Overlord had required every bit of logistical support available and its success was not yet assured. The port in Arromanches, brilliant in concept, was still untested. The plan to resupply fuel oil via pipelines strung along the floor of the Channel had thus far not worked, and such resupply had therefore to be accomplished by the traditional method, oil tankers, which tied up even more shipping assets.

Operation Dragoon would present a whole new set of challenges. France's southern coast in Provence was well defended, and the areas suitable for amphibious landings were narrow. Another problem was distance: Operation Dragoon would commence hundreds of miles away from Eisenhower's armies in northern France and even farther from the German border.

The *Wehrmacht* had well-prepared defensive positions along the Rhône and could therefore be expected to fight tenaciously as they withdrew northward. Meanwhile, they would attrit attacking forces and compel the Allies to expend enormous quantities of ammunition, supplies, and equipment. By the time General Wilson's army approached the German border, his forces could very well be spent.

As Eisenhower weighed the two options, Dragoon in southern France or an advance through Yugoslavia and Hungary, he reflected on his orders. They authorized only military considerations. They did not allow for political concerns such as Stalin's post-war ambitions.

The concept of pushing through Yugoslavia included political concerns: how to arrest Stalin's post-war ambitions. Further, if Overlord failed, or if Dragoon or Yugoslavia did not produce a winning drive into the heart of Germany, Stalin might seek a separate peace with Hitler. In that case, the Western Allies would likely lose the war.

The general banished such considerations. *Stretch our resources, or mass them for a single thrust at the heart of the enemy? My guiding principle has always been to destroy enemy combat forces. Geographical points are only considered if they are important to enemy operations or to us as centers of supply and communications to support our own actions.*

Another aide approached the general. "Sir, we're receiving more urgent messages from General Koenig and from de Gaulle's staff in Algiers asking about support for the Resistance forces in southern France. They make a strident point that those Resistance groups were activated on your orders on the belief of a simultaneous landing in Provence to support Overlord. They're requesting immediate air support for specific targets in southeastern France, particularly in an area called the Vercors."

The general listened absently.

Only yesterday morning in the wee hours before dawn, amidst driving rain and reports of raucous storms over the Channel, he had taken the advice of his chief meteorological adviser, Group Captain JM Stagg, that a break in the weather over Normandy would occur early on June 6. On that basis, he had ordered the execution of Operation Overlord, the invasion of Normandy, the largest amphibious operation ever undertaken. It involved fifty-three hundred ships, three thousand landing craft, fifteen hundred tanks, and twelve thousand airplanes. Each piece of equipment represented thousands of hours of toil and sacrifice, as well as many tears on the home front.

The operation would launch one hundred and fifty-six thousand flesh-and-blood men onto Normandy's beaches in the face of blazing gunfire. Some were combat veterans, but the majority were fresh troops. The bullets propelled to meet them did not differentiate between novice and experienced soldiers. Thousands of veterans and raw recruits would bleed out their lives within the first minutes of descending into the rough surf from the mouths of their landing craft.

After he had given the order to execute Overlord, the general had gone quietly to his desk in his private quarters. There, alone, by his lamplight, he composed two letters. In the first, he congratulated Allied troops for their incredible victory against unfathomable odds. In the second, he took full responsibility for the worst military failure and tragedy in history.

Now, standing surrounded by staff but still alone with his thoughts, he continued to stare at the map. At 06:00 hours that morning, Overlord had launched. The question of which letter he would eventually send still lingered.

"Sir, what response should I give about support?"

Eisenhower glanced at the officer. "The request for immediate air support?"

"That, and Dragoon's timing."

The general diverted his attention back to the map. Two days ago, he had ordered General Koenig, Commander-in-Chief of de Gaulle's Free French army, to activate the Resistance groups in southern France. He had done so while knowing that Operation Dragoon would not occur simultaneous with Operation Overlord. His reason was to keep the *Wehrmacht* off-balance while troops came ashore at Normandy.

For the Germans to believe that rumors of a second operation were not a ruse, Resistance members had to believe them as well. Minutes counted for the success of Overlord, and the longer that German units could be kept in the south, the more probable that Allied troops would establish a permanent presence in France.

But reports had floated up of open combat between veteran German units and loose Resistance groups. The French Resistance in the north were fully supported, but in the south, they were on their own despite promises made.

In formulating his organization and command concept for Overlord and subsequent operations, the general had decided that a single commander, General Sir Bernard Montgomery, would oversee coordinated land and sea operations for the landing. Once ashore, the armies would continue along their natural routes directed by their own ground commanding generals who would then report directly to Eisenhower.

Out of strategic and tactical concerns, Eisenhower retained direct command of the air forces. The missions of strategic versus tactical air assets were distinctly different. Use of each type was critical and required close coordination. Every sortie involved different considerations, whether on the French coast or deep into German territory. No room existed for mixed priorities.

In particular, the general was determined that no strategic air forces would be diverted to support tactical operations. The long-range bombers must concentrate on destroying arms and munitions factories and other industrial facilities in Germany's Ruhr Valley and the Saar Basin, and the tactical air forces must deliver ordnance at the points of greatest need to clear the skies above combat troops. He had learned the hard lesson from Salerno that when minutes counted, no time existed for negotiating support between senior commanders. Only the supreme commander, he himself, General Eisenhower, would decide.

"Sir, how should I respond," the officer persisted.

Eisenhower turned tiredly toward him. He took a sip of coffee and let out a breath. "Tell them that the southern amphibious landing will occur, but that all air assets are currently fully committed elsewhere."

The aide regarded the general without expression. "Is that all, sir?"

"That's all."

As the young officer departed, Eisenhower returned to his office. There he composed a message to General Wilson ordering him to proceed with the planning of Dragoon, to be executed on August 15, 1944, two months hence.

8

June 19, 1944
Central Pacific Ocean, West of Mariana Islands

US Navy Commander Josh Littlefield steadied himself on the rolling deck of the USS *Lexington*, Task Force 58's flagship, as he peered through thin veils of smoke at hundreds of small, dark, puff-ball clouds against the far sky. They were the visible remains of proximity-detonated 5 In. rounds that had exploded within feet of enemy aircraft. The ocean frothed with the debris of enemy aircraft brought down by US anti-aircraft fire and the deadly effective F6F Hellcat fighters.

"The Japs have lost their edge," Josh muttered while stemming envy of his fellow pilots engaged in life-and-death dogfights at a distance halfway to the horizon. Flying was his passion, and flying in combat was where he believed he made his greatest contributions to the war effort, but his superiors thought otherwise. He had distinguished himself not only as a brilliant tactical pilot but also as a strategic thinker. The latter capability led to his assignment as a high-level operations officer.

Once before he had been assigned to Operations. That had been aboard the USS *Enterprise* under Admiral Halsey. Then, two years ago at the Battle of Midway, every available pilot was needed in a final assault on the Japanese fleet threatening that naval outpost. Subsequently, Josh was promoted and returned to flight duties, first as a flight commander, and then as a squadron commander.

As the war continued, the US Navy had studied and experimented with various concepts of command and control and had settled on one now firmly established on every capital ship, including the *Lexington*. Known as the Combat Information Center, it was a room aboard the ship manned by twenty-seven officers and enlisted sailors, each highly skilled in specific, complementary disciplines. Among the assignments were monitoring radio traffic, keeping track of the positions of every vessel in the fleet relative to the flagship, plotting geographical positions, and observing the status of fighters in the air. And for every man watching over his element of information on the friendly side, another did the same for every detail of intelligence gained on the enemy.

In essence, the CIC served as a filtration system fed by every conceivable sensor, including radar; reports from reconnaissance flights seeking to pinpoint Japanese warships' positions by direct observation; and from submarine spotter reports. In addition, the CIC received transmissions from naval intelligence derived from various sources including intercepting and decoding Japanese radio traffic, a capability developed near the beginning of hostilities.

The CIC was led by an evaluator, a US Navy captain who directed the activities of the monitors and analysts in his charge. He had final say on whether a piece of intelligence was complete, corroborated, and relevant to ongoing operations. He sent his analysis and recommendations to the fleet admiral, in this case, Admiral Marc Andrew "Pete" Mitscher.

The evaluator's chief assistant was the CIC officer. At this moment, aboard the Lexington, that was Josh. Against his objections, he had been promoted into the position after his commendable actions in two battles at Truk Lagoon, the latter being four months ago. Ahead of the first of two engagements there, he had, without authorization, flown a "training flight" over the lagoon and found that the Japanese lacked radar on their anti-aircraft guns. During the second, he led a squadron of Hellcats on a successful attack that had aided in permanently wresting the former enemy naval headquarters from Japanese control. Truk Lagoon had been the site from which the entire Japanese fleet operations were commanded.

His many hours of combat flight experience combined with a foray into ground combat with Marine infantry units against Japanese forces at Guadalcanal, as well as action in North Africa, had marked him as an ideal candidate for the position. He understood the weapons on both sides of the battlefield, and how to apply them on his own side for best effect.

"You've played around in the sky long enough," the admiral had said gruffly but with a touch of humor when Josh objected to the assignment. "It's time you kept your feet on a rolling deck and did some real work. Besides, you're near the end of your luck—you've been shot down twice, and I need your brain here while it's still working."

The admiral well understood Josh's obsession with flying. Mitscher had been a pioneer of naval aviation, having been one of three pilots to attempt a first trans-Atlantic flight in 1919 on behalf of the navy, and he had been involved with naval aviation developments over the next two decades, including the concepts and doctrine for carrier warfare. Regardless, he understood the importance of the thinking side of naval aviation, and he valued Josh as someone who understood nitty-gritty details as well as the big picture of naval combat operations.

Not mollified by Mitscher's backhanded compliment, Josh had nevertheless accepted his lot and had thrown himself into his tasks in the CIC. Because the men selected to work there were chosen for competence and dedication, his job was generally easy, mainly requiring him to interact with the various CIC sections and ensure quality analysis and recommendations that would result in sound decisions.

Mitscher was a man cast in the mold of Admiral "Bull" Halsey, even resembling him in stature, countenance, and demeanor. Thin-faced with rough skin and piercing eyes, he looked for and brooked no nonsense. Described by Halsey as "a fighting fool," he had commanded the *Hornet* at Midway, and he had been the air commander over an assortment of army, navy, Marine, and New Zealander aircraft during the thick of fighting at Guadalcanal and in the Solomon Islands. He had then been assigned to develop the concept of a "fast carrier task force," the first of which he now commanded.

The model organized several task groups within the larger task force. Each group contained three to four carriers and their supporting vessels. Added together, they brought Task Force 58's strength to seven fleet carriers, eight fast carriers, four hundred and seventy-five fighter planes, two hundred and thirty-two dive bombers, one hundred and eighty-four torpedo bombers, fourteen reconnaissance aircraft, and eighty-four other ships, including screening destroyers, cruisers, and fast battleships.

Never had a mightier naval task force been assembled, and yet it was only one element of the US fleet steaming to do battle with the Japanese Imperial Navy. Admiral Chester Nimitz, Commander-in-Chief of the Pacific Ocean Areas and the United States Pacific Fleet, directed activity across the vast deep. He had divided his area into two subordinate commands: Northern, under Vice Admiral Frank Fletcher; and Central, under Admiral Spruance.

General Douglas MacArthur, equal in rank and authority to Nimitz, commanded the Southwest Pacific Theater. Thus the Japanese faced two independent avenues of advance, keeping them off balance.

The Central Area under Spruance included the Mariana Islands, which was the Pacific Fleet's current main objective. The string of landmasses spanned four hundred miles and included Saipan, Tinian, and Guam. All three contained flat ground ideal for airfields to support US long-range B-29 Superfortress bombers. From those vantages, they could strike Japan's home islands.

So critical were the Marianas to Japan's defense that intercepted Japanese messages informed US intelligence that the imperial command considered their islands to be Japan's last line of defense. If they were lost, the unthinkable for Japan would become possible—it could lose the war.

Six days earlier, US Marines had landed on Saipan. A vicious battle raged there now with thousands of casualties on both sides.

Recalling his days of ground combat with the Marines on Guadalcanal, Josh shuddered. He remembered the sparse living conditions in hovels dug into the sides of a dirt ridge; incessant bombing; and the bloodcurdling "bonsai" screams of thousands of Japanese soldiers in last-ditch, suicidal charges bent on driving American Marines back into the sea. Vivid in Josh's mind was one Japanese soldier who leaped at him only to be impaled on a rifle and bayonet that Josh had grabbed from the hands of a dead US Marine only seconds earlier. Some nights, even now, two years later, he jerked awake in a sweat, wondering how he had survived. That was the cauldron, multiplied many times over, into which the ground forces now waded ashore at Saipan.

Nimitz had assigned to Spruance the objective of capturing and securing the Marianas. Spruance, a cerebral man who planned carefully and executed cautiously, was the only admiral in his fleet who had not been an aviator.

Alternating command over the same fleet of ships and aircraft, he and Halsey had together island-hopped across the Pacific, driving the Japanese navy farther and farther west. Spruance's mission now was to deliver the kill shot that would destroy the Japanese navy's ability to fight anywhere beyond close proximity to its own coastline. In Mitscher and TF 58, he possessed a formidable weapon to accomplish the task.

For that purpose, in addition to Mitscher's task force, Spruance also had under his command Vice Admiral Turner's TF 51, the Joint Expeditionary Force. It had previously fought tenaciously and victoriously at Tarawa and Makin islands, and now led the ground assault in the Marianas. Spruance also had Vice Admiral John Hoover's TF 57, Central Pacific Forward Area, capable of building airfields and launching long-range bombing raids and strike forces deep into enemy territory. In addition, TF 17 under the command of Vice Admiral Charles Lockwood supported the 5th Fleet with its submarines that prowled the Pacific for enemy ships and provided location reports.

In thinking about the forces arrayed against the Japanese, Josh marveled that the US could lob suppressive fires on the Japanese airfields in the Marianas from miles away. That meant Japanese pilots on the ground in Guam took their chances between being destroyed while their aircraft sat idle on the tarmac or getting hit while they took off. A safer bet was to seek refuge in a bomb shelter.

That was the crux of another advantage of the US versus Japanese fighter pilots. The American flyers arrived on station with roughly four hundred and fifty hours of flight time. Many of them were combat veterans. By contrast, most of the seasoned Japanese pilots had been lost at the Battle of the Santa Cruz Islands and other momentous air battles across the Pacific. Their replacements had only a few flying hours and little if any combat experience. Added to that, the Japanese Zeros were aging while the Hellcats were new and state of the art. In head-to-head aerial combat, the Japanese pilots were no longer equal contestants. The proof was in the numbers.

The aerial battle that Josh now watched raging over the ocean resulted from the fourth Japanese raid of the day against TF 58. The night before, Mitscher's scouts had located the main body of the Japanese fleet steaming to meet its foe. The admiral judged that he was in a perfect position for and requested permission to launch a surprise attack in force to destroy the Japanese fleet.

Admiral Spruance, after taking time to assess the situation, declined consent because the 5th Fleet's mission was to protect the ground force already fighting on Saipan, and because TF 58's pilots were not experienced at night carrier landings, an operation that would be necessitated by the time of day of the proposed raid.

Enraged, and supported in his anger by the other admirals of Spruance's 5th Fleet, Mitscher had been urged to disobey orders and launch the attack. Josh had been present on the bridge during the exchange of messages. He watched Mitscher's jaw tighten and his eyes narrow.

"I could wipe out the Japs' offensive capability in one raid," Mitscher messaged.

"And you could lose half your aircraft in night landing operations for which you have no experience," Spruance replied. "And furthermore, you'd leave our flank exposed, which in turn would jeopardize our ground forces."

"Our radar will warn us of that," Mitscher countered. "We have enough forces to deal with it. Otherwise, you'll play defense instead of offense."

"Admiral Mitscher," Spruance replied, "my task is to protect against what the enemy *could* do. It is not to take action against what I think the enemy might do. If your attack didn't work and our ground forces were wiped out, we'd fail at our overall mission."

"I am confident that will not happen. I will destroy the Japanese fleet."

"We know that the Imperial Japanese Navy wants this battle as much as we do," Spruance responded. "We know their plan. So far, they've executed it just as we expected. We won't deviate from ours. You have your orders."

Mitscher had glared at the signals officer. Other officers on the bridge expressed their disgust. "Ignore those orders," one senior officer said. "Stage the attack."

Mitscher glared at him. "That would be insubordination," he growled. "We follow orders." As he walked away, he added tersely, "He has a point."

After the outburst, Josh had slipped down to the CIC, removed a file from a classified cabinet, and sat down to peruse it. He had gone over it many times, but in light of the heated exchange he had just witnessed, he wanted to scan it again.

The origin of the document and how it came to be in American hands was like something out of a spy novel. It had been under lock and key at Japanese Commander of the Fleet Admiral Koga's headquarters in Palau. Koga had assumed command after the Allies shot down the airplane in which Admiral Yamamoto was flying. On March 29, a reconnaissance plane reported that American ships had been spotted heading in Palau's direction. Given that the island was isolated in the Pacific, Koga decided to move his headquarters to Davao, six hundred miles farther west.

For security reasons, he and his deputy, Vice Admiral Fukudome, flew out in separate planes. Fukudome carried with him a small wooden box. Both officers encountered a typhoon, and both went down. Koga did not survive. After eight hours in the water floating on a seat cushion in the Bohol Strait near Cebu, Fukudome was rescued by local villagers. He had lost the small wooden box during the crash.

Within days, Japanese soldiers arrived at Cebu demanding information about rescued officers and recovered documents. When the villagers pleaded ignorance of any documents, many were subjected to executions as reprisals.

Meanwhile, down the beach from Cebu, a villager at Perilos spotted an object in the water. It was Fukudome's small wooden box. When he opened it, he found a Japanese document wrapped in fine, waterproof leather. Fearful of what it might contain, he quickly placed it in the hands of an American, Lieutenant Colonel Cushing, who worked with local Cebu guerrilla organizations.

After several days, and upon learning of what appeared to be intense Japanese interest in recovering the box, Cushing opened it and found the document. It was written in Japanese. Unable to read it, he messaged General MacArthur's Southwest Pacific headquarters with pertinent information. A month later, a submarine picked it up, and a week after that, it arrived in the hands of MacArthur's intelligence section. Its translators immediately pored over it.

Josh took a deep breath. *Et voila! The full Japanese plan.*

Although weeks had gone by since a translated copy of the plan had landed in Admiral Nimitz' hands, there were no indications that the Japanese suspected that the Americans had it or that they had changed their plans. Message intercepts indicated that they continued to believe that their final line of defense had to be the chain of islands that included Saipan, Tinian, Roda, and Guam—the Marianas.

To defeat the Allies, they planned to lure the Americans into the Southwest Pacific and attack them with the full weight of Japanese imperial forces. To accomplish that objective, they would assemble a force roughly equal to their estimate of the American fleet's strength. Their planes had a longer range than the Americans', and with nine carriers, two hundred and six fighters, one hundred and nine dive-bombers, and seventy-eight torpedo bombers supported by forty-six ships, they could hit from the flank and deliver a knock-out blow.

Japan had not counted on US radar capabilities, which had grown exponentially during the war years. In times past, conventional wisdom predicted that the force that struck first had the advantage. US radar disrupted that paradigm. Low-frequency radar gave early warning that an attack was on its way. As the enemy force drew closer, high-frequency radar identified the type of aircraft. Rather than scrambling to launch aircraft to meet a close-in surprise attack, the US pilots flew three hundred miles west to engage the enemy at TF 58's leading edge. Meanwhile, US warships pelted the land facilities in Guam, Biak, and Ulithi.

The resulting clash was one that both titan navies had anticipated, but the outcome was lopsided in favor of the Americans. Josh suspected that by now, the Japanese rued their eagerness to engage.

TF 58 pilots spotted Japanese Raid I at 08:30 hours, at a distance of three hundred miles, and approaching from the west. Every available Hellcat sortied to meet the attack, and every airborne aircraft on search and patrol missions was directed to clear from the airspace so that the fighters could return and refuel as needed.

Watching the battle unfold on the scopes, charts, and maps in the CIC, Josh saw that the Japanese pilots' poor training and lack of experience was apparent from the start. Inexplicably, rather than zooming straight in to close on their objectives, when they came within seventy miles of their enemy's carriers, they orbited at twenty thousand feet. Josh could only surmise that the pilots' fear and inexperience might account for their delay. Regardless, it allowed TF 58's fighters more time to launch and reach their intercept altitudes of seventeen to twenty-three thousand feet.

The Japanese planes attacked in two groups comprising sixty-nine aircraft: sixteen Zero fighters escorted forty-five bomb-carrying Zeros and eight B6N2 Tenzan Model 12 torpedo bombers, known to the Americans as "Jills."

Josh listened to the crackling radio traffic. "Got one. He's goin' down."

"I got one too. Wait. Got another one."

"I got five already, and we ain't engaged for even five minutes yet."

The raid ended almost as quickly as it began. TF 58 had lost three Hellcats, but the Japanese had paid for those losses in spades—eight Japanese fighters, thirty-two fighter bombers, and two torpedo bombers, all plummeted below the ocean's surface. None had come close to the American carriers.

9

Same Day, June 19, 1944

Josh watched as Raid II appeared on the radar screens. Again, the enemy was detected at three hundred miles out. This force was much larger than the first one, and as it closed and TF 58's fighters scrambled aloft, its composition became clear: one hundred and twenty-eight aircraft, including forty-eight Zero fighters, twenty-seven Jills with torpedoes, and fifty-three Yokosuka D4Y dive bombers. The latter aircraft was specifically designated by the Japanese to bomb aircraft carriers, and was known among American flight crews as "Judy."

Josh knew that Japanese planes were lighter and thus enjoyed a longer range than their American counterparts. If they launched from the Marianas, as this latest raid appeared to have done, they could conduct their attack and then fly to Ulithi or Yap, two islands farther south, to refuel and rearm for another strike. This "shuttle" bombing method, a tactic the Allies used effectively in Europe against the *Luftwaffe* with US bombers launching from Great Britain and refueling and rearming in the Soviet Union for another run over Germany, could double or triple the effectiveness of a regular attack, and in this case attrit US fighter strength.

The only option was to defeat them on their first run.

A deep, electronic-laced voice boomed over the intercom. "Attention! Attention! All pilots report on deck for duty aloft. I say again. All pilots report on deck for duty aloft."

Josh spun around and faced the evaluator, a questioning look on his face.

"Are you a pilot?" the commander demanded with a facetious half-frown.

Josh nodded.

"Then go. We'll handle things here."

Josh grabbed his bag of flight gear from under his desk and rushed out of the CIC. In the passageway, a tumult of pilots bumped against each other as they scurried headlong to retrieve their helmets and flight suits and made their way to the upper decks.

The wind nearly knocked Josh over when he emerged from the *Lexington's* command island onto the flight deck. Already, Hellcats screamed by as they launched from a standstill at the aft end of the runway and flew over the bow within seconds. He rushed to a deck handler on the starboard side in front of rows of Hellcats, lined up abreast, waiting to be launched. A column of pilots had formed in front of the crewman, who directed them to their assigned fighters.

Ordinarily, flyers preferred their own planes. They had decorated the dashboard with family photos and personalized controls with set distances between seat and pedal. On this occasion, all such considerations were tossed aside for the urgency to launch quickly.

Minutes later, in his flight suit and helmet and fully strapped in, Josh sat in the cockpit of a Hellcat, three rows from the front. He flipped switches, made eye contact with his deck handler to check clearance, and punched the ignition button. The starter groaned as the propeller began to rotate. Then the engine roared to life, and the prop spun to invisibility.

Josh waited.

Ahead of him, one by one, the Hellcats peeled off the port side of the front row, taxied into launch position, revved the engine, and waited for the flagman, far down the flight deck, to signal to launch.

The front row cleared, and then the second row. Josh waited as three fighters ahead of him, each in turn, flew over the bow of the *Lexington*, dipped toward the waves, and soared into the sky. Then it was his turn.

He taxied into position, feeling the airframe vibrating as he once again waited. His heart pounded; sweat beads formed over his brow and ran in rivulets along his temples. His engine roared at full throttle.

If his engine stalled or incurred any mishap during his takeoff run, his actions were clear. He would clamber out of the cockpit as fast as possible and aid the ground crew in pushing the aircraft overboard.

At the other end of the flight deck, the flagman watched the waves. When the *Lexington's* prow dipped into a furrow between waves, he lifted his flag to alert the pilot. As the prow lifted halfway, he waved the flag, and another Hellcat raced along a white line painted on the port side. If the timing was right, the aircraft would leap over the forward edge as the prow reached its zenith atop the wave.

Josh grasped the stick. The flagman waved. Josh released the brakes, and his Hellcat screamed along the deck and over the edge. The ocean's roiling waves rose to meet him, then his wings caught the air and he sailed into the sky, rising to meet the ad hoc squadron hastily forming above the carrier.

When receiving his plane assignment, Josh had also received a radio frequency. He tuned to it and called, "Squadron Leader, this is Wannabe. Joining at your rear."

Almost immediately, he heard the reply. "Roger, Wannabe, glad to have you aboard. We're at full capacity. Heading at two-sixty degrees."

"Roger." Josh had no idea who was leading the squadron. It would be someone qualified, but in the haste to get planes aloft, those pilots not already specifically assigned for today's flights followed and obeyed the orders of whichever commander they ended up flying with, irrespective of rank. Josh's callsign was well known among TF 58's pilots. He had gained it during his ground action with the Marines at Guadalcanal. In its aftermath, someone had joked that he was a "Marine wannabe." The label had stuck.

As the squadron flew slightly south of due west, Josh familiarized himself with the cockpit. He had taken his last practice flight only yesterday expressly for the purpose of remaining familiar with the various checklists and switches, and the controls. With roughly an hour to go before any expected encounter with the enemy, he took the time to adjust his seat and check the controls. Satisfying himself that all was copasetic, he took a deep breath and settled in for the flight.

A black-and-white photo on the dash caught his attention: a matronly brunette seated on a chair with two children standing on either side of her. Below, scrawled in blue ink, were the words, "We love and miss you." It was signed in three different pens, "Martha," "Sandy," and "Tom."

Josh wondered who the pilot was. The children looked to be within two years of each other and around the age of ten. He found himself conjecturing whether their father would live out the day. He pushed the thought aside. However, in their place came, unbidden, thoughts of his own family—especially his siblings, Zack and Sherry.

The last Josh knew of Zack, he had been in Italy. But Rome had fallen to the Allies just two weeks ago, and D-Day in Normandy followed the very next day. Was Zack involved in any of that? Was he still alive?

Once again, Josh shoved the unpleasant thoughts aside, only to be replaced by concerns over Sherry. His sister was one of the Flying Angels, the nurses who flew into forward combat zones to treat soldiers so badly wounded that their only hope of survival was immediate treatment by these angels of mercy. By pure chance, Sherry had treated Zack on one such flight after his tank had taken a direct hit. The planes that flew these nurses and their wounded soldiers were clearly marked with red crosses, but the Germans had been known to ignore the markings, ascribing such targeting to error.

Then there were his cousins, Paul, Claire, Lance, and Jeremy. He had been assigned with Paul briefly in Tunisia, but he knew nothing of the others aside from the fact that they all looked very much alike and were involved in the war. Zack and Sherry had met the other British Littlefields and wrote fine things about them in their letters.

Josh's uncle, Stephen Littlefield, born an American who had taken British citizenship after flying for the Royal Air Force in WWI, was their stepfather, so in a strict sense, the British and American wings of the Littlefield family were not blood-related. However, both had thrown their all into winning this war against Fascist, Nazi, and statist-Shinto brutality, and they felt the family connection.

The thought of family was suddenly overwhelming. With the loss of his mother less than two years ago and his father before that, he yearned to see his brother and sister, and that yearning extended to Paul and his siblings.

Family and friends. Isn't that why we fight?

No! He pulled himself from his reverie. *We fight for our comrades to our left and right. Our wingmen. We keep them alive. They keep us alive. All other considerations are secondary.*

Glancing at his watch, he saw that forty-five minutes had elapsed since he had joined the squadron. He flexed his arms and legs to keep them loose.

His radio crackled. "This is Squadron Leader. Ten minutes to contact."

As did the other pilots, Josh squawked his mic to acknowledge and scanned the far horizon. Time now condensed. Only seconds seemed to have passed when his radio crackled again. "This is Red Dot. I see 'em. Eleven o'clock low."

"Squadron Leader here. Roger. Got 'em. We're coming out of the sun. Let 'em pass, and we'll hit their rear from above. Keep 'em in sight."

Josh scanned in the direction indicated and spotted the enemy flight, still just specks against the sky, flying at a slight angle well below and against the squadron's direction of flight. Seconds later, they expanded into dots, and then their wings and tails became recognizable.

Something indefinable about the way Japanese pilots handled their planes alluded to their inexperience. As Josh watched them, he tried to distinguish the element that gave them away. Perhaps they were too low, too slow, or too separated from each other. They were certainly not on a course to take them directly to their target. The sum of factors made the attacking formation look tentative.

Josh shoved the thought into the back of his mind. Doing otherwise could lead to overconfidence, which, in turn, could lead to disaster.

The squadron leader started a wide turn. "Keep your eyes peeled to the west," he cautioned. "Don't want to miss anybody."

They continued the turn until they were lined up several miles behind the Japanese formation. "No dogfights," the leader warned. "They'll beat you in the turns. Diamond formation. Pick your targets. We'll shoot our way through and circle wide. Two more squadrons are right behind us. They'll pick off any still flying when we're done."

Josh re-checked all his gauges, fuel levels, ammunition loads, and triggers. Once more he scanned the sky. The Japanese planes were ahead of him now, and he could distinguish between the Zero escorts, those with bombs, and the Jills and Judies.

Josh almost felt sad at how easy the targets were lining up to be. He would shoot at machines, but they were flown by flesh-and-blood pilots. The sense of deliberately attempting to down aircraft that might result in killing other human beings was not lost on him. The Japanese seemed unaware that they had been sighted and were now in their enemies' crosshairs.

"Fire at will."

The Judy in Josh's sights loomed large. He pulled the trigger. His plane shook as his six .50 in M2/AN Browning air-cooled machine guns spat out a stream of tracers. They arced across the sky behind the Judy and plowed into her fuselage.

Josh fired another burst.

The Judy's nose dropped. Smoke swirled from her engine. Aircraft around her blew into fragments as Hellcats unleashed a torrent of hot steel that found their marks.

The Japanese dispersed, some planes climbing, others diving, but already, their numbers had been cut by a third. Josh's original target plunged into the ocean.

He raised his nose. Another enemy plane, a Zero bomber, crossed his gunsights. Josh pulled the trigger. Seconds later, it trailed smoke as it dove into the dark waters.

"Wannabe, this is Blue Dog. You got one on you."

Instinctively, Josh dropped the Hellcat's nose, raised his eyes, and scanned the skies back to his left.

"He's behind and to your left," Blue Dot said. "Might be the only veteran in the bunch. He knows his stuff. He arced behind us right after we first hit."

Josh cut sharply to his right and dove in a corkscrew.

"This is Blue Dog. Keep jinking and hold your general direction. I've gone wide right. I should get to him before he gets to you, but it'll be close."

Josh flew high enough above the wavetops to allow quick up and down changes. He also jinked erratically left and right to keep from presenting a steady target.

"He's coming around behind you," Blue Dog called. "I need a few more seconds."

Heavy plinking on Josh's left wing informed him, even before he felt the effects, that his Hellcat had been hit. Fortunately, he was not wounded.

"This is Wannabe. He got me, but so far, I can still fly."

"Wannabe, this is Squadron Leader. Head for home. Blue Dog got your bogey. He won't bother you again."

Josh's plane vibrated fitfully. He checked his left wing. Liquid dripped from its aileron. His fuel gauge for that wing showed a drop in its level. "Squadron Leader, this is Wannabe. I'm losin' gas."

"Can you make it all the way?"

"I think I can. It's dripping, not spilling. It could be close, though."

"Can you climb to where you could glide for a while?"

"I'd use up too much fuel. At the rate it's leakin', my best bet is to stay down until I have to come up to land."

"Roger. We'll keep watch. Not much enemy left."

Josh breathed a sigh of relief. The attack had been defeated. He flew well above the waves now. Glancing skyward, he saw several Hellcats orbiting, and took comfort in their solicitude. Then he concentrated on keeping his crippled aircraft aloft and flying straight and level toward the *Lexington*.

He crabbed against the wind, further eroding fuel economy. When the level in the damaged wing was nearing empty, he closed it entirely so that none from the right wing would flow into it. Meanwhile, he searched ahead for a glimpse of the tall aircraft carrier.

He flew past the picket ships, those stationed ahead of TF 58 with radar and guns to both detect enemy actions and suppress fire from its land bases. Just being inside the task force security perimeter gave comfort that, if he had to ditch in the ocean, he would be rescued quickly.

At last, he saw the *Lexington*, a most welcome sight. As he drew near, the ship appeared so big and solid—and so tall.

Josh checked his gauges and gulped. He was almost flying on fumes, and he would have to climb to land the Hellcat on the deck. Already, the engine coughed occasionally, but at least the ship was facing the same direction he would need to land.

Josh began a slow climb, interrupting it every time the engine sputtered. Gradually, he overtook the ship. As he approached, other Hellcats returned and landed safely. Josh keyed his mic. "Squadron Leader, this is Wannabe. Can I get priority?"

He checked his fuel gauge again. It showed no interval between the needle and the thin line marking an empty tank.

The stern of the *Lexington* filled his windscreen and he tossed from side to side in its turbulent tailwind. Since he had to travel faster than the ship to clear the rear edge of the flight deck, he could not cut his speed to conserve fuel which, theoretically, no longer existed. But if he used the last drop of fuel before clearing the stern, he could crash into its steel wall.

He flew closer and closer, the gap narrowing to feet, and then inches, and then he was beyond the stern and snagged by one of the arresting cables. The plane dropped to the deck. Josh lurched forward in the cockpit and then sat still, breathing heavily and wondering if he really still lived.

A deckhand hurried to help him out. "How much gas I got left?" Josh asked.

The deckhand went to check the tanks. "None."

Josh stumbled through the passageways on his way to the CIC, shaking off his third close encounter. He passed a ready room for one of the squadrons. Posted on a blackboard in large white letters was the directive, "Get the carriers."

Numbly, he registered that to win this epic battle, not only must the fighters be knocked out of the air, but their home bases and the aircraft carriers must also find their ways to the bottom of the ocean. A burst of laughter caught his ear, and he realized that, as opposed to his own sober demeanor, the general atmosphere surrounding him was festive. He passed a cheerful fellow pilot, Lieutenant Ziggy Neff from Missouri.

"I got four kills today," he told Josh. "It was like a turkey shoot back home."

Josh smiled wryly. "And that's probably how this battle will be remembered," he replied, "the Great Marianas Turkey Shoot." Several other officers in the passageway laughed uproariously with Neff. Josh was too tired to join in.

He continued to the CIC, and when he entered, a burst of applause greeted him. "You made it all the way home this time," the evaluator said, smiling as he clapped an arm around Josh's shoulders and shook his hand. "Welcome. We monitored your radio all the way back. We're glad you made it in one piece."

Amid much shoulder clapping and praise, Josh made his way back to his desk. He looked up at the status board through tired eyes, and stared in disbelief. Although thirty to forty Japanese planes had penetrated and attacked American warships below TF 58's overhead security, none had scored a direct hit, and only light damage had been incurred. Of the one hundred and twenty-eight aircraft in the second strike, ninety-seven had been shot down, including thirty-two fighters, forty-two Judies, and twenty-three Jills. The few that had threatened the fleet close-in had been unable to deliver their payloads accurately. Josh saw no entries for US losses. His had been the closest call.

He monitored the next two enemy raids from the CIC. No general call for all pilots was issued. The attacks were equally ineffective. The third consisted of forty-seven aircraft, forty of which returned to their carriers shortly after their initial attack. The remaining seven fell to their American foes.

Josh found the fourth raid to be interesting to watch, both from the deck and on the radar screens. It contained thirty Zero fighters, ten additional Zeros with bombs, thirty-six dive bombers, and six Jills. They appeared on the screen heading in a direction where no American warships plied the waters. Then, at a point where, presumably, they discovered their error, they split into three groups. One of them headed for its airfield in Guam but it was quickly intercepted by Hellcats. Thirty of forty-nine other enemy aircraft were knocked out of the sky. Incoming reports indicated that the remaining nineteen were crippled, although they were able to land.

Fifteen other Japanese planes located and attacked the carriers *Bunker Hill* and the *Wasp,* but quick maneuvering and effective anti-aircraft gunnery frustrated their efforts. Only one enemy aircraft escaped, having done no damage to the US ships.

As the last raid wound to its end and final figures were added to the status board, Josh studied it again. It had been a bad day for the Japanese. They had lost three hundred and sixty-five of four hundred carrier aircraft and an unknown number of ground-based planes from Guam. Worse still, three of their nine carriers were sunk, and two were severely damaged.

Josh looked at the columns showing American losses. Only one hundred and thirty aircraft had been downed. Fortunately, no appreciable damage had been exacted on any American ships. However, the next column was sobering. Seventy-six airmen had been killed. Seventy-six American families would soon be grieving.

Despite the resounding victory, Josh regarded the numbers with misgivings. The ground battle on Saipan still raged with the death toll counted in the thousands, and the Japanese Imperial Navy still controlled the waters west of the Marianas. He took some comfort in knowing that the enemy fleet was no longer capable of projecting its power east of that island chain. The next major targets for strategic bombing were Japan's home islands. That could be contemplated when Saipan and the rest of the Marianas were secure and US B-29 Superfortress bombers could base there.

10

June 27, 1944
Saint-Martin-en-Vercors, France

Stern-faced, Major Huet stood behind his desk to address Eugène Chavant, Jeremy Littlefield, and the commanders of the four military sections of the Vercors, Captains Geyer, Beauregard, Ullman, and Prévost. The major had brought under his personal command Abel Chabal and the men over-watching the Germans near Villard and Saint-Nizier. Also present were members of Huet's staff.

"This week began with sixty enemy aircraft landing and basing at Chabeuil," he said. "Then the news became steadily worse. The next day, several of these planes took off and bombed Plan-de-Baix. The distance from their airfield to that town is roughly the same as it is to Vassieux. An advantage for our defense is the mountain range between Chabeuil and Vassieux, but we can't count on the high peaks and ridges to protect us forever. Reconnaissance flights are constantly overflying them. I assure you that the *Luftwaffe* is seeking the best way for aircraft to enter our plateau.

"German bombers also hit Beaufort, sixty miles northeast of Grenoble, and then came back south and struck at Combovin, just a few miles from Chabeuil." He grimaced. "Don't ask me about the rationale behind the flight pattern. I don't understand it either, but obviously the overall objective was to intimidate. At Combovin, they made a direct hit on the headquarters of the Resistance group responsible for defending the southwest foothills of the Vercors." He arched his brow. "German intelligence has been very good, which suggests that the Resistance has been infiltrated."

His face softened. "Our people are brave. At Combovin, Lilette Lesage rescued five wounded *maquisards*. She drove them into the countryside, left the main road, drove over cart tracks into the mountains, and hid them."

Jeremy knew Lilette. She was a twenty-year-old ambulance driver, tanned from being outdoors constantly, with dark hair, brown eyes, and a lively disposition. He had seen her that very morning setting off in her ambulance, wearing a blue frock.

The major's expression hardened into a somber mask. "Unfortunately, an observation plane spotted the group and directed German troops to their location. The soldiers executed the *maquisards* and left Lilette for dead with a wound in her thigh."

Huet's eyes moistened and his lips quivered as his compassion for Lilette and the lost *maquisards* combined with disgust for the Germans. No one stirred as he continued, "Fortunately, Lilette was rescued and is recovering in hospital."

His eyes flashed, but his expression otherwise remained impassive. "We've seen the enemy's savagery before, at Échevis, at Les Barraques, at Vassieux, even here at Saint-Martin, and now at Saint-Nizier. It continues to spread, and the *Wehrmacht* is driven to desperation because of the invasion at Normandy and the one it knows must come in Provence. And our plateau is General Pflaumm's main objective."

A knock on the door interrupted Huet. It opened and a senior sergeant indicated, by his demeanor, an urgent matter. The major crossed the room, consulted in whispers, and then returned to the front. At the door, the sergeant led in another man who looked exhausted, disheveled, and in shock.

Huet himself had paled as fury surfaced under his controlled visage. "I've just received the worst news yet. But rather than tell it to you secondhand, I prefer that you hear it from an eyewitness." He indicated the man who had just entered with the sergeant.

The man stood, quavering. He looked into a faraway place and not directly at anyone, and when he spoke, he stammered, and his voice broke.

"I-I come from Saint-Donat in the Drôme Department, ten miles south of the Vercors." He stopped speaking and turned to the sergeant. "May I have a cigarette?" His hands shook as he took one and lit it. His eyes closed and his head and shoulders bobbed slightly in gratitude as he exhaled the first puff of smoke.

"Yesterday," he went on in haunted tones, "we were attacked. Our town had been active in the Resistance, and we were chosen to be an example. German fighter planes came in low over Saint-Donat and machine gunned everyone in their path.

"Then—" His voice broke again, and for a few moments he appeared unable to continue. "Then," he rasped, "they brought in the Mongols."

He explained in halting, sometimes murmured speech that the Mongols were POWs from the eastern provinces of the Soviet Union. As an alternative to being confined in prison camps, they had been offered the opportunity to form into punitive units, be transported to Germany, and let loose under *SS* supervision to savage the public in centers of resistance.

"They ransacked houses and shops," the man cried, his speech turning to wails as his body shook violently. "They machine gunned anyone they saw. They lined up people against buildings and toyed with them, sometimes torturing them before executing them. They, they—" He gasped for breath and fought for composure. Fury burned from his eyes as he relived the horror he had witnessed. "They went from house to house and raped every female they could find. Mothers, old women, little girls—it didn't matter." Tears flowed freely from his face, and he collapsed back onto a chair.

Huet sat unmoving, his face impassive. At last he gasped, "My God!" and lapsed back into silence.

A stunned hush settled over the room. Jeremy stared at the floor in front of him, trying to comprehend what he had heard. He knew Huet's thoughts now and those of everyone in the room. The man had just foretold what was in store for the whole of the Vercors should the *Wehrmacht* succeed in overwhelming the plateau.

Without Allied support, the rape of the Vercors is certain.

When the man from Saint-Donat had been led away to safe quarters and the company of sympathetic villagers, Huet sat quietly at his desk. Jeremy watched him, astounded at the officer's composure. Only the major's eyes gave away the stirrings of the mind.

"The enemy is gathering to attack from the northeast and from the south," Huet said at last. "They'll come in first with an air assault at Vassieux and La Chappelle. We have no reason to believe that we'll receive Allied support—"

"Our support will come," Chavant broke in softly. "I received assurances directly from Jacques Soustelle in the name of General de Gaulle. They'll come."

Huet did not reply directly to Chavant. "We must assume that we're on our own," he said to the entire group. "New *maquisards* arrive every day. Keeping spies out and everyone sheltered and fed will be a challenge, and we still have no more weapons. My chief of staff, Captain Tannant, investigates each new volunteer, but we're up to six thousand people from other places now, men and women, and most join the fight."

Captain Geyer, commander of the 11th Cuirassieres Regiment, stood. He was known for his independence and flash, a cavalryman who, before Huet's arrival, had led horseback raids on German facilities in the valleys until retributive assaults on Les Barraques and Vassieux had prompted him to re-think his tactics. By then, he had alienated the Vercors population, who saw his actions as provoking the German reprisals. As a result, he had moved his camp to *La Forêt de Lente,* the largest virginal forest in France. His relations with Huet were strained, but the major recognized a good fighter and retained him in his command.

"Sir, may I make a recommendation?" Geyer asked.

The major nodded.

"Time is short. We don't know when the Germans will strike. Despite Monsieur Chavant's assurances, we have no evidence that any support is coming."

"It's coming," Chavant broke in angrily.

Geyer started to protest, but Chavant shouted over him. "If you hadn't gone on those silly raids earlier this year, we might not be in this mess. The people of Échevis, Les Barraques, and Vassieux might still be alive. You prodded the wolf."

"That's stupid," Geyer fired back. "Are we going to condemn Abel Chabal for all the raids against us and the people in the valleys because he flew that flag over Moucherotte for everyone in Grenoble to see, including General Pflaumm."

"Enough," Huet commanded. "We have no time for this." He faced Geyer. "What is your suggestion?"

"That we disperse our forces to the most defensible terrain and prepare for guerrilla warfare."

Huet's response was immediate but measured. "Captain, your suggestion is noted, but we're not going to act on it, at least not immediately." Seeing a sullen reaction, Huet went on. "I have here a message that will surely interest you." He reached for a slip of paper on his desk and scanned it. "We are to be receiving a group of parachutists tonight—"

A chorus of derision met his announcement. "We've heard that before."

"I'm a doubting Thomas."

"How many promises are we expected to believe?"

Huet raised a hand for quiet. "Regardless of our doubts, we must prepare to receive the group. Perhaps help is really coming."

He set the note aside. "Getting back to Geyer's suggestion, our prime responsibility is to safeguard the people of the Vercors. They will feel unprotected if we vacate to outlying camps. Mobility is difficult, so the reality is that if we adopt primarily guerrilla tactics, we might not arrive where we're needed in time to do anything other than count the casualties.

"Instead, we'll man the passes, continue to collect intelligence on German movements, train our recruits, and keep pressing London and Algiers for support. We've been promised a regiment of paratroopers. They can come quickly, and when they do, more support will follow, including heavy weapons and anti-aircraft guns."

He paused and blew out a deep breath, then looked directly at Chavant. "On the other hand, we must consider that no support will arrive, at least not in time to save us."

Chavant reacted angrily, and Huet held up a hand. "We must consider the worst case, Eugène. As much as we'd like to rely on promises made, we'd be negligent not to plan for the circumstances that stare us in the face."

Chavant nodded dolefully and dropped his head.

Huet resumed. "The enemy still doesn't know our strength or equipment levels, or they'd have been here already, and they would not have left only a light occupation force up by Saint-Nizier and Villard. They're still probing. We have to make best use of whatever time we have, and if help does arrive, they'll find in us a disciplined unit capable of carrying out actions we jointly undertake. To that end, we'll prepare as if we are a proper military district, with assigned areas of command and responsibility."

Huet addressed the cavalry officer directly. "Acting on your suggestion now would be premature for the reasons outlined, Captain Geyer, but it has merit. We'll establish contingency plans, and if we see that we're about to be overrun, I'll give an order, and each unit will withdraw to designated areas and conduct guerrilla tactics as each subordinate commander deems fit. But only when I give the order. Am I clear?"

Reluctantly, and with an expression barely concealing his irritation, Geyer acceded with a nod.

"I'll close this meeting now. Return to your commands. We'll send new recruits to each of you following vetting. Ramp up your training programs. Until we have arms for all, make your *maquisards* earn their rifles by being the best shots. And prepare your contingency plans as we just discussed. I'll send out more specifics, and then I want to review, coordinate, and consolidate a final plan within a week."

Huet surveyed the faces in the room. "Gentlemen, my firm belief is that the Allies will win this war, but we will not be able to stop all the suffering that will occur on our beloved Vercors. Our job now is to hold the enemy at bay, and failing that, to minimize our foes' success until their fate is so clear that they must retreat to Germany of their own accord. That is how we will survive. That is how the Vercors will survive."

When the meeting broke up, Jeremy wandered onto the street in front of the Hôtel Breyton. As he was descending the few front stairs, he encountered Captain Geyer also making his departure.

"Hey, Labrador," Geyer called. "Can we talk? We haven't had much opportunity to become acquainted."

"Of course," Jeremy said with a measure of uncertainty. He had not formed an independent assessment of the brash cavalryman, but he knew of the antipathy that existed between the officer and Huet, the animosity that Chavant bore for him, and the general abhorrence of the population who blamed him for provoking General Pflaumm's raids. "What's on your mind?"

"I believe your job is to keep lines of communication and supply going, with emphasis on intelligence gathering, between your area of responsibility and your headquarters in London. Is that correct?"

Jeremy nodded. "You've summed it up succinctly."

"So, are you not reporting accurately or is your headquarters just not listening?"

Not surprised at the man's directness but taken aback by it when experienced on a personal basis, he searched Geyer's face for signs of rancor. Seeing only a neutral expression, he replied, "That's a fair question, Captain. I'm doing as thorough a job as I know how in the circumstances and I believe I'm being heard. That leaves one other option: that resources are already stretched."

"And they're just not telling you?"

"We're in a war that spans the world. Priorities are always in flux. I'm expected to do the best I can with what I have."

Geyer scoffed. "Which is pitifully little, and as Huet points out, we have a population to protect. I believe that he is going about it the wrong way."

Seeing Jeremy draw back in reaction to his comment, Geyer went on. "I'm a soldier. I obey orders, but that doesn't prevent me from having an opinion. I see the major trying to build up a headquarters on the scope and scale of a regiment. He's pursuing conventional army solutions that are inadequate to the threat. Clearly, guerrilla tactics are now called for. Frankly, I'm appalled—"

"He's expecting that support will come at some point—"

"We're already past that," Geyer interrupted steadily. "The Germans haven't attacked in full force yet because they're gathering their forces. The activity at the Chabeuil airfield indicates that. We should prepare for the worst case—"

"I don't disagree with you, but some people believe that your raids on the plains invited German attacks on the Vercors."

Geyer stared stonily at Jeremy. Then his expression broke, and he looked chagrined. "I know. I made mistakes. I believed in hitting the enemy where I could at every opportunity." He took a deep breath. "I'm more cautious now, and I've moved my camp deep into the forest where I keep the men in constant training." He thrust his head toward Jeremy with narrowed eyes. "My actions don't mean that I don't care for the people of the Vercors or that I intended to endanger them. But now, I believe that guerrilla tactics are all that will save us. The opportunity to protect the Vercors without high civilian casualties is sliding by, and I'm horrified that regular army methods are being employed in what is not regular warfare."

"Huet considered your concept and incorporated it as a contingency."

Geyer smacked his lips impatiently. "Regular and guerrilla tactics are not the same. You don't turn untrained men from one type of warfare to another in an instant."

A shout from one of Geyer's men across the street interrupted the conversation. The captain glanced at his watch. "I have another engagement," he said. "I must go."

Jeremy watched the cavalryman hurry across the street, mount a horse he had captured from the Germans, and gallop away in a cloud of dust. Then Jeremy turned and continued through Saint-Martin's streets, looking into the faces of the townspeople as he passed them. He had seen many of them almost daily over the past five months, and he regarded them in the strange way that shared happiness or tragedy causes people to feel that they have known each other all their lives. Since January, he had shared the thrilling anticipation of Operation Montagnard, the liberation that it would bring, and the special place in French history it would create for the Vercors. Now he saw on their faces common expressions of fear, uncertainty, and stoicism as the reality of their situation sank in.

His thoughts turned to Amélie in Lyon. She would not be content to remain safe and protected while her younger sister fought with the Resistance in Normandy or while Jeremy was operating somewhere unknown to her. She had been devastated by the capture of another operator, Jeannie Rousseau, for whom she had been the courier and only barely escaped herself. She had sworn to find her friend. Whether she did or did not, she would not give up the fight for France until Germany had been routed or... Thinking of Amélie's smile, her auburn hair, and honey-colored eyes caused Jeremy's throat to catch as he contemplated the worst case.

For a fleeting moment, he thought how easily he could slip unnoticed over the high ridgelines on one of the mountain paths and make his way back to Lyon. He was practiced in moving overland through occupied territory with its guards and checkpoints. He had even impersonated a *Gestapo* officer on three separate occasions. He could be with Amélie and avoid the certain fate of so many on the Vercors.

He banished the thought. Were he to abandon the people who most needed him during this crucial time, living with himself would be impossible.

He trudged back to the Hôtel Breyton, up the stairs to the third floor, and into the signaler's office. There, he sent yet another urgent message demanding immediate support. His lot was now cast irrevocably with that of the people of the Vercors Massif.

Just past midnight, Major Desmond Longe, commander of an SOE liaison team, parachuted into an open field outside of Vassieux to a reception he could not have anticipated. He was joined by three members of his own team and fifteen American Office of Strategic Services, or OSS, paratroopers led by Lieutenant Vernon Hopper.

To the residents of the Vercors, the appearance of these Allied soldiers represented the advance team of the long-awaited paratrooper regiment and the beginning of the full execution of Operation Montagnard. With wine and music, they feted the tired newcomers until dawn.

When the celebration had quieted, Jeremy approached Major Longe, a lanky officer who exuded competence. "When is the regiment going to arrive?"

Longe regarded him quizzically. "I know of no regiment deploying here. My men and the Americans are here to help train the *maquisards*."

With a sinking feeling, Jeremy asked, "What about the southern invasion on the Provence coast? When will that occur?"

Once again, the major shook his head. "Everything and everybody is going over to Normandy. We've put a hundred and seventy-five thousand men on the ground there, but I've heard of no operation like the one you described planned for here—and given that I'm here for your support, I'd know about it."

Feeling his heart sink into his stomach, Jeremy merely nodded bleakly. "I see."

11

July 3, 1944
Saint-Martin-en-Vercors, France

The town bustled with excitement, tempered by the sense of peril of unknown size lurking beyond the forested escarpments, rolling foothills, vertical limestone cliffs, and high mountain peaks that had thus far prevented a German occupation of unspeakable brutality. All knew it was coming, but today, the citizens of the Vercors would declare and celebrate their freedom and independence.

A man appointed as a commissioner of the republic by General de Gaulle's headquarters in Algiers, Yves Farge, had arrived that day to much anticipation. Along with Colonel Descour and Major Huet, he would establish his own HQ in the town and preside over a ceremony to formally recognize the Vercors' existence as an independent country.

Since the fall of Saint-Nizier, a pall had descended over the Vercors. Vicious *Wehrmacht* incursions had continued, as well as daily surveillance overflights. The major attack would come, but when or from which direction, no one could be certain. A rhythm of life had set in with ominous undertones—when something was needed that was not available within the area, a band of *maquisards* descended from the Vercors and took it, either by the willing generosity of residents or theft from German stores and convoys.

An enterprising sergeant organized a group of teenage boys to raid farms in the plains and bring back as many eggs as they could. With so many new mouths to feed on the Vercors, the breakfast staple was in short supply.

In another foray, a raiding party seized all the uniforms in a warehouse. Although stopped at a German checkpoint on the way back to the Vercors, they succeeded in returning intact with their cargo. Issuing the uniforms to *maquisards* and veterans alike resulted in a huge upward psychological shift.

On another excursion, a raiding party drove ninety miles to Lyon, and in a well-coordinated attack, freed fifty-two Senegalese POWs who had been pressed into service as waiters in a German officers' mess. Known for their imposing statures, discipline, and military tenacity, the Senegalese soldiers customarily served as bodyguards for important persons. Despite the distance and danger in traveling to Lyon, the addition of the Senegalese to the Vercors fighting force was deemed desirable, and the rescue mission stoked the resistance fighters' sense of defiance.

Amazingly, the raid was completed without incident. The Senegalese then happily assumed the task of guarding the headquarters of Colonel Descour, Major Huet's immediate superior.

Apart from the raids to secure supplies and rescue captives, a battle had taken place at Pont Chabert bridge located at the north end of the Routes des Ecouges, a roughly five-mile descent deep into a canyon between parallel mountain ranges. There, the road crossed the bridge over a deep gorge and turned sharply into a dark, curved tunnel a third of a mile long and chiseled out of solid rock. Surrounding the bridge and the tunnel, steep cliffs rose hundreds of feet to a ridgeline.

Unlike the slopes of Saint-Nizier, the terrain was so unforgiving that an attack by this route seemed unlikely. Only accomplished cliff-climbers could hope to ascend the steep walls. To effect a pincer maneuver was impossible.

Nevertheless, Captains Beauregard and Henri Ullman had driven out to review their position overlooking the narrow passage. As they did, they saw motion and heard engines echoing from the mountainsides, and then spotted a gray column of German troop carriers and other heavy equipment wending its way along the canyon floor toward the far end of the tunnel. On exiting the near end, the formation would turn onto the bridge and begin the long ascent on the Routes des Ecouges. As Beauregard observed the convoy through binoculars, his throat caught, dreading what he saw—towed mountain artillery, a game changer.

The ensuing battle lasted for several hours. Fortunately, Beauregard had two veteran Russian machine gunners with direct lines of fire into the near mouth of the tunnel, and they laid waste as the Germans emerged. However, with heavier weapons and more manpower, the Germans pressed their advance and secured a bridgehead just beyond Pont Chabert. They brought their machine guns forward and laid down covering fire while their artillery maneuvered into position.

At first, the German artillery overshot the French positions, but soon the rounds landed with deadly effectiveness on Beauregard's men. Then, just when the Germans appeared prepared for a full-scale attack, they withdrew.

Although relieved that his position had not been overrun, Beauregard understood the reality: General Pflaumm's troops had once again probed an unlikely avenue of approach, identified the French strongpoints on this route, and refined their assumptions of the Vercors' strength in manpower and weaponry. Obviously, the German commander was exploring all possibilities.

Jeremy sat in the Hôtel Breyton café with Chavant discussing Beauregard's news of the German incursion at Pont Chabert, the plight and morale of the Vercors' citizenry, and a ceremony to be conducted shortly. Chavant had completely overtaken the café with security posted outside. Thus, they were surprised when the door burst open and they heard a heavy clomp of boots, followed by a cheery, "*Bonjour, mes amis!*"

Recognizing the voice, Jeremy sprang to his feet and whirled around to greet his immediate SOE superior, Francis Cammaerts. "Roger!" Jeremy exclaimed, using Cammaerts' codename. "What a surprise, and how good to see you."

Chavant stood as well and greeted Roger with a broad smile. "It's been too long, my friend." He gestured toward Jeremy. "But you left us in competent hands. Labrador serves us well."

Roger towered over the two men, his narrow face exhibiting a controlled smile, his slanted shoulders and lean figure indicating a man in superb physical condition. Although having a tall stature was less than desirable for a covert operator, he had outlasted most of his peers. By fighting alongside the *maquisards* and displaced French veterans and doing all within his ability to keep them supplied with money, equipment, and weapons, he had won the hearts of the people within his area of responsibility, of which the Vercors was only a part. Any member of the Resistance from south of the plateau, extending north past Lyon, and incorporating seven French departments would gladly house, feed, and protect Roger. He came and went without advance notice, and thus he avoided ambush and betrayal.

Five months had passed since Jeremy had been assigned as his deputy in the Vercors. Jeremy had adopted Roger's methods, and by virtue of his constant work on behalf of the Vercors' defense, he had gained a measure of the affection and regard that his mentor enjoyed.

"It's been touch and go here," Jeremy said when they were seated and Chavant had poured three goblets of wine. "As you must know, we're expecting an attack."

"I do know," Roger said, "which is why I came." He smiled. "And to attend today's celebration." He grew serious again. "The fight might be worse and come sooner than we anticipated." He sipped his wine and took a moment to frame his thoughts. "Unfortunately, because the war is wide and being fought fiercely on the plains, I can't stay long. But I wanted to give personal warning about what might be coming this way."

He let out a long breath. "Yesterday, I observed something over Montélimar. That's a village—"

"I know the place," Chavant broke in. "It's about thirty miles southwest of Vassieux overlooking the eastern bank of the Rhône."

"That's the one. It's constrained by geography, but it has room for an airfield." He took a deep breath and let it out. "The Germans were using it to practice with DFS 230 gliders. They carry ten fully equipped infantrymen and mount an MG 34 machine gun on the top. The idea is that as they land, the man just behind the pilot will stand through an open hatch in the roof and provide covering fire for the other troops as they deploy. The pilot is also an active infantryman."

Roger took a short breath before continuing. "They've done something different this time. They've attached parachutes to the back end of the airframes." He arched his brow. "These aircraft are small and rickety. They have light metal frames and wide wingspans. Just the basics, and a cloth skin." He leaned forward. "So, here's the worrisome part. Instead of landing by circling in the sky as gravity and drag slows the aircraft and brings it to the ground, the parachute acts as an airbrake to slow it down for a fast, straight-in landing."

Chavant and Jeremy picked up on the implications immediately. "We've been worried about an air assault," the Frenchman breathed. "We had in mind airborne machine guns and dropped bombs. But you're saying that they could bring in many troops quickly by air using these gliders. They'd avoid our blockades at the passes as if they weren't even there."

Chavant let out a long sigh. "And still no news of support. Do you have any?"

Roger shook his head. "I'm sorry. I don't. Along with Jeremy, I've been pressing London, and your French command here keeps sending urgent messages to Algiers. I can tell you that the fighting at Normandy is fierce. The Allies keep bringing men, supplies, and equipment ashore at Arromanches. Unfortunately, a storm blew away the second such port two days after it was built, and the fighting there has taken longer than expected. The Allies are still fighting to capture the port at Cherbourg. Then we'll hit the enemy with a force that's stronger by several magnitudes."

Chavant grunted. "That's all nice to hear," he growled with a tinge of fury, "but the British still haven't taken Caen. Even if a breakout happens there soon, it does nothing to help our people *here*. We acted on promises. We committed on promises. We provoked the enemy on promises. Any idea of when the southern invasion will take place?"

Again, Roger shook his head, his face somber. "I don't."

"So, we received Major Longe's SOE team and Lieutenant Hopper's American paratroopers," Chavant growled in disgust, "but we're essentially in the same position that we were before their arrival—underpowered to take on the onslaught that is coming." He grunted. "Well," he said with measured resolve. "You came at a good time. General Zeller is here, and Colonel Descour."

He caught himself. "I should say General Descour. He's been elevated, and so has Huet, who is now a lieutenant colonel." A smile crossed his face. "Come to think of it, I hear that you've also been promoted to lieutenant colonel, Roger. Congratulations."

Roger smirked. "News travels. That was only done so that I could speak with authority to all those generals." He glanced across at Jeremy. "I also carry a message from SOE headquarters that this young captain has also advanced. At my insistence, he is now Major Littlefield. He carries the responsibility; he ought to carry the rank."

Nonplussed, Jeremy struggled for words. "That wasn't necessary, sir."

"It's done, nevertheless," Roger replied. "Now, shall we get on with business?"

Chavant clapped Jeremy on the shoulder. "Much deserved." He cleared his throat. "As I was saying, Zeller and Descour will attend our festivities to announce the Free Republic of the Vercors, properly recognized by the exiled Free French government in Algiers. Already, we have roadblocks with signs indicating our border and men checking identifications. For the rest of France, after today and until the full republic is restored, we will be a foreign country.

"Huet will be at the ceremony, and naturally, Geyer will lead a parade on horseback. We're big into military parades these days. It's about all we have to lift our spirits, and Geyer is such a priss. He always insists on riding at the front of them."

He sighed. "I hope I'm not being a Don Quixote tilting at windmills, but we've set up a police authority, a post office, and other government organs including a foreign office. Of course, when victory finally happens, all of that will subsume into post-war France, but meanwhile our people need to feel that our own laws govern us."

Chavant leaned forward with a vexed look. "Roger, we have a problem among ourselves. We have people who lean politically left and others to the right, and they are suspicious of each other. I put Vincent Beaume in charge of investigating accusations of collaboration or spying. He was a good choice because he believes in the rule of law." He chuckled. "Vincent has an irritating personality, but he's forceful, and the job is much larger than either of us thought it would be. We have several hundred prisoners to house and feed. They're detained because someone accused them, and some people want their immediate execution without trial.

"But what do we do with them when the attack comes? Beaume himself was threatened because he would not execute a schoolteacher without trial."

Chavant's chair scraped the floor loudly as he shoved from the table to his feet in exasperation. "A young schoolteacher. Do you believe it? She's not even accused of collaborating, but to have helped a collaborator. We have no evidence that she knew who she was helping. I suspect that she's a good-hearted soul who would help anyone.

"The Vercors is a tinderbox," he continued. "If we don't get help soon, or if the Germans linger too long, we could end up doing their dirty work for them by killing each other."

Chavant crossed to a window and looked out. "They're good people here, Roger, but the pressures are excruciating. Everyone knows someone who's been executed or killed by the Germans in firefights or raids, sometimes with the help of collaborators. We know we've been infiltrated. And now you just told us that the external threat is even greater and probably more imminent. Without aid, we'll be destroyed soon, and no one has anything of substance to tell us. Meanwhile, we'll declare ourselves a free country and hope for the best—while the *Wehrmacht* watches and prepares, and London and Algiers send back more bromides and promises."

Jeremy eyed Chavant sympathetically. New lines creased the Frenchman's face and his shoulders were hunched. Publicly, Chavant exhibited continued confidence in Allied intentions to invade southern France, drop a regiment of paratroopers onto the Vercors plateau, and fully execute Operation Montagnard. This was the first and only time that Jeremy had heard Chavant express doubts.

Roger stood and crossed the room to place a hand on Chavant's shoulder. "You carry the weight of your people, my friend. They chose their leader well. Jeremy and I will do all in our power, including pulling triggers when the fight gets close."

Chavant looked at him cheerlessly. "It's already close," he said hoarsely. He reached up and grasped Roger's hand. "I appreciate the thought."

He straightened his shoulders and lifted his head upright. "Now, we have a ceremony to attend." He pointed out the window. "Look at the cliffs, so clear against a blue sky. It's a glorious day in the Vercors, and a happy one. Shall we go?"

"Wait, one more thing," Roger said, "and this comes under actual good news. I requested an SOE-trained female agent, and I'm happy to say that one is arriving soon." He glanced at Jeremy. "This is no slight on you. We have a lot of women in the Resistance now. I need a trained one to teach others how to be most effective and protect themselves."

"I'll look forward to working with her," Jeremy replied.

"She's Polish and speaks five languages fluently, including English, French, and German. She's a proven asset and is said to be Winston Churchill's favorite spy. I won't be here when she arrives, but I'll link up soon afterward. Her codename is Pauline."

Chavant and Jeremy exchanged glances. "We'll watch for her," Jeremy said.

"I'll fill you in about her later. Right now, we should be going to the ceremony."

As he watched the excited crowd gathering in the square in front of the church and overflowing into adjacent streets, Jeremy had to admire the spirit of these people living under threat of annihilation. The American paratroopers and the British SOE team, too, were lined up to observe the festivities. Cheers broke out when Eugène Chavant, their *Patron*, took to the podium to introduce the guest speaker.

The affection shared between the people and their leader was apparent, and as Chavant mounted the platform, Jeremy recognized unusual courage in the man. He spoke to them calmly and confidently, not as an official or administrator but as their neighbor and friend. He said only a few words, mentioning nothing about the increased threat just made known to him. This was, after all, their day to celebrate freedom, and no reports had surfaced about any probes or imminent attack.

"Let them enjoy," he had told Jeremy and Roger as they accompanied him to the square. "If it's their last day, let it be a good one."

He said only a few words to introduce Yves Farge. "We knew him before the war as a distinguished journalist and one of the leaders of our Resistance in France's south. He championed our Operation Montagnard. He comes to us now as our commissioner on General de Gaulle's Committee for National Liberation to join in the fight on our plateau with his headquarters in our newly formed Free Republic of the Vercors."

Farge spoke of the suffering of the French people under the German yoke, the embarrassment of being routed in their own country, and the long fight as they sought, with the Allies, to recapture Europe, liberate conquered countries, and expel the Nazi threat. Then, under the shade of an old lime tree, he proclaimed the creation of the Free Republic of the Vercors. People cheered thunderously as he finished.

As Chavant re-took the stage, the crowd again erupted in applause, and then quieted as he spoke. "People of the Vercors." His voice was deep and strong, its resonance registering on the faces of his audience. "Today, on this third day of July 1944, the French Republic is officially restored in the Vercors. As of today, the decrees of the Vichy government are abolished, and all the laws of our Republic are reinstated."

The crowd again broke into loud cheers. He waited for them to subside, and then continued. "Since our plateau is in a state of siege, the Committee for National Liberation asks the people to do everything possible, as it will itself, to help the military commander—" He gestured toward Lieutenant Colonel Huet, who, wearing his new insignia of rank, snapped to attention. "To help him, as he has the crushing responsibility of defending us against a barbarous enemy."

He paused as he looked across the faces of people he knew and loved so well. "It is in your home that our great republic is reborn. We can be proud of it. We are certain that you will fight for it. As my first duty as president of our free republic, I am sending a message to General de Gaulle that affirms our allegiance to the French provisional government in Algiers."

He was silent again. Then he thrust a fist into the air and thundered, *"Vive la Republique Française!"*

The crowd roared back, *"Vive la Republique Française!"*

As Chavant had predicted, a military parade, complete with a band, formed on one end of the street and marched to the other. Captain Geyer led on his splendid horse, in full uniform with his sword drawn and held in salute. The people cheered, and the day ended without adverse incident.

Jeremy and Roger walked together back to the Hôtel Breyton. "That was nice."

Roger nodded. "I'm reminded of something the American colonial, Benjamin Franklin, said when the American Constitution was passed. It was something along the lines of a republic being a wonderful thing, if you can keep it."

Jeremy grimaced. "Keeping it will be a challenge," he said. "Pflaumm will no doubt hear of today's proceedings."

"He will, and so will Adolf Hitler," Roger replied. "Neither will be pleased."

July 8, 1944

Jeremy joined a search party in the low hills surrounding Vassieux to find a group that had parachuted onto the plateau during the night. Crosswinds had blown the Hudson bomber that delivered them off course, and it had thus dropped them west of the intended field. The arriving group consisted of four French engineers, one of whom, Captain Tournissa, was to supervise construction of a runway at Vassieux capable of handling Allied bombers.

Fortunately, Tournissa was unhurt, but the winds had been so blustery that all the parachutists hit the ground hard. As a result, one of his officers was taken straight to hospital with a broken shoulder.

The fifth member of the group was Pauline, the SOE operative whom Roger had mentioned. When Jeremy first saw her, she was limping along a hillside path, aided by a *maquisard*.

"Pauline?" Jeremy called, concerned with her discomfort. "Are you all right?"

Pauline grinned through a pained face. "Yes, of course." She laughed, and her natural warmth exuded. "I landed flat on my tush. I'm afraid I've bruised my tailbone." She extended her hand. "Labrador? Madame Fourcade said I should expect to see you." She smiled slyly. "She told me to tell you that Amélie is safe and well."

Observing Jeremy's startled reaction, Pauline said, "I've met your fiancée. She's a lovely girl."

In spite of himself, Jeremy failed to repress a broad grin. "Yes, well, I'm very lucky. And I'm very pleased to meet you, Pauline."

They struck up a lively conversation as they struggled down the slopes. Pauline took her pain in stride and strove not to slow down progress. "I feel so silly. It's not as though I broke a shoulder like that other poor bloke."

Jeremy found her Polish accent and the use of British colloquialisms charming, and her fluency in French was similarly endearing. "I know your true identity," she said as she toiled over the rough terrain, "so you might as well know mine. My legal name is Christine Granville. I was born with the name Maria Krystyna Janina Skarbeck." She laughed. "That's a mouthful, I know. I changed it when I became a British citizen. I just liked the sound of 'Christine Granville,' and I needed a name that would not identify me with my family in Poland. My parents were quite prominent, and since I went back there undercover, it was better that I had an entirely different name." She glanced sideways at him. "'Pauline' will suit our purposes here. And I'll call you Labrador."

She was slender with an oval face that sharpened at the chin and was framed by short, dark hair. A ready smile that started with her eyes, her musical laughter, and easy interactions with everyone on the search party, whom she thanked profusely for retrieving her, immediately earned their affection.

As Jeremy learned more about Pauline, he understood her effectiveness as an agent. She was an accomplished horsewoman, a snow skier and mountain climber, and her speech was such that she was obviously cultured, yet she mixed with the local population as if she were one of them.

"I'm anxious to see Roger and find out what plans he has for me," she said.

"He's away in the high Alps training some *maquisards*," Jeremy said. "You'll need some time to rest and heal."

"I'll be fine. At least brief me on the local situation and take me around and introduce me to the people I'll need to know."

"As it happens, the man in charge of vetting everyone in the Vercors, Monsieur Beaume, has organized crews to construct Captain Tournissa's runway. They include an encampment of Polish refugees who've settled on the Vercors and happily volunteered to work on the project. I'm sure they'd love to meet you."

"And I'd love to meet them. That project sounds ambitious."

"But necessary. If we're to use the Vercors as envisioned in Operation Montagnard, the runway must be able to service Allied aircraft, big and small." They reached flat land and a small convoy of trucks that would take them back into town. Then, as they passed the proposed site for the runway, he pointed it out.

"It's going to be eleven hundred and fifty yards long and a hundred and fifty yards wide," he said. "Frankly, I don't see how the captain can accomplish it in the scheduled time—six days from now. But Beaume has mustered huge work crews from all over the plateau. The Germans will know we're building it within hours of the start. They fly over here daily. I'm guessing they'll disrupt its construction.

"A week ago, we received an SOE team and some OSS paratroopers, and already they've been in a skirmish with the Germans. One *maquisard* was killed during the fighting, and one captured. The second one was tortured and executed in front of the villagers at Lus-la-Croix-Haute. They were forced to watch as his eyes were gouged out and every bone in his body was slowly broken."

Silence hung between them before Jeremy continued. "That's what every person on this plateau faces if the Germans break through the passes." He let out a long breath. "The raid was one of many probes, but the Germans are always gathering more intelligence on our capabilities." He laughed sardonically. "And lack thereof."

"We had a funeral for those two *maquisards,"* he continued after a pause. "It was very somber and dignified. The OSS and SOE teams were there." He chuckled softly. "The priest who presided, Le Barbu, is a huge man. His parishioners call him the fighting priest because he's in the war for them. As the bodies were lowered into their graves, side by side, he bent over to pray for them, and when he did, his cassock slipped up, and I saw that he had a row of grenades strapped to his belt."

Pauline smiled. "So everyone is in the fight?"

"Whether or not they want to be."

They remained quiet a few more moments, and then Pauline said, "I've had extended conversations with Captain Tournissa. If anyone can get that runway built, he can. I've seen some impossible things during this war."

"That's good to hear. I was an engineer building roads and airfields north of Dunkirk when the war began. I'm rusty, but I'll help him all I can."

"I'm sure he'll appreciate that." Pauline shot him a sharp glance. "You must have been in the evacuation from Dunkirk?"

Jeremy let out a wry laugh. "No. I wasn't so lucky. I was in Dunkirk, but I came out later by another route. I'll tell you about it sometime."

12

Same Day, July 8, 1944
Saipan, Mariana Islands

Eighteen-year-old Marine Private First Class Guy Gabaldon lay still, peering through the night and listening for any sound of the enemy. Battle had raged for possession of this Pacific island for more than three weeks, since June 15, when US Marines first invaded. Five hundred and thirty-five ships had escorted nearly one hundred and thirty thousand US troops to seize the island and its airfield from Japanese occupiers.

Gabaldon soon learned that the casualty count was extraordinarily high on both sides of the battle. Against a growing US presence and dwindling supplies and reinforcements, the Japanese had fought fiercely, sacrificing themselves rather than being taken prisoner. According to Marines who had arrived on Saipan before Gabaldon, the enemy's fear of Americans, fueled by Japanese propaganda, had rubbed off on the native Chamorros. Hundreds of them, including whole families, flung themselves from high cliffs onto the rocky shore rather than face the cruelty and torture expected from their potential American captors.

At stake were the airfields on Saipan. For the Americans, they would be bases from which B-29 Superfortress bombers could launch against the

Japanese home islands. For the Japanese, it was a key element in their last line of defense.

Gabaldon had arrived two days earlier as a scout-observer with an intelligence unit of the 2nd Marine Regiment of the 2nd Marine Division. He was average in size with dark hair, recessed eyes, and a gregarious personality, and he had been assigned to the Pacific specifically because of his Japanese language fluency. On his first night ashore, he had been posted to guard duty on his unit's periphery. He had left his post to scout enemy territory alone during the night, and on his return the next morning, he had brought with him two Japanese prisoners.

Gabaldon had grown up in Los Angeles, a Mexican living in a predominantly Japanese district. The neighborhood was rough, and he was in many fights, but he noticed that his Japanese counterparts were always respectful and studious. He reached out to them, and they welcomed him into their circle of friends. Over time, he learned their culture and language, and he was dismayed when, at the onset of the war, he had seen so many of them sent off to detainment camps.

Since arriving on Saipan, his natural curiosity as well as his assignment to the intelligence unit prompted him to delve into both the casualty figures and the matter of the natives committing mass suicide. He was pragmatic, having no compunction against killing an enemy, and he had done so on multiple occasions. He had even kept sabers and watches from his kills as war booty, but in his mind, the demonstrated propensity for Japanese barbarism flew in the face of the gentle Japanese culture he had come to know and appreciate.

His first encounter with Japanese troops had occurred early in the afternoon of his first day ashore. During a firefight, he saw his first dead Marine, a man he had joked with a few hours earlier aboard ship before debarking. They had talked about girls back home. Now, that same Marine slumped against a tree, a neat bullet hole through his helmet, his body growing cold.

The experience had jolted Gabaldon, and that night, for reasons that defied logic, he had gone in search of enemy soldiers. He found two guarding the mouth of a cave, and he called to them in their own language. "You're surrounded. Lay your weapons down, and you'll live. Refuse, and you'll die. Come forward with your hands up."

To his surprise, the pair of soldiers had eagerly surrendered. They were exhausted, half-starved, and on further interrogation, he learned that Japanese soldiers generally were terrified of American flame-throwers. Over the weeks of battle, as supplies dwindled and Japanese ability to fight diminished, they had retreated into caves. The only means the Americans had to extricate them were tossing hand grenades or spewing flame-throwers aimed into the mouths of the caves until nothing inside could possibly remain alive.

Gabaldon learned that Japanese soldiers had been propagandized to expect no mercy from American forces and, instead, to anticipate capture as a prelude to a long and torturous death. Hence their preference for taking their own lives and those of as many of the enemy as possible.

When he arrived back at camp the next morning with his prisoners in tow, Gabaldon's commander, Captain John Schwabe, had been furious. "Don't you ever do that again," he said sternly, but not unkindly. "We're Marines, a team. You don't fight on your own. You're not a prima donna. If you do a stunt like that again, I'll court martial you."

Undeterred, on his second night, Gabaldon again ventured into the darkness. When he returned the next morning, he escorted fifty more prisoners into camp. Again, his commander confronted him. This time, Schwabe scanned the faces of the POWs, then turned to Gabaldon and scratched his head. "All right, Private," he said, "you've got something going for you." He gestured toward the captives. "Hell, we ought to get a load of intel from them. Continue your lone-wolf activities. Just be careful."

Tonight was his third such outing.

He waited at the edge of the periphery past dusk, and then crept on his belly through tall grass until he reached a stand of trees that had been reduced to stumps by the battles of the last three weeks. There, he rose to a crouch and made his way carefully down a shallow bank to a creek he had encountered on his first foray.

An almost full but waning moon provided sufficient light such that, with his practiced eye, he saw plainly the path to follow. It led along the bank of a creek he had encountered on the first of his outings, toward known Japanese positions. On the logic that the enemy still needed water, he trailed alongside of it.

The beaches and gentle slopes of the eastern side of the island where the Marines had landed gave way to rocky hills interspersed with wild foliage on the western side still occupied by the Japanese. The caves where they hid were among those rocks.

Intermittently Gabaldon stopped to listen and to smell. On both previous nights, he had encountered the aroma of soy sauce, and he had followed it to its source. He repeated the tactic on this night.

More than an hour into his lone patrol, he heard soft voices. Crawling forward, he perceived a soft glow from a tiny fire emanating from behind leaves. He lay still, listening. After several minutes, he determined that two men sat together, no doubt on guard duty, and conversed.

He crept closer until he saw their outlines in the dim light of their fire. Slowly, he drew his M1 rifle forward and sighted on one of them. Mentally, he retraced his steps so that he could make good an immediate escape if need be. Then, as he had done the first two nights, he called out in Japanese. "You're surrounded by US forces. You have no escape."

The two soldiers lurched forward.

"Don't move," Gabaldon commanded. "I can shoot you right now." He counted on the surrounding rocky hillside and foliage to disperse the sound of his voice so that its origin could not be immediately pinpointed. "Lay your weapons down and raise your hands in the air. We promise fair treatment, food, and shelter."

The two soldiers glanced at each other in fright. Then they laid their rifles on the ground, raised their hands, and stepped forward.

Covering them with his M1, Gabaldon raised himself from a crouch. "Come forward," he said. He guided them a safe distance away and ordered them to sit. "How far away is your cave?"

"It's around a curve in the rocks. Two other guards are on the other side."

"How many are in the cave?"

Both soldiers shrugged. "Many."

They were both young, scrawny, and unkempt, apparently suffering the effects of constant threat and exposure to the elements. Neither appeared prepared to attempt action against Gabaldon. Essentially, they were two kids pressed into unwelcome service. The gentle respect that

Gabaldon had known among their kindred in Los Angeles showed itself now.

Careful to keep his rifle covering them, Gabaldon too sat on the ground. "There's no honor in sacrificing your lives or committing *hari-kari*. Your army and navy abandoned you. Where's the honor in that? Why do you fight so fiercely?"

The soldiers glanced at each other. "The Americans will torture and then kill us," one said fearfully. "Our commanders told us. It's better that we die first."

"Look at me," Gabaldon said. "I'm Mexican. I have dark skin. I'm well fed. I wear the American uniform. I can tell you that mistreating prisoners is absolutely forbidden. The penalties are high. I could have shot you both, and I didn't."

The Japanese once again exchanged glances. "Our comrades are starving," one said. "We're almost out of ammunition. The emperor has ordered *gyokusai*."

Puzzled, Gabaldon asked, "What's that?"

"*Gyokusai*. It's an order only the emperor can give. Every Japanese soldier on the island will gather into one formation carrying every weapon available with every bit of remaining ammunition. They will fix bayonets and charge into the center of American positions. We are each ordered to kill at least seven Americans before we fall in battle."

Dumbfounded, Gabaldon took a moment to absorb what he had just heard. "When is that supposed to happen?"

"Tomorrow night, at midnight."

Gabaldon swallowed hard. "Will your comrades do this willingly?"

Both soldiers shook their heads. "We just want to go home. But anyone who doesn't participate will be shot for cowardice."

Gabaldon took a few moments to mull. "Do you think others in your group would surrender if given the chance and offered food, shelter, and safety?"

Both soldiers nodded enthusiastically. "Most would. We're tired of fighting."

Gabaldon took a deep breath. Leaves on the few standing trees rustled, and moonlight glistened on the soldiers' dark hair. "All right. One of you go back to the cave. I'll wait here with your companion."

As one started to rise, Gabaldon stopped him. "If you don't come back, or if I sense anything hostile, I'll shoot your friend."

The soldier nodded and disappeared into the night.

Per normal routine, the Marines in camp were up and alert, manning their positions as the sun rose over the eastern horizon. Wind blowing out of the west was reduced by the rocky hills to a stiff breeze.

First Sergeant Davis rubbed his eyes to assure himself of what he saw. Then he called to the company commander. "Captain Schwabe, you're gonna wanna see this."

The captain emerged from his hooch and stared in the direction that the sergeant pointed. Marching toward him was a single Japanese soldier with a white cloth held high on a bamboo pole. Behind him and to one side, PFC Gabaldon stood, his rifle ready as a platoon of Japanese soldiers, hands empty and raised in the air, marched by him and into the center of the encampment. They were dirty, obviously underfed, and scared.

Schwabe watched in amazement, and then his eyes shifted back to Gabaldon, who was busily waving another platoon forward. It was followed by a third and then a fourth. "What is he," the captain muttered, "the Pied Piper of Saipan?"

By that time, the first sergeant had made his way to Gabaldon. "We need someone to take over for me, First Sergeant," Gabaldon said. "More are comin', but I've got important information the captain needs to hear."

The first sergeant stared in shock. "How many more?"

"I don't know. Hundreds."

13

July 10, 1944
Guam, Mariana Islands

While the sun began to descend over the distant horizon, US Navy Radioman First Class George Tweed crouched behind thick foliage cloaking his lookout. It was situated outside a crevasse three hundred feet above Guam's jagged, heavily vegetated coast.

He sucked in his breath.

Moments earlier, using a three-inch pocket mirror and with the sun in a straight line of his position behind two US destroyers, he had aimed his beam across the nearest ship's bridge, hoping to gain attention. Both warships had ventured within several hundred yards of shore.

Earlier in the month, Tweed had located a battery of three Japanese six- or eight-inch shore guns. He could not be sure of their size—he had determined their position from their sounds when the batteries fired off rounds during gunnery practice before American bombing and strafing raids began. They were on Adelup Point, roughly four miles southwest of his hideout. When he first spotted the American destroyers earlier in the day, they had been within the enemy guns' point-blank range.

While cruising to their current position below Tweed, the two ships had sailed past an anti-aircraft and machine gun nest halfway between Tweed and Adelup Point. It had opened up on the destroyers. They had returned fire with their own big guns.

Tweed cheered to see the Japanese position obliterated, but he prayed silently that the big shore guns at Adelup would not open up on the ships —even at this distance, they remained within easy range. He guessed that the battery did not shoot because it was saving its powder for the inevitable US amphibious landing, and the Japanese commander did not want to give away the guns' position. On the other hand, if the Americans identified the guns' whereabouts, they could blast them out of existence and save the lives of many Marines and soldiers who were sure to invade within days.

Two makeshift semaphore flags lay on the ground at Tweed's feet. For many days, he had stood in this same place and signaled to American destroyers patrolling the coast. No one aboard any of them had seen him.

Today, he thought to try the mirror. Given the time of day and the sun's hue as it descended to the horizon, the mirror danced a strong reddish reflection over the bridge's windshields.

Suddenly, he saw the destroyer's main guns rotate and elevate. They aimed directly at him.

They've seen me. They think I'm another machine gun nest!

Forcing his mind and body to stay calm, he dropped the mirror and grabbed the semaphores. He was not practiced in their use, and he cursed himself for not keeping up his proficiency during thirty-one months of hiding from the Japanese. He signaled with the flags slowly, deliberately, spelling out each letter he could remember and hoping that the communications specialists on the ship could figure out any errors.

"Please answer by searchlight."

Being a US Navy radioman first class, Tweed was an expert at Morse code.

Almost immediately, a single flash from the US Naval destroyer's searchlight signaled, "K."

Tweed sucked in his breath. That was code for "Go ahead."

Controlling his excitement, he semaphored, "I have information for you."

In an instant, the searchlight signaled again, a beautiful, welcome, "K."

Tweed's mind whirled. He took a few quick breaths to further calm himself. Despite that his actions had been consciously taken, in light of the response, they carried a dreamlike quality. Once again, with anxious deliberation, he manipulated the semaphores, hoping to spell out, "The Japs have a battery of coast guns mounted at Adelup Point."

Then he added, "The Japs kill every American who falls into their hands."

For the next half hour, while the ships circled, Tweed used the semaphores to provide reports. The signalman on the destroyer replied in Morse code using the searchlight. Tweed reported what he could on enemy troop strength and locations, types and placements of shore obstacles, mine fields, tank traps, and any other information he thought pertinent that could be delivered in this manner.

Enemy build-up had accelerated since March, three months before the bombing run he had watched four weeks ago over Agaña Harbor. During those months, Japanese fighters in formations had flown over incessantly, the high-pitched whine of the Zeros becoming so frequent that he no longer paid them any mind.

Since the start of the buildup, thousands of Japanese troops had disembarked onto Guam, and they set about buttressing the island with steel-reinforced concrete fortifications at strategic points. Eleven bunkers were constructed on the ranch where Tweed hid out, and the Japanese command had established a lookout less than a mile away from his cave. By May, he had estimated that, in addition to aircraft, pilots, and ground crews, over twenty-five thousand combat soldiers as well as tanks, artillery, coastal guns, ammunition stores, foodstuffs, and fuel stocks had arrived on the island.

As Tweed watched for the next flashed message, the water behind the destroyers churned, and their bows lifted.

Panic gripped. *They're leaving.*

Desperately, while hot tears rolled down his cheeks, he grasped the semaphores and spelled out methodically, "Can you take me aboard?"

Then he leaned forward against his lookout, scrutinizing the ships for a reply.

Tweed had come about his circumstances when, thirty-one months earlier, simultaneous with the attack on faraway Pearl Harbor, another assault took place at Guam. He had jerked awake to the pop and muffled explosions of field guns.

The Marines had no such field guns on the island.

Japs!

Tweed leaped from his bunk into chaos as his fellow sailors and Marines servicing the island's administration scurried to assess the situation and determine what actions to take. "It's escape to the jungle or be captured," Al Tyson, a fellow sailor and Tweed's best friend, called out. "Several of us are heading into the bush."

"No Jap is going to jab my rear end with a bayonet," Tweed called back as he buckled his belt on his khaki trousers, "but I'm going to get permission. I won't be accused of deserting under fire."

He dashed out of the barracks while still fumbling with his clothes and rushed across a road, through a hedge, over a fence, and into the mansion's back garden. Entering the residence through the back door, he encountered Commander Giles, aide to USN Captain George McMillin, Guam's military governor.

"We'll surrender in a few minutes," Giles said. He remained perfectly calm. "We've only got a hundred and fifty Marines and four hundred of you sailors, and you're not trained for ground combat. Neither are the two hundred Chamorros in the insular service. That's not enough men to fight it out with the Japs, and we can't defend the local population. You can stay here, or you can head into the jungle."

"That's what I wanted to hear, sir. I'll take the jungle."

"Do you have a pistol?"

"No."

Tweed waited only long enough to see that no weapon would be offered, then he made his getaway in an old jalopy with Tyson and Gevarra, a Chamorro who worked for the island's insular affairs office. The three drove out of the capital under Japanese machine gun fire. They dropped

Gevarra at his ranch with advice to take his family and flee. Then they drove southeast toward Yoña.

Tweed had come to Guam in 1939. During that time, he had developed a great fondness and respect for the Chamorros, finding them to be proud Americans, both generous and protective of what was theirs. They would willingly share food or whatever else they had, but woe to the man who stole from them.

Tweed realized very quickly the implications of his current circumstances. The Japanese took possession of the island's food stores. That meant that the Guamanians themselves had to forage in the jungle, and every inch was owned by someone. If Tweed ate something found in the bush, he would be stealing food from someone else. Therefore, he must rely on the generosity of the Chamorros.

He found them willing to help to a fault. They hid him and Tyson, fed them, and kept them safe despite the danger to themselves.

As days of occupation turned into weeks, news spread that six US Navy servicemen had escaped into the bush during the initial assault. In addition to Tweed and Tyson, Yeoman First Class Yablonsky, Chief Aerographer Jones, Chief Machinist Mate Krump, and Machinist Mate First Class Johnston had also taken to the jungle.

The Japanese were hunting them down. The peril to anyone helping the fugitives became tragically manifest as the Japanese rounded up large numbers of Chamorros, tortured them, and executed many in the most brutal ways, including beheadings and guttings.

With local help, the six sailors were able to find each other and stayed together for the next eight months. Then, in September, Krump, Jones, and Yablonsky were betrayed by collaborators. The Japanese tortured and beheaded them.

The following month, Tyson and Johnston were also betrayed. They found themselves surrounded by fifty Japanese soldiers. Knowing the fate of their deceased companions, they fought rather than face torture. They were machine gunned down.

Tweed was then the lone American serviceman on Guam. He was known widely among the islanders. They had dubbed him Juan Cruz, a codename to be used if they had to refer to him when an enemy was present. Over the next twelve months, they moved him to new hideouts eleven times and made his quarters as comfortable as possible under the circumstances.

One hideout was deep within a large patch of China lemons, which were thick, almost impenetrable shrubs with three-inch-long thorns. Within the patch, they obscured Tweed's hideaway even from the sky. His hosts built a wooden hut with a rainwater capture system for drinking, bathing, and cooking. A girl of nineteen, Tonie, walked ten miles to deliver to him a large watermelon, a live chicken, and canned foodstuffs.

Others brought him two broken radios and a typewriter in similar state, as well as a mimeograph machine. He repaired the typewriter, and he fixed the radios over which he received news from the Voice of Freedom at Corregidor until the Philippines fell. While the broadcast was still active, however, he typed out the news he heard, reproduced it on the mimeograph, and published an underground newspaper he dubbed the *Guam Eagle*.

Meanwhile, the Japanese intensified their search for him. Reports multiplied of beatings, tortures, and executions. Guilt plagued him over the plight of those who protected him and kept him sheltered and fed.

Then he received a note from a Mrs. Johnston, delivered by confidential courier. She had been a schoolteacher on the island. Her late husband, unrelated to the sailor who had fought fatally against the Japanese machine gunners, had been a prominent resident who, before the war, had owned one of two theaters in Agaña. Mrs. Johnston had requested by confidential means to be included among those receiving the *Guam Eagle*. Her note this time was an invitation to dinner.

She was a kind woman who loved Guam and the Chamorros. During the conversation, Tweed spoke of being guilt-ridden over the people who suffered pain, loss of family, and death because of him. One example he mentioned was a young girl who refused to bow before a portrait of the Japanese emperor. A colonel beat and stomped on her so brutally that she was crippled for life.

"Mr. Tweed," Mrs. Johnston said, "the people of Guam feel that as long as you hold out, the Americans will return. If you surrender, they will believe you have lost faith and think the Japs have won. They will give up hope. You can never surrender."

Shortly thereafter, Tweed had to move again. Then in late 1942, Antonio Artero, son of one of the most prominent ranchers on Guam, moved him into the high crevasse among the cliffs on the northwest coast of the island. Two large boulders, thirty and forty feet high respectively, added cover and concealment to the thick foliage surrounding the entrance. It had no ceiling, being open to the sky sixty feet above the floor, but it ran thirty feet back into solid rock.

Antonio brought corrugated tin sections to fashion a low roof so that Tweed could sleep sheltered from the rain. Periodically, he brought food. Tweed fashioned a table and chair from jungle materials, and there he lived, in isolation other than Antonio's visits, for nineteen long months, until the appearance of the US naval destroyers.

While Tweed waited for a response to his request to board the warship, Mrs. Johnston's face flashed through his mind. Two years had passed since he had seen her, and he still felt the warmth of her kindness and her urgent admonition to never surrender.

A lump formed in his throat as he recalled her and Tonie, the girl who had hiked ten miles to bring him food, and all the other Chamorros who had risked their lives to save his. The lump choked his breathing as he imagined the men who had escaped with him: Al Tyson, Jones, Yablonsky, Krump, and Johnston. Johnston had given Tweed his pistol. It had not left Tweed's side in two years.

Tears continued down his face.

And still no response from the destroyer.

Slowly, Tweed turned away from the ocean and toward the entrance to his crevasse. Then, a single blip from the searchlight caught the corner of his eye. He whirled and stared.

He saw motion at the side of the ship. A long object was lowered into the water. *A whaleboat! They're coming to take me home.*

He grabbed his semaphores and signaled, “Thirty minutes to get to the beach.”

14

July 13, 1944
Saint-Martin, the Vercors, France

Lieutenant Colonel Huet hurried into his new headquarters in the Villa Bellon, situated in the heights north of Saint-Martin and hidden among trees. He had moved there to be less of a target and thus less of a threat to the town's residents. Night had settled and trees outside rustled in a gentle breeze.

Already assembled were his staff, subordinate commanders, Jeremy, and Pauline. Also among them was the leadership of the SOE and OSS teams respectively, Major Longe and Lieutenant Hopper. "We're in the thick of it now," Huet began, even before sitting down. "You know that a single aircraft dropped a stick of bombs on La Chapelle last night. They killed four people. And just two hours ago, a whole squadron of FW 190s attacked Vassieux. They killed fifteen people and damaged the church. Then they flew on to hit La Chapelle again and strafed the streets. Fortunately, they dropped only one bomb there, which was a dud. Our men fired back with machine guns and damaged one plane that left a trail of smoke over the mountains."

He took his seat. "I'm sure the *Luftwaffe* thought it was hitting our headquarters at La Chapelle yesterday because we set free a suspected spy near there. She would have seen the targets that were hit. Among them were some of our administrative buildings. She might have mistaken them for our headquarters and delivered a flawed report to the Germans.

"In any event, that was the first air strike directly into the interior of our plateau, and today we were hit by two additional ones. Word spread. People are scared.

"The German window to attack is closing as a breakout from Normandy becomes probable, and as we get closer to a southern invasion."

Derisive hoots and desultory comments arose from the assembled officers. Huet waved a hand to quiet them. "I believe the invasion will come. It must, because the Allies need a thrust from Provence to support the attack east from Normandy. At least that's the way I see things." He sighed and glanced at the ceiling. *But perhaps the southern invasion will not occur in time to save the Vercors.*

Huet picked up a sheaf of papers from his desktop and held them out. "I've been over your contingency plans and listened to your briefings for transforming to guerrilla warfare. I've approved them all." He made eye contact with each of his commanders. "Make sure your soldiers know what that means and what actions to take."

He glanced heavenward and made the sign of the cross. "God help us when it happens. Our friends and their families will be massacred, and we'll be able to do little to save them. Until then, we continue as we have, as a disciplined, fully military organization, and that's regardless of whether our fighters are veterans or fresh *maquisards*. We're all in this Resistance and wearing the same uniform—" He broke into a rare and spontaneous chuckle. "At least pieces of it."

To a ripple of laughter, Huet's face reverted to deadpan serious. "And we must fight as a unified force, or we're doomed from the start."

Silence hung over the room. No one spoke.

Jeremy studied the faces as best he could without turning his head. They were solemn, serious, cognizant, and deadly determined.

A chair scraped. Longe stood. He addressed Huet. "Sir, may I speak?"

The French commander assented with a nod.

Longe took a deep breath as he gazed around at the assembly of fighters. "Sir, when I brought my team here, we had been briefed very little and expected a disorganized throng of recruits lacking any training at all. We were surprised on the very first day to find a disciplined army of five thousand men and women organized into geographical commands with personnel, intelligence, operations, communications, and logistics sections. But your task has been not only to feed and shelter a fighting force at the front. You've had to feed the whole population of the Vercors and all the *maquisards* who've made their way here.

"We've been on the passes with your defenders. We've trained the new volunteers. We've even fought the Germans with them. We've found, in every instance, an army, a real army, which numbers now around six thousand men and women. They're under-equipped, lacking in arms, and some are better trained than others, but all are willing to learn and fight, and they throw their hearts into it.

"Against all odds, you've built a fighting force to be reckoned with. The proof is the caution that General Pflaumm takes in his approach to conquer this place, the Vercors." He took a deep breath and straightened to his full height. "I'm saying, sir, that my SOE team and I are proud to fight alongside you. We'll be with you to the end."

When he finished speaking, a hush once again settled over the room. Then Lieutenant Hopper leaped to his feet and applauded vigorously. Soon, he was joined by all the officers in the room.

"Sir," Hopper called over the commotion. The room quieted. "Sir," Hopper began again. "I can't let our British cousins grandstand here without adding our own American comments. May I?"

With a half-smile and a nod amid a round of laughter, Huet assented.

"We've observed and commented among ourselves about exactly what the good lieutenant colonel just said," Hopper announced. "You can count on our unit to fight with you through whatever comes, and we'll be proud to do it."

Once again, the room erupted into applause and cheers. Huet let it continue a few moments and then held up his hands. "Thank you both, our British and American brothers," he said. "It's gratifying to think that we've regained a measure of respect from our Allies. We, in turn, are happy to fight alongside you.

"Now listen," he said, and his tone changed abruptly as he strode to a window to stare out into darkness. "Tomorrow is Bastille Day. Our civil authorities want to celebrate it with another parade at La Chapelle. I've advised against it. The plans for the event are well known inside and outside of the Vercors, and the Germans know that the fourteenth of July is important to us. We received a report from Grenoble about two German officers overheard to remark that the people of the Vercors will definitely remember this particular Bastille Day." He smacked his lips sardonically. "I'm sure they weren't wishing us good weather.

"We can't stop the parade, but I've ordered the location moved to a road alongside a forest so that, if attacked, the people will have cover and concealment. If the parade comes off, we can most assuredly expect a strike of some sort whether by air or land. I suspect it will be an air assault to disrupt the festivities.

"The runway in Vassieux is nearing completion. The Germans have undoubtedly seen it. That's all the more reason for them to attack. That's all I have for now."

Huet half-smiled and redirected his attention to Geyer. "Captain, I expect that you'll lead the parade on your horse?"

The cavalry officer reddened slightly but came to attention and responded with only a slight touch of defiance. "That is correct, sir."

Huet's eyes warmed. "That's good. Be sure you can be called to action at a moment's notice."

"As always, sir."

Jeremy took it all in. When Huet had adjourned, he glanced at Pauline. She sat, fully composed, but with a profound look of resolve on her prim face. "What are you thinking?" he asked.

She grinned. "That we've got our work cut out for us."

15

Same Day, July 13, 1944
Grenoble, France

General Pflaumm stood next to the flagpole flying the red Nazi banner in the middle of the parade ground of his 157th Reserve Division headquarters. He dropped a pair of binoculars from his eyes and let them thump against his massive chest. Then he raised them again, looked through them, and focused the lenses once more on the massive French flag with the emblem of the Free French Republic of the Vercors sewn into the white panel. He grunted derisively. "Soon they'll learn," he murmured to no one.

He turned and stalked across the field, back to his headquarters building. An orderly in gray *Wehrmacht* regalia at the front door snapped to attention, clapped the heels of his highly polished boots together, delivered the requisite "Heil Hitler" with an upstretched arm, and moved rapidly to open the door.

Pflaumm entered and walked swiftly and deliberately through the halls, deigning to acknowledge a favored few subordinates but otherwise frowning on anyone blocking his path. When he entered his office, *Oberst* Schwehr, his operations officer, was waiting for him. Schwehr would inflict Nazi vengeance on the Vercors.

"You have news?" Pflaumm demanded.

Schwehr smiled smugly. "Nothing that we didn't know, sir. The Bastille Day celebration is one they'll never forget. It will be their last."

The general smiled in satisfaction. "Let's drink to that and enjoy some cigars too."

Schwehr dutifully rose from his seat, crossing to a small table holding a tray of tumblers and a bottle of schnapps while Pflaumm reached across the desk and extracted two thick cigars from a humidifier. Then he removed a set of spectacles from his fleshy face, leaned back in his chair, and ran his fingers through his thick black hair.

"You know, Schwehr, these troubles with the Vercors started just as Normandy was invaded. I had only two hundred troops under my command then. Keep in mind that the Vercors is two hundred kilometers around its circumference. We had no air support, scant logistical support—we were a garrison whose main job was to keep the peace. Yet I was ordered to do whatever it took to contain and squash the terrorists, and to do it while the *panzers* and most other support were sent up to deal with Normandy." He shook his head. "I'll freely admit that, at the outset, the task seemed overwhelming." He savored his cigar as he put flame to it and drew on it until the end glowed. "But now," he said, blowing out a puff of smoke, "I think we'll succeed. I can feel it."

Schwehr brought the drinks over to the desk and handed one to Pflaumm. "I'll drink to that, *Mein Herr*," he said. "You've planned thoroughly, prepared carefully, and you were provided the authority you needed to muster the resources."

"And you determined that the terrorists' major weakness was not in the main passes, but rather in the high mountains of the southeast where there are no roads."

Schwehr accepted the compliment with a nod. "We'll still have to push the bulk of our ground forces through the passes, but there are hundreds of mule paths, and our *Gebirgsjägers*, our mountain troops, will have little difficulty advancing along them. We'll hit their defenses from the rear."

He grinned maliciously. "The parade at La Chapelle will take place on schedule."

"And our response to that is ready?"

Schwehr grinned. "It will be loud and clear."

"Keep an eye out for surprises." Pflaumm gave a short laugh. "The brazenness of these criminals is amazing. They actually believe that their barricades across roads into the plateau will stand up against the *Wehrmacht*."

Schwehr laughed. "You mean the signs announcing entry into the Republic of the Vercors posted there for what—nine days now?" He sneered. "We'll see how long those stay in place." He lit his cigar, and enjoyed a few puffs. "We know where their strongholds are now. We have a good idea of their strength—" He chuckled. "And now they're even doing the courtesy of building an airfield for us."

Pflaumm chuckled as he nodded agreement. "That brings up a good point. They wouldn't construct that strip at Vassieux if they didn't expect incoming support. Plus, the Allies rely a lot on their paratroopers, which can land almost anywhere. That type of support can come quickly, unannounced."

Schwehr looked perplexed. "I'm stumped over why it hasn't happened already. The Vercors offers huge advantages for an enemy to work behind our lines—"

The general interrupted, "Which is precisely why we've put such a high priority on securing it. We can't afford to let that damnable plateau slip into Allied hands." He tamped his cigar on an ashtray. "Of course the same goes for any uprising against German authority."

16

July 14, 1944, Bastille Day
Vassieux-en-Vercors, France

By early dawn, Jeremy had already toured the defenses, such as they were, around Vassieux. The assigned *maquisards* were as ready as they could be. Before leaving Saint-Martin late the previous evening, Chavant showed him a telegram he had received from "friends in Algiers." It read, "On this July 14, festival of liberty...give all around you our admiration and good wishes."

The newly inaugurated president of the fledgling Free Republic of the Vercors had grunted. "It's a nice sentiment," he said gruffly, "but it's not going to destroy the enemy planes at Chabeuil, start the invasion at Provence, or bring us the paratroop regiment. We get lots of pretty words, but nothing of substance to protect our people."

A low roar of aircraft engines caught Jeremy's attention, and a stream of adrenaline pulsed through his body. The men around him jumped into their covered positions. Those manning the machine guns checked their ammo belts, charged their weapons, and aimed them toward the northern horizon.

A line of dark objects broke over the mountain ranges and descended toward the plateau. Then, as the sun rose and gleamed off the wings, individual bombers became visible. They were huge, and they flew low and fast, the sound of their engines rising to an ear-splitting pitch.

Jeremy counted quickly as they passed overhead and was sure that more than seventy bombers flew in the formation. The undersides of their wings were dark, but they dropped no munitions, sweeping on by as the people below watched warily. Then the aircraft circled, apparently lining up for another run, and as they did, Jeremy clearly saw the markings on the underside of their wings.

"Don't shoot," he shouted, and sprang from his position. "They're Americans. Don't shoot. Look! The big star in a circle. Those planes are American."

More fighters took up Jeremy's call, and then as the defenders emerged from their hiding places, jumping for joy, pounding each other's backs, the bombers' bellies opened and dark objects fell from them. Almost immediately, parachute canopies bloomed, and the sun gleamed off the sides of hundreds of large metal cannisters as they floated gently toward earth.

"Look at the parachutes," a man yelled excitedly to Jeremy. "They're our colors: blue, white, and red. Thank God for the Americans! We can celebrate our Bastille Day."

As if on signal, huge numbers of cars and trucks and people running over open fields converged around the ground where Captain Tournissa's runway was under construction. The cannisters lay all about, and the excited people reached them and began loading them on the trucks.

Just as suddenly, a higher-pitched roar of engines sounded from the west, one that the residents readily recognized. In a panic, they looked skyward toward Chabeuil. A squadron of FW 190s crested the mountain range and dived low over the valley floor.

People scattered. They flung themselves flat on the ground, under the vehicles, or in the shelter of whatever other meager cover they could find and hunched their heads under their arms.

The German fighter planes opened with their machine guns, mowing down anyone still on their feet. Screams of terror and cries of agony rose into the sky as the planes completed their first pass and circled to continue the attack.

At the periphery, the Resistance machine guns opened up, and those members with rifles shot ahead of the aircraft as they had been trained, into the planes' paths.

After the first pass, Jeremy rushed onto the field on the back of a truck. "Cut away the chutes," he shouted. "They're easily seen from the sky. They mark the cannisters and anyone around them as targets."

The German attack continued with several passes. Between each, the *maquisards* hurriedly cut away the canopies as Jeremy had instructed, loaded the cannisters onto trucks, and fled the field. Other men and women rushed to pick up the wounded and move them to safety. Still, the assault continued, with more wounded, more dead, and more bright red spills of blood dotting the field under a clear blue sky.

La Chapelle-en-Vercors, France

Pauline glanced around the room at Hôtel Bellier, decorated with the American Stars and Stripes, the British Union Jack, and the Free French Flag. News of the attack had reached La Chapelle, but since action seemed centered at Vassieux six miles to the south, the town's leaders had decided to go ahead with the parade.

Because hostile action was anticipated at Vassieux but the ceremonies at La Chapelle had been a social occasion, Jeremy and Pauline had decided between them that he should be close to the military action in case an attack occurred. Pauline's attendance at the parade, on the other hand, could afford her an opportunity to become acquainted with some of the women that she might work with. In either event, their presence at the most vulnerable locations would serve as visible evidence of Britain's continued support.

Word of the massive American drop had spread swiftly to much enthusiasm, which turned to dread as news of the German air attack followed. But so far, the assault had not spread beyond Vassieux. The festivities at La Chapelle remained on schedule.

The room where Pauline sat had filled for a formal, albeit early lunch.

A quartet of violinists provided soft music, and Vincent Beaume would preside. She had met him, and although he was a pleasant man, there was an insistence about his personality that, Pauline perceived, could be offsetting. She had heard that he had irritated Huet with persistent reports of problems with detainees, and yet it was he who had obtained the intelligence confirming a Bastille Day attack on the Vercors. Furthermore, he had faced down the group that had threatened him for not immediately executing the schoolteacher suspected of betrayal, and that was after they had tortured the poor woman by burning the soles of her bare feet with hot coals to force a confession.

Beaume was not a large man, and he looked very much like an accountant, with close-cropped graying hair around a balding head. He wore heavy black spectacles and sported a sweeping mustache. Chavant had appointed him as the Chief of the Second Bureau with oversight of several departments including the *gendarmeries.* Still, the notion of real civil authority being vested in local officials who were now the Vercors' national leaders had not yet seeped into the population's psyche.

By force of personality, Beaume had succeeded in securing the teacher's release, and upon further investigation, he found that she was innocent. That bit of information about Beaume created a warm place for the man in Pauline's heart.

She watched him as the luncheon began and the aroma of roast beef wafted on a gentle breeze blowing through open windows. The tinkling of crystal and the quiet ring of silverware against plates mixed with the soft tones of the violins as attendees munched and conversed, mostly about the attack at Vassieux.

The music ceased. Beaume mounted the speaker's platform. "Ladies and gentlemen..."

Boom! An explosion somewhere in town rocked the room. People screamed. Some bolted to peer out the windows.

The roar of a bomber engine vibrated the building, and shortly, another bomb hit the town. Pauline surveyed the panicked guests for anyone who was injured. Seeing none, she circulated through the room to double-check, and then headed outside. The street had emptied. No person was in sight.

She returned to the room. Beaume was still standing motionless at the rostrum. And then he began singing "*La Marseillaise.*" "*Allons enfants de la Patrie...*"

Panic stopped. People halted where they were, turned toward the unassuming man on the platform, and joined him in chorus. "*Le jour de gloire est arrivé!*"

Saint-Martin-en-Vercors, France

Huet's conference that evening was grim. The lieutenant colonel remained calm as he listened to angry comments made among his subordinates before he convened the meeting. Jeremy and Pauline had arrived, as had Beaume, all the commanders, and his own staff.

Also present was Dr. Fernand Ganimède. The doctor had established a hospital at Saint-Martin and had treated the majority of the wounded from the various German incursions, including the engineer with the broken shoulder, the tortured schoolteacher, the brave ambulance driver, Lilette Lesage, and many brought to his facility today.

Rumor circulated that Huet's headquarters had been attacked by fighter planes that came so close he could see the goggles on the pilots' faces. Huet had been having lunch with several of his staff during the attack. He had stood, offered toasts to the American and British officers present, then he had re-taken his seat and proceeded with his lunch. Without adequate weaponry, he said, he had little other recourse.

Now, Huet called for order. He began with a half-smile. "Captain Geyer, I understand that you'll have to wait until next year to lead a Bastille Day parade."

Geyer stood with an expression halfway between sheepish and his normal stoicism. "Yes, sir, that is a fact. The people of La Chapelle were too busy surviving. The parade did not take place."

Huet arched his brow. "People sought shelter all over the southern section of the Vercors today. Almost every town and hamlet was hit. I know of none that was not hit. The German fighters even attacked cars and trucks moving between villages." He stared out a window to his left. "They sent a loud message, and they made sure we heard it." He regarded Geyer once again with his half-smile. "I'm sure you'll have your chance next year. Have a seat."

As Geyer complied, Huet continued. "We have to believe that General Pflaumm intends to launch his main attack soon. We don't know when he'll have assembled sufficient forces to ensure success—more troops are still headed to his command. But by now, he knows where our defensive positions are and has a good sense of what equipment we have—and I'd guess he's heard inklings of Operation Montagnard. If that's the case, then he might have heard that we're expecting a paratroop regiment. That could be what's holding him back." He broke a wry smile and arched his eyebrow. "His information on that point is no better than ours—at least I'd like to believe that.

"Regardless, his main assault will come soon. Perhaps tomorrow." He stopped speaking and gazed across his audience. "Therefore, I've prepared a statement for you to read to your fighters." He picked up a paper from his desk and read, "'Soldiers of the Vercors, the time has come for you to show your mettle. It is the hour of battle. We will fight from our posts. We will engage the enemy wherever he is at all times, and above all, when he least expects it. We will harass him without ceasing.

"'The eyes of the country are fixed on us. We have faith in each other. We have right on our side. The ideal that has motivated us and unites us will enable us to win.'"

He stopped talking. Silence had descended. Huet broke it. "Just before this meeting, I received a message from Algiers. I won't bother to read it to you. It promised two teams of officers and sergeants, fifteen men altogether, with six shoulder-fired recoilless rocket rifles—I think the Americans call them bazookas—and some other material. The poignant part was the last sentence, inquiring by what priority this support should be sent and to which drop zones." He drew a deep breath and let it out. "Very obviously, neither Algiers nor London understands our precarious situation. We are on our own."

Moments passed, and Huet continued. "So, we have additional preparations to make." He nodded toward the doctor. "Dr. Ganimède is worried that his patients will be helpless victims if Saint-Martin is overrun. Therefore, he wishes to move his hospital to Tourtre, two miles southeast of here. The village is in a forest, and the American OSS team is camped there, a good thing for security. He'll need help making the move, so"—he turned to his staff—"please see that he gets it."

Huet then gestured toward Beaume. "*Monsieur* Beaume has a problem in that his population of detainees has grown. If we are overrun, I intend to set them free. Meanwhile, we must move them to a safe place as well." He turned again to his staff section. His officer in charge of logistics nodded without saying a word.

Geyer stood and started to speak.

Huet anticipated his question. "Captain, you want to know when we'll devolve to guerrilla mode?"

"Yes, sir?"

"When I order it. Any other questions?"

Geyer shook his head and re-took his seat.

Huet gazed across his audience. "Everyone, keep doing what you're doing. That will be all. We're adjourned."

Jeremy and Pauline walked together back to the main part of Saint-Martin. "Huet is incredibly calm for a man carrying his responsibilities under astounding pressure," Pauline noted.

Jeremy nodded. "He's an incredible leader. He opposed activating Operation Montagnard. He thought coordination to receive reinforcements and confirmation that the paratroopers were on their way should have been done first. He was overruled. If Algiers had followed his advice, the Germans would probably not have attacked the Vercors. They were too busy with Normandy and might have overlooked the danger of the Vercors as an Allied base."

He breathed a sigh. "What I see is that the Vercors is low on the list of Allied priorities if it was ever there in the first place. Promises came without the slightest evidence that they were ever intended to be fulfilled.

They walked on in silence, then Jeremy said, "I'd hate to think that these people were used in an intelligence operation to induce the *Wehrmacht* to tie up resources that otherwise would be used on the western front."

"Don't think that," Pauline warned. "You'll go crazy. We need clear heads."

"I know. You're right. And Huet continues to do a great job along with Chavant. He had to contend with initial bad relations between Chavant and Geyer—"

"Now there's a man with an inflated ego."

"Geyer?" Jeremy laughed. "He is, but I've come to appreciate him. He's a fighter, a good leader with his men, and he follows orders whether or not he likes or agrees with them. If I'm ever in a tight spot, he's someone I'd want fighting next to me. That being said, if I'd been in Huet's shoes a month ago, I'd have fired the captain. But Huet set aside personal feelings in favor of what the captain could do, and Huet was right."

Jeremy glanced at Pauline. In the darkness, she was merely a vague figure illuminated by starlight. "What about you? Are you settling in?"

Pauline laughed. "Settling in? To what? Where? I'm fortunate that a farm family offered me a room, and they are wonderful. But without Roger here to give me direction, I'm only guessing at what he wants me to do. I'm a spy, not a soldier. The female *maquisards* I've met take their training seriously and they'll be good fighters—if they ever get weapons. I can teach them surveillance techniques and how to analyze intelligence, and of course I've learned to fight in close quarters. But unless these women are going on spying forays, I have little to teach them.

"It's frustrating. I've been here over a week. I've seen the attacks, I've learned to love the people here, but I don't know how to help them."

"Don't feel bad," Jeremy consoled with a chuckle. "I was here for three weeks before Roger showed up to tell me my job, but believe me, he has a plan and it'll be a good one. I'll tell you what I learned before he arrived that was invaluable. You're probably picking up on it already."

"I'm listening."

"The people of the Vercors adore him because he's made himself one of them. They'll tell you readily that they'll take a bullet for him—women say that as well as men. He's shown by his dedication and actions that their safety and freedom—winning the war so that they can go back to their normal lives—is uppermost in his mind. With that perception of him, they'll do anything for him. And I'm told that the people in the other regions he oversees feel the same."

"Yes. I sensed that, but I hadn't articulated it," Pauline said. "I think the people feel the same way about you."

Jeremy scoffed. "I'd like to think so, but I stand deep in Roger's shadow. Any regard coming my way is the result of the respect he's built."

Pauline chuckled. "You've developed your own share of goodwill. The people love and trust you, despite the broken promises coming from the UK."

"I'm a ray of hope, that's all."

"Have it your way," Pauline said, laughing. "I will say this, Captain Geyer could use a measure of your humility. Amélie chose well."

Jeremy's breath caught. "How is she? I miss her."

"She misses you, Jeremy. I was with her for only a few minutes. We were both about to go on our next missions, and when she heard that I might see you, I could see in her eyes how much she loves you."

Jeremy forced a breath out of his constricted chest. "Do you know where she was going?"

"You know the answer. I don't and couldn't tell you if I did. But I can tell you that she was healthy, well fed, and seemed calm." She laughed again. "I say that because we've all become experts at looking calm when we're consumed with terror."

"You too?"

"Especially me."

They reached the center of town and an intersection. "This is where I turn off," Pauline said, gesturing in a direction. "I'm just down the road that way a kilometer."

"I'll be riding a motorcycle back to Vassieux tonight. That's the most vulnerable point for air and ground assaults. I'll set up there until I hear otherwise."

"What happens tomorrow?"

"Same as today, and the day after that, and so on until Pflaumm attacks in force. Meanwhile, we wait to see which comes first, the assault or our support, and we keep preparing as best we can."

Pauline's voice rose in exasperation. "And what should I do in the meantime?"

Jeremy chuckled. "Roger should be here in a few days. I'd suggest you stay close to Huet's headquarters, get to know Chavant, and get them to introduce you to the influential women in the Vercors' Resistance. Roger gave you a sterling recommendation. They'll be happy to guide you until he arrives."

Pauline harrumphed impatiently. "I'll have to be satisfied with that for the moment."

17

July 16, 1944
Bletchley Park, England

"You should see this," Claire Littlefield said on entering Commander Travis' office. "The German High Command got wind of an impending operation in the offing at Normandy—Operation Goodwood. It seems that our 21st Army is gathering major elements on our left flank to force a breakout from the bocage country onto the plains south of Caen. The *Wehrmacht* is shifting huge amounts of armor there to block us."

Travis frowned. "Hmph. They know our plans and are sufficiently confident in their intel that they're transferring troops and equipment? That's troublesome. Have we got a leak?"

"That seems likely, sir."

Travis scoffed. "Those bloody Americans can't keep a secret if—"

"It's not the Americans, sir," Claire said quietly. "I'm afraid it's probably coming out of our British units." She grimaced. "Most likely the 21st Army Group."

"General Montgomery's command?" Travis said in shock.

"It could be the attached Canadians—"

"Get that out to the field via the Ultra channels immediately. Monty must close that breach, and he and his commanders must be informed that they'll face greater opposition than they might be expecting." He leaned back in his chair and mulled. "I'll pass the word higher to make sure it gets the right emphasis. Anything else?"

"Nothing pressing, sir. I thought you should be informed immediately."

"Of course." He sighed. "Things were looking so good when we landed on Normandy's beach. People thought we'd have the war won by Christmas. The truth is, if we don't break out of that bocage area, or if Hitler learns that we really have no plans to come through Calais—" He took a deep breath and let it out. "He'll release the *Panzer* Group West and throw us right back into the Channel. That's worrisome."

He brought himself back to the present. "How is your family getting along?"

"You're always so considerate to ask, sir," Claire responded calmly. She had learned to expect his frequent inquiries. "Nothing from my parents since the Red Cross messaging stopped. I heard from Paul a few weeks back. He was in a field hospital in Normandy. He said he was recovering from a concussion after a misfired artillery round struck near him at a place called Bréville."

"Oh, that's been in the news. As I recall, Lord Lovat was wounded in that affair, severely enough to bring him home. And two of his officers were killed."

Startled, Claire's eyes widened. "He didn't tell me that. I missed that news."

Seeing the worry on her face, Travis looked chagrined. "How thoughtless of me. My apologies." A reflective look crossed his face. "If Paul is still in France, he must be all right, or he would have been sent home too."

Claire sighed. "I suppose you're right." She closed her eyes momentarily. "I'll be so thankful when this war is over."

Travis regarded her kindly. "You've held up remarkably, Miss Littlefield. How's the rest of your family?"

"Not much has changed since my last update. Will that be all?"

Travis smiled broadly. "You know I must ask about Timmy. How's he getting on?"

Claire's eyes brightened and her lips parted into a beaming smile. "He's the light of my life. While this war is on, he's a daily reminder of why we bother."

"Ah, yes, that is the reason, isn't it?"

After leaving Travis' office, Claire walked quickly to force thoughts of her family from her mind, but they were quickly replaced by an image of Timmy. Hitler's buzzbombs had flown over Britain's cities for many weeks, but they had recently become less frequent and caused minimal damage. Even so, they created terror and confusion, and the prospect was always present that they could become more effective.

One of them had exploded near Claire's house. Timmy, who had taken the bombs in stride for never having heard one explode nearby, was terrified. Claire had not been home at the time, and when she arrived several hours later, she found Timmy and Elsie still sheltering in the basement. He had refused to leave until Claire came home, and even then, he looked around with troubled eyes.

"We'll be all right," she had cooed, but after five long years of war, her characteristic optimism was waning. Time had passed since she had uttered her favorite saying, "Things will get better. You'll see." That night, Timmy had gripped her hand and refused to let go until he had fallen asleep as she read him a bedtime story.

Now she castigated herself for allowing emotion to trump stoicism during her conversation with Travis. *You can't do that. You lead decoders and analysts.*

She reached the door into her work area and paused to take a deep breath. Then she let it out, forced a smile, entered, and took her place at her desk.

18

July 20, 1944
Grenoble, France

"I'm prepared to give you a final briefing on our plans," *Oberst* Schwehr said.

Sitting behind his desk, General Pflaumm gestured with a cigar. "I suppose you've heard about our counterattack against the Allies at Normandy."

"I have, sir," Schwehr replied enthusiastically. "They thought they'd break out of the bocage, but our great fighters put a stop to that. We have them bogged down there, and we'll soon push them back the way they came."

Pflaumm nodded with a malevolent smirk. "Go ahead. Let me hear your plans."

Schwehr's eyes gleamed. "The coordinated attack will commence at four major points at 06:00 tomorrow morning. Our units at Saint-Nizier will push down through Lans and Villard, neutralize every village that could threaten our supply lines along the northeast rim of the Vercors, and then push south onto the plateau.

"We'll also have a column of *panzers* attacking across the southern rim.

They're staged to advance through Die and strike into the mountains, crossing into the plateau at Col de Rousset.

"Also, as we discussed previously, our *Gebirgsjägers* will navigate through the mule tracks in the east at Pas de Chattons and Pas de la Selle. They're between the high peaks, Le Grand Veymont and Mont Aiguille. Those troops will hit the strongholds at the main passes in their sector from the rear. They'll rappel down the cliffs and cut off escape. That area is heavily forested below the cliffs, so our men will deny sanctuary for anyone trying to hide out there.

"Finally, in the west, we'll attack from Pont-en-Royans to link up with our forces coming from the north along the Gorges de la Bourne."

Pflaumm listened contentedly. "When does air support begin?"

Schwehr held a finger in the air and smiled, enjoying his day in the sun. "Four hours after the ground attack begins, our gliders will descend at the heart of the plateau, at Vassieux. The troops they carry will dominate the airfield still being built there, take the town, and control all access into the area. When it's secure, they'll leave behind an occupying force and then split the remainder into two groups. One will push north through La Chapelle and Saint-Martin to cover the advance of our forces climbing out of the Gorges de la Bourne. The other will head southeast to support our forces coming onto the plateau through the pass at Col de Rousset.

"At every step of the way, they'll be supported by fighter and bomber aircraft."

Pflaumm drew on his cigar. "How long will the main operation take?"

Schwehr shrugged. "Without unforeseen circumstances, a few days, maybe, but if the Allies bring in heavy support, that's another question. My intent is to drive hard and fast, and have it complete almost before word of the campaign is communicated outside the plateau."

The general arched his brows. "That'll be difficult. The people there control their own phone lines, and they're in touch with London and Algiers via wireless."

"Yes, sir, and that's why, from the outset, we'll deal harshly with the farms, villages, and people near the major towns. From my view, anyone who lends aid to the terrorists are themselves terrorists and will be dealt with accordingly. We'll burn them out, execute them, do whatever it takes to subdue them."

Pflaumm considered quietly. "If we're successful, you'll have surrounded an armed camp. That means men with weapons, and women too, and we don't know how many fighters or how heavily armed they are. How will you handle mop-up operations?"

"We've mustered the resources we need. Once the periphery of the Vercors and the major towns are secure, we'll go through every house, every forested area, step by step. We'll post guards around any and all sources of drinking water, drive holdouts into the mountains, and starve them out.

"We'll deal with anyone who helps them. That should end things rapidly."

Pflaumm leaned back in his chair, reviewing the plan while Schwehr stood by. At last the general rose and crossed the room to pour two glasses of schnapps. When he was done, he handed one to the *oberst*. "Let's drink to a successful operation," he said. "What else do you need?"

"Only your order, sir."

Pflaumm raised his glass and clinked it against Schwehr's. "Execute."

19

July 21, 1944
Eisenhower HQ, France

"I wanted a personal conversation, Monty," General Eisenhower said. He kept his voice deliberately mild. "No one else needs to be here for this."

General Montgomery stiffened. "Are you going to relieve me, sir?"

Eisenhower shook his head slightly. "I haven't made up my mind yet. This discussion is off the record. I want to know what happened. Just a few days ago, you told General Allen that the 2nd Army was very strong and could get no stronger. I believe that was the gist. You said you were looking for a real showdown on the eastern flank, to let loose a corps of three armored divisions into the open country on either side of the Caen-Falaise road. Since then, you've conducted the biggest tank battle in history, we've lost hundreds of tanks and suffered thirty-five-hundred casualties—the reports are still coming in, so we don't know how many are dead—and we haven't moved an inch.

"Your VIII Corps had twelve infantry battalions available, three of them mechanized. They could have supported the nine tank and three infantry reconnaissance battalions you had out there, yet five of the twelve saw no action at all. I'm having a little trouble with that."

Montgomery remained quiet, stung by the indictment despite Eisenhower's mild tone. At last he said, "We'll finish taking Caen today."

"That was the objective we were supposed to secure on D-Day," Eisenhower rejoined, his voice becoming slightly heated. "Here we are seven weeks later, and we're finally going to liberate the city. Your Operation Goodwood was supposed to capture the part of Caen we didn't already control and position us on the Bourguébus Ridge to threaten Falaise.

"In other words, break us out of bocage country onto the plains south of Caen so our tanks can maneuver and create a gap we could pour our armies through. That didn't happen. Why not? This was your plan. Why didn't it work?"

Montgomery took a deep breath. He was aware of his reputation for grandiosity and a "my way is the right way" mentality. This was not the time to exhibit those traits even though they had served him well in North Africa and Sicily.

He had been the overall ground commander on D-Day. In that capacity, he had directed the establishment of the beachhead perimeter and managed the build-up of men and resources along the coast. In both tasks, he succeeded brilliantly.

Eisenhower, on the other hand, had never commanded troops in combat prior to taking charge of the Mediterranean Theater in advance of the Allied invasion in North Africa. On completion, he had transferred his headquarters from Gibraltar back to London to assume the position of Supreme Allied Commander—Europe to plan Operation Overlord, the invasion of France.

Does Eisenhower know that he's viewed by senior British officers as an exalted desk clerk who leaves the real running of the war to combat-experienced subordinates, a good many of them being British? He ditched the thought. This was no time to indicate that he shared even an inkling of that perception. "General, I drew the German *panzers* in. That relieved pressure on the Americans on our right flank as they campaigned on Cotentin to take Cherbourg."

Eisenhower lifted an eyebrow. "That wasn't the objective."

"But it happened, and we'd be negligent not to exploit the opportunity."

The American general took his time to reply. "Bradley's Operation Cobra will break us out of bocage. But let's stay on the subject. After three days of heavy fighting, thousands of casualties, and an incalculable loss of equipment, Operation Goodwood took us nowhere."

The British general inhaled sharply and let his breath out slowly. "Sir, you tasked my army group, including the Canadians, with taking Caen and the surrounding countryside. We faced a dug-in force of seven infantry divisions, seven *panzer* divisions including four *Waffen SS* units, and three heavy *panzer* battalions. That means we went against six hundred tanks including all the Tigers available in France."

"You had three corps to do the job," Eisenhower replied steadily, "and you expressed confidence that you had sufficient forces. I hate to bring this up, but we had Ultra-level intelligence that the Germans learned of the operation and prepared to meet it. You've got an intelligence leak."

Montgomery jammed his hands in his pockets, and his shoulders slumped slightly. "I believed I had enough strength," he said, "and I'm quite disturbed about the breach." He blew out a breath. "This is not easy for me, but I admit I made mistakes." He straightened his shoulders and looked directly into Eisenhower's eyes. "I understand that my errors cost lives. I'll take that to my grave." He paused, and his jaw tightened. "Sir, if you're going to relieve me, let's get it done."

Eisenhower remained silent while eyeing Montgomery. At last he said, "You've served your country and the Allies well, Monty. I won't make any major command changes now. Get that security issue contained and get ready for the next operations. They'll be on us within days, and we'll be preparing for Falaise."

Montgomery took the news matter-of-factly. He saluted, waited for Eisenhower's return salute, and departed. On his way out, he passed General Bradley, commanding general of the US 1st Army, who was on his way in. As soon as the Allied ground troops landed and established the beachhead, Bradley fell directly under Eisenhower's command. General Patton's 3rd Army was due to arrive by August 1. Together with the 1st army, the two would form the US 12th Army Group under Bradley.

Montgomery and Bradley greeted each other cordially but did not linger to visit.

Eisenhower received Bradley warmly. "Come in." The two had been classmates at West Point. "I'm glad you're here. Walk me through Operation Cobra."

Bradley nodded grimly. "Sir, before we get started, I want to say that my job will be a lot easier in the western sector because of what Monty did on the eastern flank. He drew the bulk of German armored units that way, destroyed a lot of them, and now my soldiers won't have to fight them."

Eisenhower returned his steady gaze. "Point taken. Getting to the subject at hand, Patton's 3rd Army is on its way into Normandy as we speak."

Bradley chuckled. "That's going to be an interesting challenge." In North Africa, Patton had been Bradley's superior. Now he would be Patton's boss. "I don't believe there's been a man born with a bigger ego since Julius Caesar, and that's allowing for Bernard Montgomery and Douglas MacArthur!"

Eisenhower smiled mildly. "He might even think he's Caesar's reincarnation."

Both men laughed. Patton's belief in reincarnation, and his fascination with Roman history and their generals in particular, was no secret. "Keeping him out of combat for the last year was good for him," Eisenhower observed. "Now he's raring to go, and he won't be slapping any more soldiers. And I don't think he'll kick up a fuss if he disagrees with you or me on a point. He doesn't want to be sidelined again."

Eisenhower referred to a pair of incidents at field hospitals in Sicily where Patton had slapped two soldiers he accused of cowardice and malingering. The public outcry in the US had forced disciplinary measures including Patton's public apology and relief from command. "We made good use of him with his ghost army in England. That ruse worked spectacularly. Hitler still believes we're coming for him through Calais. The longer we keep the *führer* believing that, the longer he'll keep his *Panzer* Group West in that area of France." He moved to a map on his wall. "I was worried about the carpet bombing at Saint-Lô being too close to our troops. Looking back, my worries were justified. We hit a lot of our own men."

Bradley blew out a long breath. "I know, Ike." Out of respect for Eisenhower's position, Bradley seldom addressed his classmate in a familiar way, but he sensed the heavy burden that the supreme commander carried. He could use a friend.

Bradley scrutinized the map and put his finger on Saint-Lô. "I'm sorry about what happened there, but I still see the bombing sweeps as a risk we had to take. Luck went against us, but I didn't see another way of breaking out of bocage country. I still don't. That patchwork of hedges and fields was killing our men. If we had kept at it, the Germans would have attritted us down to an ineffective force—and you know another counterattack is coming sooner or later."

Eisenhower's eyes faded into a haunted look. "But we dropped so many bombs on Saint-Lô, and we couldn't get the villagers out first. And a lot of our ordnance fell on our own boys. We lost hundreds, including General McNair, and he's the highest ranking officer we've lost in this theater to date."

Bradly took his time to respond. "We took the risk and created the gap through the bocage that we needed. Patton will push through and head west to neutralize Brittany's ports at Saint-Malo, Brest, and Lorient."

Eisenhower grunted. "After he punches past Saint-Lô, his instincts will urge him to turn east and push for Falaise, Paris, and beyond to the Rhine. He won't like going west, but we've got to lock up those three ports. The Germans are still in there."

Bradley smiled grimly while rubbing the back of his neck. "Maybe Patton can isolate them. When he's done in Brittany, he'll thrust east with one of his three corps to Argentan and become the southern pincer to catch the German 7th Army between there and the British 2nd Army north of Falaise. That narrow corridor won't be much space for the *Wehrmacht* units escaping from Brittany and the Cotentin Peninsula. The Brits and Poles are maneuvering to push them west into that Falaise pocket." He grimaced. "Once Monty chases the Huns out of Caen, we'll be in open tank country, and then he can turn up the pressure."

Eisenhower agreed gravely. "That channel between Falaise and Argentan is awfully narrow. We'll need to close the gap to kill or capture the *Wehrmacht's* Army Group B and all the straggling units. If we don't, a lot of them will escape to fight again."

20

Same Day, July 21, 1944
Eniwetok Naval Base, Eniwetok Atoll, Pacific Ocean

USN Lieutenant Commander Josh Littlefield breathed a sigh of relief, but immediately understood that he might regret the impulse. He had just read a message from his boss, the evaluator, in the CIC.

Barely a month had passed since he had been in the thick of sea battle west of Saipan. The team in the CIC was excellent. He could not ask for better, and he knew he was good at planning and overseeing operations. But his heart was in flying, even if that was where he incurred the greatest threat to his life. He had not become a fighter pilot to stare at radar screens, charts, and graphs from behind a desk.

With the Imperial Japanese Navy reduced to a defensive posture west of the Marianas, and with Allied victories over Saipan and Tinian secured at unspeakable costs in lives and equipment, the *Lexington* had cruised to anchor within the Eniwetok Atoll eleven hundred miles east of the Marianas. It launched sorties in support of other operations including on Guam, but the demands on the ship and its resources had greatly diminished with a concurrent decrease in demands on the CIC.

The reduced operational tempo left Josh with spare time, and he found himself reading intelligence reports to keep busy. One he had found interesting regarded a young Japanese-speaking Mexican Marine private, Guy Gabaldon, who had single-handedly secured the surrender of hundreds of Japanese soldiers before the final day of ground fighting at Saipan. Estimates of the number of prisoners he had captured ranged from eight hundred to fifteen hundred, though Josh noticed that Gabaldon made no claims himself. His company commander made the initial claim, supported by others in his chain of command.

In addition to bringing in the captives, he had also delivered intelligence of an impending *gyokusai,* which Josh learned was a suicidal mission to kill as many of the enemy as possible. The *gyokusai,* a massive *bonsai* charge, had all but destroyed two US Marine battalions. By the time Saipan had been secured, American casualties were estimated at over thirteen thousand, including three thousand dead. Probable Japanese deaths approached twenty-seven thousand. No Japanese plans had become evident either to retake Saipan or rescue their stranded soldiers.

Josh shook his head soberly. *Gabaldon saved many American lives.* Captain Schwabe had nominated the private for a Congressional Medal of Honor, and Josh thought he certainly deserved it.

Josh read another report about a Navy Radioman First Class, George Tweed, who had survived on Guam for thirty-one months while hiding from the Japanese. He had been rescued by a destroyer, and he had supplied superb intelligence that was also expected to save many lives during the impending invasion there.

Josh glanced at his calendar. The amphibious operation at Guam had commenced that morning. Silently, he wished all the fighters well.

Reading of Gabaldon's and Tweed's exploits brought to mind Josh's own time with the Marines on Guadalcanal, and suddenly a sense overcame him that he was not doing enough in the war. He knew the arguments against the notion: he had flown countless missions, taken down enemy aircraft, trained the Doolittle-raid pilots, helped flip the Vichy-French army to the Allies in Algeria, participated in sinking a Japanese carrier . . . and was shot down three times.

He groaned as the last thought flashed by. Technically, he had been shot down only twice, he reminded himself. The last time, he had limped the

Hellcat back to the *Lexington. Come to think of it, I never learned whether the plane was repairable, or for that matter, who the squadron leader was, or who the pilot was that saved my butt.*

His mind returned to the Marine ground fighters. He knew the lives they lived because he had experienced it on Edson's Ridge at Guadalcanal. And while he had known moments of high drama in that battle, the Marines and soldiers, day in and day out, lived in foxholes with the stench of death added to that of jungle rot, eating C-Rations much of the time and savoring a hot meal whenever possible. In comparison, his current situation was luxurious.

With more time on his hands, Josh kept up with news of the war on the other side of the planet. Still unknown beyond planners directly involved in the European and Mediterranean Theaters was whether the Allies would continue up Italy's boot, invade Europe through southern France, or push up through the Balkans and attack Germany from the east. Conjecture on the alternatives was a favorite topic of discussion at mealtimes, but no one had insight more valid than anyone else's, and Josh deemed his own judgment on the matter too ill-informed to be reliable.

More than anything, he wished for word from Zack and Sherry on how they were doing, and beyond them, how his British cousins were getting along. He resolved to travel to London and Sark at war's end to meet them all.

His thoughts were interrupted by a knock on his door. Upon opening it, an orderly handed him the message that brought an immediate sense of relief. His request to be transferred back to flight status had been approved, and he would command another squadron.

21

Same Day, July 21, 1944
Vassieux-en-Vercors, France

The roar of aircraft engines at midmorning was different than any Jeremy had heard before, but coming out of the west from Chabeuil, it portended an ominous warning. He rushed from the farmhouse where he had been on alert.

For the past week, he had worked with the *Maquis* at Vassieux, checking defensive positions around the town and the airfield, preparing fields of fire, drilling volunteers in infantry tactics, coaching on effective use of rifles and machine guns, instructing in hand-to-hand combat with and without bayonets, and generally doing all he could to prepare the defenders against the imminent attack.

When not engaged in training, Jeremy took to his motorcycle to tour the defensive positions in the main passes. Roger had arrived in Saint-Martin two days earlier and sent a message that he fully supported Jeremy's actions. "I've also worked with Pauline here," he wrote. "You gave her good advice on working through Huet and Chavant. She's a great addition to our team."

Word reached Jeremy of simultaneous attacks from four major directions below the rim of the mountains protecting the Vercors. Now, dark shadows of Junkers JU 52 transport planes swept across the sky, dragging behind them small gliders which then released their towing cables and slid toward the ground. Jeremy counted them as they descended. They included three larger gliders that had already been released, and Jeremy had not seen the aircraft that had towed them.

He rushed to the farmer's phone to call a report to Roger at Huet's Villa Bellon headquarters. While waiting to be connected, Jeremy heard small-arms fire outside and then a much steadier, heavier rhythmic pounding of machine guns from the landing field.

When Roger answered the phone, Jeremy yelled, "The Germans are here." He panted. Sweat poured from his forehead. "Twenty-five gliders in all. Most of them were the DFS 230s you described, but there were three larger ones. They look about double the size."

"Probably Go 242s. They carry twenty troops each. That puts the incoming strength there at just under three hundred, and we can expect more to arrive by ground transportation. With air support, our troops won't hold them for long. We're getting reports of a sizeable force coming out of Saint-Nizier as well."

He paused. "Jeremy, I want you to come here—"

"But sir, I'm needed here—"

"Jeremy," Roger said sternly, "we'll need you to coordinate elsewhere. We can't afford to lose you in combat."

Jeremy's anger sparked. He controlled it. "Sir, I've lived with these people. I've trained and fought alongside them. I can't leave now when the heavy shooting starts."

"I don't have time to discuss, Major," Roger replied sharply. "I'll expect to see you here at first opportunity. That's an order."

His cheeks flushed with anger, Jeremy rushed outside. Ringing in the back of his mind were Huet's words in the message to the Vercors *maquisards*: "We will engage the enemy wherever he is at all times..."

And I'm being ordered to quit the battlefield.

The airfield was in plain view, and he was at the south end of it at the edge of town. All the gliders had landed. The Junkers had towed them over the pass at Col de la Chau, banked south to release them for a north-to-south landing, and then flown over Vassieux as they departed the area.

The gliders were spread across the field, and the soldiers atop them combed its periphery with their MG 34s while their comrades poured out through two wide doors on the left sides of their gliders. The ground troops began a sweep across the field and up a short bluff into the village.

Jeremy watched, aghast, as the carnage commenced. Fighters flew low and strafed the town indiscriminately. Bombers followed, dropping deadly ordnance, and within minutes, homes and buildings in Vassieux, including the church, were in flames.

Panicked by the roaring bombers, fighters, explosions, and machine gun fire, the population ran wildly about, seeking cover. But there was no place to go. Many of them already lay dead or wounded in the streets.

Maquisards positioned to defend the northern flank exchanged fire with the marauders, but as their ammunition dwindled, they fell back, Jeremy with them. Mindful of Roger's order to join him in Saint-Martin, Jeremy maneuvered to the northeast edge of town where he had left his motorcycle inside a barn. There, reluctantly, with the sound of battle and the screams of terrified mothers and children ringing in his ears, he headed out on a circuitous route west and then northwest through Le Château, up into the hilly country that skirted La Chapelle, and finally staggered into Villa Bellon four hours after departing from Vassieux on a journey whose straight-line distance was little more than ten miles. For much of the way, he was barely out of earshot of fierce battle.

On arrival at Villa Bellon, he found Pauline and Roger in the operations room with Huet. The three looked haggard. While the commander studied the map intently, Roger briefed Jeremy on the situation. "Vassieux is overrun," he said. Seeing Jeremy's downcast eyes, he said kindly, "I'm sorry, Jeremy. Everyone here and there did all we could, you included. Don't let the guilt of surviving get in the way of clear thinking. We still have thousands to try to save. Without support at Vassieux, the outcome there was preordained."

"As it will be in the rest of the Vercors," Jeremy said tersely.

Roger peered at Jeremy and handed him a message. "Two things to let you know. The Americans took Saint-Lô yesterday. The German containment at Normandy is broken. The Allies are headed this way."

Jeremy nodded, almost with disinterest, his mind wrestling with the horrific sights and sounds of the deaths of friends and the destruction of their homes at Vassieux. "What's the second thing?"

Roger handed him a slip of paper. "I sent this message out to London last night."

Jeremy took it and read.

"Fierce battle for capture of Vercors imminent. Without your help result uncertain. Urgently request reinforcements of one parachute battalion and mortars. Also immediate bombing of St Nizier and Chabeuil. Come to our aid by every means."

Jeremy finished reading, quivering with anger and grief. "Did you hear back?"

Roger shook his head. "I sent out another telegraph this morning as soon as the attack started at Vassieux, which was almost simultaneous with the actions at Saint-Nizier." He handed it to Jeremy. "Just read the last three lines."

"Those in London and Algiers understand nothing about the situation in which we find ourselves and are considered as criminals and cowards. Yes repeat criminals and cowards."

"You've aptly characterized those 'leaders,' sir," Jeremy muttered.

Six days earlier, Lieutenant Colonel Huet had seen the first indications of Pflaumm's major plan of attack. On that day, *Wehrmacht* forces destroyed a tunnel at Engins in the northwest; it demolished one of two roads and occupied the other, both leading from Grenoble onto the plateau in the northeast; and it blew up a bridge over the Isère River below Royans in the west. Those and other operations blocked six of the eight passes onto the plateau and left the remaining two under German control. Then, over the next forty-eight hours, a steady stream of reports into Huet's headquarters informed of continued buildup of German forces around the periphery of the Vercors at the outside base of its mountain crests.

One account was particularly startling. In the southeast, the Germans had occupied the pass at Col de Grimone, a commanding position overlooking Lus-la-Croix-Haute, the very hamlet where the villagers had been forced to witness the tortured death of a *maquisard*. The *Wehrmacht* soldiers' actions on the pass demonstrated that this was no hit-and-run raid —they were prepared to launch a sustained attack.

Obviously, Pflaumm intended to cordon off the Vercors to prevent escape. The daily aerial reconnaissance, the build-up at Chabeuil, and Roger's sighting of the strange gliders indicated a strong, imminent air assault. And the number of troops and armor on every road in the plains with access through key points into the Vercors pointed to unremitting sustained operations after the initial assault.

The objective was unmistakable. When Pflaumm's maneuvers had been completed, he intended that no opportunity would remain on the Vercors for armed resistance to the Nazi regime. He had demonstrated by his frequent raids how he would handle the civilian population as well as those who fought to protect it.

Less than seventy-two hours ago, reacting to reports of almost constant contact between Resistance forces and German probes already on the plateau, Huet had imposed martial law. Major Longe had worked on multiple messages to London advising of the urgent situation and imploring for air support. He received back only the now customary silence.

Now, Jeremy remained quiet while he peered at a map on the wall. Huet stood in front of it, also studying it closely. The two men were alone in the operations room.

"It's obvious what they intend," Jeremy said after a few moments. "Villard was left undefended. The Germans took the men out of there by force three days ago for their labor camps in Germany."

Images flashed through his mind of people lining the road as Beauregard's and Abel's soldiers withdrew from Saint-Nizier and Lans. That was barely a month ago, and the villagers had celebrated their defenders. *Little did they know...*

Jeremy drove the visions from his mind. "If the thrust to the northwest takes the pass at Perrin," he went on, "it'll turn south toward Méaudre. Then, the two arms will jointly attack at the Gorges de la Bourne there." He pointed at the location on the map. "And that is crucial terrain. When they break through there, they'll block escape and have a free route onto the plateau from the north."

Huet listened to Jeremy's comments. "That's my conclusion too," he said. "Their plan is clear." He heaved a sigh. "Once again, Captain Beauregard's men will bear the brunt, at least in the north." He traced a southbound route on the map. "They'll ascend from the gorge through Valchevrière. That's Abel Chabal's area." Without turning his head, he mused out loud, "You know, we just promoted Abel to lieutenant. That was long overdue, and now he will face the full force of the enemy drive to the south."

Jeremy's throat constricted. Valchevrière, a community of coal miners, was the hamlet he was first brought to in the Vercors, where he had waited three weeks for Roger's arrival. He had worked with those people and spent many evenings with them in the small tavern. The village had since been evacuated and lay empty.

The lonely hamlet rested on a cleared knoll surrounded by forest, and had twenty stone buildings, including homes and the tavern. A small white stone church with a belltower stood apart from the other buildings on its own promontory at a break in the trees between two mountainsides. Beyond it was a spectacular view of the mountain ranges, at the bottom of which was the Gorges de la Bourne.

Jeremy recalled the friendly atmosphere when he had arrived. It had been so relaxed compared to the rest of German-occupied France. The people had reveled in their independence and freedom in the midst of Nazi tyranny.

In his mind's eye, Jeremy saw his friend, the quiet chief sergeant, now a lieutenant, who had arrived to defend Saint-Nizier while singing "*La Marseillaise*" with his thirty commandos. Together, Jeremy and Abel had attacked and defeated a machine gun position that had provided covering fire to German forces in an initial probing maneuver. They had fought side by side when General Pflaumm's troops had overrun the village. Together, they had buried four of Abel's men.

Jeremy recalled racing in full flight on Abel's command, across an open field between two enemy salients attempting a pincer to capture or kill them. Abel's tactic had worked. Most of his commandos had escaped, but the fourth man had been lost.

It had been Abel who had ordered the flag raised on the Moucherotte. It had caused consternation among local Resistance leaders, irritated General Pflaumm, and sparked defiance among the citizens of the Vercors and those living on the plains.

Jeremy's throat constricted further, and he realized suddenly that he had grown as close to Abel as he was to his own brothers, Paul and Lance, and to his sister, Claire. He and Abel had relied on each other for their very lives in close quarters. The bond between them had been sealed. And now, his friend, his brother, the man who had undoubtedly saved his life in that race across the field, was in mortal danger.

Roger entered the room with Pauline. Jeremy immediately approached him. "Roger, let me go join Abel."

Caught by surprise, Roger studied Jeremy's face. At last he said, "That's not a good idea—"

"Look, Roger," Jeremy interrupted. "The Vercors is encircled. The soldiers are on the plateau in large numbers. You've seen the reports. They've even rappelled down the cliffs in the southeast district. We're hemmed in.

"At some point, Huet will give the order to disperse. When that happens, each district command will withdraw to its designated area, forage to survive, and try to either do hit-and-run operations or find a way to escape over the mountain crests. That includes this headquarters. There's no coordination for me to do now, so let me join Abel's unit to make myself useful." He added with a striking tone, "I won't avoid combat again."

Taken aback by Jeremy's final statement and his tone, Roger reluctantly agreed. "All right. The war continues elsewhere, and things are not going well for the Germans in the rest of France. At some point, they'll have to leave the Vercors. I'll need you alive and well. You know how to reach me through London."

Jeremy nodded.

Roger extended his hand. "Good luck, Major."

Jeremy shook it. "Thank you, sir."

Pauline had listened to the discussion quietly. Now she followed Jeremy out to his motorcycle. Dusk was settling in.

"I won't get to do the job I was sent here for," she said. "Events moved too fast."

She suddenly flung her arms around Jeremy's neck and squeezed him. "I've known you for such a short time, but you've become like a brother to me. And now, I fear I will never see you again." Her body shook. "Promise me. Promise me that you'll live and go back to make Amélie very happy."

Jeremy held her without response.

Pauline peered into his eyes. Tears rolled down her face. "I dream of the day when frequent, final goodbyes are in the past."

Seized with emotion and at a loss for words, Jeremy held her for a few moments longer. "We'll meet again," he said gruffly. "Stick with Roger. He'll get you out of here safely, and then he'll have a new mission for you."

Fighting off sadness, Jeremy disentangled himself from Pauline's embrace. He mounted the motorcycle and rode into the gathering dusk.

Shortly after nightfall, he parked the bike behind some bushes at the top of the road that led into tiny stone Valchevrière, still several hundred meters away at the base of a steep slope. He descended on foot, mindful that Abel's men were expecting enemy probes. However, he was approaching downhill from the south, and Pflaumm's troops were expected to advance uphill from the north. Rather than stationing in the village, the commandos had occupied the area around an outcropping of rock, a belvedere, that overlooked the village.

From this position, an alternate route into the Vercors plateau could be controlled easily with few men—if the attacking force could be constrained to the road and had no other support. A single lane wound through a thick forest of firs, creating an arduous path for vehicles of any size. Its narrow approaches were bordered by huge boulders, and the mountain slopes rising from them were laden with glacier-strewn rocks that could be used to make impassable the road that paralleled the Gorges de la Bourne.

However, if an invading force were to navigate the difficulties successfully and ascend above the belvedere, it would encounter a road that wound around steep hairpin turns and crossed three jagged ridgelines. Then it would descend steeply into the valley through the rugged Roche Rousse cliffs near Saint-Martin. It would then threaten the heart of the Vercors.

As he reached the rear of Abel's defensive lines, a guard recognized Jeremy and escorted him to Abel's headquarters. It was nothing more than a spot on the ground where the lieutenant and his signaler piled their gear. Huet had handpicked Abel and his commandos for this position two days earlier, and placed them under the command of Captain Jean Prévost, an originator of Operation Montagnard.

The site provided an expansive view to the north with a clear line of sight into Valchevrière and beyond into the Gorges de la Bourne. The Germans would be detected long before they reached this position.

A rock wall behind Abel's men protected their rear, and the inclines to their front and sides were steep and not easily accessible. With the right weapons, the position should be defensible by a small unit against large forces for an indefinite time. However, Abel's commandos were down to small arms, a single machine gun, a bazooka, and not nearly enough ammunition.

Jeremy's escort, a sergeant, was a crusty veteran of many battles. He was pleased to see Jeremy, but as they threaded down the path to the belvedere, he said, "Lieutenant Chabal is not the same. He's changed."

"In what way?"

The sergeant shrugged. "He doesn't joke with us anymore. He's as thorough and careful as ever, but I think he doesn't expect to live through this battle."

"Then we'll change his mind," Jeremy replied brusquely, feeling far less confident than he hoped he sounded.

On reaching the belvedere, he was slightly shocked to see Abel. Like the rest of his commandos, the officer was gaunt and exhausted, but that was expected. What Jeremy had not anticipated, however, was the air of fatalism that was immediately evident in Abel's demeanor and speech.

Abel clasped Jeremy's hand in a warm welcome. "Ah, my friend and brother, you've joined us for our final battle."

Jeremy eyed him with a forced deadpan expression. "Let's hope it won't be that."

The two men moved to the side where they could talk between themselves quietly. "I'm realistic," Abel said. "Look at this terrain. With the right weapons and enough men, we could hold out forever." He shook his head and let out an exasperated breath. "But we don't have them. The Germans have skilled mountaineer units, their *Gebirgsjägers*, and they'll use them here. They'll move past our flanks, and when they're above us, the battle's over." He paused. "They might not even have to do that. Pflaumm's troops have already pushed past Villard. They could show up on the high ground behind us at any time."

Jeremy grasped Abel's shoulder. "Your men are worried about you."

Abel laughed. "They're always worried about me—that I joke too much or not enough. *Merde*, if I acted too confident now, they'd think I was being careless and not sizing things up accurately." His face turned serious. "The truth is, a lot of us will die when the battle comes, probably tomorrow. In fact, I have a final instruction to deliver to my men. You can join and listen if you'd care to."

Ten minutes later, Abel's command was gathered around him. "This has to be quick," he said. "The German mountain troops are good at night maneuvers, as we saw at Saint-Nizier, so we need to get listening posts back out. But I want you all to hear what I have to say."

He took a deep breath. "This is going to be tougher than anything we've experienced to date. If things work out badly or if I'm killed, those of you who survive should make for the ridge at Le Coinchette." He pointed south. Then, without another word, he strode into the darkness.

Jeremy watched him go. Abel had given the distinct impression of someone who was overcome by sentiment and wanted to be alone. But Jeremy well knew the mental tricks that a dark night in terrifying situations could play on the stoutest of hearts and minds. He waited a few minutes, and then followed.

His friend welcomed his presence. The two talked long into the night about family, friends, plans for after the war; and then, while sitting against tree trunks, their heads drooped, their eyes closed, and they both fell into restless sleep.

22

July 22, 1944

Before dawn, Abel rousted Jeremy. “Let me show you what we’ve done.”

Heavy with fatigue, Jeremy clambered to his feet and rubbed granules from the corners of his eyes. Then he followed Abel.

Keeping low and using shrubs and trees to screen their movement, they edged to the precipice. “We’ve mined the roads and cut down trees to clear our fields of fire,” Abel said, pointing out the battlefield preparations. “We’ve also built several log shelters for our machine gun and the bazooka. We can shift between them to meet the tactical situation when the firing starts. Have I overlooked anything?”

Jeremy studied the preparations carefully. “If I see something, I’ll let you know.”

The full platoon was up before the sun tinted the eastern sky. If they moved about at all, they did so quietly, being careful not to clang metal objects against each other. They ate cold rations, and otherwise, they waited and watched in their positions.

Three hours passed. The sun rose high in the sky.

A shot from below echoed against the rock wall behind the belvedere.

Jeremy held his breath.

Suddenly, an Alsation soldier, one of Abel's men whom Jeremy knew only as Mulheim, called out in a loud voice to the German soldiers in their own language. "*Zoldaten*! *Kamaraden*! Listen. Don't shoot. I am going to stand up."

Watching in astonishment, Jeremy had no idea what to expect.

"Look," Mulheim called. "We're wearing uniforms. We are not terrorists."

Jeremy almost laughed out loud. The French army uniforms the commandos wore were from the warehouse the *maquisards* had raided in Grenoble.

"You see, we are regular troops," Mulheim went on. "We were parachuted in and there are a lot of us." He paused a moment, and then started up again, calling in an even louder voice, "Hitler was killed two days ago."

Jeremy had heard vague rumors in Huet's headquarters that an assassination attempt against Hitler had succeeded at a place in Poland called *Wolfsschanze*, or Wolf's Lair. The story had raised hope, but given current circumstances and the continued press of Pflaumm's troops, no one gave the rumor much credence, and it had slipped from Jeremy's mind.

"The *Reich* scuttled its fleet," Mulheim shouted, and then, to Jeremy's amazement, he heard Germans below saying, "*Ja? Ja*?" They sounded old and tired, perhaps men with families, ready to accept an end to the war.

"The Geneva Convention requires you to lay down your arms and come out," Mulheim called, "one by one, with your hands on your heads."

Jeremy listened, still amazed. *Is this going to work?* He wondered if the report about Hitler and the alleged scuttling of the fleet were true.

Seconds stretched to almost a full minute. The only sounds were a breeze and the birds' morning songs. Jeremy dropped his head back. *What sweet music.*

Then a furious voice broke the peace. "*Dummkopfs*," the man bellowed. "*Schießen*!" A fusillade erupted with machine guns, rifles, grenades, mortars...

Jeremy ducked down. His rifle was already thrust through a hole in the defenses, and he searched over its sights for a target. Spotting a man running uphill, he zeroed in and squeezed the trigger.

The soldier went down. Jeremy had no time for regrets, but he noted that the man looked overweight and might have been struggling up the hill. He had been an easy target. *Could Germany be down to older replacements?*

After five years of fighting in places far from its borders, the notion seemed plausible. Jeremy searched for his next target.

Behind him somewhere, he heard the bazooka and half-smiled. Abel had reserved the recoilless rocket launcher for himself. It was designed to defeat armor and was generally ineffective against infantry, but since no *panzers* would come this way, Abel used them against whatever target he deemed fit for such a round. Whether he did any damage, Jeremy could not tell, but Abel seemed bent on trying what he had against machine guns and mortars.

The battle continued for four hours with the Germans pressing closer and closer. And then Abel's fear of insufficient resources in all categories became stark. He sent a squad to provide cover from an outcrop of rocks overlooking Abel's position.

They never arrived.

The Germans occupied the location first and eliminated the squad. Now, they occupied the high ground, and rained down hot steel on the belvedere.

Abel called to Jeremy and beckoned to him. "We're surrounded," he said when Jeremy reached him at the base of the cliff wall behind the belvedere. Bullets whizzed by from above, below, and both flanks. "We can't hold much longer, and we have no place to go. This isn't your fight. You should escape now."

Before Jeremy could reply, Abel lurched backward. His face registered shock as three bullets struck him, two in a leg and one in an arm. Furiously, Abel sat up, mounted the recoilless rifle on his shoulder, found a target, and fired.

Then, almost as an afterthought, he pulled a piece of paper from his shirt pocket. "I almost forgot," he said through gritted teeth, his eyes wild with pain. "This is a list of Resistance members. It can't fall into German hands." He wadded it tightly and tossed it over the edge of the belvedere.

Jeremy watched it disappear. All around, the chaos of battle continued with the zing of bullets, the rat-tat-tat of machine guns, and the explosions of mortars and mountain artillery. Over the cacophony, Jeremy heard a grunt. Turning, he found Abel lying lifeless, his eyes unseeing, a new bullet wound in his forehead.

Jeremy whirled toward the signaler. "Send a message to Captain Prévost," he snapped. "Tell him that Abel is dead and we're about to be overrun. Let your second-in-command here know. He is now in charge."

Saint-Martin-en-Vercors, France

Huet's normally impassive face turned stone-cold as he read a message. Facing him, Chavant, Roger, and Pauline sensed increased tension.

"Lieutenant Abel Chabal is dead," Huet said in clipped words. "The blocking position above Valchevrière is breached. It's time to order dispersion."

"And still no support," Chavant said, his deep voice now filled with bitterness. "I must get back to town. We'll need to move the hospital and evacuate our people from all over the plateau into the forests as quickly as possible." He stood to leave and bowed slightly. "*Mademoiselle* Pauline, gentlemen, thank you for everything you've done. I hope to see you in better times."

"What about you?" Huet asked.

Chavant looked out a window and gestured toward the mountain peaks. "I know all of them," he said. "I know how to move at night, and my friends out there stand with me. I'll survive." He stood a moment as if in deep reverie, then held his thumbs inside his suspenders and patted his chest with a wry smile. "Do you know it's only been sixteen days since we declared the Free Republic of the Vercors?" Breathing in deeply, he said, "Ah well. *Vive la France*!"

With that he strode through the door, closing it behind him.

"For the first time, he's lost hope of rescue," Huet said softly. "With the loss comes bitterness for being betrayed." He looked at Roger. "There's nothing more for you to do here. You have a whole network outside of the Vercors to run. You should leave and put your effort where you'll do the most good. The future of France still depends on winning the whole war."

He sighed deeply. "When France is saved, the Vercors will revive." He extended his hand. "And now, if you'll excuse me, I must issue that dispersion order."

Roger rose from his chair, shook Huet's hand, and saluted. "Sir, my honor has been to fight with you."

"And mine to fight with you, my friend." Huet returned the salute, half-smiled, and said, "I'm sure we'll see each other again."

Pauline also stood. She crossed the room and kissed Huet on both cheeks. "I'm sorry I didn't get here sooner," she said. "I've fallen in love with your plateau."

Huet waved off the comment. "You came when you could. Go. I have to work."

Roger held the door as Pauline passed through. Before closing it, he peered back into the office.

Huet sat at his desk, on the phone, calling for his signaler. "Send out the dispersal order through our couriers, and then come back here."

After he hung up, Huet scratched out a final message for London and Algiers. "We have held out against three German divisions for fifty-six hours," he wrote. "Until now, we have lost only a tiny piece of territory. The troops have fought courageously but desperately, for they are physically exhausted and almost out of ammunition. Despite repeated requests, we are still fighting alone and have received neither support nor aid since the start of battle. It was obvious that sooner or later the situation would become desperate and deteriorate into terrible misfortune on the Vercors plateau. We have done all that could be expected of us but are filled with sadness for the enormous responsibility of those who, from far away, deliberately engaged us in such a venture."

He had just finished composing the note when his signaler knocked on his office door and entered. "Code and send this out immediately," Huet ordered.

July 25, 1944
Grenoble, France

"Good day to you, *Herr* Field Marshal," Pflaumm greeted Gerd Von Runstedt, commander of Army Group South. He spoke over his phone, his voice resonating with success. "I'm pleased to report on the activity within my command."

While he listened to the field marshal's response, he leaned back in his chair, puffed on a cigar, and watched the smoke swirl above his head. "You heard correctly, sir. Resistance to the southwest of Grenoble is broken. The terrorists have evacuated the camps and villages and are in full flight. They're trying to slip away to the northwest toward Paris. We're still pursuing some of their remnants east of Valence."

He listened as Von Runstedt asked a question, and then continued. "Our air support was magnificent every step of the way."

He paused for another question. "Yes, sir. The terrorists evacuated the towns and villages they had occupied. They left in haste, leaving arms, ammunition, and even food. They've divided up into small groups and are attempting to escape through our encirclement. I can assure you that my operations officer, *Oberst* Schwehr, has issued orders to pursue with all vigor. The troops are entering every home, looking behind every tree, and guarding every mud puddle. Very few terrorists, if any, will escape."

He listened again. "Thank you for your congratulations, *Mein* Herr. They are most appreciated. Before we hang up, may I ask, how are things on the western front?"

His face became grim as he listened to the response. Von Runstedt told him that the Americans had broken through the Normandy perimeter south of the Cotentin Peninsula at Saint-Lô.

After hanging up, Pflaumm pulled his bulky figure from his chair and crossed to the small table that held the schnapps decanter. Being alone, he poured a single glass of the clear liquid. He lifted it to savor the scent and took a sip as he contemplated the news about Saint-Lô. A huge smile crossed his face as he reveled in his achievement. He held the glass high in the air and tossed the drink into his open mouth.

23

Same Day, July 25, 1944
The Vercors, France

During the five days since the battle above Valchevrière, Jeremy and the three commandos who escaped with him moved silently through the forested terrain. At times, they lay still for hours while German patrols passed within feet of them. Abel had predicted that the skirmish would be all but over when the Germans gained the high ground above the belvedere. Within minutes, only three of Abel's thirty men and Jeremy were still alive, and one of them was wounded. The survivors managed to crawl together on their bellies to the right flank of the battle area and hide in thick brush until the Germans were satisfied that the objective was secure and had moved on.

Even then, the four men had stayed in place through the long afternoon, into the late evening, and long after dusk. Then they had set out painstakingly slow to ascend the mountain's steep slope and start a long trek to Grotte de la Luire, where Dr. Ganimède had moved his field hospital following Huet's dispersal order.

The wounded man traveling with Jeremy and his group had taken a bullet to the leg and needed medical attention. Their first aid supplies would soon run out, and if the man did not receive medical care, infection would set in.

Over the next seventy-two hours, the group struggled at night over bare rocks and thick forest undergrowth on the mountain slopes. They took turns standing guard during the day while the others slept, and they braced the wounded man as they slogged over mountain trails.

Although Jeremy was unfamiliar with the area, the other three men knew it well. One of them had often hiked the region and led them to hidden streams where they drank desperately needed water. They had started out with a few rations, but by the end of the second day, those had been depleted, and they dared not forage for fear of attracting a German patrol. Their ammunition was also gone, so hunting was not an option even in the absence of the Germans. They persisted, hungry, and with strength waning upon each agonizing step. At dawn of the third day, they stole along a narrow path leading into the mouth of the grotto.

Approaching cautiously to be sure they did not walk into a position already overrun by the Germans, they found that all was quiet. Then a nurse emerged furtively from the side of the cave's wide mouth. She carried a water jug and was apparently on her way to refill it. When she saw the four men, she was terrified momentarily, but on recognizing them, she immediately led them into the cavern.

Jeremy lingered at the mouth of the grotto, observing that a stand of trees obscured the front, that the mountain wall ascended steeply on one side of the entrance and descended precipitously on the other side. However, the hillside on the approach was shallow, and only one path led into it.

No alternate escape route.

Jeremy also worried that, although well hidden, the cave might be seen from the air, at least as a dark depression.

He entered and found Dr. Ganimède and two nurses tending to the injured man, who fought against crying out as they cleaned his wound, but the agony was too great. Infection had begun. The skin around the bullet hole was sensitive to the touch.

Jeremy toured the cave, admiring that the clinic had been situated well back from the entrance where the air was cool. Ganimède and his staff had cleared loose rocks, swept the floor, set up a table for minor surgery, and segregated patients by types of injury.

Jeremy stopped for a few minutes to greet some of the wounded whom he knew. Among them was the French officer who had broken his shoulder on landing during his parachute entry onto the plateau.

Jeremy also visited with Lilette Lesage, the ambulance driver who had tried to escape into the forested hills with her charges and had been shot and left for dead. Her normally tanned face was pale, her brown eyes fearful, and she wore the same blue frock, faded now, that she had worn when the German soldiers had hunted her down. Jeremy was glad to see that she was able to limp about, although with much pain.

"Do you think we'll get out of here safely?" she whispered.

Disguising his own uncertainty, Jeremy merely replied, "I think so."

The doctor approached him and guided him to an area where they could confer. "I sedated the man you brought in, cleaned his wound, extracted the bullet, and treated it with antibiotics." He observed Jeremy gazing about. "Things are desperate. You're welcome to stay, but we're running out of food and medical supplies. We've sent anyone who could walk to other smaller caves." He heaved a sigh. "They're better off. The patients who are still here can't leave, which means that my staff can't either." He sighed again. "This place is marked on the maps, like all the large caves on the Vercors. The Germans will eventually search all of them."

Jeremy grasped the desperate situation. "How many people?"

The doctor shook his head. "Thirty-seven wounded. That includes twenty-eight *maquisards*, one of the Senegalese, two women who were wounded in the Vassieux bombing, Lilette, four Polish men forced to fight for Germany, the French officer who broke his shoulder, and an American OSS officer. Then there's my staff of seven nurses and three doctors, a Jesuit priest, my wife and son, and myself."

Jeremy inhaled. "So many. How old is your son?"

Ganimède's face tightened. "Seventeen."

Jeremy sighed deeply. "I'm out of bullets, and so was the rest of our group. I came along to help bring in the patient. At nightfall, I'll head across the plateau to find Huet's headquarters. I know generally where it is.

I'll bring back supplies and protection. The other two men will try to escape over the eastern rim of the plateau and join a *Maquis* south of Grenoble. I'll come back for you."

Ganimède regarded him gravely. "Let's get you some food. You'll need strength."

Starving, exhausted, and lacking sleep, Jeremy stumbled into Huet's camp along the mountain wall on the west side of the plateau above Les Barraques at dawn the next morning. Two of the lieutenant colonel's lookouts had spotted him struggling up the mountainside, and together, they helped Jeremy up the remaining steep climb. Huet had immediately ordered a full plate of food to be brought to him.

Between mouthfuls eaten desperately, Jeremy described the battle at Valchevrière, Abel's last minutes, and the conditions at Grotte de la Luire. "The people there won't make it without help," he said. "I'm going back tonight. Just give me some food and ammunition to take with me."

"We'll talk," Huet replied. "Meanwhile, get some sleep. You won't be good for anything if you don't. We'll wake you."

Jeremy slept in fits and starts, images of the horrors he had seen rising in wisps of nightmares. Abel's face appeared, lifeless and staring. Jeremy bolted awake with a burning desire to see his parents, but then he could not remember what they looked like. He thought of Amélie, trying to picture her face, but saw only darkness. He caught himself wondering if she had ever been real or just imagined.

Finally, he slipped into deep sleep only to be awakened, seemingly only minutes later. Surprised to find that he had slept for twelve straight hours, he staggered into Huet's tent.

A bowl of steaming beef stew awaited him.

"Listen to me carefully while you eat," Huet said.

Jeremy stared at him dully but nodded. The stew was adequate, but prepared under survival conditions, it lacked flavor. Nonetheless, he ate ravenously.

"Vassieux barely exists," Huet began. "Nearly two hundred homes were burned to the ground or destroyed by the bombing, the shops ransacked, and God only knows how many dead. Saint-Martin is in similar ruin. Reports I'm receiving indicate the same happened all over the Vercors, with tiny villages incinerated."

Jeremy looked up in bleak silence.

"Eat," Huet commanded. "You'll need all your energy tonight. Pflaumm's soldiers are guarding every watering hole. They set fire to any farm they suspect of helping us. They rape every female they find regardless of age. Do you remember the girl who coded messages for Major Longe?"

Jeremy set his spoon down and nodded, prepared for the worst.

"They gutted her and strung her entrails around her neck. They also burned five *maquisards* alive in a farmhouse. They raped a fourteen-year-old girl eleven times, and a *Wehrmacht* doctor monitored the pulse of another one between rapes to be sure she was conscious for each one. They're rounding up all the cattle and flying them to Germany from Captain Tournissa's airstrip, and they're taking any young man deemed not to be a terrorist for forced labor. The others, they're shooting."

Jeremy suddenly bolted from the table and gagged by the door. Then he gasped for cold air to stem nausea.

Huet came and stood by him. "I'm sorry to tell you while you're eating, but you need to understand the savagery of our enemy, and you *must* eat. To do any good at la Luire, you'll have to leave soon."

When Jeremy had regained some equilibrium, Huet guided him back to the table, where he nibbled at the food.

"We've been playing the odds, Labrador," the lieutenant colonel continued. "What were the chances that the Allies would come before the Germans invaded the Vercors? Was an Allied southern landing planned for southern France at all? I've had my doubts.

"Then, what were the odds that we could hold back *les boches* until we received support? The list goes on, and it's long, but we're still playing the odds."

He watched Jeremy absorb his words. "There *is* good news," he continued, "but before I tell you, you mentioned that two of Abel's men survived with you unhurt."

Jeremy nodded. "They went to another *Maquis* south of Grenoble."

"Any of us could have done that. We know these mountains."

Jeremy stared at Huet without comprehension.

"Those two had no food or ammunition. If they had wandered around looking for a unit here, they might have been caught and executed. They made the right choice.

"Now, here's the good news. The Americans broke through the German perimeter at Normandy. General Patton is advancing rapidly with his army. We heard it over the BBC. I don't have details, but he'll probably block Germany's forces somewhere around Grenoble. General Pflaumm will have to pull units out of the Vercors to meet the threat. We'll be in position to take the offensive—if we don't starve first."

Jeremy shoved the stew away.

"Eat," Huet commanded. "You need strength. We're playing the odds, Jeremy. We're betting that we can survive long enough to bring the fight to the enemy as they retreat. We're hoping to be strong enough to stave off more atrocities. Their previous reprisals were to intimidate against resistance. As the Allies advance, the *boche* will seek revenge, and if it's possible, they'll be even more brutal."

He shoved the stew back toward Jeremy. "Now, about la Luire. Dr. Ganimède knew when he moved the hospital there that we had no men or ammunition to spare. He played the odds that it wouldn't be detected. So far that's been the case. But German soldiers are systematically combing the forests. They're determined to find and destroy anyone they can label a terrorist.

"We're sending food for the hospital with you. Some bullets too. You're free to stay there to provide security. But understand this: you could be on a suicide mission. If the Germans come in there, you'll be the only one shooting back."

Jeremy stared at Huet. Then he shoved his chair back and stood. "I'm ready."

Huet smiled somberly. "Sit back down and finish your soup."

Jeremy left Huet's camp with plenty of time to hike the miles and arrive at the cave before dawn. However, en route, he twice encountered German patrols and had to wait them out. On the second occasion, the patrol settled in for a break directly in his path. He waited for them to move on, but having relaxed, they were in no hurry to resume their nocturnal circuit.

When an hour had passed and they remained in place, Jeremy attempted to detour around them. He was not familiar with the terrain, though, and he became disoriented and concerned that he might be heard. His compass was no help for navigating around bluffs and folds in the mountains. The map he carried showed only main roads and major terrain features, which he could not see in the dark. Forced to wait out the night, more German daylight patrols delayed progress into the afternoon.

Then the buzz of a light Fieseler Storch reconnaissance plane caught Jeremy's attention. He hid among thick bushes and parted the branches to search the sky. His heart sank as the Storch circled. It scouted above the area around Grotte de la Luire, circling several times.

Can't wait. Choosing speed over caution, Jeremy hurried over the rough ground, skirted through trees north of still-smoldering Saint-Martin, and headed south.

The Storch continued circling.

Jeremy stepped up his pace, recalling that Lilette Lesage was spotted by a Storch pilot who guided enemy soldiers to her location. His stomach tightened. *They've found la Luire.*

Maintaining stealth became difficult, but he could do no good if he was killed or captured. Then, three miles out, as he paralleled the road down to the path leading to the cave, he heard rifle shots.

He stopped, listening.

All was quiet. He proceeded forward. After several minutes, he heard machine gun fire, and then more intermittent rifle shots.

A truck labored up the hill toward him. Jeremy ducked behind shrubbery and watched. The back of the lorry bore a canvas top over its cargo bed, open at the rear. Two *Wehrmacht* soldiers rode at the back, and two more followed on motorcycles. As it passed, Jeremy strained to see inside the cargo area.

The slanting sun shone into the back of the truck sufficient for Jeremy to see a mass of people cowering inside. As he stared, a single terrified face came into stark focus over a faded blue frock. Lilette Lesage.

Jeremy's muscles tightened. The truck lumbered on uphill, followed soon thereafter by more vehicles exiting the vicinity intermittently. He held his place among the foliage until silence once again descended, broken only by the wind's whisper. Then he continued down the hill.

He gagged as he cleared the last curve and approached the hidden path. There in a wide spot, the patients on stretchers had been placed in a neat row and executed, two shots each to the forehead. They lay in pitiable repose with arms and legs dangling at odd angles.

A little farther on, he found those who had been able to limp out of the cave. They had been formed into a tight group and machine gunned. Their blood had pooled in a low spot on the road or spattered against nearby trees with bright red, still-dripping smears. Their bodies were ripped apart with entrails scattered, the contents of their stomachs already raising the stink of death.

Jeremy bent over and retched, dry heaves continuing in waves after he had coughed up the remainder of last night's stew. Standing in the clearing, he was exposed but so overcome with shock that he found himself incapable of seeking shelter.

By degrees, he caught his breath and lifted his head, forcing himself to view the ghastly sight, to see exactly who had been shot. His wounded comrade from Valchevrière was there, and so was the French officer with the broken shoulder.

Jeremy looked into each face, some too ghastly to recognize. Others were people he had worked with over the past months, but none were Dr. Ganimède, his wife or son, or any of the nurses.

His senses recovering, Jeremy moved into the trees and crept down the path toward the cave. All was quiet aside from the natural sounds of the forest.

A scarlet blot ahead to one side of the path caught Jeremy's attention. A swarm of flies buzzed around it, and the familiar smell of death floated toward him.

He braced for the worst.

Forcing himself forward, Jeremy again fought off nausea as he came upon the body of the Senegalese soldier. The man had been bludgeoned to death.

Gripped by the horror, Jeremy stumbled on to the mouth of the cave. Inside were items indicating a field hospital: the operating table, the remaining medical supplies, and a small store of food. Otherwise, there was no sign of the violence that had taken place within the last hour.

Jeremy did not linger. He began the arduous trek back to Huet's camp.

24

July 30, 1944
Saint-Guinoux, France

British Lieutenant Lance Littlefield regarded Jean Monmousseaux, codenamed Faucon, with skepticism. “I’ve never heard of the Jedburghs. Who are they?”

Faucon shrugged. “It’s some kind of Allied team. An American and two Frenchmen. They’ve been trying to contact Resistance groups in Brittany.”

Lance eyed him questioningly. “Go on.”

“They found their way into a farmer’s barn, and he got word to a Resistance member who informed us. They’re in rough shape.”

“Could it be a *Gestapo* trap?”

“Possibly, but doubtful,” Faucon said. “This part of Brittany and the northern end of Loire have been cleared of Germans. Most of the Cotentin Peninsula was overrun by the Americans, including Cherbourg, a month ago. This team is in Le Ferré. That’s not far—less than an hour’s drive.”

“Then we should go see them.”

Looking very much like his brothers, Paul and Jeremy, and his sister, Claire, with their medium statures, dirty-blond hair, and strong facial features, Lance had been the most carefree of the siblings, though all four had enjoyed climbing among the cliffs of Sark while growing up. Against his parents' wishes, Lance had enlisted in the British Army before the war began, seeking adventure. At the outset of hostilities between Germany and Poland, his unit had been transferred to northern France in the area around Dunkirk.

One of two-hundred thousand soldiers left to fend for themselves after the evacuation at Dunkirk, he had evaded capture and made his way south to Saint-Nazaire leading nine other men, including Derek Horton. Most of the group escaped to England, but Lance had engaged in sabotage with a fledgling French Resistance group. Their mission had succeeded, but Lance was captured.

After two escape attempts, he had been consigned to Oflag IV-C within Colditz Castle, a POW camp intended for escape artists, located in the far northeastern part of Germany. After more escape attempts, Lance had arrived safely back in England, but he had promptly volunteered for the commandos. During a raid in Norway, he was captured again and found himself back in Colditz Castle. Once again, he escaped and made his way across Germany, into France, and to Faucon's home at Val de Cher in the Loire Valley.

Faucon, a scion of a prominent multi-generational vintner family in the valley, was also a veteran of Dunkirk. Tall and muscular with rugged features and thick hair, he carried himself with confidence beyond his thirty years, and he commanded the respect of a natural leader.

He had been enraged at France's humiliating capitulation to the Nazis. On returning to Val de Cher after the dissolution of most of the French army, he had formed a Resistance group. Using the family winery to cover his activities, he developed a robust Resistance organization in the Loire Valley.

Shortly after his latest escape, Lance and Faucon joined another Resistance organization at a farm near Vannes, closer to where they expected the Allied invasion might take place. Most of the new group's members were combat veterans.

Less than a month ago, on the evening before D-Day at Normandy, they had been sent to Saint-Brieuc in Brittany to secure a drop zone for French commandos parachuting in to direct a local sabotage campaign and prepare for the arrival of a battalion of British Special Air Service paratroopers. Although the main invasion turned out to be in Normandy, the night was one that Lance and Faucon would never forget. Their *maquisards* performed remarkably, completing each sabotage mission without incident and earning high praise from the French commandos.

The British paratroopers landed and established a beachhead in Brittany. However, they had been unable to expand it. Lance and Faucon found themselves fighting defensive battles as *Wehrmacht* units in the area counterattacked. East of them on the Cotentin Peninsula, the battle for Cherbourg had been costly as the Germans and the Allies fought each other bitterly for control of the port facilities.

When finally the Cotentin was liberated, the Allies turned to Brittany and drove the Germans from pockets where they had been trapped. Though most of the Germans escaped, a strong unit was still trapped at Saint-Malo in a fortress of pillboxes and steel-reinforced shore-gun casements that were part of Hitler's Atlantic Wall.

As Lance and Faucon drove toward Le Ferré, Lance reveled in a forgotten sense of unfettered freedom in the liberated countryside. He breathed in deeply, and the air seemed sweeter as he leaned out the window and let the wind blow against his face.

They traveled south and then east, and Lance savored the view rather than watch for enemies out to kill or capture him. Villagers and farmers drove implements along the roads. Garages and auto repair shops had opened, with mechanics and helpers busily poring over engines under the hoods of long-hidden vehicles.

"People are getting back to normal," Lance remarked.

Faucon smiled wanly. "France has a long road ahead," he lamented.

A sedan passed in the opposite direction. It had been crudely painted in drab green with huge white letters. Lance turned to take a closer look. "What's that about? I've seen cars with 'FTP' painted on them, and others with 'FFI.' They're filled with young men, sometimes with a woman or two, but they all have serious expressions, like they're on a mission."

Faucon sighed. "As I said, France has a long road ahead." He took his time to formulate a reply. "The French Resistance started as loose local organizations all over the country, initially trying to survive and save each other. They connected, and everyone heard de Gaulle's call to resist."

He glanced across at Lance. "I'm simplifying. You Brits sent agents, arms, equipment, and money, and requested our help to rescue downed airmen and escaped POWs and get them home."

Lance nodded. "That's how my brother, Jeremy, became involved with Madame Fourcade in Marseille."

Faucon chuckled. "I think Amélie had something to do with his dedication to the cause, but you're right. I enjoyed working with him those weeks he was with us in Val de Cher. Amélie too."

Both Amélie and Jeremy had spent time with Faucon's organization at separate times. "Getting back to your question," Faucon continued, "de Gaulle took command of the French Army in Algeria back in January. One of his first acts was to declare that Resistance groups were part of the French Forces of the Interior, the FFI. He gave its leaders rank according to how many fighters they commanded. That's why you see some very young colonels and some very old captains."

"What about the FTP?"

"I'll come to that, but first, the *Maquis*. Two years ago, the Vichy government—" He looked across at Lance. "You understand what that is?"

Lance nodded. "The French government over the part of France that wasn't occupied by the Germans. It colluded with the Nazis."

"Exactly. And two years ago, to satisfy Hitler, it issued a requirement that all men of military age had to be sent to work in Germany. Rather than comply, thousands of them took to the mountains and lived off the scrubland. They formed into groups called '*Maquis*,' and their members were called '*maquisards*.'"

"That's simple enough."

"As for the FTP," Faucon went on, "they're the *Francs-Tireurs et Partisan.* Most are patriots and fierce fighters, but Communists lead them. I think most care nothing about ideology or politics—they want to restore our country. But their highest leader in France is a man who takes his orders from Moscow."

Startled, Lance exclaimed, “Joseph Stalin?”

Faucon nodded. “And the FTP recruited the largest number of fighters.”

Lance frowned. “Why is that?”

Faucon chortled. “They promise eutopia. The leaders don’t really support de Gaulle, but they’re cautious about opposing him—they know how popular he is.

“The people in those cars you saw are not at each other’s throats yet, but there’s a split between them. With the *Wehrmacht* on the run, members of both groups are hunting down Germans and anyone they think collaborated with them. Then they will turn on each other. More French blood will spill, by our own countrymen.”

“That’s terrible,” Lance interjected.

“Some executions are deserved,” Faucon continued, “but they’ll be done outside the rule of law. Innocents will be killed.” He shook his head sadly. “The horrors for France are not over, and we still have to battle inside Germany. The Third *Reich* must be stamped out.”

They drove through towns and villages that had been untouched by combat and others that had been reduced to ash. Among those that had survived intact, Lance perceived a sense of permanence, reflected in well-constructed streets despite having fallen into disrepair. He saw the strength in stone houses and shops, some having weathered centuries. He savored the sense of culture manifested by medieval cathedrals’ tall spires and intricate architecture and in the elegance of municipal buildings.

Lance sighed. “You know, I joined the army for adventure. I got more than I expected.” He shook his head. “We’ve seen so much death and destruction.”

They met the Jedburghs in a barn near a tree line on the edge of Le Ferré. Arriving in the mid-afternoon, they found the team sitting on rickety wooden chairs, surrounded by farmers, and drinking Calvados.

A French major rose to introduce himself. “I am Major Jeanpaul, commander of Team Gavin.” He indicated two uniformed men who rose and stepped forward. “These are my teammates, Captain Bill Dreux and Lieutenant Paul Masson.” After greetings, Jeanpaul took Lance and Faucon aside. “Which one of you is in charge?”

The two looked at each other blankly. "We hadn't much thought about it," Lance replied. "Faucon leads a Resistance group—"

"And Lance is a British commando and a former POW," Faucon interjected. "He escaped a few weeks before the invasion and stayed on to fight with us."

Lance shrugged. "The Allied armies were coming this way."

Jeanpaul peered at him. "Your French is good. You speak without much accent."

"He's from *Sercquiais*," Faucon cut in. "It's an island off the French northwest coast that the British call Sark."

"Ah. I know it. By Normandy." Jeanpaul glanced back at the farmers still surrounding Dreux and Masson, and he allowed a slow smile. "It's been the same wherever we go. The farmers come to us at breakfast, lunch, and dinner. They don't have much food to offer, but they all seem to have Calvados. They each bring a bottle with them that they'd hidden from the Germans. All the farmers around here want to see the French officers and the American paratrooper." He sniffed. "They want to show their gratitude for being liberated."

Lance regarded Jeanpaul. The major was of average height, slender, and in excellent physical shape, but he had obviously encountered recent physical challenges. Dark circles ringed his eyes, and his cheeks were sunken in. Nevertheless, his military bearing appeared both deliberate and natural, his demeanor stern and sensible.

The major called to Dreux. As the American made his way over, Jeanpaul added, "Captain Dreux's mother is French. He lives in the French Quarter of New Orleans in the United States. People still speak mainly French there." He glanced at Lance. "He speaks it well. My English is not so good, so may we continue in French?"

Lance nodded. "My pleasure." He turned to the American captain and extended his hand while noticing that the farmers were vacating the barn.

"They know we have things to discuss." Dreux chuckled. "They'll be back at dinner time, if we're still here, with more Calvados and whatever food they can scrounge. We'd be rude not to drink with them, but I have to be careful to sip it slowly. They want to hear about the war in other places."

Lance liked Dreux. He appeared serious and no-nonsense but had a sense of humor and held an obvious affinity with the French farmers. He was the tallest man in the barn, but thin—his American combat uniform hung on his gaunt frame.

"Without them and other people like them, we'd be dead." Dreux turned to watch the farmers file out. "When we landed and figured out we were in the wrong place, a farmer sheltered us in his barn and brought us food. The area around Courcité was thick with Germans. The farmer took us to his priest, who hid us in the attic of his parsonage for three days. The town was full of krauts, and we had no way out and no place to go. The priest made contact with the Resistance and got us out of there and on the road to Saint-Malo. Then, another farmer sold us his car." Dreux paused and grinned. "We brought plenty of cash from London."

Amid straw strewn across the dirt floor and a pungent odor of farm animals, the group took seats on the rickety chairs. "Tell us about the Jedburghs," Faucon said. "What do you do?"

Jeanpaul laughed quietly. "You mean what are we supposed to do?" He grunted. "It's a newly deployed asset, a cooperative effort between the US OSS, the British SOE, and the Free French army's intelligence services. Some Dutch too. We're sometimes referred to as General Eisenhower's secret army.

"The concept was developed last year. Recruitment and training took time. General Koenig, de Gaulle's appointed commander-in-chief of the French army, commands the service. In that regard, he reports to Eisenhower. Since de Gaulle incorporated the Resistance into the FFI, the structure officially puts Eisenhower in command of the French Resistance. The benefit is that we bring in trained combatants to work with existing Resistance groups to conduct guerilla warfare. We'll replace team members as casualties occur.

"The concept is to provide better coordination and effectiveness. Instead of random targets, the Resistance will hit Allied designated ones. In return, the Allies provide money, weapons, ammunition, and food.

"The first teams deployed just before D-Day. General Eisenhower held up until then because he didn't want to give even a hint of the invasion's time and place. My team came over at night on July 13, two weeks ago."

"How are the teams organized," Lance asked. "What are your missions?"

Jeanpaul grunted. "Theoretically, we'd have an American, a Brit, and a Frenchman on each team. Two of them are supposed to be officers, the senior of them to be in command. The third man operates the wireless. In our case, we have one American and two Frenchmen."

Dreux chuckled. "I suppose there weren't enough Brits to go around." He added seriously, "One stipulation was that every team must have at least one French officer to speak the language and gain the confidence of the local *Maquis*."

Jeanpaul agreed. "Eighty teams dropped behind the lines all across France, thirteen in Brittany alone. Churchill told us to set Europe on fire. Tons of equipment are being dropped and stored. The teams make contact with local Resistance groups. On a single night soon, we'll receive a message over the BBC, and every team will attack its targets all over France. After that, we'll continue looking for targets of opportunity.

"The specific mission of Gavin Team—the team I command—is to destroy six bridges near Saint-Malo. Another group, Team Guy, was supposed to operate jointly with us to take out six more bridges. It dropped close to us from another plane."

"Where is Team Guy?" Faucon asked.

Dreux scoffed. "Good question. They must have had a bad landing too. We were never able to contact them on the ground."

"That's irrelevant now," Jeanpaul said, lifting a hand to interrupt the captain. He turned to Faucon. "What is the situation at Saint-Malo?"

Faucon took a deep breath. "It's a German stronghold, but they have no resources to escape out to sea. The Americans surrounded the landward side of the city, but *les boches* show no sign of surrender. In fact, other *Wehrmacht* units fought their way in to join them from other locations." He exhaled. "Eventually, we'll have them, but we don't know what it'll take."

Lance had drawn back at Jeanpaul's mention of a plan to destroy the bridges. "Major, taking out those bridges would be a catastrophe. The Allies need them to move supplies into the interior. If you blew them, you might get shot for treason."

Jeanpaul frowned. "The situation changed rapidly after we landed. At the time, all that terrain was behind enemy lines. We were supposed to be dropped closer to Saint-Brieuc and contact the organization there."

"Then you would have contacted us," Faucon broke in. "What happened?"

"We were dropped near Courcité. That's seventy-five miles east of our drop zone. We were behind enemy lines with no transportation, no local contacts, and our radio was destroyed when it hit the ground."

Faucon scoffed. "Who got the target wrong?"

Jeanpaul stood abruptly. "Let's not waste time pointing fingers. We were faced with moving ourselves across enemy territory without assets and without local contacts. That's what we set out to do."

"Did your plane fly off course?" Faucon pressed. "Was it the wind?"

"No," Dreux broke in tersely, and received a sharp look from Jeanpaul. "The major is being proper. I don't have to." Jabbing a finger in the air, he continued angrily, "I lay our entire fiasco at the feet of the staff in London. They planned our mission and picked the drop zone. I hope they did a better job for the other teams." Turning back to Faucon, he continued. "Even before we left London, we had concerns about those twelve bridges and their effect on Allied transportation. By then, D-Day had happened and the beachhead was established on Normandy. The London staff should have known that crippling those bridges would slow down movement inland." He glanced at Jeanpaul and added, "I'll spell out details in my report when we get back."

"Which is when?" Faucon demanded.

Dreux shrugged and deferred to Jeanpaul. "When we receive orders to return," the major said. "Until then, we're at your disposal." He scrutinized Faucon and Lance. "Whatever plans you have, we can help with them."

Faucon locked eyes with Jeanpaul for an extended period. "I want to believe you," he said slowly, "but I need to see your papers."

Jeanpaul and Dreux exchanged glances. They reached into inner pockets on their jackets and produced letters signed by General Koenig as Commanding General of the French Forces of the Interior on behalf of the Supreme Allied Commander, General Dwight Eisenhower. The letters identified the officers by name and ordered any and all assistance from anyone who could help complete their missions.

The group fell silent as Lance and Faucon read the letters. Dreux retrieved a bottle of Calvados and poured a round. The major remained standing.

Dreux sipped his brandy while watching Lance and Faucon. When they looked up, he smirked. "I'm a lawyer by profession. I'd never shot a rifle in a hostile environment until several days after we landed at Courcité."

His expression abruptly changed to deadly serious. "You should know," he continued, "that Major Jeanpaul is a battle-seasoned warrior. He's known as a *sacré baroudeur*, a hellacious fighter. His reputation is that he's always at the front in a firefight. I can attest to that personally."

Jeanpaul eyed Dreux and lifted his cup of wine in an appreciative gesture. "He's not wearing his ribbons now," Dreux went on, "but I've seen them. He's got a Legion of Honor, a Croix de Guerre with four citations, and a British Military Cross."

Jeanpaul raised a palm in a placating gesture. "You go too far."

Dreux turned and faced him directly. "With respect, sir, they need to know the quality of the officer who just joined them."

He turned back to Lance and Faucon. "The major graduated from the same academy as Charles de Gaulle, Saint-Cyr, and he fought at Dunkirk where he was wounded and taken prisoner. He escaped to Africa and commanded a French battalion against Rommel's Africa Korps. The fact is, he gave up a battalion command to volunteer for the Jedburghs because he wanted to be one of the first French officers to fight on his home soil, and he didn't know when his unit might arrive."

Lance listened, remembering his own various captures, imprisonments, and breakouts; the initial despair of guns pointed at him at close range and hearing the words, "For you, the war is over." Visceral images flashed by of initial dark days of isolation in the "cooler" where he nursed the overpowering drive to escape.

The major interrupted his thoughts. "Captain Dreux oversells me, but don't let him undersell himself. I selected him to be on my team because of how he trained, and because he speaks French fluently. We've been in skirmishes together since landing at Courcité. He's proven himself."

Faucon listened carefully. If Jeanpaul's story checked out, the major outranked him in the same army and was far more experienced in combat.

Slowly, he rose to his feet. “Sir, with all my heart I want to believe you. But you could be enemy agents.”

Jeanpaul arched his brows and nodded. “I admire your caution.” He brought himself to attention. “Until we’ve resolved this, which can be done by messaging London, consider me your prisoner.” He pointed to his carbine leaning against the foot of his chair. “Please, take my weapon.” He turned to Dreux and Masson. “Surrender your weapons,” he ordered.

25

July 31, 1944
Saint-Guinoux, France

A reunion between Teams Gavin and Guy the next day had been a happy occasion, particularly since they were now among friendly forces in a liberated part of France. Their original objectives of blowing the specified bridges were abandoned.

Overnight, Faucon had queried London via wireless regarding the backgrounds of both team's members. On receiving a positive reply, he presented himself to the major at attention and saluted. "Sir, my apologies for the scrutiny. Your identities are verified. I place myself and my team under your command. What are your orders?"

Caught off-guard by Faucon's action, Lance stared at him in astonishment. Then he too saluted Jeanpaul. "Sir, I presently have no commander. As a British officer in the Allied forces, I am at your disposal."

Jeanpaul peered at the two studiously. Then he returned their salutes and extended his hand. "Let's go over the situation in Saint-Malo."

Team Guy had also found itself behind enemy lines without transportation. Their radio landed safely, but their carbines were destroyed. Nevertheless, they had fared better for having quickly found locals who could take them to Saint-Guinoux. Unfortunately, the third member of the team had landed hard, suffered a broken leg, and on reaching friendly lines, had been returned to England by the first available flight.

Captain André Duron, Team Guy's commander, was a tall, boyish-looking officer with blond hair and an easy smile. Although reserved on first encounters with new acquaintances, once rapport had been established, he revealed a personality that could be jovial one minute and deadly serious the next, as appropriate.

August 1, 1944

Lance felt Faucon shaking him. "Wake up! The Americans are here."

Lance felt the ground tremble and heard the creaking of tracked war machines rumbling by. He swept a blanket aside, spun on his cot, and felt for his boots with his foot while pulling a shirt around his shoulders. "Which elements?"

"The advance units of the US 6th Armored Division. The 83rd Infantry Division is right behind them. They must be here to liberate Saint-Malo. We've cleared out most of the areas outside the city, but it's fortified. Without tanks and artillery, we're powerless to take it. The Americans are moving rapidly, and Saint-Malo must be the objective."

A few minutes later, Faucon, Lance, the members of Teams Gavin and Guy, and many *maquisards* gathered at the roadside to cheer the vast numbers of armored and infantry vehicles trundling by. Then, Faucon and Jeanpaul left to reconnoiter closer to the city.

Hardly an hour had passed since the first vehicles' arrival when a message came by courier to Jeanpaul from Major General Robert Macon, the 83rd Infantry Division's commander. Since neither the major nor Faucon were present, Captain Dreux received and read the note. The general wanted to see the major. The matter was urgent, the message stated, though the purpose was unspecified. Dreux went himself, taking Duron and Lance with him.

General Macon greeted them jovially. His looks did not match his demeanor. He was tall, lean, and all business, but he went about it in a friendly way. "I heard we got some special forces officers in the area. Jedburghs—is that what they call you?"

Dreux affirmed.

Macon observed the three officers before him, taking stock of them. "So I got a Frenchman, an American, and a Brit all on the same team. And you're trained in that commando stuff, plus you can get along in French. I like that."

He walked over to a map on his wall and spread his hand over a large area of Brittany. "We've pretty much got this area cleaned out except for Saint-Malo itself. The krauts are hemmed in there. They have no escape, but intel came down that their orders are to fight to the last man, and they've still got lots of men and lots of bullets."

He grinned. "They're fighting like hell, and every one of their units caught outside their perimeter is beatin' hell for leather to get inside." He whirled on his small audience. "Here's my problem. My intelligence section got reports from higher stating that only two thousand men were in my area." He scoffed. "We've already taken twice that many prisoners, so intel got it wrong. But we've got to clean out that city, and my guess is there's over twelve thousand still in there."

He pointed to two places on his map that displayed friendly and enemy positions in red and blue, respectively. "We've got the 6th Armored Division supporting us on our right flank, but I need your forces to sweep through on the left. You've got to be aggressive and you've got to drive the enemy out of their hidey-holes and either capture or kill 'em. How many *maquisards* you got?"

Dreux responded slowly. "About two hundred and fifty."

"That's good. Send out combat patrols starting tomorrow morning. Harass the tar out of the krauts, but don't get in any major battles. We'll drop a load of artillery on them before you go in. They ain't got a lot of troops in that area anyway, and they're beat down, but they've got to go. Any questions?"

Dreux took a deep breath. "We might have a problem meeting your objective."

Macon drew back. "You're supposed to be on the ground ready to go. You've got the manpower. What's the issue?"

"Weapons, ammunition, regular supplies, food. The Germans stripped everything, sir. The men are willing to fight, but they need something to fight with."

Macon glared at him and then called to his adjutant. "Get Colonel Jones in here," he barked, and when the officer appeared, he ordered, "Get these officers whatever they need. Don't hold back. Give 'em all the captured equipment we seized and fill in the rest from our own stores."

He paused to reflect. Then he went back to the map and pointed out a particular town. "I also need a reconnaissance patrol to scout out this pretty little town, Dinan, eighteen miles north of here on the Rance River. I hear that krauts are holed up in there. If that's true, I want to know what it's gonna take to get 'em out."

When the two Jedburghs and Lance rolled back into their camp at Saint-Guinoux

with truckloads of supplies and equipment, Major Jeanpaul set aside his normal stern demeanor and smiled happily at the abundance that was suddenly in the two Jedburgh team's possession. Faucon pounded one fist into his open palm in enthusiasm.

While Duron briefed Jeanpaul and Faucon on the missions Macon had assigned, Lance took Dreux to one side. "Where did you get that figure of two hundred and fifty *maquisards*?"

Dreux chuckled. "I made it up."

Lance stared at him in shock.

"Look," Dreux said, "you and Faucon have contact into FFI and FTP groups. Get the word out to the best of their leaders. When they learn that we have this trove of equipment, they'll show up with the numbers we need."

He sighed, and his wistful tenor caught Lance's attention. "You know," Dreux said, "before you guys interrupted our little party with the farmers in that barn at Le Ferré, we weren't sitting on our haunches waiting for someone to rescue us. While we were trekking across the countryside to get here, we met some *Maquis* groups. We led their fighters on combat patrols and engaged in firefights."

Dreux's face became somber. "I felt like a Boy Scout leader on some of those patrols. Some of the *maquisards* were as young as fourteen. Their tactics were bad, their equipment was poor, but their fighting spirit was great."

His eyes narrowed and his jaw quivered as he re-lived jarring memories. "We were leading children into battle," he said quietly. "I had to bury a couple of boys who would have been rosy-cheeked if they hadn't been half-starved." He paused. "We buried a dead American soldier we found in an empty field. I have no idea how he got there. His throat was slit. He died fast with his rosary in his hand, probably thinking of home."

He sniffed and remained silent for a few moments. When he spoke again, his voice broke. "Those *Maquis* boys are gonna fight," he said. "There's no stopping 'em. They want the Germans out and they want France to be France again. The least we can do is arm and train them the best we can, make sure their planning and tactics are sound, and lead them. If we don't, they're gonna go anyway, and probably get themselves killed. They deserve every piece of luck they can get."

"You're right," Lance said softly. While he had never led young boys in battle, he had met many of them and looked into their eyes. Some were already veterans. Their expressions fluctuated between fervor, despair, and determination. Some had been horribly wounded but carried on, enjoying their honored places among their comrades. The new recruits effused both enthusiasm and fear and regarded the veterans with awe.

Some never returned.

Lance had witnessed, too, the abject grief of mothers mourning lost sons—and daughters. Just as sad as the loss of the young boys was that the *Maquis* included girls as young as the youngest boys, with sometimes the same tragic results.

Jeanpaul called Lance and Dreux over. "Faucon identified the two *Maquis* leaders he trusts the most," he said. "Get them in here quickly. The FTP guy will push for a greater share of Macon's spoils. I'll tolerate none of that, and he will subordinate himself to me, or he'll be out. We'll distribute strictly based on mission needs."

He turned to Lance. "Duron is short an officer. He's requested that you be assigned to his team—permanently. That'll take some communicating with London, but meanwhile, we'll assume approval and go forward. So, until we hear otherwise, you'll be Duron's exec. Any objections?"

Surprised, Lance spun around to meet Duron's steady gaze. The two had become friends quickly, and Lance knew they could work well together. On the other hand, Lance had worked closely with Faucon for the past five months, including the heady operations on the eve of D-Day. Before then, Faucon had twice facilitated his escapes. Since then, they had engaged side by side in guerrilla warfare, watching out for each other during innumerable combat patrols.

Faucon, the aristocratic vintner turned Resistance leader, caught Lance's eye and smiled somberly. "*C'est la guerre*," he said. "We go where the mission demands."

Lance nodded. A dull ache formed in his stomach similar to the one he had experienced on leaving behind his comrades at Colditz POW camp. *We're always leaving people we care about, and we don't know if we'll ever see them again.*

"It's settled," Jeanpaul intoned. "Let's get on with planning." When he had the full group's attention, he began. "Team Gavin will conduct the maneuvers on General Macon's right flank. Faucon, you know these *Maquis* leaders. For this mission, you'll be my exec. I'm looking to you to see that the *Maquis* carry out my orders faithfully. We anticipate having a force of better than two hundred fighters. The subordinate leaders must perform as planned. Time is short. We don't have time for arguments or negotiations, and we can't risk someone deciding he's got a better idea in the middle of battle.

"Captain Dreux, you'll develop the overall operations plan with me. Then, work with Faucon to scope out the requirements and the distribution of supplies and equipment, keeping in mind that we'll have a patrol going to Dinan simultaneously.

"Lieutenant Masson, find out how many radios are with the new equipment. See if they work and distribute them in accordance with final plans. Make sure to coordinate with the Dinan patrol to meet its needs.

"For everyone on Team Gavin, let me know quickly if there is anything else we need. I'll communicate with General Macon or his staff as needed."

Jeanpaul turned his attention to Duron. "Captain, you'll organize a platoon-sized reconnaissance patrol to determine the number and strength of enemy troops in Dinan. Lieutenant Littlefield knows the local *Maquis*. Lean on his experience." He smiled slightly. "He's a British commando with raids in Norway to his credit."

Duron turned to Lance, eyes wide in surprise. "I didn't know."

Lance brushed aside the comment. "Just one raid," he said quietly.

"We have a lot of work to do," Jeanpaul announced grimly. "Let's get started."

26

Same Day, August 1, 1944
Utah Beach, Normandy, France

Lieutenant Colonel Paul Littlefield stood to one side and watched as General Philippe Leclerc greeted the soldiers of the 2nd French Armored Division. The general joked and laughed, enjoying these first moments of his return to France in the sand just above the water's edge. Then he stood aside and gazed around while breathing in deeply, savoring the sea air, the sights of his homeland, and the feel of having his feet firmly planted on French soil.

Leclerc was of average height, and his thin face sported a small mustache. He exuded vigor despite the walking cane he relied on to compensate for a limp. He moved easily among his men, and their eyes glowed with adulation for the legend he had already become.

He caught Paul's eye and called to him. "You're with us now, Colonel. Come, celebrate our homecoming with us."

Paul ambled over, and the general introduced him to the soldiers standing around. "This is Lieutenant Colonel Paul Littlefield, my new—" He paused and turned to Paul, laughing good-naturedly. "What should I call you, my liaison? To whom? General Bradley? We're part of his army group. General Gerow? He'll be my immediate boss the moment that V Corps activates. To his boss, General Patton, who specifically requested that our division be placed in his command? He arrives today too?"

He turned to his men. "Like me, Lieutenant Colonel Littlefield is a wounded duck, shot up in North Africa and blown up a few weeks ago near here. He was with our French commandos when they came ashore on D-Day. Like me, walking for him is a little more of a challenge at present. The difference is that I fell from a horse six years ago. My friend the lieutenant colonel was wounded in combat."

While his soldiers clapped and cheered, Leclerc stood back to observe Paul, and then continued. "Like me, he can't seem to stay away from the war. Maybe that's why we were put together by the fates. Make him welcome—" He held up a palm as a thought crossed his mind. "Wait!" Then he whirled around to face inland and raised his arms wide apart. "Let's welcome him to our home, France."

Amid a round of cheers, Paul waved his hand over his head and nodded appreciatively. As the celebration waned and men disbursed, Leclerc turned to him. "My command car should be above the beach. Let's walk up there."

Paul could not help being amused at the mental picture of two officers limping off the shore together. They continued conversing as they walked.

"I guess you're my special assistant. I asked for a mid-level combat officer who knew our language and understood both the British and the American military. I've read your dossier. You're a commando—"

"Technically not, sir. I was trained at the X Academy in Canada."

"The spy school. Close enough. And technically, you commanded our French commandos. *Capitaine* Kieffer brought you to my attention. And you were instrumental in getting our French forces in Algeria away from Vichy command."

"Sir, my part was insignificant."

Leclerc held up his hand. "It was sufficiently momentous that you were assigned to the task. And I know about your combat in North Africa. You have Kieffer's recommendations, and others come from Lord Lovat, General Montgomery, and all the way from Winston Churchill. I'm pleased to have you working with us."

"I hope not to disappoint. What are my duties?"

"You speak French and English equally well, German too. Mistakes from language or cultural differences could be fatal in extended combat. I need your help to make sure that those are kept to a minimum." He laughed. "I've seen that you British and the Americans don't always comprehend each other even though you speak the same language."

They reached Leclerc's command car, an open-topped M3 half-track troop carrier. "Will you join me standing behind the cab?" Leclerc invited. "I want to see the people."

The streets were lined on both sides with crowds from wherever France had been liberated. They had come to see their own French armor division come ashore and convoy inland, sixteen thousand strong, complete with five thousand war machines, including Sherman tanks.

Men and women, old and young greeted them with wild cheers, embraces, kisses, food, and wine. Old women cried. Tears ran down the cheeks of ancient warriors, veterans of WWI.

Paul was sure that he would never again see anything quite so moving. He watched Leclerc lean over the sides and grab hands, accept kisses, touch small children. The mutual affection between him and his people was palpable.

Pain jabbed Paul's right leg, caused by the lurching of the half-track over the rough roads, which aggravated his wounds. His face froze into a grim mask that he concealed with a forced smile, but his eyes watered and he had to lean against the side of the vehicle to hold himself steady.

After being hit by the friendly artillery misfire at Bréville, Paul woke up in a field hospital. He had been thrown twenty feet by the explosion, but fortunately he had landed on soft ground. Nevertheless, he suffered from a concussion and three shrapnel wounds on his right leg. One piece had nicked his fibula, which made walking very painful. He had refused to be sent back to the UK, requesting instead to be assigned temporarily to General Montgomery's operations staff. When his doctor refused, a quick personal note to the general resolved the issue in Paul's favor. Montgomery had previously selected Paul personally to command an infantry battalion in Africa.

While convalescing, Paul was dismayed to learn that Lord Lovat had been badly wounded in the Bréville incident and that two of his officers were killed. *Capitaine* Kieffer had visited while Paul was still in the field hospital and related the news. Kieffer had also just learned that General Leclerc sought a special kind of liaison officer. "I think you'd be ideal, if you're interested," Kieffer told Paul. "I could pass along your name with my recommendations."

"It's worth looking at," Paul replied, and arrangements were made. Now, having met Leclerc for the first time in person, Paul was impressed by the charismatic general who believed that national honor required French leaders to be at the front of the fight for France's liberation.

His name at birth was Philippe de Hauteclocque. As a descendant of a patrician family with a long history of martial service to the country, he had been born into his passion for France, and he graduated from Saint-Cyr and Saumur, France's military academy and cavalry school respectively.

Receiving a head wound in battle and then captured while fighting Germans in Libya, he escaped to England. There, heeding de Gaulle's call to arms, he changed his name to Philippe Leclerc to protect his family, and then fought with distinction against the Nazis in Equatorial Africa. His actions there included leading a thousand-mile march of his unit from Chad to join the British at Tripoli.

While fighting in Libya, Leclerc had vowed to free Paris, and he pursued every opportunity to be at the battlefront, most recently by taking command of the 2nd French Armored Division. Along the path of his career, he had gained among his superiors the sobriquet, the "Impatient Lion."

Leaving the crowds behind, the half-track rolled across the countryside and arrived at the general's temporary headquarters inside a clump of trees. Leclerc clambered out. Paul followed, painfully.

On the ground, Leclerc gazed around at the soldiers still setting up camp, at the combat vehicles still pouring in from the beach, and at the wide fields beyond the trees stretching down to the gleaming ocean speckled with warships and landing craft. His eyes bright, an eager expression on his face, he rubbed his hands together. "Playtime is over," he muttered to Paul, who was standing at his shoulder. "Now for the fight."

27

Same Day, August 1, 1944
Paris, France

Dressed in the black flowing robes with the white collar and headband of a nun's habit, Amélie Boulier melded into the shadows of the railway platform of Paris' Gare Lyon. The depressed atmosphere was palpable but with a subtle change to what she had known in previous times. She had noticed it settling in since news of the successful Allied beachhead at Normandy. Before then, the German guards inside the station had stalked about arrogantly, enjoying, by their mere presence, the fear that registered on passengers' faces. They still prowled in packs of threes and fours with their submachine guns slung over their shoulders, but now their shoulders slouched, their eyes had lost their glint, and they peered about with uncertainty approaching that of the occupied population.

The people too had changed in general demeanor. Gone were the set jaws and stoic stares from the past four oppressive years. Instead, through hooded eyes, they exchanged cautious expressions of hope and fear for what might lie ahead in their darkened City of Lights.

I wonder if the soldiers notice. They seem to stop people less.

Still present in the train station were the screech of steel wheels on rails, the hiss of steam, and the scream of whistles as locomotives muscled long trains in and out of the station. Red banners with black swastikas still festooned the walls, but as Amélie scanned them, some appeared faded. The aura of authority seemed to have dissipated ever so slightly.

The Germans know their days here are numbered.

As the train she sought steamed to a halt, Amélie held her stance, hands folded in front of her, head slightly bowed. As passengers off-loaded, she watched for two women. They would be easy to spot. One was dressed exactly as Amélie was, in a nun's habit. The other would be wearing all black apparel, that of a grieving widow.

She did not have long to wait. The pair of women were seated near the front of the train, and fellow passengers moved aside to let them pass ahead of the crowd.

On her way into the station, Amélie had observed the German guards examining travel papers at the barriers. She spotted one who appeared less strident than his companions, so she maneuvered to enter through his checkpoint. As she produced her immaculately fabricated counterfeit documents, she explained that she would be escorting an arriving widow and asked if she could please bring her and another nun back his way to be cleared. The guard remained impassive, but he had glanced around furtively at other nearby officials, and nodded faintly.

Amélie made eye contact with the widow and her escorting nun. Immediately, she raised her hands and rushed to embrace them. "My poor dear," she cried, loudly enough for anyone nearby to hear. "I'm so sorry for your loss."

The woman's body shook as she clasped her arms about Amélie. "It's so good to see you," she murmured in a steady voice. "Let's get on to Georges' apartment."

On arrival at the flat, both imitation nuns were quick to remove their habits. Each of them was now dressed in a worn skirt and blouse. They greeted each other with genuine warmth while the ostensible grieving widow, Madame Madeleine Fourcade, went into another room to change out of her black grieving attire.

"Ah, my little sister," Amélie told Chantal, "years seem to have passed since I saw you last."

"Three months," Chantal replied.

"And since then, you've delivered that sketch map to London and fought at Normandy with the Resistance." She stroked Chantal's hair. "You've grown up so much since that scared girl of fourteen only four years ago. You're indomitable."

"You're my mentor," Chantal said, laughing, and pulled away. "Let me look at you. You're thin."

Amélie grimaced. "Everyone in Paris is thin. Conditions here are even worse than they were in Lyon. Women line up at dawn to get their family's ration of bread."

"I noticed the grimy streets on the way over here," Chantal replied, "and I saw the oddest thing—two men pulling the rear half of a chopped-off car with a person riding on the exposed seat."

Amélie nodded. "That's what serves as a taxi these days. Hardly anyone is allowed petrol. Even the small delivery trucks are converted to run their engines on wood-burning stoves in their trunks. For the most part, people travel by bicycle or walk."

"This is my first visit to Paris," Chantal interjected. "It's not at all what I imagined. The boulevards are wide, but they're dirty and need repair. The public buildings look dingy and dilapidated."

"There aren't as many German officers sitting in the outdoor cafés on the Champs-Élysées either," Amélie replied. "That's a good thing." She added wistfully, "I came to Paris once with Father. It was incredibly beautiful then."

Aside from subtle signs of the difference in their ages, the two girls could be twins. Both had slight figures, auburn hair, and honey-colored eyes.

Fourcade rejoined them in the sitting room. "I've been away too long," she said as she took a seat on a divan. "London didn't want to let me come back. I had to do a sleight of hand and go around SOE to get back here." She sighed. "They mean well in those offices there, but they sit in safety and comfort and imagine what it must be like over here, but really, they have no clue. Hitler's V-1 rockets hit less often now, and they were more a bother than a danger when measured in casualties. So, aside from lingering food shortages, the UK is out of danger for the most part."

"Well, you're looking good," Amélie broke in. "Tell me the news, beyond what I've heard on the BBC."

Fourcade, the woman who had built and led Alliance, was also small. Her hair was drawn tightly against her scalp, and her features were such that she could touch them up with makeup, turn on the charm, and brighten a room, or just as easily slip into obscurity within a crowd.

Three times her organization had been devastated by *Gestapo* raids resulting from informants who had infiltrated. Three times she had rebuilt it, twice with the aid of Georges Lamarque, the man whose apartment the three women now visited together.

"I'm happy to see you both," Amélie said, "but besides the news, why are you here? Why now?"

Fourcade took a deep breath. "Before I answer that, let me say that, despite your caution and loss of weight, you seem more relaxed than I've seen you in times past."

Amélie tossed her head and arched her eyebrows. "The result of aging?"

Fourcade chuckled. "You're so old at twenty-four—"

"Maybe becoming hardened?" Amélie said wistfully. "Perhaps some optimism. We know the war is moving this way. The sense that Paris will be liberated is inescapable. People feel it. Every house has a bottle of champagne or wine hidden away somewhere to celebrate liberation when it comes. Every woman has a special dress put away for when Paris is finally free again."

"I feel it too," Chantal broke in. "I saw the Germans pushed off the beaches at Normandy. They ran like scared rabbits." She scoffed. "I'll never forget the faces of the soldiers who had taken over the *Feldgendarmerie* at Bayeux when we broke in on them. They never expected to see French people holding weapons aimed close to their faces.

"It's one thing to fight a disarmed, starving population," she continued, still scoffing. "It's another to face a well-equipped army shooting back with the populace helping them. The Germans lost against the Allies, they were pushed out of North Africa, Italy changed sides, and the war there is nearly over."

Noticing Amélie staring at her in shock, she said, "What's wrong?"

"You did what at Bayeux?" Amélie brought a hand to her forehead. "Dragon was supposed to keep you safe."

"I left him no choice," Chantal responded. Dragon led the Resistance group Chantal had joined to help an artist who sketched eighty miles of Normandy's beaches for the Allies. She sniffed. "Anyway, I still haven't taken the chances you have."

"The difference is that I didn't go looking for those situations—"

"But those situations found you and so many of our countrymen," Chantal retorted. "If we don't look for ways to fight the Germans, they'll rule us forever."

Chantal's face reddened, and her voice rose with passion. "We've seen the slave workers of the Todt organization. They're Polish, and they're shipped all over the place to build fortifications or roads or whatever the Germans want. They're hardly fed, and they're worked until they drop dead. That's our future if we don't defeat this evil."

She took a deep breath and closed her eyes. "I'm sorry. I have to do my part just like you do." She sniffed as tears formed in her eyes. "You've been a mother to me since our mother died, and especially after that *boche* pig killed Father, but I'm grown now. You have enough to worry about."

Amélie crossed the room to embrace Chantal. "I'm so proud of you. I just couldn't bear to lose you." She wiped a tear from Chantal's eye. "Now tell me, what do you hear from Horton?"

Chantal's face took on a bleak expression. "Nothing," she said in a hollow voice. "I've heard nothing of him since he left for Italy back in January." Her voice broke. "I try not to think about him. I was in an area above Arromanches, and I saw the Allies building a huge port there. They did it so fast, floating in large sections. It was amazing. I used to look at all the soldiers coming off those great piers and wonder if Horton was one of them." She sighed. "If he was there, I never saw him."

She squeezed Amélie's hand. "What about Jeremy?"

Amélie drew back and shook her head. "Nothing since we were all together in Lyon at the beginning of May. I don't know where he was assigned."

Fourcade had observed the exchange quietly. Now she interjected. "I can give you a little encouragement," she told Amélie. "I can't say where

Jeremy went, but I can tell you that, at last report, he was healthy and doing a wonderful job. He's very highly thought of among the *Maquis* that he works with."

Amélie breathed another sigh. "I can only hope that he's not at the Vercors. There's an awful slaughter going on there right now. The Germans are positively chortling about it. They want it to be an example of what any community who dares to oppose them can expect. The reports coming through the underground confirm the German claims. It's awful. I also hope he's not in that mess at Normandy."

Amélie rubbed her eyes.

Fourcade looked away.

Chantal noticed and glanced questioningly at her.

Fourcade averted her eyes and resumed, "As I was about to say, we sent another agent to the organization he's with. You met her. She's codenamed Pauline—"

Amélie swung around.

"Nothing to worry about," Fourcade continued with a slight smile. "She's a wonderful woman, and she carried with her a message to Jeremy that you are alive and well. I'm sure he'll appreciate that."

"I need a drink," Amélie said, and crossed to a cabinet. "Anyone else?" She rummaged around in the cabinet and then announced, "Georges is just about out of everything, like everyone else in Paris. But I found a little claret."

When the three had settled back into their seats with their wine, Fourcade said, "You asked about the news beyond BBC. I'll relate what I can, but to tell you the truth, I won't be telling you much because what I know is surmised.

"I think the Allies plan on bypassing Paris."

Seeing the sisters' shocked expressions, Fourcade nodded somberly. "It makes sense from a military perspective. The Germans won't let Paris go easily. Hitler is already making noises about fighting to the last man. That's coming down through British intelligence channels. If the Allies get into a protracted fight here, the city could be destroyed—you should see Saint-Lô. It's rubble. The whole city."

She let out a long breath. "Beyond that concern, the thinking is that if the Allies drive north to the Rhine, they'll isolate the Germans still occupying Paris and force them into surrender. They think that will shorten the war. If instead, they fight their way into Paris, they will use up resources and extend the war."

Amélie and Chantal stared bleakly at each other. "What of the people here?" Amélie said in abject wonder. "Are we supposed to just wait for our deliverance? What makes anyone think that Hitler won't take out his vengeance on Paris? This city was his prize, his trophy. Look what he's doing in the Vercors! He will most certainly do something similar here. Can't Allied generals see that?"

Fourcade rose and paced while raising her hands in frustration. "I've thought the same thing. Still, I can see some sense in what they're saying. The wild card is Hitler. What will he do?"

They sat in silence a few minutes, and then Amélie asked, "What are your plans now, Madeleine?"

Fourcade smirked in irony. "The senior command asked me to organize Resistance patrols north of Paris on the main route to the Rhine." She retook her seat. "I can't ask our people to do that without my own participation. German units are already withdrawing through there to Germany. The Allies are moving fast east of Normandy. I think it'll turn into a rout. The *Wehrmacht* is desperate, angry, and it will fight desperately to get home." She took another breath and arched her eyebrows. "So I'll be there organizing."

Amélie regarded her in consternation. "Madeleine, we can't afford to lose you."

Fourcade smiled distantly. "No one is indispensable. Besides, I haven't been to the north of France in some time."

"What about—" Amélie interrupted herself.

"Henri?"

Amélie nodded. "Have you heard anything?"

"Sadly, no." For an instant, Fourcade's shoulders drooped and she looked as forlorn as anyone Amélie had ever seen her. Then she snapped herself back into self-control. "Believe me, I will never stop looking, but I think I know the worst."

Major Henri La Faye and Fourcade had worked together in Marseille.

He had been a dashing fighter pilot in Vichy-France's Algerian air force. He defected to General Charles de Gaulle and joined Alliance as Fourcade's chief of staff. In that capacity, he had recruited many senior officers from both the active Vichy military and from the deactivated veterans of France's pre-armistice national army.

Henri and Fourcade had fallen in love. Several months ago, they had flown separately back to London for joint meetings with SOE. When he was scheduled to return to France, Fourcade had walked him to the aircraft. As the plane lifted off, she had experienced a terrible sense that she would never see him again.

Moments after being warned to leave the clandestine airfield where he landed, Henri disappeared. No one in the Resistance networks had heard from him since.

"I'm so sorry," Amélie comforted. "I'll help you search."

Fourcade wiped her eyes and grasped Amélie's arm. "You're a wonderful friend." She remained quiet a moment, then regained her poise and said, "That brings us to Jeannie Rousseau. What is the latest?"

"We've located her," Amélie replied. "She's imprisoned at Fresnes, just south of Paris."

Jeannie was a beautiful, multilingual graduate of the Paris Institute of Political Science. She veiled her intellectual brilliance and photographic memory behind charm, grace, and a deliberately coquettish manner that had ingratiated her to senior German commanders. The result was extraordinary in terms of her effectiveness as a spy. Earlier in the war, while employed in the German headquarters that had planned the invasion of England, Jeannie provided highly accurate reports on German plans and dispositions. The information she provided enabled Allied leaders to respond in a way that convinced Hitler to forego the invasion.

Surviving *Gestapo* suspicions and an investigation, Jeannie had moved to Paris, where, with the help of Georges Lamarque, her favorite professor, she had gained employment within the German High Command. There, she had seen, memorized, and transmitted through the Resistance Hitler's plans for the V-1 and V-2 rockets to be launched against the UK.

Both at Dinard and then in Paris, Amélie had been her trusted courier, and the two women had become each other's dearest friend.

Barely two months ago, on a dark night at a house along a canal in Saint-Brieuc on the Brittany coast, the Royal Navy's attempt to bring them both to London had been betrayed. Jeannie had sacrificed herself to warn Amélie away.

Amélie's escape had been arduous, and over a week later, when she arrived safely at the apartment in Lyon that served as Fourcade's headquarters, she was skin and bones. She had vowed then that she would not rest until she found Jeannie.

"Georges went to Raoul Nordling. He's the Swedish consul general—"

"I know him," Fourcade said. "He's a good man, and being from neutral Sweden, he has—or had—a certain sway with the Germans."

"He still does," Amélie interjected. "It's waning a bit, but the *Wehrmacht* is still sensitive to perceptions of war crimes. Monsieur Nordling was able to get a list of prisoners at each of the prisons, including Fresnes."

Startled, Fourcade asked, "Jeannie's name was on the list?"

"Yes, that surprised me too. She must have given her real name when she arrived at the prison. It didn't connect with any of her aliases. They kept her anyway."

Fourcade shook her head in disbelief. "The girl is a wonder. Do they even know why they're holding her?"

Amélie shrugged. "I suppose not. They'd hold her because she was delivered to them." She scowled. "They're a cruel lot, those prison managers and guards."

Fourcade gave Amélie a discerning look. "What happens now?"

"We have to keep track of Jeannie. The Germans are starting to move prisoners east into Germany, both male and female. Fortunately, they keep good records. Nordling is in constant touch with them, and I have the impression that the *Wehrmacht* command here has been softer than in other places."

Fourcade smacked her lips sardonically. "Well, it is a plum assignment."

Chantal had been listening to the discussion quietly, and now she interjected. "Where is Georges?" She looked around the sumptuous apartment. "I only met him one time in Lyon. This is a very nice place he has."

"Somewhat in need of repair, thanks to the Germans," Amélie said with a tinge of anger. "The floors need re-doing, the rugs are becoming threadbare, and the paint is cracking on the walls. Georges is fastidious. He must hate living this way."

Georges Lamarque was a distinguished mathematics professor at the university where Jeannie had graduated. Tall and fit with a square jaw and a permanent smile, his notability had allowed him to maneuver around Nazi strictures. Soon after the *Wehrmacht* occupied Paris, he joined the Resistance and started up a national network, the Druids, which he subsumed into Fourcade's network.

Fourcade sighed. "I can't tell you where he is. I can only say that he continues to do good work for us."

Amélie knew how Fourcade and Georges had worked together. When the *Gestapo* infiltrated and raided Alliance and reduced it to only five members, killing hundreds of her friends and followers, he was one of those still remaining and was able to help Fourcade quickly reconstitute the network. As a result, he was her close friend, confidant, and a most trusted aide.

Fourcade's thoughts went to Georges. He too had perceived a change in the fortunes of war favoring the Allies. In discussion with him, she mentioned her mission to organize patrols north and east of Paris and that she needed someone to unite disparate Resistance groups in and around Nancy. He had immediately volunteered.

She had accepted but had since suffered the same apprehensions she had sensed about Henri. She closed her eyes momentarily. *I hope they're both all right.*

Amélie noticed Fourcade's sudden turn to introspection. To lighten the mood, she turned to Chantal. "What about you, little sister?" she asked with forced jocularity. "What brings you to Paris at this dour time?"

Chantal stared at her in obvious discomfort. "I—I can't say. I'm not allowed to."

Amélie froze. She gazed at Chantal and a look of sadness crossed her face. She and her sister had never deliberately kept secrets from each other. Only now did they realize that, in this war, operational secrecy trumped the bonds of sisterhood. The conversation ended abruptly.

Amélie shifted her eyes to Fourcade, who met her gaze in non-committal silence. Amélie glanced back at Chantal. “My, my,” she murmured, “you really have grown up.”

28

The mission elements that Chantal could not disclose had been revealed to her in a discussion with Fourcade prior to boarding the train to Paris. Her task was one that Chantal felt less than confident she could complete.

"You must try," Fourcade had enjoined her. "At this late date, there is no one else we can bring in. The qualifications are quite specific and rare. You won't be told who your boss is until you report for duty. He needs someone not known in Paris, who's been trained in London's spy school, and has secret operations experience which includes participation in combat. That's you."

The Allies were stalled east of Normandy, Fourcade had explained, but their further advance was inexorable as they poured more men and equipment into combat. Cherbourg was taken with its port facilities intact, and the docks towed into Arromanches were performing remarkably. Between them, they were delivering onto France's shores an unstoppable power that would overwhelm the *Wehrmacht* in size and capability. Already, Allied air forces had seized air superiority from the *Luftwaffe* over Normandy and a hundred miles inland.

"Word is spreading and reaching the capital," Fourcade said. "The Nazis can't stop it. People are still coming and going from Paris; they're calling friends and family or sending written messages by courier to bypass censors. Expectation is building that Paris will be free. Soon."

The fear, she explained, was that in the vacuum that would follow a German exit from the capital, fighting between French factions could descend into an insurgency, resulting in a full-scale civil war. Already, individuals and groups were jockeying for power in a post-war France.

Chantal had reacted in alarm. "That sounds treasonous."

Fourcade nodded grimly. "Most people are sincere in advancing visions of what a free France should be. Others are power-hungry. Those people will always exist. Hitler is the personification of such thinking. So is the Soviet Union's Joseph Stalin."

Chantal responded in surprise. "But he's our ally."

"Only because we needed him. During peacetime, he ruled his people every bit as savagely as Hitler does. He'd have lost against the Germans without US aid."

Fourcade laid her hands gently on Chantal's face and held it while looking deep into her eyes. "You're perfect for what we have in mind, Chantal. You can do it."

"Do what?" Chantal replied irritably. "And who is 'we?'"

Fourcade mulled for a moment over how best to respond. "I'll put you in touch with members of the Resistance in Paris. For several days, all I want you to do is mix with them. Become known to them, but very quietly. You're not there to lead. Then, when the time is right, I'll send you to the man who will explain everything."

Chantal had held Fourcade's steady gaze. "All right, I'll do it."

29

Same Day, August 1, 1944
VII Army Headquarters, Rome, Italy

Général d'armée Jean-Marie Gabriel de Lattre de Tassigny strode across Major General Alexander Patch's office. He held out his hand in greeting, but his face hinted at profound dismay.

Although not a large man, his bald head and rounded, stone-sculptured features over broad shoulders gave the impression of one, and he lived and breathed France. In the last great war, he had been wounded five times including at Verdun, and he was cited eight times for courage under fire, receiving France's highest and most honored award, the Legion of Honor.

At the beginning of the current war, he was the youngest general in the French army. He remained in major commands after the French Armistice and ascended to take command of Vichy-French troops in Tunisia. He became a controversial figure to the Allies when he was the only general who refused an order to flip his forces to oppose the Germans in North Africa. Instead he ordered them to fight the Allies.

As a result, he was arrested but escaped, and he subsequently defected to de Gaulle's Free French Army, composed of all formerly Vichy-French units in North Africa. De Gaulle had since charged General de Lattre to take command of the French II Corps for the southern invasion of France as part of Operation Dragoon.

"I'll come straight to the point," de Lattre told General Patch after their handshake. "I've studied the invasion plans, and nowhere does it include French forces in the initial assault. Operation Dragoon will see the return of the French army to fight for France's existence on its own native soil. The honor of France demands that we be included from the outset." He added with a vaguely sullen tone, "A French general should be in command of the Allied invasion force, but General de Gaulle has already been denied that privilege. At least we should take a significant part in the mission."

General Patch listened while eyeing de Lattre somberly. "And you will," he said. "Come over to the map and let's go over the plan together."

Patch was almost a mirror image of de Lattre, with short-cropped hair atop a balding head, broad shoulders, and a quiet-bulldog demeanor. During the Great War, he had fought in the Second Battle of the Marne, the Battle of Saint-Mihiel, and the Meuse-Argonne Offensive, the latter being the largest battle in the history of the United States Army to date. His leadership qualities were observed by then Colonel George Marshall, who was now a four-star general, the US Army Chief of Staff, and President Roosevelt's closest military adviser.

At the beginning of the current war, Patch was a colonel in command of a regiment, but he was soon promoted to the rank of brigadier general and charged with training raw recruits at Fort Bragg, North Carolina. Two years ago, by then a major general and despite recovering from a severe bout of pneumonia, he had formed the Americal Division and relieved the valiant, exhausted, and malaria-ridden 1st Marine Division at Guadalcanal in the Pacific Theater. He personally led in the Battles of Mount Austen, the Galloping Horse, and the Sea Horse to capture several fortified hills and ridges from Japanese forces. By February 1943, he had driven the enemy from the island.

Still suffering from the effects of pneumonia accompanied by dysentery and malaria, he nevertheless took command of VI Corps, which he trained in Oregon. He then transferred the headquarters to Algiers in the Mediterranean Theater to prepare for Operation Dragoon. Five months ago, he had relinquished that command to take over as the commanding general of the

US VII Army with orders to plan and execute the southern invasion of France.

Patch guided de Lattre over to a large wall map showing the southern French coast from Cannes in the east and sloping southwest to Porquerolles Island at the western boundary of the operations area. He indicated a wide arrow pointing at Saint-Raphaël. "That's where Camel Force, the 36th Division, is going in. That unit is one of our most battle-hardened elements, and it has two successful amphibious landings under its belt at Sicily and Salerno. Those troops fought all the way up through Italy's mountains. They were at Anzio and were the first full division into Rome. Its commanders and soldiers know what they're doing. They'll secure our right flank."

De Lattre started to speak, but Patch stopped him with a gesture. "Please, bear with me." He pointed at another arrow aimed at Saint-Maxime. "That's Delta Force, the 45th Division. It was also at those landings, and in Italy and Rome. It'll thrust up the Rhône Valley at the center and bear the brunt of meeting the German Nineteenth Army.

"Then there's the 3rd Infantry Division." He indicated an arrow pointing at Saint-Tropez. "That's Alpha Force. It led the invasion in North Africa and was there at Sicily and Salerno." He moved his hand to indicate the other two divisions. "While those two reinforced at Anzio, the 3rd was part of the initial force and, as you know, despite what happened later at Anzio, the initial landing was picture perfect. It'll secure our left—"

De Lattre had listened, restraining his impatience, but now he interrupted. "Our French troops also fought in Italy—"

"Bravely and competently," Patch broke in. "We could not have had the success we did without them. But my point is that these three divisions are our most experienced at amphibious operations. If we don't get onshore, push inland, and establish a permanent presence, we're nowhere."

De Lattre pursed his lips as he stared at the map.

Patch noted de Lattre's restrained irritation. "Look, General, it's not that we don't want you in the initial force or that we think your troops aren't up to it. The fact is that we've maxed out our available amphibious capability in getting those divisions ashore. We've got that whole other war in the

Pacific, and it's using up most of those assets. We go with what we've got, and getting those divisions onto dry land must be the priority."

Resignedly, de Lattre nodded.

Patch broke a half-smile. "Don't think all is lost," he said kindly. "Your II Corps is top priority for the second wave and is assigned to capture both Toulon and Marseille."

"But that won't be until after—"

"General de Lattre, if we don't take those two cities, the whole operation will fail. Don't forget that the overall objective is to push the German Nineteenth Army north, destroy as much as possible along the way, link up with the armies heading east out of Normandy, and set a trap to cut off the *Wehrmacht's* retreat before it gets to Germany. There's plenty for all of us to do."

De Lattre glanced at him with questioning eyes.

"General," Patch went on, "intelligence reports indicate that Hitler ordered the destruction of the port facilities in those two cities if they can no longer be defended. If that happens, we will lose our re-supply capability, and we'll run out of gas, food, and ammunition while our soldiers are in the heat of fighting. If that happens, our operation will stall, and the Nineteenth Army will either overrun us and throw us back into the ocean or escape back into Germany.

"Overwhelming force is the fundamental principle of war we're relying on. No one knows when we'll reach that critical mass, but not executing this invasion would leave southern France with a huge army still harassing your people and able to strike our men crossing northern France. So, assuming for the sake of argument that Operation Dragoon is critical to the entire Allied effort in Europe, then capturing Toulon and Marseille are crucial to Dragoon.

"You can see then that your mission is crucial to overall Allied success."

De Lattre continued studying the map in silence. Then he turned to Patch. "You're very convincing." He exhaled. "I feel a little patronized—"

"Not at all. That's the way things are." Patch arched his eyebrows, peered directly into de Lattre's eyes, and added, "General Truscott assigned the bulk of his VI Corps to your mission under your command, and I approved his plan. He's known to be a careful planner, a fierce fighter, and a commander who cares deeply for his troops. The fact that he assigned that many combat assets, including his soldiers, to your command has got to demonstrate some level of our confidence in you and your French soldiers."

De Lattre nodded stiffly, reluctantly mollified.

Patch clapped his shoulder. "We're about to set your homeland free, together." While he spoke, he crossed to a table with a decanter and poured brandy into two small glasses. "Keep in mind that General Truscott is organizing a task force patterned after the French 'combat command' concept—I think you call it a 'CC.' Hell, he inspected and studied your CC Sudre in North Africa and then lobbied for two months to get it assigned permanently to his VI Corps. When he was turned down, he decided to form his own under General Butler, who is developing the idea as we speak.

"We've used task forces regularly, but they've been put together from units that worked and trained together. Truscott's concept goes a step further by putting in place a permanent headquarters that has no combat assets of its own. Corps headquarters will support it with staff and communications. The units assigned will be based on the combat situation, and they report solely to its commander, in this case Butler, for the duration of its mission. The task force will go as light or as heavy as required by the mission. I think it's a good idea." He pointed a finger at the French general in a jocular manner. "And it came from your French forces."

He grunted as he handed a brandy to de Lattre. "Anyway, I like your fighting spirit. Let's drink to your success in Toulon and Marseille."

De Lattre smiled for the first time and lifted his glass. "And then on to Paris."

30

August 4, 1944
Saint-Lô, France

The depth of destruction visited on this city shocked Paul to his core. Saint-Lô had been an important crossroads for the *Wehrmacht* as it moved equipment and supplies to its troops along the seacoasts. Until thirteen days ago, like Caen, it had been a major impediment to the Allies' ability to move out of bocage country and into the tank-friendly terrain south of Normandy. Then the Allied carpet bombing ensued.

The destruction of Saint-Lô was complete, and gained the moniker, "The Capital of Ruins." Paul had been through towns and villages that had been flattened, but nothing he had seen before compared to what he beheld now. Looking across the devastation from the top of a hill, he wondered if it could ever be repaired and restored to a desirable place to live.

He had accompanied General Leclerc on a tour of the battlefield. They had stopped at the top of a hill overlooking the town. The road's surface itself had been ground into place by combat vehicles as they drove over debris—the original lane had been obliterated and covered with rubble. Winding downhill, the makeshift motorway traversed through buildings whose bricks lay in piles of wreckage such that the town's streets were indiscernible. Combat engineers had guessed where the avenues were supposed to be and bulldozed a passage so that military traffic could go through.

Paul glanced at Leclerc.

The general stood stone-faced, observing the devastation.

Paul thought he knew some of what passed through Leclerc's mind. When the Allies landed in Normandy, three of their first-day objectives had been Cherbourg, Bayeux, and Caen. Immediately thereafter, they had expected to take Saint-Lô. Once those places were secured, they would control the major port facilities, roads, and railways across northwestern France.

That did not happen. When the fighting bogged down at Caen, the battle lines drew to a stalemate resembling WWI trench warfare. To break out of the bocage, a gap had to be created to allow General Patton to penetrate deep into German territory. To that end, Omar Bradley, Commanding General of 12th Army Group, proposed saturation bombing in an area four miles long and two miles wide. The proposal included use of a new type of incendiary composed of various acids that, when mixed together, formed a highly combustible gel that poured easily into containers. When they impacted, the resulting flames rose high and wide, consuming everything they touched.

They called it "napalm."

Beautiful, picturesque Saint-Lô, nestled among the rolling hills and surrounding forests, lay in the path of that carpet of incendiaries and explosives.

Paul took a deep breath and let it out quietly. *General Leclerc is thinking we did this. And we did.*

Beginning two weeks ago on the night of July 6, Allied bombers flew over the town and targeted areas incessantly, dropping over three thousand tons of bombs. Their main objectives had been the railroads and the power station. The purpose was to deny reinforcements and resupply to the *Wehrmacht* in Brittany, and to obliterate German defenses that were blocking an Allied breakout from bocage country.

Precautions had been taken in the form of leaflets dropped to warn the city's population. However, high winds blew them to other communities. Saint-Lô residents remained uninformed.

Downhill from the two officers, an ancient, massive fortress rose from the left side of what remained of the road. Leclerc pointed it out. "Charlemagne built those ramparts over a thousand years ago," he muttered just above a whisper.

Paul observed the stronghold and then followed the makeshift road with his eyes. It ran past the battlements to the bottom of a valley, curved to the right, and then split. A continuous convoy of jeeps and supply trucks rumbled over the pockmarked road littered with rubble and took the left fork. The convoy extended across flat ground, crossed a bridge over the Sire River, headed back uphill, and disappeared over the horizon, miles away.

The right fork straightened and ran up along the side of a hill overlooking what must have been, only days ago, a verdant valley. A single row of two-story houses with brightly colored trim stood on the uphill side of the road to the right, perhaps three to five miles away. From that distance they appeared to be untouched by the war.

Between those far houses and where Paul and Leclerc stood were miles of desolation. Hardly a single wall stood erect and those that did were pockmarked where thousands of bullets had struck, and some had holes blasted through. On the valley floor, stone outlines gave witness to where homes had stood, families had grown, and children had played.

On the way into town, Paul had seen l' Église Notre-Dame, the thirteenth-century stone cathedral that was the very symbol of Saint-Lô. Its tall steeple had been demolished halfway up and its sanctuary caved in from bombs.

Leclerc, his face taut, indicated that he was ready to go. As they reached the half-track, his chest heaved. He faced Paul directly and swept an arm across the hellacious landscape. "People died here," he hissed. "Thousands of them. Women. Children. Innocents." His voice shook and his lips trembled. "I promise you this. Their sacrifices will never be forgotten, and they will not have died in vain."

31

August 5, 1944
Dinan, France

Lance Littlefield watched as Captain André Duron left the shelter of their hiding place and strode alone into the middle of one of Dinan's main streets. Despite the ravages of four years of occupation, the walled town had managed to retain its ancient beauty with mid-summer flowers in planters lining the cobblestone walkways and narrow streets, and vines draping the sides of buildings and hanging from window ledges.

Situated along the graceful Rivière Rance, the gentle lapping of flowing water added to the ambiance enjoyed by the German occupiers. The pleasant atmosphere could not be fully suppressed by the enemy's presence so long as bombs and bullets remained distant sounds. Its stone houses alluded to centuries of communal solidarity; and its storefronts and cafés, painted brightly in reds, yellows, greens, and myriad other colors, although chipped and faded, lent a vivacity that defied Dinan's circumstances. In a photogenic province, this town was a crown jewel.

Duron, Lance, and their guide, Roland, had approached cautiously from the northeast by a circuitous route to avoid German observation posts.

Three days ago, on receiving their operations order, they had worked all through the night, selecting members for the patrol, drawing and checking ammunition and equipment, planning and rehearsing their route to the objective and actions on arrival, and going over every perceived detail that could make or break the mission.

All the *maquisards* were ecstatic to receive good weapons with plenty of ammunition, as well as full rations. Mindful of Dreux's melancholy over leading young boys into combat, Lance advised Duron to avoid them except in rare cases that could be justified by combat experience that might add to a probability of success.

"You know those who don't come with us will fight on the left flank at Saint-Malo," Duron had observed gravely.

Lance nodded. "We're taking the ones with experience," he replied. "We have a smaller margin for error." He sighed. "At least I can rationalize that way."

They set out the next day under the thunder of American artillery pounding the ancient port city of Saint-Malo. General Macon had estimated that the battle would take three days. He wanted to receive the reconnaissance report by the time it ended.

Lance was impressed with Captain Duron. The man knew his business. He had planned and prepared carefully, briefed his squad leaders fully, and conducted brief-backs and rehearsals until he felt confident that his patrol could accomplish its mission.

The *maquisards* he selected were high-spirited, still reveling in the good fortune of their new weapons and supplies. Encouraged by that happenstance and understanding that failure to comply with orders would result in dismissal, they had thrown themselves into preparations and crossed their line of departure with bright, attentive eyes.

The distance, roughly eighteen miles, was not great even on foot, but Duron took his time. They traveled in two columns abreast, and Lance took up his station between them close to the rear of the formation. They first headed northwest to Les Rousselais, an isolated farming community, and then cut east to Tressé to spend the night. Then they would trek through the Côtes-du-Nord Department, planning to approach Dinan from the northeast.

Traversing small fields bounded by bocages presented challenges, but

Duron and Lance had worked out tactics. After surveilling an area they needed to cross, scouts went ahead. When an all clear was called, the two columns would maneuver ahead by separate routes using the hedgerows for cover and meet at a designated rally point. The method was tedious and slowed forward progress, but it provided the greatest probability of avoiding enemy contact.

As they approached Tressé, they left most of the bocages behind and entered the cool shade of forestland where they could move faster. They camped in a friendly farmer's barn near the town and set out the next morning for Taden, another farm village near Dinan. From there, Duron intended to stage his observation posts.

Arriving without incident in the early afternoon, Duron and Lance set the men in hidden vantage points where they could observe activity in charming, beautiful Dinan. The river flowed slowly through it, glimmering in sunlight.

Lance settled into his position. From far off, he still heard the dull thud of artillery explosions at Saint-Malo, and he wondered how that battle progressed. The noise had been a constant as the patrol tramped to Dinan, but it had been muffled by distance and the sounds of many boots plodding through fields and forests over rocks, twigs, and dried leaves. The soldiers had generally avoided civilians, but the few they met along the way had been thrilled to see an American and a French officer, and their own young fighters, fully equipped and maneuvering with discipline.

As Lance watched from his observation post, it was easy for his mind to wander because not much was going on inside the town. There was no vehicular traffic, and pedestrians were few. When they appeared, they scurried about their business, and they seemed to glance around furtively.

Thoughts of Sark and his family crossed his mind. Suddenly, he couldn't remember the last time he had seen any of them. *It was Christmastime, but was that last year or the year before?* The memory was a blur.

Since then, he had either been raiding, fighting, escaping, or evading. At a younger age, he might have been thrilled to have learned about the life that was in store for him. Having lived it, thinking of all the dark days at Colditz Castle and the friends lost along the way now made him weary.

He thought of the young *maquisards* that Dreux had grieved over. They had fought, but not out of a sense of adventure. They fought as best they knew how with the meager weapons at their disposal to repulse a brutal invader, and far too many of them would never come home.

Lance huffed out a breath of air. *So, what are you going to do when this is all over?* He shook his head. *I don't know. War is all I've known as an adult. I've never even had a serious girlfriend.* He tried to picture the faces of girls he had known, but none came to mind. He scolded himself. *That's sad.*

An overpowering longing for home gripped him. He shook it off and went to check the men at the observation posts. At dusk, a few rested *maquisards* relieved others still in place. Duron withdrew the rest and gathered them in a barn where they would spend the night.

A quick query confirmed what Lance had witnessed. Not a single German soldier, officer, or *Wehrmacht* vehicle of any sort had been spotted. The people had moved about warily, but otherwise normally. Further, the owner of the barn had informed Duron that pockets of Germans were still around, but most had withdrawn from the area, and he believed that only a few, if any, remained in Dinan. Obviously, he said, the people were not yet confident to celebrate, but there was a sense that their war might be over. He added that when the artillery sounds still floating in from Saint-Malo ceased, then perhaps the people would celebrate.

Early the next morning, Lance and Duron crept to the rim of a rocky outcropping and viewed the town through binoculars. Several young *maquisards* asked to go along, and Duron allowed them.

Considering Dreux's concern for the boys, Lance looked at them differently now. His stomach tightened with visions flitting through his mind of their young faces lying bloodied and lifeless in a barren field.

The air was crisp, the first sign of approaching autumn, and the Basilique Saint-Sauveur's spire rose through an early mist over what appeared to be an ancient Roman aqueduct. The river, channeled on both banks by rough-hewn stone embankments with picturesque homes on either side, meandered on its way to the sea under an old stone bridge. Flowers, still moist with dew, greeted the day with a panoply of hues, their fragrance floating on the air. They complemented the striking colors of the doorframes at the front of the shops along the brown cobblestone streets. Birds sang, despite the dull thuds of far-off battle.

Lance took in all the beauty around him juxtaposed against the anticipated danger and the calamitous effects of war. *When bad people want to rule and displace good people, it becomes necessary.* He sighed. *But God I wish it wasn't so.*

Duron prodded him. "Do you see what I see?"

Lance took a long breath and nodded. "The streets are deserted—not a single person out and about."

Roland, one of the *maquisards,* nudged Duron. He was a lanky, dark-haired lad. "I know how to get into the town without being seen," he said. "I have family in Dinan. I know the town well. There's a dike across the Rance downriver from here. I can show you the way."

Duron glanced at Lance, who shrugged and muttered, "Why not?"

To the disappointment of the other fighters, Duran left them behind, taking only Lance and Roland with him. An hour later, the trio emerged on the opposite side of the river onto a narrow street lined with stone apartment buildings.

All the windows were shuttered.

A cat meowed. Dogs barked from a faraway place. Otherwise, silence reigned.

The three men crept to an intersection of a main street and stood in the shadows, listening and watching.

Duron took a deep breath and turned to Lance. "You can come with me or stay here. Your choice."

Without waiting for a response, he stood straight, squared his shoulders, and marched to the middle of the larger thoroughfare. There, he halted, executed a military right-face onto Rue Beaumanoir, and continued marching down its center.

Lance watched in amazement. He heard a window creak, and then a shutter banged against a wall. Fearing for his comrade, Lance whirled on Roland. "Stay here," he barked. Then, he ran out onto the main avenue and lifted his carbine toward the open window.

He heard footsteps behind him. Against Lance's order, Roland had followed.

A girl's voice rang out. "It's an American. The Americans are here." The excitement in her voice was palpable.

Lance saw her now, quite pretty in the morning sunlight. She gazed toward Duron, who still marched proudly through the center of Dinan. "*Non*," the girl shouted even more excitedly. "He wears the French flag. He's French. Our own army is here."

Shutters clattered against walls as windows flew open and hundreds of French flags appeared. Bouquets of flowers flew through the air. People poured into the street.

Roland caught up with Lance, and together, they hurried alongside Duron. Without missing a step, he glanced at both of them and grinned.

Someone started singing "*La Marseillaise*." A hush fell over the crowd, and then as one, the citizens of Dinan picked up the stirring tune and lyrics and belted out their pride in their country. The trio from Team Guy halted and joined in.

When the anthem was done, the crowd roared even louder. The Team Guy trio started off again, amid ever-growing throngs, marching abreast of each other down Rue Beaumanoir to a spacious square, the Place Duguesclin.

Lance had never experienced so many girls who wanted to reach out and touch his face, arms, and shoulders, or run their fingers through his hair. They threw themselves against him and kissed him on his cheeks, on his lips.

Duron, meanwhile, after extricating himself from a similar pleasant occurrence, found a stern-faced man standing in front of him with his hands on his hips. He was obviously a recognized leader, for the people stood back. "Is the war over?" he demanded with heavy sarcasm. "You're enjoying a party, but I still hear the sound of guns at Saint-Malo."

Duron smiled sheepishly. "You're right. We came to find out if there are Germans still here and their strength." He held out his hand. "I am Captain Duron."

The young man eyed Duron skeptically. Without changing his expression, he shook Duron's hand. "I am Gaston, leader of the local Resistance." He was medium height with a muscular build, dark hair, and sharp blue eyes.

"Then you're the man we need to speak with."

"Let's get to business." Gaston glanced at Lance and Roland, and with a quick flick of his hand, he bade all three to follow. Against the backdrop of the still-cheering crowd, he led them to a nearby café. There, he held the door while the others sauntered in. He also allowed several other men to enter. Then he closed the door and directed the proprietor to lock it while he led the group into an inner room.

Standing in the middle of the far end, Gaston waited for everyone to find a seat. "If you really are with the Allies," he said at last, "then you are welcome, but we've been infiltrated before."

Duron stood. "We came on a reconnaissance mission," he said. "I'm promising nothing and I'm not asking for anything. I saw that the streets were empty and thought your townspeople might be encouraged by the sight of a French soldier in uniform." He indicated Lance and grinned. "The Brit followed me, and so did Roland."

Gaston's expression softened, and he switched his gaze to Roland. "We know Roland. He's a Resistance fighter in this area. We know his family." He rubbed the back of his neck. "Still, I need to be sure."

Duron nodded and brought out his letter issued by Generals Koenig and Eisenhower. Gaston read it, looked up, and read it again. He took a deep breath and let it out slowly, a look of relief crossing his face. "The last of the Germans that were here left during the night," he said, "but they still have units in the surrounding areas. Our streets were empty because the people were scared of the fighting going on at Saint-Malo. Will it spread this way?"

"Not if we act fast," Duron replied. "The American 6th Armored and 83rd Infantry divisions are fighting at Saint-Malo. General Macon personally ordered this mission. After those divisions are finished at Saint-Malo, they'll send tanks and infantrymen this way to clear out what's left of the Germans."

Gaston paced the floor while he considered Duron's words. Then he turned to his own men. "Tell them what you know," he ordered. "Everything." His lips formed a small smile, and he indicated one of his members. "This *maquisard* got all their local gun positions and sketched them out. The Germans thought he was stupid, so they let him wander around. I promise you, he is not stupid. I checked his work personally."

The two groups conferred for two hours, going over sketches and questioning troop numbers, types, and weaponry. When both leaders were satisfied that they understood matters the same way, Gaston led them out a back way. "Pleasant as the girls are, if you go out the front, you'll never get to deliver this intelligence."

As they parted ways, Gaston shook hands with Duron and Lance. "Thank you for coming." He tousled Roland's hair. "Good job bringing them here. You're all grown up."

Roland grinned and swung a fake jab at Gaston's stomach.

Gaston regarded him fondly. "Maybe soon you'll have the chance to enjoy what's left of your teenage years."

Watching the exchange, Lance interjected, "We'll tell the general to hurry. Dinan is liberated, but it needs protection."

32

August 9, 1944
Paris, France

General Dietrich von Choltitz, the new commanding general of Paris, stared into the darkness outside his window of the Meurice, the luxury hotel that had been converted into Germany's headquarters for the military occupation of France's capital city. He had just come from dinner at the sumptuous residence of his predecessor, General Hans von Boineburg-Lengsfeld, who had been relieved of the position six days earlier.

Choltitz' reputation had preceded him as a *ganz harter*—a hard-boiled guy—manifested in his battlefield record. He had been promoted to general during the seven-month siege of Sevastopol ending early in July two years ago. In that battle, he lost all but three hundred and forty-seven of forty-eight hundred men, and at its end, he bled from a wounded arm. But he had defeated the Soviet defenders and conquered the city.

General Lengsfeld, known as a dilettante, lived under suspicion of having participated in the plot, three weeks earlier, to assassinate Hitler at *Wolfsschanze*. The general had not been involved, but upon receipt of a message relating erroneous news that the dictator was dead, he had ordered the arrest of the twelve hundred *SS* and *Gestapo* officers in the city.

When later, he heard Hitler's piercing voice over the radio, he knew his days were numbered. The severity of his punishment remained to be seen.

Prior to the failed assassination, Lengsfeld had been ordered to defend Paris from the Allied onslaught. He had submitted plans to the German High Command for defensive positions south of the city designed to deflect an attack around Paris. His plans were deemed inadequate.

With two strikes against Lengsfeld, Hitler demanded that the general be replaced. The *führer* personally selected Choltitz, deeming the new commander's mission so important that he summoned the general to east Prussia to receive personal instruction. "Paris must be defended," he said when the two men met. "In every war across France, when Paris was lost, the war was lost. It controls the crossroads through it and the plains to the north."

Choltitz understood viscerally that Paris, beyond its strategic value, was the crown jewel among Hitler's conquests. After the *Wehrmacht* marched into France's capital, Hitler went there personally to survey the Eiffel Tower and visit Napoleon's tomb, among other sites. He liked to compare himself to the French conqueror, noting that both were foreigners to the countries they ruled, both had invaded Russia while preparing to invade England, and both had captured Vilna on the same day of the year.

Before leaving Paris, the *führer* had ordered two other actions: the transfer to Paris of Napoleon's son's remains from Vienna to be reinterred alongside those of his father, and the destruction of all monuments to the Great War. He did not care to leave reminders of Germany's defeat in 1918.

Standing in front of Hitler at the "wolf's lair" near Rastenburg, Choltitz listened to the haranguing of a man he had once admired but who now appeared withered, angry, and even insane. But the general came from a long line of aristocratic Prussian military officers. In his heart and soul, he was a combat soldier, and he followed orders.

Now, peering out his window at the Meurice and staring at the darkness surrounding the City of Lights, a vision formed in Choltitz' mind of the angry little man with the peculiar mustache giving the general his last instruction. "If Paris cannot be saved, level it. Flatten the city. Use demolitions, and destroy every building, every museum, art gallery, cathedral, school, hospital—" Hitler had grabbed Choltitz' arm. "Do you understand? Leave nothing standing."

The dictator had then conferred on him levels of power never before granted to any commanding general in any city under Third *Reich* control, including Paris. It granted him authority to requisition men and materiel and to take any and all actions to defend Paris or otherwise to convert it to rubble.

Another recollection played in Choltitz' mind on this evening in Paris, of an officer he had met on the train coming out of Rastenburg. By coincidence, the two had served together at an earlier time, and Choltitz' acquaintance was now a military attorney who had authored a newly promulgated law. It required that if an officer failed to perform his duty and the infraction warranted it, his family was to be arrested and, depending on severity of the failure, executed.

Now, thinking of the military attorney he had encountered on the train, and in light of the information the officer had passed along regarding the newly promulgated law, the "chance" meeting seemed beyond coincidental. A warning had been delivered: Choltitz was to obey orders concerning Paris, or his punishment would extend to his family.

Another recent memory tugged at him. Before traveling to his destination, he had stopped at home in Baden-Baden to see his wife, Uberta, herself the offspring of another long line of Prussian officers, and their two daughters, Maria and Anna, fourteen and eight years of age respectively. He doted on them, but aside from giving them a box of jams and jellies sent courtesy of the *führer*, he had little time to spend with them or with Uberta. He completed preparations and departed for Paris.

Choltitz now reflected on his conversation with Lengsfeld and another young German aristocrat who had attended their dinner. Lengsfeld had fought at Stalingrad and had seen the destruction. "Use my plans," he urged. "Avoid fighting in the city itself. Do nothing that could bring irreparable destruction to Paris."

Choltitz had remained stiff, his short, stocky frame filling his seat. He had his coffee without expression, but when shortly he rose to retire for the evening, he glanced about at the sumptuous furnishings and turned to Lengsfeld. "I need a headquarters, not a residence."

33

Same Day, August 11, 1944
Alençon, France

The jerries were on the run. Paul could feel it despite exhaustion after eleven hard days of moving and fighting since General Leclerc had landed on Utah beach with his 2nd French Armored Division.

Events had moved so fast in the past month that Paul could barely keep up with them. Finally, after two months and multiple major confrontations, Caen had fallen.

After Bradley completed Cobra to break out of bocage country, resistance crumbled against General Patton's XX Corps of his 3rd Army, which he deployed into Brittany to seal off Brittany's ports and cross the river at Avranches. Then he sent XV Corps east to liberate Le Mans, freeing other communities along the way.

On the same day that Caen fell, word from an Ultra message came through intelligence channels informing that, against advice of his generals, Hitler had ordered a counterattack. Operation Lüttich would launch across the Allied front to retake ground that the 3rd Army had captured after Cobra. Its final objective was Avranches, crucial for a *Wehrmacht* return of control in Brittany. The main battle had centered on Mortain, a town nestled among rolling hills twenty miles east of Avranches.

Without air support and facing overwhelming Allied air attacks as well as determined ground counterattacks by US First Army, the German drive stalled. News trickled in that the Germans were now planning to withdraw Army Group B. It included three *panzer* and two infantry divisions, a mix of five *panzer* and infantry battlegroups, and one hundred and fifty tanks and assault guns, minus an indeterminate number of casualties, captured soldiers, and destroyed equipment. Its commander, *Feldmarschall* von Rundstedt, was hell-bent on pushing his forces back to Germany.

Their expected route would remain in the north, traversing through Trun, Chambois, and Saint-Lambert, then skirting around Paris to the northwest, and finally driving east toward the Rhine River. That route would lead through a gap between Falaise and Argentan so narrow that in some places it was only seven hundred yards wide and included a small stream with steep banks that formed a natural barrier to vehicular traffic, including and especially tanks.

Four days ago, General Montgomery, anticipating the mass German retreat, ordered his major commands to converge around Falaise-Argentan to envelop the enemy. Three corps from US General Hodges' First Army would form the southern arm. Two British and one Canadian corps under British General Dempsey's Second Army would form the northern one. A third British corps, reinforced by the Polish 1st Armored Division, would drive the Germans from the west into the tiny Falaise Gap. The overall objective was to close the pincers at Chambois, east of Falaise, trap Army Group B in the resulting pocket, and capture or destroy the fleeing German army group.

For its part in the oncoming battle, Leclerc's 2nd Armored Division was detached from V Corps to support XV Corps in its drive to liberate Le Mans. Once accomplished, Leclerc received orders to deploy north to expel forces at Carrouges, which straddled a route that the US 1st Army's main body would need to traverse to position itself as the southern pincer near Argentan. On the way, he would pass through Alençon, which also must be held for the bridges that could otherwise afford retreating *Wehrmacht* troops safe passage across the Sarthe River.

General Leclerc was in a decidedly good mood when he returned from a commanders conference to his headquarters northeast of Le Mans. "We're going north," he told Paul. "The scenery is magnificent this time of year." He grinned, and Paul sensed his excitement. "We're leading this time," Leclerc exulted. "We'll be supported by the US 5th Armored and the US 79th and 90th Infantry Divisions." His eyes gleamed. "We're going to Alençon. It will be the first French city to be liberated by French forces."

When all was ready, Paul climbed into the back of Leclerc's M4. He had become accustomed to the general's audacity bordering on impulsiveness, but he recognized the man's unswerving commitment to being in the fight, leading where possible, and doing all he could to restore the honor that France's army had lost when it succumbed so easily and quickly to the German *blitzkrieg* four years ago.

"I've instructed my units to watch out on our right flank," Leclerc continued. "We'll be passing by the Ecouves Forest on our way to Alençon. Several German units are encamped there. One of the supporting divisions will roust them out."

He directed his driver to head toward a hillock from which he could watch his tanks and troop carriers spread out and begin the trek north. There, he dismounted and stood where he could observe progress through a pair of binoculars. Paul joined him.

Then the general handed the field glasses to Paul and pointed out where his tanks were deployed. "I've never been to Alençon, but according to my map, the Sarthe River is wide there. The Germans will want the bridges.

"It's an interesting place with several castles and prominent buildings. William the Conqueror came through in the mid-eleventh century. I don't know the details, but I've heard that when he demanded the castle's surrender, the people inside mocked him for being the grandson of a tanner by waving animal skins from the parapets. In retaliation, he cut off the hands and feet of thirty-two villagers. The castle then surrendered quickly, and so did the neighboring town."

Paul grimaced. "That's grim. It sounds like, temperamentally, he had a lot in common with Hitler and his Nazis."

"At least in Alençon he did." Leclerc looked around as the patrol started off. "Our latest intelligence is that no Germans are there now, but don't be surprised if we run into some. They're on the move."

By way of response, Paul patted his carbine and gestured toward the .50 Cal machine gun. "We'll be ready. The tables have turned. Now, they are the hunted."

As Leclerc's division approached Alençon shortly after nightfall, a dark-haired, round-faced youngster, roughly twenty years old, approached the lead elements and was swiftly escorted to Leclerc's vehicle. "My name is Raymond Ciroux," he announced. "I'm a local Resistant. No Germans are in the city now, but they've had patrols there. I think they'll be using our bridges on their way back to Germany."

Paul watched in amusement.

Raymond was obviously nervous. On seeing the American war machines and soldiers in American uniforms, he thought he had encountered an American unit. When greeted by French soldiers instead, he had been both overjoyed and disbelieving that such could be possible. Then, when presented to a French general, his eyes became reverential, his cheeks turned rosy, and he kept wiping his sweaty palms on his worn trousers. "I can guide you around and through the city and show you that no Germans are there now."

Leclerc regarded Raymond with mild sternness. "How do I know you are not a collaborator? You could lead us into a trap."

Raymond's eyes became big and round. He took a deep breath. "As God is my witness, I'm a French patriot. I can prove it. The Germans blow up bridges when they move east. Ours are whole, and they're not set with demolitions." He gulped. "If I'm lying, you can shoot me."

Leclerc allowed himself a small smile. "All right. Where is the nearest bridge?"

"Pont Neuf. Just inside the south city limit. There are two more bridges to the left and right of it, and more up and downstream. I'll show you all of them."

"Do you realize that my men could come under sniper fire?"

Wide-eyed, Raymond nodded.

"And if that happens, we will have you shot as a collaborator?"

Again, Raymond nodded.

Leclerc glanced at Paul. "Do you want to come along?"

Paul smiled. "I wouldn't miss it."

Pont Neuf proved to be just as Raymond had described it, as did the bridges on either side, each separated by a few hundred yards. With his security team led by *Capitaine* Henri Da, Leclerc and Paul followed in a jeep. As the two-platoon infantry patrol moved through the sleeping town, one of the squads encountered a German reconnaissance vehicle. They surrounded it and captured three German soldiers.

When the prisoners were brought to Leclerc, he was surprised at how demoralized and cooperative they were. Their rations had become scant, they said, their ammunition was running out, and they just wanted the war to be over—the Third *Reich* was a bad dream. Most significantly, they told him that their unit planned to occupy and hold Alençon for its river crossings.

Leclerc moved swiftly. He radioed back to his operations officer, Major André Gribius, and ordered the tanks moved forward to occupy positions covering every bridge and an infantry cordon established around the town. "Bring the full 2nd division forward. Position the support divisions to the left and right, and be ready with artillery to strike on the opposite side if needed. We'll send coordinates. Lastly, set up my headquarters somewhere along Rue Pont Neuf." Then he added, "We have three POWs to move to the rear. Get the adjutant to handle them."

The next morning, as they emerged from their homes and were greeted by French soldiers, the citizens of Alençon cheered. The *Wehrmacht* units had moved on without contesting possession. Alençon had been liberated without a shot.

Paul's reserved demeanor relaxed as he joined in the celebration of a joyous population extending their thanks for this unexpected first taste of freedom in four years. He shared in their pride later that morning when Raymond, in combat uniform, took his oath, with General Leclerc officiating, and joined the 2nd French Armored Division.

"I'll be an assistant tank driver," Raymond said happily through laughter. "I've never even touched one, or a machine gun."

"We'll teach you," Leclerc replied. "Now on to Carrouges."

34

August 13, 1944
Auteuil, France

Chantal knocked in the prescribed recognition sequence on the attic door of a fifth-floor apartment building in the western suburb of Paris. She knew only that she was there to meet the man whom Fourcade had told her about two weeks ago before coming to the capital city.

Chantal was to be his liaison to unknown parties, but she was not sure what a liaison did. Fourcade's explanation had been sparse, making the duties sound very much like those of a courier, but apparently more was expected in terms of her judgment. Chantal found that perception to be disconcerting irrespective of Fourcade's assurances that she was up to the task.

She heard the scoot of a chair scraping on the floor and light footsteps coming across a wooden floor. A bead of light appeared through a peephole as an inside cover was flipped aside. Moments later, the door opened a crack, and then widened most but not all the way.

A tall man with dark, wavy hair stood appraising her without expression. Then he smiled warmly. "Please, come in." He swept a long arm, gesturing for her to enter. "You are Papillon?"

Awed by the man's calm presence and reassured by his use of her codename, Chantal nodded. He was young, perhaps thirty, she guessed, maybe a year or two younger, but he carried himself with the dignity of a much older man and with an easy grace that did much to put her at ease.

As she stepped inside, he closed the door. "I've been anxious to meet you," he said as he followed her into the single, long room. "Madame Fourcade and the man you know as Dragon both recommended you highly for this job. Dragon told me how you helped the artist Robert Douin with his sketches of the Normandy coast. I understand you were also involved in the reconnaissance at Bruneval that gave insights into German radar technology. Both of those missions were significant to winning the war. My congratulations."

Chantal stood, uncertain of what she should do. The sloped roof of the attic cast shadows into corners from a weak light that hung from its rafters. Dormer windows had been shuttered, and heavy blackout drapes hung over them.

"I'm sorry," the man said. "This isn't very comfortable, but for the moment, it's the best we can do. I move from place to place for such meetings. We're unlikely to meet here again." He took a wooden folding chair leaning against a wall, opened it, and indicated for Chantal to take a seat.

As she sat, she asked, "Would you please tell me what I am here to do?"

The man stared at her. Then his face broke into an amused smile. He turned a chair around from a table and sat down. "No one told you?"

Chantal shook her head. "Not in detail."

He laughed. "My name is Jacques Michel Pierre Delmas. My *nom de guerre* is Chaban, and I have the honor of representing Charles de Gaulle in Paris. He saw fit to make me a general in his secret army. I command nothing, but my current task is to ensure that no insurrection arises in Paris." He paused and leaned toward her. "You are to help me in that mission."

Taken aback, Chantal gulped. "General de Gaulle?"

"The one and only," Chaban said. "I asked for someone with very specific qualifications. You were sent." He chuckled. "I understand that you can meld into a crowd, and that you do a wonderful impersonation of a little girl—on demand. Or, you can stand your ground if need be, and you have no problem handling weapons."

Color rose to Chantal's cheeks. "I do what the occasion calls for."

"Then you'll be perfect." He pulled his chair close to hers. "Let's get down to business. The task we face is impossible." He took a deep breath. "How much do you know about the political situation within the Resistance, particularly here in Paris?"

Chantal shook her head. "Not much. Madame Fourcade explained some of it to me, but I found it quite confusing. I thought we were all fighting for France."

Chaban frowned. "You're a patriot. That's good, and victory is near, at least in Paris. The people can smell it. But factions are already staking out political territory. Like us, they want to throw the *boche* out, but some want power after we're liberated. Our job is also to prevent civil war. Those orders come not just from General de Gaulle but also from General Eisenhower."

Chantal leaped to her feet, breathing hard. "General Eisenhower?" she exclaimed. "I know nothing of politics and don't want to. I'm a fighter, I only want to see France free. But orders coming from Eisenhower are, are—" She grasped for words.

Chaban raised his hands in a placating gesture. "You'll do well." He indicated the chair. "Please sit. I'll simplify."

When Chantal had re-taken her seat, he went on. "I need for you to gather and pass along information. That's all. But I need you to understand the context, who the players are, and how to interact with each one.

"Here's the situation: Senior Resistance leaders created the Committee for National Resistance, or CNR, to coordinate and direct the activities of the French Resistance. General de Gaulle is represented on the committee by a man named Alexandre Parodi. The president of the committee is Georges Bidault.

"Don't worry too much about the names. If time allows, and I'm not sure it will, you'll learn them. I'll brief you on the people who are important for our purposes.

"The two main groups on the CNR are the Gaullists and the Communists. The loyalties of the Gaullists are obvious, but the loyalties of the Communists are influenced by a group known as the FTP and are therefore questionable. The trouble is that they've been very active in resisting the

Germans. They've built a huge organization that runs a large part of the Resistance in France generally and in Paris in particular. They're very strong in the unions, growing daily, and we have reason to believe that they take their orders from Moscow—Joseph Stalin."

Chantal scoffed. "Moscow? Stalin? How can that be?"

Chaban smacked his lips. "How much do you know about the Soviet Union?"

"Nothing, really, but I don't see the sense of throwing off one foreign ruler only to invite in another one. Madame Fourcade says that Stalin is as bad as Hitler."

Chaban smiled. "That's as simple as it gets, and your logic is sound." He pursed his lips. "Have you heard about the German operation in the Wola neighborhood of Warsaw eleven days ago?"

"Vaguely. I heard that something happened there, but I don't know any details."

Chaban cocked his head to one side and lifted his eyebrows. "It was a slaughter. As the Germans advanced into Warsaw, it systematically massacred between forty and fifty thousand residents. They even forced the surviving men to burn the bodies to cover the evidence. Then, the Germans leveled the city." He paused. "Here's the main point regarding Stalin and Warsaw. His army was just a few miles away, and he could have stopped the bloodbath and the destruction. He did nothing."

Chaban let the statement sink in, and then continued. "So much for a Soviet ally. You might recall that the UK and France went into this war to save Poland.

"The bigger issue where we're concerned is that there's no reason to think that the Germans wouldn't do the same thing to Paris. One of their demolitions experts is in town. We know who he is, Captain Werner Ebernach of the 813th *Pionierkompanie*, but he travels under heavy escort. If we tried to stop him directly, we'd invite certain destruction of those sites he's already prepared. In addition to the explosives already in Paris and what he brought with him, he's requisitioned over three hundred torpedoes he found stored in a kilometer-long tunnel belonging to Pilz. That's a munitions factory in Saint-Cloud, a few miles east of here. With those torpedoes he has sufficient material to blow every bridge in Paris.

"He's placed heavy explosives in the Louvre, under Notre-Dame, and in and around all our historical monuments and buildings, every bridge into the city, and all the factories around its periphery. Also, as of five days ago, Paris has a new commanding general, Choltitz. He gained prominence with the *Wehrmacht* and was promoted to his current rank for his destruction of Sevastopol. If there's anyone who would execute an order to blow up Paris, he's the one."

Chantal listened in a daze. She took a deep breath. "Sir, you're scaring me."

"Good. I need for you to grasp how serious the situation is." He walked to his desk, picked up a piece of paper, and handed it to Chantal. "This is a message I sent to London a few days ago." He took his seat once again.

As Chantal read, she felt the blood drain from her face.

"Paris situation extremely touchy. Strikes of police, railroads, posts and developing tendencies to general strike. All conditions necessary for an insurrection have been realized. Local incidents, whether spontaneous, provoked by enemy, or even impatient resistance groups, will be enough to lead to gravest troubles with bloody reprisals for which Germans seem to have already taken decisions and assembled necessary means. Situation worsening with paralysis of public utilities: no gas, hour and half electricity daily, water lacking in some parts of town, food situation disastrous. Necessary you intervene with allies to demand rapid occupation Paris. Officially warn population in sharpest most precise terms possible via BBC to avoid new Warsaw."

Chantal looked up at Chaban, dread in her eyes. "What will we do?" she whispered.

Chaban leaned toward her. "Do you trust de Gaulle?"

Chantal took her time to respond. "I think so. I'm from Dunkirk. I was there and saw the British evacuation and the German onslaught that followed. I remember how terrified and desperate we all were. I was too young to understand all that was happening, but a German soldier tried to rape me. My sister found him on top of me and beat him off with a shovel."

She stopped talking and stared. Finally, she said, "I've said too much."

"No, please go on. What did your sister do?"

Emotion overcame Chantal, and she took a breath. "She killed him with that shovel," she said bitterly. "Then a German officer came after our family." Her voice broke. "We fled with our father, so that officer arrested and executed some of the men in our neighborhood. He was looking for us."

She bent over, shaking with grief. "He killed our father."

Chaban rose slowly and placed a comforting hand on her shoulder. "And then you killed him," he said softly.

Chantal brought both hands to her face and fought back tears. Her head bobbed slightly in tormented confirmation.

"You tried to save your father," Chaban said softly. "Madame Fourcade told me. You pushed the German officer over a cliff."

Sobbing, Chantal nodded. "I was fourteen," she cried, unable to stop herself. "We lost both of our parents."

Chaban leaned over and put both arms around her shoulders. "You're brave."

After a few moments, Chantal pushed away. "You asked if I trust de Gaulle," she said, her voice hoarse and halting. "We heard him on the radio, calling on all of us to fight for France, for our homes, for our country. We joined the fight, my sister and I."

Her voice regained strength. "I don't know the general, or even what he looks like. But I know his voice from listening to the BBC on forbidden radios for four years, and he inspired us through that dark, miserable time. I'll trust him until I have reason not to, and I'll never trust anyone who wants to submit France to foreign rule. That's not what we fought for. I want a free France."

Chaban stood back and scrutinized Chantal. "I see why Fourcade selected you. I knew your age, and I had my doubts, even when I first saw you. But I think her judgment was correct. Let's get to work. I need to brief you thoroughly."

He returned to his seat. "I should tell you that the Allies will bypass Paris. They won't come until the war in France is won and the Germans here are isolated. I was in London two weeks ago. I went to convince the Allies to liberate Paris immediately. I failed. We won't receive military support anytime soon."

Chantal listened with rising dread. "Madame Fourcade had figured that out. Hearing you state it as fact is disastrous. What will we do?"

"Have you been to see some of the Resistance groups in the city?"

Chantal nodded. "Madame Fourcade arranged several introductions through her contacts. They were all low key. Nothing much made out of my being there. It was more like I was just another recruit. In some cases there were other new people, so I didn't come off as anything special. Oh, and I got a job in the telephone exchange at the Prefecture of Police."

"That's excellent, and not accidental," Chaban said. "I'll talk about its significance shortly, but let me caution you not to reveal political beliefs at all, to anyone. If asked, act dumb and pliable—"

"I can do that," Chantal said, and laughed for the first time.

"Good. The Communists might try to recruit you. Play along but be careful. Two weeks ago, they tried to recruit a young man, Yvon Morandat. He refused, and then a week later, he was nearly run over by a car while riding his bicycle. He's convinced that the Communists deliberately tried to kill him—"

"One of our own?" Chantal demanded in shock.

Chaban nodded and sighed. "I'm afraid so. Some people will do anything for power. But you have to be careful around the Gaullists too—"

"You're a Gaullist—"

"Yes, but understand that the stakes are very high. We're talking about who will lead the nation when the Germans leave. The Americans plan to establish a military governorship. De Gaulle will not accept that. Neither will the Gaullists, nor the Communists. Each group has its own committee that appoints representatives to the CNR. De Gaulle's representative there, Parodi, the man I mentioned earlier, is good.

"All the others on the CNR have designs on how power should be structured, post-occupation. I'm sure that neither of the two major groups intends to include the other. The Communists will attempt to sideline de Gaulle, and the Gaullists will try to shunt him into an advisory role while staking out central positions for themselves. The CNR is not the same as the general's Committee for National Liberation, the CNL. The CNL is de Gaulle's committee, which appointed Parodi to the CNR."

Chantal listened intently, but she began shaking her head in bewilderment. "I don't understand. Why would this CNR do these things? Why wouldn't they work with de Gaulle. The people have suffered so much. It feels like a betrayal."

"It could end that way. We've got to stop it. The people are with de Gaulle. We have to pave the way for his entry to Paris to assume authority. He's formed a government-in-exile, appointed ministers who already act on behalf of France, and formed an army of over half a million men that includes our troops from North Africa who had been under Vichy control. We have two divisions fighting now, one under General de Lattre to liberate Toulon and Marseille, and another under General Leclerc at Normandy. Those divisions will come this way, but perhaps not in time to save Paris. It's up to us to act here."

Chaban's passion rose, captivating Chantal. Her eyes glistened as she watched and listened to him.

"As you say, de Gaulle inspired our people during their darkest days," Chaban continued. "Who else can say that? I know the man, and I can tell you without a single doubt that he is for France. He loves our country and our people, and everything he does is to free us from these *boche* slave masters."

Chantal took a deep breath. "I believe you," she cried with a sudden surge of determined energy. "Tell me what to do."

Chaban's eyes lit up. "I get caught up too. Planning for a free France is exhilarating." His face grew solemn. "Our first fear is of an insurrection against the Germans. Parisians expect the Allies to liberate us. That won't happen until the rest of France is secure. Our people grow impatient with the hellish living conditions the Germans created. But we don't have nearly enough arms or ammunition to take up the fight ourselves—about one rifle for every two members in the Resistance. If we fought the Germans now, we'd be slaughtered, and that would happen without considering their tanks and artillery weapons.

"The next fear is civil war. Assuming we boot the *boche*, the Gaullists and Communists are likely to start shooting each other."

"That's frightening."

"It is. That's where you come in. I need early warning. Right now, you can move among both groups easily. I need to know when there is an inkling of plans coming together to take armed action against the Germans.

"We talked earlier about the police. Both the Communists and the Gaullists want to control the Paris police force. That's twenty thousand men. Whoever controls them will control Paris, although, yesterday, Choltitz disarmed them. In retaliation, they've gone on strike. But they're a disciplined group that can fight.

"Being on the ground and in the telephone exchange, you'll hear what's happening before I learn anything from the CNR. The two groups won't inform each other. I need to know as soon as you hear of anything happening."

Chantal took time to absorb and think through all she had heard. Finally, she said, "I have a question. I can't be the only one doing this—"

Chaban chuckled. "Your experience shows, despite your age. We have various informants, some good, some not. I'm counting on you to bring me reliable information on which I can act. That's all I can say about other sources."

"Will the members of the CNR know about me?"

Chaban shook his head. "No. I'm the only one who'll know your status. Those you meet in the Resistance will know only what you tell them, and your role with me must be kept secret."

Chantal drew a deep breath and let it out. "I understand. But what if we fail? What if we do all we can and the insurrection still happens?"

Chaban smiled distantly. "We have contingencies."

Chantal sat wordlessly for an extended time, mulling. The notion that she could be significant in saving Paris seemed beyond imagining. Her life had been at risk since the German invasion north of Dunkirk. Chaban's plan for her seemed neither more nor less risky than anything else she had done, irrespective of the proximity to de Gaulle and Eisenhower. She breathed out slowly. "I'll do my best."

"Good. Let's establish how we communicate and I'll identify the leaders you'll need to watch for."

35

Same Day, August 13, 1944
Digne-les-Bains, France

Claude Renoir, grandson of the late great painter and now serving as a Red Cross driver currently taxiing SOE operative Lieutenant Colonel Francis Cammaerts, codenamed Roger, and two of his colleagues to Seyne, glanced in his rearview mirror. "There's a car pulling in behind us," he warned. "I think it's the *Gestapo*. They look like they want to stop us."

Roger turned in the front passenger seat and glanced out the back window. "You are correct," he said jauntily. "No use trying to outrun them. Pull over. Our 'authentic' fake papers need to get us through once more."

He had been traveling for days with Renoir and two subordinate SOE field operators, Xan Fielding and Christian Sorenson. Early that morning, the three had met in the village of Apt with officials of de Gaulle's Free French government-in-exile who delivered to Fielding a large sum of money to be distributed for living expenses to Resistance members around Roger's current headquarters at Seyne-les-Alpes.

The morning drive had been so pleasant that the war seemed far distant, the atmosphere like being on holiday. Their reverie ended abruptly on reaching the outskirts of Digne when an Allied air strike hit the town. Sirens sounded, and Renoir sought shelter for the Red Cross-emblazoned car.

On leaving the Vercors twenty-three days earlier, Roger and Pauline had been driven by car to the western rim of the Vercors with several *maquisards*. There, they descended on foot to the valley along the river Drôme. Heading south to Die, they passed through Saint-Nazaire-le-Désert and Savournon, and finally arrived at Seyne. Having traveled one hundred and thirty-five miles in twenty-four hours, much of it on foot, they collapsed, exhausted, and slept for hours.

They had no time to dwell on the atrocities at the Vercors or its betrayal. A new assignment awaited Pauline when she awoke. She was to go south of the French-Italian border. Roger reluctantly saw her off on the back of a veteran Resistance member's motorcycle. There, she was to help plan and organize a Resistance operation for upsetting German traffic between two roads in the Italian Alps. The group she joined had over two hundred members. It was the only one in the vicinity capable of dominating the mountain heights in the region and denying them to the Germans.

The mission coincided with a major German offensive during which Pauline passed through German lines several times. Three times, she was detained for questioning. She had perfected the ability of morphing into the role of a naïve peasant girl, complete with a scarf around her neck; and twice she secured her own release by playing the part perfectly.

On the third occasion, she and a group of partisans were detained. Her captors intended to lead them to a detention facility. Pauline had then held her hands over her head with a live grenade and threatened to blow everyone "to hell" if they were not released. Her German guards scampered away.

When her mission in Italy was completed, Pauline traveled to Col de Madeleine, a high mountain pass where a German-held fortress dominated the supply routes into Digne. Learning that it was manned largely by impressed soldiers from her native Poland, she had taken one and a half days to scale the nearly two-thousand-foot heights. There, calling loudly to her countrymen in their own language over a megaphone, she convinced them to desert the *Wehrmacht* and join with the Resistance. Her success scuttled German plans for an attack over the pass against American forces moving northeast.

Meanwhile, Roger traveled to Gap to prepare for and attend a secret meeting on August 8. He represented the Allies using his real identity as Colonel Francis Cammaerts and met with the military leadership of two *Maquis* groups, La Bâtie-Neuve and La Rochette. In attendance were Colonel l'Hermine and six other commanders. *Chef* Paul Héraud, code-named "Commander Dumont," presided over the conference.

Héraud had become a legendary operator in the Hautes-Alpes, having unified the two *Maquis* groups and then leading them. A mountain climber since his youth, he was in tough physical condition with a high forehead and piercing eyes. He had come to the Resistance early in 1941 and organized the department into sectors. His combination of physical ability, intellectual pursuit, and personal charisma had won over the loyalty of countless *maquisards* of various political stripes. They set aside their differences to liberate France.

When the war had begun, Héraud had refused to accept that France was permanently subdued. He studied the art of war in depth and set up leadership schools and training for Resistance fighters. Since Roger's arrival in France, the two had worked together extensively, and their trained fighters had gone on to sabotage factories, track down collaborators, provide security for the friendly forces and individuals, identify landing fields for clandestine aircraft and paratroopers, and organize units for recovering Allied supply drops. Héraud's cells had operated as far south as Gardanne and Marseille, and he had also cooperated with activities in Sector R2, another area within Roger's responsibilities.

At the meeting, Héraud had presented a plan for the liberation of Gap that was detailed, thorough, and immediately accepted. Unfortunately, the following day, he was killed in a German ambush.

Roger thought about Héraud as he journeyed on this beautiful day back toward Seyne, where he would reunite with Pauline after these many days. "These 'many days,'" he muttered to himself sardonically. *We only left the Vercors three weeks ago. It feels like decades.*

He thought again of Héraud's killing. Was it the result of betrayal or a coincidence? If a betrayal, by whom? He grunted. *We'll probably never know.*

He let out a breath. The thought of betrayal brought to mind the events on the Vercors, arousing bitterness. *We know who promised and who failed to deliver.*

He dismissed the thought as not useful. *I wonder where Jeremy is.*

Then, as Renoir drove into Digne, the Allied air strike commenced.

Sirens blared. Renoir steered the car off the main street into the cover of trees. With the Red Cross adorning its sides and roof, he doubted that it would become a direct target, but the chance of being hit by a nearby explosion was not insignificant.

"Split up," Roger ordered. "We'll meet at the largest intersection on the eastern edge of town. Renoir, drive the car there and watch for us."

The hasty plan had worked. All had reached the opposite edge of Digne safely, but no sooner had they regrouped and started off again than they were stopped at a checkpoint by a group of Mongol sentries that had been dragooned into forced labor by the Germans. Far from their homes in the Soviet eastern provinces, the Mongols were now employed in regulating the daily activities of residents of France. Unable to read the identity papers but apparently unwilling to demonstrate that such was the case, the guards let all four men go.

Roger studied the Mongols unobtrusively, wondering if any of them had participated in the marauding of Saint-Donat ahead of the assault on the Vercors plateau. Once again dismissing an idle thought, he settled into his seat. They had barely started up again when Renoir informed them of the *Gestapo* car behind them.

Next Day, August 14, 1944
Seyne-les-Alpes, France

Pauline's sense of well-being overrode her exhaustion as she entered the gorgeous little town. It sat on rolling hills at the base of snow-capped mountains ranging in a U-shape around it. Pauline gazed at the peaks, enjoying their beauty yet glad to be out of them for a while. Here in Seyne, she could unwind. Arriving at a whitewashed house with a red-tile roof, she greeted her host, Monsieur Turrel, and flopped into a chair to relax and take in the view from the wide downstairs veranda. When Turrel brought her a glass of wine, he found her fast asleep.

She was awakened by an anxious Claude Renoir shaking her shoulder. "I'm sorry, Pauline, but you must wake up."

As her eyes fluttered and started to close, he shook her again. "Pauline, the *Gestapo* has Roger. They detained him yesterday ago. We must rescue him."

Pauline sat up straight, her eyes wide open, fatigue forgotten. "When, where, how?" The questions flooded her mind, and she fought to order them.

Another man, Dr. Jouve, was with Renoir. Pauline had met the doctor before but did not know him well.

"We were stopped in Digne," Renoir said. He explained that somewhere along the trip before arriving in Digne, Fielding had decided that, if they were stopped, carrying the large amount of money provided to them for the Resistance groups might arouse suspicion. Therefore, he decided to split it up into three bundles, with himself, Roger, and Sorenson each carrying one of them.

"That turned out to be a big mistake," Renoir said. "The *Gestapo* had no problem with our papers," he explained. "They searched us and found the money. Initially, that was not a problem. They asked how we knew each other. I told them that they were just men along the way seeking a ride. Fielding said that he had never met any of us before. But then, a *Gestapo* officer in civilian clothes who had been inspecting the money noticed that the bills were all from the same sequence of serial numbers.

"He asked us, 'How do three men who've never met have large sums of money belonging to the same series?'"

Renoir took a deep breath. "They let me go because I'm a legitimate driver for the Red Cross, and I was easy to check out. But they took Roger, Fielding, and Sorenson for questioning."

Pauline forced her mind to take in all that she had heard. "Do you know where they took them?"

Renoir shook his head. "Probably to the local *gendarmeries*. The *Gestapo* doesn't have a large presence in Digne, so they don't have any holding facilities."

"What's the distance from here to Digne?"

"About twenty miles."

"Then first we need to establish that our friends are there, in that jail. I think I know how to do that." Pauline glanced at her watch. "We still have time today," she declared, leaping to her feet.

"I'll drive you," Renoir volunteered.

"You can't go back into Digne. You'll be picked up. But we've got to get Roger out. When they find out who he is, they'll torture him, and he'll be the first to tell you that every man breaks. More lives, Resistance cells, and operations are at risk." She stood up straight and placed her hands on her hips. "Get me a bicycle."

Renoir stared at her. "Pauline, you're terrified of bicycles. I'll drive you."

She shook her head. "I'll get over it. You can't drive me, and I don't have a permit to drive a Red Cross car. We can't afford a slip-up. Get me a bicycle."

While Renoir went to comply, Jouve approached her. "*Mademoiselle*," he said, "I have a contact at the *gendarmeries*, a Captain Albert Schenk. He's Alsation and speaks German fluently, so he acts as a liaison officer between the French and German authorities. He's a double-agent, but he might help you."

"Or he might turn me in."

Jouve nodded. "That's a possibility."

Pauline grunted. "I'll keep his name at the back of my mind."

Word reached another of Roger's colleagues about his plight. Captain Havard Gunn, a rugged Scottish soldier of the Seaforth Highlanders and seconded to one of the Jedburgh teams, was sixty miles east of Digne at Valberg when he heard the news. Immediately determined to break Roger free by an armed raid if necessary, he recognized that he did not have the resources to bring it about.

On that same day, the 1st Allied Airborne Task Force, under the command of General Robert Fredericks, parachuted into the Argens Valley between Le Luc and Le Muy. They landed behind the Massif des Maures, a key piece of terrain overlooking the Allies' intended amphibious landing beaches near Saint-Tropez and Saint-Raphaël on France's Mediterranean shore as the vanguard of Operation Dragoon. Their mission: to block German forces from reinforcing coastal defenses.

Gunn, knowing well the immense damage that could be meted out if the Germans discovered Roger's identity, set out from Valberg to seek the highest Allied officer he could find. Late in the afternoon, he was escorted to see Fredericks at a sprawling farmhouse near Le Mitan, just over two miles north of Le Muy.

Fredericks had barely arrived when two officers brought Gunn into his office, set up in the largest of the farmhouse's bedrooms. He regarded Gunn without comment, taking in his Scottish regalia complete with kilt.

"This guy demanded to see the commanding general," one of the officers said. "He claims to be an SOE agent and that he worked with our OSS guys. He says he has information crucial to this operation."

Gunn immediately recognized Fredericks as the legendary commando who, as a lieutenant colonel in 1942, had been tasked to raise the 1st Special Service Force, a new US-Canadian regiment-sized commando unit intended for an operation in Norway.

Physically and mentally tough, Fredericks combed his dark hair close to his scalp, wore a trimmed mustache, and kept his square jaw meticulously shaved. He was fearless in battle and ardent in the care of his troops, for which they were deeply loyal.

When the mission to Norway was scrubbed, the unit was first sent to the Aleutians and then to Italy. There, Fredericks led reconnaissance and combat patrols against the enemy at Monte la Remetanea, Monte Sammucro, and Monte Vischiataro. During those actions, he was wounded three times.

He earned his place in history by taking Monte La Difensa. The mountain was crucial to the Allied advance northward, but it was fiercely defended by the Germans. From a plateau at its crest, the *Wehrmacht* had placed artillery and heavy machine guns with clear views of all approaches from the south. At the rear of the position were vertical cliffs hundreds of feet high.

Fredericks volunteered his regiment to approach the cliffs under cover of night, wait until dawn, and scale them. He joined his men in the attack from behind, and drove the Germans beyond a rocky ridgeline that had been their main line of defense. Left with no cover, the *Wehrmacht* unit surrendered. Fredericks had executed the plan so successfully that the Allies occupied the summit, and the Germans dubbed his commandos "The Devil's Brigade."

Because of his successes, he became a favorite of General Clark, who, when planning the 5th Army's entry into Rome, sent Fredericks, by then a colonel, and the Devil's Brigade to reconnoiter, becoming the first Allied unit to enter the Eternal City. Then, two months ago, Fredericks had relinquished the commando regiment, was promoted to brigadier general, and took command of the 1st Allied Airborne Task Force. He had just jumped into southern France with his paratroopers.

Knowing Fredericks' reputation, Gunn counted on an open ear, but the general was skeptical of Gunn's insistence that Roger be rescued. "Look, Captain," Fredericks said, "I'm sympathetic to rescuing anyone from the Germans. But the Allies' main body for this invasion has not even landed yet. Tell me why I should traipse all the way to Digne to rescue one man."

"Because he's not just any man, sir. He's the heart and soul of the Jockey network, one of the most effective Resistance organizations in France." Very quickly, Gunn outlined Roger's involvement in organizing the network, consisting of twenty thousand Resistance members operating from north of Lyon to the French southern coast, and executing hundreds of sabotage missions. He told of Jeremy's work in the Vercors, which Roger set up and oversaw; and of Pauline's success in the Italian Alps and in turning the Polish troops at Col de la Madeleine.

"Sir, Roger will readily tell you that every man can be broken. What's in his head could sink a lot of operations, delay victory in France, and cost thousands of lives. It's in Allied interests to save him."

Fredericks scrutinized Gunn. Then he turned to an aide standing by his office door. "Get this checked out," he ordered, "top priority." Turning back to Gunn, he said, "Let's see what comes out of London and then do what makes sense."

36

Same Day, August 14, 1944
Seyne-les-Alpes

Pauline pedaled uncertainly down the road on a rickety bicycle in the guise of a peasant, her scarf wrapped around her neck. She laughed at her own irrational fear of the bicycle—after all, she was an accomplished horsewoman and mountaineer. Yet she detested bicycles in the same way that she detested firearms. She had used both in the field on SOE missions, but she never felt comfortable with them. She disliked the noise of gunfire and the need to constantly clean guns, and she avoided their use and bicycles whenever possible. And now she would cycle to Digne, a twenty-mile ride, and she would probably need to do the trip several times. "*C'est la vie,*" she murmured.

She arrived in the town in midafternoon and made her way to the *gendarmerie*. People, concerned about friends and relatives who had been detained, milled about in front of the office.

Pauline approached a guard. "My husband is in here," she said. "How can I get to see him?"

The guard gave her a dismissive glance. "You can't. It's not allowed."

Given his hard-nosed expression, Pauline did not press the matter with him. Instead, she wandered around observing the sentries. While she meandered, she deliberately hummed a song, "Frankie and Johnny." It was one that she and Roger had sung together many times during dark circumstances or to pass the time while traveling between destinations. The words and the melody lifted their spirits. If Roger was within earshot, he would recognize the song and Pauline's voice.

Suddenly, from the recesses of the jail, she heard the stentorian tones of Roger's voice belting out the first line of the song. "Frankie and Johnny were sweethearts..."

Pauline froze in place. *Roger's alive, and he knows I'm here.*

Repressing an urge to show any emotion, she continued to survey the guards. Against a wall, she spotted an older one with graying hair and a kindly face.

She approached him and said, "My husband is in here. I'd like to get some small things to him that he'll need to keep himself clean, and maybe a little food."

The man shook his head.

"Then can you take me to Captain Schenk's office?" she asked.

The old man peered at her, but his eyes softened. "I can do that. Wait here."

He came back a few minutes later and told Pauline that the captain had agreed to see her. She had rehearsed in her mind what to say. *He's French. Impress him. Don't implore.*

Schenk sat at his desk leaning over a document with pen in hand. He did not look up when Pauline was announced.

She advanced to his desk and watched him momentarily. Then she slammed her hand flat on the document the captain was reading.

He glanced up in shock.

"My husband is a high-level British spy held in your jail right now with two others," she hissed. "I'm also a British spy. You must have heard the rumors that Allied troops had dropped above Saint-Tropez." She jabbed a finger onto Schenk's desk. "The Allies are coming. They will be here, in Digne, within days. If my husband is killed or harmed, you will pay. If the Allies don't arrest you, the Resistance will torture and hang you in revenge for all their compatriots you've imprisoned and executed."

Schenk continued to stare. Then a small smile crossed his face, and he leaned back in his chair. "You do know that I could have you arrested right here, right now?"

Pauline leaned toward him. "And you must know that you've been identified within the Resistance as a double-agent, and we can leave proof where the *Gestapo* can find it. People are waiting to hear what I accomplish in here right now. If I don't come out soon, in healthy shape, and with an agreement, things will go badly for you."

Schenk's face darkened while he pondered. If the Allies invaded on the southern shore, as expected, and pressed northward, local retribution would be unleashed. He could suffer. Finally he said, "I have no authority to order your husband's release or that of his colleagues. Perhaps Max Waem can help."

"Who?"

"He's Belgian and the official interpreter for the *Gestapo*." Schenk pursed his lips. "It'll cost you."

"Money?" Pauline asked. She let out a derisive laugh. "How much?"

"Two million francs."

Pauline did a quick mental calculation. *About seventeen thousand US dollars.*

Her mind raced. Time was short. The *Gestapo* was undoubtedly checking Roger's identity papers at this very moment, and the money would have to be transported from London by a Lysander night flight. "Done," she said. "Set up the meeting with Max. I'll bring the money." She leaned over the desk and brought her face close to Schenk's. "If you betray me, I will hunt you down and shoot you myself."

That night, after a grueling nighttime trip back to Seyne over the rough road, much of the time pushing her bicycle, she radioed a message to London, stressing the urgency. The next afternoon at four o'clock, she waited in Schenk's apartment for Max's arrival. Schenk had insisted on that location to avoid eavesdropping.

He came late, dressed in full black *Gestapo* uniform, a small man with aquiline features. Pauline began by thrusting a handful of broken wireless/telegraph crystals at him. "I'm in constant contact with British forces," she said matter-of-factly. She repeated what she had said to Schenk about the coming Allied invasion. "You have limited time before their troops come to Digne, and then things will go badly for anyone connected with harming my husband or his colleagues."

After three hours, during which the price for cooperation never changed—a sign that Pauline held the upper hand—Max asked, "How will I be protected?"

Pauline rose from her chair across from Max. She took a deep breath. "Under authority of the British government and upon safe delivery to my custody of my husband and the two men with him, I extend to you and Captain Schenk my government's protection. The help you both provide will save you."

Pauline's chest constricted as she rode the twenty miles back to Seyne on the bicycle, which she now loathed. London had never delivered on a request for specific support in such a short time. They must deliver that night. If not...

37

August 15, 1944
Fresnes, France

Jeannie Rousseau brought her arms up to shield her face from the German officer hovering over her. Then, as her eyes became accustomed to the dim light seeping through the open door of her windowless cell, she saw that a crucifix hung from his belt under his tunic.

"I am Abbé Steinert," he told her and four other prisoners huddled together in the tiny cell. "I've come to pray with you and to offer communion to provide strength for your coming ordeal."

Jeannie regarded him dully. She had seen him on occasion since entering the prison, but she had not interacted with him, so she had no idea what kind of person he was. "What time is it?"

"Four o'clock in the morning."

"What ordeal are we about to experience that's worse than the one we're in?"

Steinert regarded her stoically. His lot was to minister to the prisoners, a duty that would challenge the staunchest among the faithful. "The entire women's section of the prison will transfer today to Ravensbrück. That's a women's prison near Berlin."

Jeannie drew a deep breath. She knew of Ravensbrück, a place where women were imprisoned for slave work in German arms factories until they dropped dead. She looked at her arms. They were already skeletal from the ravages of a single bowl of thin soup each night that was her entire day's ration. Here at Fresnes, her torment derived from forced inactivity in a crowded cell amid the stench of inhuman hygienic conditions. At Ravensbrück, she imagined, the misery would be compounded by the replacement of inactivity with forced, unceasing, back-breaking labor. She doubted that the food portion would increase.

Jeannie had arrived at the Fresnes Prison in early May following her capture at Saint-Brieuc a few days earlier. She had been arrested under a made-up name that she had shouted out as the *Gestapo* detained her, but on processing into the facility, she had given her actual name, Jeannie Rousseau. As a result, the administration had no record of why she was arrested but kept her anyway.

As Steinert had predicted, four hours after he had awakened her and her companions, the skeletal women joined a procession of other women in similar states, hundreds of them, plodding listlessly in a line to buses waiting at the main gate. As usual, shouting guards lined their way, prodding and pushing them with submachine guns, and huge German Shepherd dogs lunged at them, snarling and sometimes sinking teeth into a passing unfortunate.

The guards squeezed as many women as possible into the bus. Then the drivers followed a *kübelwagen* for the few miles to Gare du Nord.

During the transit, recently detained prisoners passed along news they had heard prior to being arrested. One piece they all shared was of the Allied invasion at Normandy. It had stalled, some said, but Caen and Cherbourg had fallen, and the Allies kept pouring more and more troops and supplies into Normandy. General Patton had crossed a river at Avranches and was heading east. A fierce battle raged at Falaise.

The most repeated bit of gossip was that the Germans were in a panic to retreat inside their own borders, and they needed the additional labor to keep up with their weapons production. That was why entire prison populations from all over Europe were being shipped to Germany.

Jeannie had no idea whether to believe any of it. At the time of her capture, an Allied invasion was still a dream, and aside from Resistance activities like her own, the Germans were in full control of every facet of life. *Could things have turned so fast?*

Despite the conditions, the news and rumors lifted spirits. A sense permeated that perhaps deliverance was still in the women's futures.

Paris, France

Amélie stood along the platform at the Gare du Nord, awaiting the arrival of the buses from Fresnes Prison. Word had spread throughout Paris that the Germans were loading cattle cars at the station and shipping the inmates to other camps and detainment facilities in Germany. She had joined groups of people waiting for glimpses of loved ones to be transferred, fearful that this might be the last time they ever saw them.

Other buses had arrived with male prisoners. The frightful sight was beyond imagining, the cruelty displayed beyond comprehension. As a bus pulled in, the passengers were shouted out, goaded along at bayonet point with snarling dogs, to join already forming similar lines and climb aboard long, windowless boxcars.

They were sad vestiges of human beings, their drab prison garbs hanging loosely on undernourished bodies. Many had distended stomachs, unnaturally large eyes, and bare patches on their scalps where hair had fallen out. They moved mostly in silence

while their families watched in horror-stricken fear.

Many wore large yellow Star of David patches, attesting to their Jewish race. Those not wearing them had been detained for other reasons, such as working in the Resistance.

With Raoul Nordling's help, Amélie learned that Jeannie had been classified as having been active in black-market activities.

The buses from Fresnes arrived. The women streamed out, some of them so thin that they were distinguishable as women only by the others around them.

Amélie searched anxiously, but as more buses arrived and more women joined the miserable throng, spotting Jeannie seemed like an impossibility. *She'll carry herself with poise, regardless of circumstance.*

Amélie scrutinized the women, looking for one who walked at her own pace unless jostled, who remained calm despite the dogs, the bayonets, and the yelling soldiers, one whose face radiated confidence and would be beautiful despite the ravages of the past months. She surveyed the lines methodically as she had been taught to do in London, observing groups of women between identifiable points in the station and quickly scanning each person before moving on to the next group.

At last, and just in time, she saw Jeannie and was shocked at her appearance. Her natural beauty still showed, but she was stooped and walked with difficulty, and her prison clothes hung from a shrunken form. She was already mounting a short, steep ramp to enter a boxcar.

Amélie ran to the nearest point that the line of soldiers allowed. She pushed herself desperately to the front of the crowd and screamed with all her might, "Jeannie! Jeannie Rousseau. I will find you. Never give up hope."

Already at the top of the ramp, Jeannie halted and turned slightly. A small smile crossed her face as she gazed in Amélie's direction. She lifted her hand to wave, and then she was pushed into the dark, crowded interior.

38

Same Day, August 15, 1944

Despite his dispassionate demeanor, General Choltitz listened attentively at a conference in *Generalfeldmarschall* von Kluge's underground bunker. As supreme commander of *Oberbefehlshaber* West, von Kluge commanded Germany's western forces in France and was Choltitz' immediate superior in the formal chain of command.

Rumor abounded that von Kluge had been connected with the assassination attempt on Hitler at *Wolfsschanze*, but thus far, no action had been taken against him. Having taken command barely a month earlier from Field Marshal von Rundstedt, who was dispirited from having failed to stop the Allied invasion at Normandy, von Kluge found himself no more able than his predecessor to halt the momentum of the enemy assault from the west.

Presenting at the conference was *Generalleutnant* Blumentritt, who laid out a detailed plan for Paris' destruction. He included a list of where Choltitz could acquire additional explosives from *Kriegsmarine* reserves. "This plan should be carried out immediately," he recommended at the end of his exposition. "If we wait, the Allies will come within range before we fully execute."

As von Kluge's chief of staff, Blumentritt carried much influence, but Choltitz was not convinced. He had no issue with the plan. It had been thoughtfully developed, professionally presented, and highly detailed.

For Choltitz, a professional soldier, the main issue was timing. He had already carried out many of the recommended preparatory actions. "Let me remind you," he said evenly as Blumentritt finished and took his seat, "that I took my orders directly from the *führer*, and his instructions were clear. He directed me to defend Paris, and failing that, to demolish the city." He paused and looked directly into the chief of staff's eyes. "Note that my first duty is to defend her."

A heated debate ensued during which von Kluge only listened. However, after it had persisted for an extended time, the field marshal lifted his hand to end the discussion. "I'll make my decision and inform you later."

That afternoon, Choltitz sat alone in his office. He turned on the radio and tuned it to the BBC. The station was forbidden to the public on threat of death, but as a senior army commander, particularly with authority to access all sources needed to complete his job, he was free to listen.

He had been monitoring the fighting around Falaise, a hundred and thirty miles west of Paris. The fighting was fierce and did not seem to be going well for the *Wehrmacht*. A general withdrawal was now in progress from the western front, and Army Group B was in jeopardy of being encircled.

The radio squawked and made humming noises, but finally became clear. The announcer ran through a report on the advance of General Patton's 3rd Army. It had taken control of Brittany and liberated Le Mans, he said, and had three corps positioned at Argentan as part of a pincer maneuver. Then, the announcer played a recording of a soft-spoken French general, Philippe Leclerc. Choltitz had never heard of him, but he listened with focused attention.

The radioman said that Leclerc was leading a thrust by his French 2nd Armored Division around Argentan. He had already liberated two towns near there, Alençon and Carrouges. The French general made no vainglorious claims. His comments were very short, but he made one statement, so calmly and matter-of-factly that its essence pierced Choltitz' psyche. "I have arrived back in France as I promised I would," his voice intoned. "And soon, I promise, the tricolor will fly again over Paris."

Choltitz' chief of staff, Colonel von Unger, appeared in his doorway. Choltitz snapped off the radio. "What is it?"

"Sir," von Unger replied, "you have a call from *Generalfeldmarschall* von Kluge."

Choltitz grunted. He picked up the receiver. "*Herr* Field Marshal," he greeted. "Have you reached a decision concerning the fate of Paris? What are your orders?"

He heard von Kluge sigh at the other end of the line. "I think Blumentritt is correct," von Kluge said. "If we wait, we will not be able to act before the Allies arrive. You are to execute your orders immediately."

When the conversation ended, Choltitz poured a glass of schnapps, lit a cigarette, and ambled out onto his balcony. Since the morning conference, he had also received written orders from high command in Berlin to proceed with demolitions.

He took a deep breath, sipped his drink, and gazed out over the fading skyline, remaining there for some time to enjoy the warm summer breeze and banish from his mind nagging images of the vast city in rubble. As he went inside and sat at his desk, von Unger once again entered. "Sir, I just received news that *Generalfeldmarschall* von Kluge was relieved of command after he spoke with you this afternoon."

If Choltitz was startled, he showed no sign. "Was a reason given?"

"Yes, *Herr* General. He fell under suspicion of participating in the assassination conspiracy against the *führer*. He's been recalled to Berlin."

"Do we know who will replace him?"

Von Unger shook his head. "Not yet, but *Herr* Taittinger, the Mayor of Paris, is here to pay you a courtesy call."

Choltitz huffed impatiently. "Show him in."

Pierre Charles Taittinger had been appointed mayor of Paris by the Vichy French government a year ago, succeeding the man who had held the position upon France's capitulation to Germany in 1941. He came from a long line of known French patriots and had served with distinction as a cavalry officer in the Great War, for which his courage was cited. His family was renowned for producing exquisite champagnes, and he was elected to the Paris Municipal Council three years before the German invasion. Upon the fall of France, whether for belief in Germany's Nazi ideology or for pragmatic reasons, he had voted with the council to authorize Marshal Philippe Pétain to draw up a new constitution, ending the French Third Republic.

Taller than Choltitz by several inches, he was an imposing figure with a high forehead, dark hair combed close to his scalp, and a heavy mustache that grew past the ends of his lips to either side of his chin. Towering over the German general, and with a nod to the interpersonal dynamics, he greeted Choltitz with gentlemanly respect.

"What can I do for you, Monsieur Taittinger?" Choltitz asked.

"I'll get right to business, sir," the mayor said politely. "I hear that your soldiers are evacuating from around many of our state buildings, monuments, factories, and bridges. A rumor is spreading that you intend to destroy them with explosives."

Choltitz gestured for Taittinger to take a seat. "You were an army officer. You understand duty. The Allies are advancing from the west. They have also, as of this morning, invaded France's south coast at Saint-Raphaël. My duty is to defend Paris against their entry here, from whichever direction it comes, and I will use every asset at my disposal to accomplish that."

In his mind, he suddenly heard again Leclerc's calm voice. "... the tricolor will fly again over Paris."

Choltitz spoke again, his voice rising with a touch of anger. "The Resistance is obviously very alive in Paris. Please advise your people that I am responsible for protecting my soldiers. If anyone fires at them, I will burn every building in the vicinity and shoot everyone in the neighborhood. I don't have a hundred thousand soldiers here now like we did only a few months ago, but I still have a hundred Tiger tanks, ninety aircraft, and over twenty thousand men." His fervor rose, and he added, "I won't leave unanswered any attack on my troops."

He stood abruptly and crossed to a map on the wall. "Come, I'll show you what I have planned."

As Taittinger joined him, Choltitz pointed at various sites on the map. "These are bridges, power plants, railroads, and communications facilities. They are strategic targets. Their destruction puts obstacles in the enemy's path. I intend to blow them."

The Frenchman looked at the map in shock. Just the targets that Choltitz had indicated would do much to destroy Paris, and the general's demeanor indicated no concern over carrying out his intentions.

Choltitz coughed. "Asthma," he gasped, and was beset with an attack. His face turned red, and his eyes watered.

Concerned, Taittinger grasped his arm. "General, perhaps you need fresh air."

When Choltitz nodded, Taittinger led him onto the balcony overlooking the Tuileries Garden. While the general took time to recover, the mayor gazed across the panorama of historical sites.

"Sir, if I may observe," he said as Choltitz' coughing subsided, "generals often encounter the opportunity for historic destruction. You stand at the threshold of such an occasion with both the means and the will to carry out unprecedented devastation. But you are also in the unique position of saving Paris for posterity. You have the opportunity to look back years from now and contemplate that you had the power to utterly destroy this city, but you chose to save it. Is that not worth as much as any conqueror's glory?"

As the general regained composure, he looked across the dramatic cityscape. Within his view, in addition to the Tuileries Garden were the Louvre, la Place de la Concorde, Notre-Dame, and many other historical and architectural treasures.

At last he turned to Taittinger, his voice softer, less severe. "Monsieur, thank you for your courtesy, and I appreciate what you've said on behalf of your beautiful city." He was quiet a moment longer, and then added, "You represent Paris well, Mayor Taittinger. You've done your duty. Now, as a German general, I must do mine."

Late that afternoon, von Unger announced another visitor. "*Generalfeldmarschall* Model." He stepped aside to allow a weathered, dust-covered officer to pass into Choltitz' office.

Choltitz looked up, startled, and snapped to attention.

Hatchet-faced Otto Model's reputation preceded him as one of the most ruthless of Hitler's field marshals, a true Nazi who put slavish fealty to the *führer* over loyalty to Germany. But he was also a field soldier of great personal courage. Early in the war, he had distinguished himself as a cunning *panzer* commander who thrived on challenges. As the war progressed, he became better known for his defensive successes, particularly on the eastern front, where, as commanding general of the German Ninth Army occupying the Rzhev salient, he held his position. His success there drew Hitler's attention. Being of humble birth soon made him one of the *führer's* favorites.

As he entered Choltitz' office, he waved his field marshal's baton. "I'm here to replace von Kluge," he announced. "Our orders are to hold Paris and the Seine River at all costs and restore order to the western front." He sniffed as he gazed about. "I just drove from Germany through Metz, and judging from the number of stragglers I saw along the way, I'd say the command needs restoration."

Based on reputation, Choltitz did not trust Model's judgment. The two settled into discussion, and Choltitz related the debate with Blumentritt that morning regarding when demolitions should be ignited. Choltitz stated his own position and the reasons why.

To his surprise, Model agreed. "Premature execution could only serve to agitate the population and make our jobs more difficult," the field marshal said. He encouraged Choltitz to take time to become familiar with his new command and to take no new actions before the field marshal had reviewed and approved them.

Thus heartened, when the meeting reached its end, Choltitz escorted Model to a waiting Horch. There, his good feeling ended abruptly.

Looking across the street through the Tuileries Garden, and to the historic sites at either end, Model grasped Choltitz' shoulder and declared, "My men took forty minutes to destroy Kovel in Poland." He took one last look around. "Paris will take at least forty hours, but when we're finished, this city will be leveled." He turned back to Choltitz with a determined leer. "We'll get the job done."

Returning to his office with rare melancholy, Choltitz found von Unger waiting for him, looking distressed. "This has been a hellish day," the general growled. "What is it?"

Von Unger hesitated. "I thought you'd want to know, sir."

Without a word, Choltitz raised questioning eyes to meet von Unger's and waited for a response.

"*Generalfeldmarschall* von Kluge shot himself."

39

Early Morning, Same Day, August 15, 1944
Off the coast of Saint-Raphaël, France

Second Lieutenant Zack Littlefield relished the warmth and fresh air washing over his landing craft as it cruised in gentle waters to the shore. Enemy fire had been much lighter than expected. Word was that the 45th Division had gone ashore earlier and had already captured a German corps, its headquarters, and its commanding general.

He could not believe the news, the weather, or the leisurely voyage from Paestum, Italy, up the Tyrrhenian Sea between Corsica and Sardinia to France's southern coast. It had been a far cry from the tempestuous crossing over the Mediterranean from Tunis for the amphibious assault on the southern shore of Sicily over a year ago or at Salerno not even two months later.

At Sicily, strong opposition had been expected, but did not occur. Then at Salerno on Italy's west coast, weak opposing forces had been anticipated. Instead, murderous German fire had met the Allied troops even before they made for shore.

At Sicily, the Germans had been duped into believing that the Allies intended to land in Greece and the Balkans and had transferred divisions from the island to meet the threat at the perceived landing sites along those coasts. As a result, the landing at Sicily had been almost unopposed.

The opposite conditions occurred at Salerno. Just before the invasion there, the Italian king deposed the dictator, Benito Mussolini. Italy abandoned Germany and the Axis Powers and joined forces with the Allies. Unbelievably, General Eisenhower had announced the Italian switch to the Allies to a worldwide audience as the assault was about to execute. In response, the Germans seized all Italian army positions and coastal defenses. Surprise was blown, and the Allied troops came ashore under blistering fire.

From many months of combat experience and those two events in particular, Zack had developed an instinct to be always vigilant. He called to his platoon sergeant. "Keep the men alert. Just 'cuz we ain't been fired on yet doesn't mean it won't happen."

He had to smile. His company's first sergeant had yelled the same thing to him when he was a squad leader struggling through the surf on landing in Sicily.

Zack was only two years out of high school, though his face bore lines evidencing his long time in combat. First had been his narrow escape from a tank that took a direct hit in North Africa. Then came the murderous battles across North Africa, followed by the slog over mountains and across rivers up Italy's spine, much of it against ferocious opposition from crack *Wehrmacht* troops.

On three occasions, he had been the sole survivor of his unit in fierce engagements with the enemy: first at Kasserine Pass in North Africa, then at San Pietro in southern Italy, and finally at the Garigliano River crossing below Monte Cassino. But his natural leadership skills, honed under fire, had been recognized, and he was promoted to lead a squad. Then he became acting platoon sergeant, the result of a fatal casualty; and at San Pietro, he had found himself the senior surviving man directing a company until he had been wounded, nearly fatally.

He had come to the 36th "Texas" Division as a replacement after his unit in North Africa was almost obliterated, and he remained with it through the tortuous fighting and trek north in Italy until at last, nine weeks ago, on the day before the Normandy invasion, he led his squad through Rome as part of the division's advance units. Finding that the *Wehrmacht* had deserted the city, what had begun as a cautious patrol in the dead of night turned into a celebrated parade of the entire Texas division, roughly twenty thousand soldiers, through the "capital of the Caesars."

After securing Rome, the 36th fought north another one hundred and fifty miles along the Tyrrhenian coast, encountering stiff resistance at Magliano and reaching Piombino on June 26. At last, the severely depleted division was pulled from combat and transported south to Paestum for much-needed rest and recuperation.

There, to Zack's surprise and trepidation, during refit and reorganization, he received a field promotion to second lieutenant and was assigned to lead an infantry platoon. He found the recognition flattering, the responsibility sobering, and a resulting transfer to the 143rd Regiment dismaying—he would leave behind the men of the 142nd Regiment who had survived with him all the way from Monte Cassino. Now he would shoulder the weight of leading forty ground-combat soldiers and keeping them alive.

Zack had originally trained as a tanker, but after the direct hits in North Africa and at San Pietro and being critically wounded the second time, he had returned to the fight as an infantryman. He preferred the latter, seeing the odds of a one-on-one battle between a foot soldier and a tank to favor the foot soldier. Furthermore, he found the thought of taking a bullet to be more favorable to burning alive in an armored coffin.

This morning, as his landing craft approached the beach, most troubling to him was that so many soldiers in his platoon had recently arrived fresh from stateside training with no combat experience, and the entire division was coming off more than a month's worth of rest. He worried that even his combat veterans might have lost the edge that could keep them alive.

His company commander had briefed the platoon leaders that the initial landing force would consist of one hundred and fifty thousand men, and the total strength would grow to over half a million, complete with their equipment and support. The 36th would land at Green Beach near Saint-Raphaël as part of Operation Dragoon and secure a beachhead. The invasion forces' immediate overall objective was to destroy the *Wehrmacht's* Nineteenth Army's shore defenses and overtake its surviving units before they could push north through France and return to Germany.

The amount of expected resistance was uncertain. Most of the enemy's armor in southern France had been transferred northwest to support forces opposing the Allies at Normandy and the shoreline north of it. However, the German Nineteenth Army was still lethal with its coastal artillery, heavily mined beaches, and infantry. Although intelligence reports indicated that the defending troops were mainly reserve units, with many of them composed of conscripted POWs from battles in Eastern Europe, they were still a deadly force numbering somewhere around fifty thousand troops.

The worst of them can shoot a lot of bullets our way.

As dawn approached and the ships of the fleet took up their positions several miles offshore, Zack had expected to hear the claps of heavy shore guns and the hisses of their rounds arcing across the sky. So far, that had not happened.

Then again, they weren't firing at us at Salerno either—until they did—and then the guns were murderous.

At roughly 06:00 hours, a low rumble sounded from the southern horizon and grew louder. Zack recognized the source. Thirteen hundred Army Air Corps bombers flying from Corsica and Sardinia formed a massive blot against the early-morning sky. They flew high over the fleet, their engines vibrating the air. As Zack watched them cross the shoreline, he made out, even at this distance, the trails of falling munitions. Then the thunderclaps of immense explosions spanned the full length of the beach and rolled out to sea in countless waves.

The bombs pounded the German positions behind the beaches for ninety minutes. Then, the navy launched spotter planes, and the ships' enormous guns hurled massive salvos at pinpointed targets.

The shoreline disappeared under a continuous line of towering flame and smoke.

The sun lifted. The guns ceased. All was quiet. Zack's watch marked 08:00.

Then the roar of many landing craft engines resounded along the coast.

The taste of seawater trickled into Zack's mouth as spray blew into his face. He looked to his left and right, taking in the unforgettable sight of hundreds of vessels speeding in a line toward the shore and their designated beaches.

At Salerno, the invading force had encountered underwater obstacles. Zack had been briefed that such obstacles had caused many casualties at Normandy. However, reports from early scouting parties and French Resistance members had informed that no such threat existed at this landing zone—the beaches were too steep.

He watched and listened for signs and sounds of resistance. He heard none.

And then he stepped ashore onto dry land. On his three previous landings, he had struggled over obstacles through rough surf turning crimson with the blood of his comrades. Here, no soldiers lay writhing in pain or with glazed eyes. No ground-level gunfire chewed up his men as they spilled from the landing craft and sought cover. No ratatat of machine guns, with attendant tracers and smoke, sent streams of steel to tear into the flesh of his soldiers.

Looking to his flanks, he saw that his adjacent units experienced the same conditions. Nevertheless, he directed his men to seek cover.

40

Same Day, August 15, 1944
Digne-les-Bains, France

"We've been jailed for two days," Xan Fielding grumbled, "and no food at all. Do you think they intend to starve us?" He was only half-joking.

Christian Sorenson took up the line of discussion. "It's as good a way as any to bring us to our end. Saves on food and energy. Even from our side of the issue, it's better than some of the things they could do to us."

Looking curious as a thought crossed his mind, he turned to Roger. "What was with your singing the other day? That started out of nowhere, and then wound down."

Roger chuckled. "You're wondering about my sanity." He hummed a few bars of "Frankie and Johnny." "It's a song Pauline and I sang together as we traveled about. It lifted our spirits. I thought it might do the same here."

"You bloody well stopped soon enough," Fielding said. "It was hurting my ears." He chuckled. "It was good for gallows humor. I got a laugh out of it."

From beyond the cell they heard the clinking of keys and exchanged apprehensive glances. A guard appeared bearing a tray with vegetable soup and brown bread. Saying nothing, he opened the door, entered, and set the tray down, all under the watchful eye of another sentry with a submachine gun trained on the prisoners. Then they both left, locking the door behind them.

Sorenson looked at the soup. "It's not bad for a last meal. We might as well dig in. We've nothing else to do."

More hours passed. To relieve boredom, the comrades exchanged stories, told of their early lives, and mused out loud about whether the Allies would ever land on the Mediterranean coast. Tiring of conversation, they attempted to nap on the cold floor.

Keys jangled again. The men rose to sitting positions against the wall, and once again exchanged glances of apprehension.

A *Gestapo* major appeared in the door with two sentries. Strangely, he wore civilian trousers below his black tunic. In his hand, he carried a pistol, which he pointed directly at them. "Out," he ordered.

"This is it," Fielding muttered.

"The soccer field is where they do the deed," Sorenson chimed in. "If we turn toward it at the end of the hall, well"—he faced the other two—"it's been my honor."

"Out," the major commanded again, his voice rising with impatience.

"Don't get edgy," Fielding said with slight sarcasm. "No need to rush."

They filed into the corridor with the soldiers on their flanks and the *Gestapo* officer covering them from the rear. As Roger passed him, the officer said in French, "You have an amazing wife."

Startled, Roger hesitated, staring at him, uncomprehending. Then he followed his comrades out of the cell. They left the holding area and headed outside under an overcast sky and a drizzle of rain toward the *gendarmerie's* gates. Two German soldiers there saluted the *Gestapo* officer.

Outside the gates, the major ordered the prisoners to turn right. They glanced at each other questioningly. The soccer field was to the left.

They reached a wooded area around a curve. While covering the trio with his pistol, the major abruptly ordered the party to halt and then dismissed the two guards. As soon as the sentries had disappeared, he holstered his weapon.

"Follow me," he said. Seeing the prisoners' hesitance, he added, "Hurry if you want to live. My name is Max Waem. I'm helping you."

The three escapees glanced at each other but followed Max wordlessly. A few hundred meters farther on, they encountered a waiting automobile.

"Get in," Max said. He took the driver's seat.

When all were inside and the doors closed, Max drove off. He wound into the countryside through gathering dusk and navigated through German checkpoints with no difficulty owing to his *Gestapo* tunic. As night settled, they pulled up to a white building.

The car's high beams shone brightly against a woman's figure, throwing her shadow on the wall behind her. She lifted her arm to shield her eyes.

In the back seat, Roger smiled. "Pauline," he breathed.

41

Same Night, August 15, 1944
1st Allied Airborne Task Force Headquarters, Le Mitan, France

"General Fredericks, you summoned?" Gunn asked.

"I did. I wanted to tell you personally that your story checked out in every detail. What you and your SOE and French army colleagues have done is remarkable."

"Then can we get on with the rescue? The Huns are likely to learn of Roger's—"

"There's no need, Captain. He's been released."

"Sir?"

"He's free and back in friendly hands. I don't have the particulars, I just know that your "Roger" is no longer in a French jail. Now if you'll excuse me, I have work to do."

Gunn stood stock still, staring. "That's wonderful news, sir. Thank you." He remained in place.

Fredericks looked him over. "Is there something else, Captain?"

Gunn nodded. "Yes, sir. Are you aware of what happened at Anzio?"

The general regarded him skeptically. "I think everyone knows about the disaster there. What's your point? I'm a little busy. We have an invasion going on."

"Please, sir, allow me two minutes, and if I've wasted your time, you can toss me in the loo, but please hear me out."

Fredericks chuckled. "Go on."

"Did you know, sir, that immediately after landing at Anzio, a British lieutenant led a platoon-sized armed patrol to scout out the enemy. They drove all the way to the gates of Rome on the Apian Way and back to the beachhead, unopposed. They never even saw German forces at any point along the way."

Fredericks regarded him piercingly. "I hadn't heard that. Go on."

"We have demonstrable evidence that if General Lucas had pressed on after landing at Anzio, we might not have encountered the slaughter that followed."

Fredericks paid Gunn his full attention.

General Lucas had conducted a superb, unopposed landing at Anzio. However, instead of pressing inland, he halted his advance just past the beach, established a defensive perimeter, and then held his forces in place while bringing reinforcements ashore. That pause had given the *Wehrmacht* time to rush opposing forces into the area and delayed taking Rome by three months, a distance of forty miles. The ensuing casualty rate was high.

"What does Anzio have to do with us here, now?"

"Sir, I'm a spy. I piece things together." He crossed to a map and pointed to Montélimar, southwest of Grenoble. "If I understand what I've overheard while waiting, you expect Allied forces to establish a blocking position here within ninety days."

"I'll have to shore up some loose lips," Fredericks muttered, clearly irritated. "That's classified information beyond your clearance. Go on."

"I drove through Montélimar to get here. For a hundred miles of that, I was on the road that Napoleon used for his surprise attack on Paris. It's called the Napoleon Route. I made the distance in a few hours, and there wasn't a single German in sight."

He pointed to the map again. "Instead of fighting north up the valleys on the western side of these mountains"—he placed his hand over the

Vercors—"if you go up on the eastern side, through Castellane, Digne, Sisteron, Gap, and La Mure, you could have your whole army north of Grenoble in a week."

Fredericks studied the map with keen attention.

Gunn was sure he had taken an accurate measure of the man. *Fredericks appreciates audacity and acts audaciously.*

"Send an armed scouting patrol to follow me, sir," Gunn urged. "I'll drive up Napoleon's Route all the way to Grenoble. If I'm wrong, your guys can shoot me so I can't divulge your plans, and they can scoot back here to let you know. But if I'm right, the Allies have an open road to Grenoble."

Fredericks swung around and regarded Gunn closely but remained silent.

"Sir, it's the same situation we had at Anzio," Gunn pressed. Sensing continued hesitance, he added, "Napoleon did it in five days on horseback."

The general reacted with narrowed eyes. He grunted. "You were right about this agent 'Roger.' You're owed the benefit of the doubt."

He called briskly to his aide, "Send for my intelligence and operations chiefs." He held his hand over the receiver and pointed at Gunn. "You! Don't go anywhere."

Mid-Day, August 17, 1944
Callas, France

Major General John Dahlquist observed skeptically the Scottish captain standing at attention in front of him. General Fredericks had sent a heavily armed patrol to escort Gunn south, skirting retreating German columns. After landing, Dahlquist's 36th Infantry Division had pushed aggressively north, and now his staff was setting up a hasty field headquarters twenty-five miles inland.

"At ease," the general said gruffly. "General Fredericks was urgent in his message requesting that I see you. What's this about?"

"The Napoleon Route," Gunn replied. "It's empty." Briefly, he repeated what he had told Fredericks.

When he had finished, Dahlquist studied him expressionlessly. Finally, he said, "Show me." He moved to the front of his jeep and unrolled a map.

Gunn scanned it for a few seconds and placed a finger on their current position. Then he indicated Saint-Raphaël. "This is where Napoleon landed," he said, and traced the route north on the map. "You're intending to press up through the Rhône Valley and block the Nineteenth Army's retreat in this vicinity." He pointed out Montélimar, and then outlined the Vercors, explaining its geographical significance. "If you skirt to the east and take Napoleon's Route north to Grenoble, you should have light resistance, and you can then send units southeast to Montélimar before the Nineteenth Army gets that far up the Rhône Valley."

Dahlquist cupped his chin in his hand as he studied the map further. "You're sure that route is open?"

"I suppose it's possible that the jerries could have moved in since two days ago, which is when I drove it," Gunn replied. "The German 157th Reserve Division is garrisoned at Grenoble, but it's been busy trying to quell an uprising on the Vercors. It could have moved units onto that road in the last two days, but not in any force.

"I got onto the route at Sisteron. From there to Saint-Raphaël is roughly a hundred miles. I didn't see a single jerry all that way." He repeated his offer to have an armed recon patrol follow him up the road and report back, and he added, "Look how easily you've moved this far. You've already got troops in Castellane."

Dahlquist glanced up, suddenly resolute. He looked around and summoned an aide. "Get this man over to see General Truscott and get an open line so I can speak to him." He glanced at Gunn. "Truscott is my commander. Tell him what you told me." He extended his hand. "Thanks for coming. This information could save a lot of lives."

Gunn received a similar reception at Truscott's headquarters. The general was chowing down on C-Rations heated on his jeep's engine block when the Scot arrived, and he offered Gunn a box. "Spaghetti and meatballs," he quipped. "Can't ask for better."

42

Same Day, August 17, 1944
Bletchley Park, England

Claire Littlefield rushed into Commander Travis' office unannounced. "Sorry to barge in on you," she exclaimed, "but I thought you'd want to hear this first chance." Her eyes were wide and bright, color had risen in her cheeks, and a dazzling smile spread across her face.

"My, my, but you are excited," Travis said, looking up from his desk and chuckling. "What has you so worked up?"

"This just came in." She held up a message while exclaiming, "I thought you might want to get this out to the major field commanders as soon as possible." She indicated the message. "Hitler's ordered withdrawal of all German troops in southern France. And Field Marshal Model, who took over Army Group B from von Kluge, just ordered a general withdrawal from western France."

"What?" Travis heaved his large body out of his chair and hurried around the desk to seize the paper from Claire. He scanned it and then gazed up at her in disbelief. "Can this be true?"

"It is, sir. I double- and triple-checked it. Hitler mandated that the 11th *Panzer* Group act as rearguard to the Nineteenth Army in the Rhône Valley;

that LXII Corps defend the Franco-Italian border with the 148th Division at Cannes and with the 157th Division at Grenoble protecting the Nineteenth Army's eastern flank; and he's stipulated that the port cities of Marseille and Toulon must be defended 'to the last man.'"

"'To the last man,'" Travis repeated in a murmur. He grunted. "Adolf loves that dramatic touch, doesn't he? But it's wearing thin."

Claire acknowledged the comment, and continued, "Model has not yet given specific instructions, but the Germans are in full retreat all over western France. The commanders are directing their troops to a route between Falaise and Argentan."

Travis peered keenly at Claire. "Very good, Miss Littlefield. They're calling the area the Falaise Gap or Pocket. The moniker has already come up through the ops channels. Eisenhower, Montgomery, Bradley, and Patton are trying to orchestrate a pincer movement there." He grunted. "They each have personal ideas on how best to bring that about." He sighed. "Generals will be generals."

He strode across the office to a wall map. "We've already captured LXII Corps in the south," he said, spreading his hand over the area. "The commander of the French II Corps, General de Lattre, is closing on both Marseille and Toulon, and we have two American divisions starting up the Napoleon Route to seize Grenoble. Their right flank is comparatively clear." He paused and rubbed his chin while studying the map. "That means our troops in southern France can pursue up the Rhône Valley in earnest."

He stared at Claire and broke into a laugh. "Look," he said, pointing to an area in northwest France. "The US 1st Army took Cherbourg and secured the Cotentin Peninsula last month. Bradley's carpet bombing at Saint-Lô opened a gap in Germany's Normandy defenses. Then General Patton's 3rd Army pushed southeast into Brittany, took Saint-Malo, and isolated three other ports there. Now one of his corps has crossed the River Sée at Avranches—"

"It seems that the action at Avranches tipped the scales," Claire interrupted. "That, and the fact that it's Patton who's doing it. The Germans still think he's the Allies' best field general."

Travis laughed. "So does he, and I'm not sure they're wrong." He gestured at the map again. "Now one of Patton's corps has turned east and is headed toward Argentan at the southern edge of that Falaise Gap, which is the very place you mentioned. When he's done there, he'll be poised to join with our southern armies somewhere south of Lyon, much sooner than expected." His eyes brightened and he beamed at Claire. "My dear Miss Littlefield, we've got the Hun on the run." He chuckled at his own inadvertent rhyme and strode to his desk, where he picked up his phone. "We must inform the commanders."

Stony Stratford, England

Claire all but flew up the garden path to her front door. She had not felt so effortlessly happy in many years. The sense of it welled from deep in her chest. She rushed through the entrance into the hall past the kitchen, and into the back garden. There she found Elsie pushing Timmy on the garden swing.

"There's my little man," she said, beaming, and lifted him. She squeezed him and then danced around the yard with him.

"You're in fine form," Elsie said, laughing. "Have you met someone special?"

Claire laughed. "Nothing like that." She set Timmy down, grabbed Elsie with one hand, held Timmy with the other, and gestured for them to join hands and prance around with her in a circle.

"This is so much fun, mum," Elsie said, puzzled, "but what brought this about?"

Realization dawned on Claire that she possessed probably the best news that anyone in the UK could have had since the beginning of the war, and she could not share it. That knowledge sobered her, but she was determined not to let it spoil her long-lost sense of pure, genuine joy. "I've decided not to let this war take any more of life's joy away from us." She smiled brightly. "Let's go into town for dinner. My treat."

Timmy jumped up and down in a child's exuberant antics. "Hurrah," he cheered. "Can we have fish and chips?"

Claire burst into a level of merriment that she had not enjoyed in years. "Let's see how long the line is."

Elsie regarded her dubiously, then shifted her eyes skyward as a buzzing sound caught her ear. "Eating out would be very nice," she said, "but we might want to wait a while. I think I hear some doodlebugs flying over. We'd better seek shelter."

Claire grimaced. "Yes, well, there is that."

She listened and determined that the V-1 bombs, dubbed "doodlebugs" colloquially for their peculiar buzzing sound, were off to the south and not likely to descend in their vicinity. They had flown over Britain daily at all hours by the hundreds for two months, but lately, they flew over less frequently and in fewer numbers.

The doodlebugs were pilotless aircraft that delivered explosive payloads. They flew on their azimuths for their designated distance. Then their fuel valves shut off and they plunged to the ground, igniting thunderous explosions. An inadvertent design feature was that they gave warning of their target area when their engines quit buzzing. Anyone below them at that moment knew to seek immediate shelter—if time allowed.

Claire surmised that the reason for their recent decline in forays was the result of the Allied push of the *Wehrmacht* east and away from their launch facilities in Normandy. She called to Timmy. "Come along. We'll wait them out in the cellar."

"Again?" Timmy moaned. His face wrinkled in disappointment and he stomped along in a five-year-old's antics, but otherwise he followed without complaint. He had sat out many hours in the cellar on other such occasions and possessed an instinctual understanding that things that go boom might be harmful, particularly when the grown-ups acted as though they thought so too.

They sat in the gloomy cellar until the sounds of distant explosions had ceased. Blackout curtains still hung in the windows upstairs. No light leaked out of them, but they no longer served the purpose for which they had been installed—to keep enemy pilots from spotting targets on the ground.

As minutes turned into hours, Claire watched Timmy with concern but without the terror she had known while escaping a firestorm in London resulting from a *Luftwaffe* bombing sweep three years earlier. The V-1s had been a failure for the Germans. Despite launching thousands that had fallen to earth on British soil, the doodlebugs caused far less damage and casualties than the mass destruction and thousands of deaths realized during the *blitz*. This "superweapon" was not going to turn the tide of events.

However, the winds of war had definitely shifted in favor of the Allies. As the realization deepened, the same thrill coursed through Claire that she had felt upon receiving the welcome intelligence of the *Wehrmacht's* general withdrawal from southern France, ordered by Hitler himself. *He knows he's losing.*

Claire's enthusiasm was sobered by her next thought. *The V-2s are still to come.*

43

August 18, 1944
Paris, France

Chantal Boulier pedaled her borrowed bicycle in Petit-Clamart, a few miles south of Notre-Dame. Keeping the object of her surveillance in sight was not difficult, and she blended with the normal foot, bicycle, and light motorized traffic easily enough.

The man she followed was Henri Georges René Tanguy, known in the CNR as Colonel Rol-Tanguy, shortened to "Rol." He was the representative of the Communist faction to the CNR and one of the men whom Chaban had identified to Chantal during their attic meeting in Auteuil four days ago.

Tall and big-boned, Rol had not been difficult to locate. At Chantal's new job in the prefecture's telephone exchange, she had quickly learned to tap into his phone line. On occasion, she had chided herself—she had no authorization and no one had directed her to such action, but she sensed that time was short, and she had little opportunity otherwise to observe Rol. *He's one of the men who wants foreigners to rule France!*

Earlier this morning, she had eavesdropped on his line and heard him arranging a meeting with four other men. His voice rang with urgency, but more significantly, all five were men whom Chaban had identified for surveillance. One of them was André Tollet, the leader of France's Communist party in Paris.

Rol stopped to assist a cyclist who was busy on the traffic circle's barren surface, ostensibly making repairs to another bicycle. Moments later, they rode off together.

Chantal followed.

The surroundings broke into a rural area, and Chantal took care to hang back, speeding up when the two disappeared around a curve or below the crest of a dip in the road. After five minutes of riding, they came to a wide vegetable patch with a single, one-room shed near its center.

While Rol entered the shed, the other man rode back in the direction he had come. Chantal scanned the field. She saw neither anyone about nor any semblance of a lookout. To check for hidden security, she left her bicycle in a stand of trees and ambled onto the vegetable patch, bending over, gathering bits of produce that had been overlooked during the harvest. No one tried to stop her. The shed had no windows, but she gave it a wide berth, dropped to the ground, and approached stealthily from its rear.

The man who had guided Rol to this place at 9 rue d'Alsace in Clamart reappeared, leading another cyclist. Chantal dropped low in a furrow and watched. The new man entered the shed, while his guide once again returned the way he had come.

Crawling with her chest to the ground, Chantal inched toward the small, rickety building. She heard voices coming from inside, three of them, so apparently one man had already been there when Rol arrived. Minutes later, the guide returned, shepherding another participant. Both men joined the group inside the shed.

Once the door closed, Chantal edged to the back of the hut.

"There'll be no smoking in here," one of the men announced, obviously taking charge. "I don't want anything to give away this meeting."

That must be André Tollet.

"We'll make this short," Tollet said. "Tomorrow is the day to launch the insurrection. My orders are to develop political legitimacy for the Communist party coming out of the unrest and the violence that is sure to follow our initial actions. As a first step, we'll seize control of the police force at the prefecture tomorrow morning and use them to restore order when rioting starts in the streets."

"The people are ready," Rol said. "They won't care who leads as long as they get to drive the Germans out of Paris. I've been promised a British overflight to drop arms. We have to get our men out and ready to receive them. We don't want them falling into the hands of Gaullists."

"We'll be forcing the CNR's hand," a third man said. "Parodi says that de Gaulle ordered the committee to prevent an insurrection while the Allies detour around Paris. The insurrection will force them to come straight here—unless they want to see the city pounded into the ground. We know what Choltitz intends."

"The police are angry and on strike because of being disarmed," Tollet said. "The CNR has caches of small arms all over the city. The Germans evacuated nearly all of their administrative staff and a lot of troops. Now is the time to start the insurrection.

"Tomorrow, our members will fire on every German they see. They'll throw Molotov cocktails and shoot at trucks, armored vehicles, and *Wehrmacht* installations. Our aim is to force the remaining Germans into their strongholds and sequester them until the Allies arrive. We have to get the people onto the streets too, shooting at anything with a swastika. When it's all over, we'll be seen as the saviors of Paris."

"Once we start," another voice chimed in, "the Germans will shoot back. Casualties will be high."

Rol scoffed. "Paris is worth two-hundred thousand deaths."

Scrunched in the dust outside the shed, Chantal blanched in horror. She had heard enough. As she turned to scramble away, her left shoe hit the base of the shed with a pronounced thump.

Inside, the voices ceased.

Chantal heard the door at the front fling open with a loud creak and a bang. With no time to escape, she climbed to her feet.

Rol spotted her. "What are you doing there?" he shouted. He closed the distance quickly and grabbed Chantal's arm. "Were you listening to our meeting?"

Covered from head to foot in thick dust, Chantal stared vacantly, her mouth hanging open. Saliva dripped from the side of her mouth. "What meeting, *Monsieur*?" she asked in the guttural tone of a dull peasant. "I didn't know anyone was in there. I was just looking for dinner." She showed the pockets on her dress, half-filled with dried vegetables she had collected from the patch. "A rabbit ran under the shed." She struggled against Rol's grasp. "I aim to get him."

Then she drew back in apparent fear. "You're not going to take these vegetables away from me. My family hasn't had any in weeks. This isn't stealing, you know. The field had already been harvested."

Rol glared down at her angrily, uncertainty in his eyes.

"Let me go," Chantal cried, wrenching her wrist from Rol's hand. "I'm going to get that rabbit." Breathing hard, she dove for the bottom of the shed and pulled dirt away from its base.

Rol grabbed her by the collar. "Go on," he yelled. "Get out of here, or I'll turn you in for thievery."

Chantal bolted across the field and did not stop until she was in the trees with her bicycle. She was still breathing hard after dusting off her clothes and starting on her way back to the prefecture, stopping in a café's lavatory only long enough to wash her face.

At the prefecture, she sat at the switchboard, an amalgam of long cables pulled from a horizontal counter and a vertical wall punctuated with metal-encircled holes. Calls were connected by pushing the male end of a cable into a female receptacle. She placed the headphone over her ear, adjusted the mic, and placed a call to a specific number Chaban had provided to be used only in case of just such an emergency.

Chantal's heart beat furiously as she listened to the electronic sound of the phone ringing at the other end of the connection. She fought to control her breathing and prepared to modulate her voice in keeping with those of the other operators sitting nearby and able to overhear her.

"Good afternoon," she said when at last a man answered on the fifth ring. Chantal did not recognize the voice, but Chaban had assured her that the phone was constantly monitored, and whoever answered would know how to respond. Chaban would be immediately informed of her message.

"This is the operator at the prefecture. I have a call for you. The caller says it's most urgent. He requests that before I connect you, I relay that if you are disconnected, he will try again tomorrow morning. He emphasized that he will call early tomorrow morning."

Silence followed. Then the voice asked cautiously, "Are you sure he said tomorrow morning?"

"Without a doubt," Chantal said. "He said, most definitely, tomorrow morning. He will place the call from here at the prefecture."

More silence ensued. Finally, the man said, "Then we will expect to hear from him tomorrow morning. I cannot speak with him now."

Blood rose in Chantal's face and her breathing came in short gasps. She ended the call and excused herself to the restroom. There, inside a stall, she retched. Fortunately, no one entered. After a few minutes, she calmed herself, washed her face, and returned to her station.

From the balcony of his office on Rue Montmartre, Yves Bayet watched Suzanne ride down a block and disappear around the next corner. He was the head of the Paris section of the Gaullist Resistance network, the counterpart to the position that André Tollet held in the Communist faction of the Paris Resistance. Suzanne was Bayet's liaison, a pretty young woman with a charming disposition.

As soon as Chaban received Chantal's message, he had relayed it to Parodi as de Gaulle's CNR representative, who in turn informed Bayet. Bayet had removed three envelopes with prepared messages from a hidden drawer in his desk. He modified each to indicate the time for action, and carefully concealed them in the lining of a moleskin handbag that had been prepared for Suzanne. She was to take the envelopes to a letterbox at a café for further distribution, and then she was to return to Bayet's office, being careful not to be on the streets past the fast-approaching German-imposed and tightly controlled curfew. Anyone still out after that time would at least be arrested and could be shot on sight.

Bayet smiled in satisfaction. He could finally use General Choltitz' heavy-handed enforcement of the curfew and Communist André Tollet's obsession for security to the Gaullists' advantage. Per agreement among the CNR membership, each Resistance group was entitled to be informed of impending cooperative action—in this case, the intended take-over of the Paris police force. By sending Suzanne on her errand, Bayet had just executed the letterbox system of communication that had been pre-arranged for use under emergency conditions.

However, as opposed to the other networks, the Communist Tollet insisted on using two letterboxes to receive such communications instead of only one. His fixation on security meant that, because of the curfew, Bayet's message would remain overnight in Tollet's first letterbox, not to be delivered to the second one until morning. By that time, Bayet's objective would be a *fait accompli*.

Suzanne continued on her journey. With still half an hour to go before reaching the café, she found herself pedaling her bicycle harder. Glancing at the front tire, she realized that she had a slow leak. She stopped and attempted to re-inflate it using the pump attached to her bicycle's frame, but the puncture was too large.

She was about to hurry on pushing the bike, but just then, a German staff car pulled alongside her. Seeing her plight and exercising Teutonic gallantry, a young lieutenant emerged from behind the wheel and offered assistance.

"I think the puncture is too large," Suzanne said, masking her nervousness behind a smile.

"Then we'll put your bike in the rear seat and I'll take you," he replied.

Suzanne hesitated.

"You need to get to where you're going," the officer said. He tapped his watch and smiled. "Curfew."

Suzanne took a deep breath. "Well then, thank you."

A few minutes later, as the car pulled in front of the café, the lieutenant turned to her questioningly. "Shouldn't you be going home?"

Suzanne thought fast. "This place belongs to my parents. I help them close down. We live nearby." She smiled demurely. "Now, thanks to you, I'll have more time to help them."

She waved as the car drove away, and when she entered the café, she told the proprietor, "I need to call Monsieur Bayet to let him know that I arrived safely, but that I won't be returning this evening. And I'll need a place to stay the night."

44

August 19, 1944
Paris, France

In the early light before dawn, two men scurried across a parapet below the gray slate roof of the Paris Police Prefecture, the stately nineteenth-century headquarters at Place Louis Lépine. On the opposite end of a long, wide square stood the eight-centuries-old stone cathedral, Notre-Dame.

Stopping for a few moments to gaze over the city, the two men saw the usual signs of Paris waking up. Thick clouds rolled in over Montmartre, threatening rain. In the streets below, wives and mothers hurried to form long lines in front of shops to receive their daily rations of bread and whatever else might be in the stores. Buying groceries had become an unpredictable nightmare.

German patrols had completed their nightly routes and retired to their garrisons. Traffic built to its normal rhythm, sparse though it was compared to the days before German occupation.

As the two men focused on streets closer in, they nudged each other, pointed, and grinned excitedly. Coming their way in small groups trailing in from every direction were vast numbers of Parisian men, Resistance members, among them policemen on strike. They had received coded alerts overnight, the result of the messages in Bayet's envelopes, further distributed in the same way that the two men on the parapet had learned of this morning's doings. Those who had pistols, rifles, or other weapons hidden away brought them. The entire throng of hundreds converged, pushed through the main gate, and assembled in the vast interior courtyard.

A Citroën was parked at its center, and lanky, blond Yves Bayet, wearing a checkered suit, stood at its front. He looked up to the fourth floor and spotted Prefect Amedee Bussière staring down. For the past few days, because of the strike, the prefect had commanded no one and had been almost alone in the great edifice.

Calling out in a loud voice that resounded from the stone walls surrounding the square, Bayet announced, "In the name of the Republic and Charles de Gaulle, I take possession of the Prefecture of Police."

Thunderous cheers broke out. A trumpet played "*La Marseillaise.*" Then, hundreds of strong, throaty voices joined in singing the stirring lyrics of the national anthem. On the roof, the two men ascended a steep, built-in ladder to the prefecture's highest point. They carried a bundle that they reverentially unwrapped and attached to a pole. Moments later, fully unfurled, for the first time since June 14, 1940, and over an official building of Paris, the French flag flew proudly in the wind.

Bayet issued pre-planned orders to occupy the entire building. An hour later, he stepped out of his Citroën and approached a small man quietly reading a newspaper on the terrace of the Café des Deux Magots. "Monsieur Luizet, we've captured the prefecture. It is yours."

Charles Luizet, appointed by General de Gaulle to be the new prefect of Paris, had parachuted into France a week earlier to assume the office. He smiled and rose from his seat. "Thank you. Let's go."

While the Resistance men had still been singing "*La Marseillaise*," Colonel Rol rode by on his bicycle intending to initiate the prefecture's takeover. Startled and enraged that it was already in progress, he rode furiously to his shop, took out from storage the army uniform he had kept hidden away all these years, and put it on. Then he rode back to the prefecture intending to impose his control over the prefecture.

He was too late. Prefect Luizet had already taken command of the police force and the Resistance members. Another man, Frédéric Joliot-Curie, had also arrived. He was the son-in-law of Madame Curie, who had discovered radium. Frédéric had brought with him the means of producing potent Molotov cocktails—potassium chlorate and sulfuric acid—to be used to defend the prefecture. Both men were known to the policemen who subordinated themselves to their authority without question.

Rol hurried away to report to Tollet. "We continue as planned," Tollet snapped. "Get our men onto the streets shooting at Germans. That will start the insurrection, and then we can figure out how to regain control."

Moments later, for the first time since the Prussian siege in 1871, the streets of Paris rang with gunfire. A German troop truck found itself under fire from apartment windows. It careened forward, past an intersection, and was fired upon once again. Then a Molotov cocktail struck its canvas top and exploded. Within seconds, the truck was engulfed in fire. Men struggled from the cab and the rear, some writhing in agony, their whole bodies aflame, only to find themselves targets of unrelenting gunfire.

Residents across Paris, having no idea of events but hearing the sounds of battle, hurried along on their errands, nervously hugging the sides of buildings lining the streets and darting between doorways. Bicycles weaved on the thoroughfares, their riders attempting to shelter below tree branches or behind trunks.

Within two hours, whole convoys came under attack, patrols had been shot up, barracks had been assaulted, and German daytime patrols retreated to their garrisons.

At mid-morning, Georges Bidault, president of the CNR, the highest political organ within the Resistance that also carried the authority of General de Gaulle, addressed a hastily called assembly of representatives, including Parodi and Tollet. It was held in a conference room on Rue de

Bellechasse. "We are here to discuss preventing an insurrection," he announced.

At that instant, gunfire erupted somewhere on the street outside the window.

"Clearly, one is already underway," Tollet growled, his face a mask of resolve, "and it will continue with or without this committee's support." He was a dark-complected man with black hair and tight jaws, shorter than most men in the room but with a pugnacious demeanor and rancorous eyes. "We don't need permission to drive these Nazis out."

Bidault glared at him. In theory, as president of the CNR carrying the highest authority of the exiled government, he was also charged by de Gaulle, through Parodi, with preventing even a hint of rebellion. If Bidault tried to quash the nascent insurgency, he would leave open the possibility of Communist rule in Paris and then all of France. Yet if he acceded, he might condemn Paris to either civil war, or worse, to total destruction at German hands, turning Paris into another Warsaw.

Reluctantly Bidault acquiesced. "By my hand," he announced, "this insurrection is hereby authorized by the French government-in-exile."

Tollet had planned carefully, and outside in the streets, the second phase of his plan commenced. Panel vans and sedans patrolled the streets with large white letters painted on their sides, FTP, for *Francs-Tireurs et Partisans*. The men wore armbands, and they occupied public buildings, took over police stations, post offices, the government halls of the city's twenty *arrondissements*, and other buildings where the public would regularly congregate or were crucial to running the metropolis.

News of the insurrection spread through Paris, and people responded in whatever ways they could. For many, that meant throwing open their long-shuttered windows and waving the blue, white, and red French flags they had hidden away for just such a day. Others grabbed anything that could be used as a weapon and joined the growing, defiant masses in the streets ready to battle the *Wehrmacht*.

Chantal's heart pounded as she pressed her hand against her earpiece. The caller repeated himself. "This is General Choltitz. Connect me to whoever is running your illegal mutiny." His voice was calm but cold as ice. "This is not a request."

Chantal looked about wildly. "Wait please."

She had entered the prefecture amid its takeover that morning, having pedaled in on her bicycle as the groups of men hurrying to the same place grew to a quiet crowd. She had stood at a window two floors below the now former Prefect Bussière as Bayet announced his occupation of the police prefecture. The deep chords of "*La Marseillaise*" sung so fervently had thrilled her even as the imminent threat they signaled brought dread for what was inevitably to come.

General Choltitz' voice registered the beginning of the German response. Behind Chantal, men had taken up positions at the windows, the barrels of their rifles and pistols thrust out over the street.

"Did you hear me?" Choltitz demanded, still speaking calmly, but the menace in his voice was palpable.

"Yes, sir," Chantal replied. Just then she heard electronic warbling, and the line went dead.

"We've cut the lines at the Meurice," someone shouted from the hall. "German headquarters' telephone communications are dead."

An enthusiastic whoop went up from the fighters. Chantal removed her headpiece and stared at the microphone. Then she looked up, caught the eye of her supervisor, and beckoned to the woman. "I just had General Choltitz on the line. He demanded to speak to whoever is in charge. Then, the line went dead."

Fear crossed the woman's face. She nodded grimly and went to find someone to take the report.

Chantal settled into her chair, closed her eyes, and let her body go limp. *The fight is on.*

Standing at his desk in his office at the Meurice Hotel, General Choltitz placed his phone's receiver firmly back in its receptacle. He turned and faced von Unger. "Our lines were cut. Get them fixed. And send a combat team to the prefecture. Order every measure to be taken to bring it back under control."

The general reflected on a call he had received that morning from *Generaloberst* Jodl, Chief of the Operations Staff of the *Oberkommando der Wehrmacht*—the German Armed Forces High Command. He was known to be slavishly loyal to Hitler irrespective of military advice from his commanders in the field.

"I've just left the morning meeting with the *führer*," Jodl had said. "He's asking about preparations for Paris' destruction."

Choltitz had stared at a stack of documents open on a table at one side of his office. They were the very detailed plans showing every edifice to be demolished and the current state of placing demolitions around them.

He had taken a deep breath, and said words he regretted as soon as they were uttered, despite being true. "I'm sorry to say that we've been delayed in igniting the explosives because my men are currently fighting terrorists all over the city."

The silence on the other end of the line was stone-cold. At last Jodl spoke. "I'm reading *Herr* Hitler's words from my notepad," he said, softly at first, but with anger building. "'The greatest importance is to be assigned to the defense of Paris, and as a result, every measure must be taken for its defense.'" He paused. "The *führer* will be furious to hear what you've just told me."

"General," Choltitz broke in, "our task is not as simple as mashing a single plunger. We're still installing demolitions, and when we are ready to initiate, we'll have to do it in stages to ensure malfunctions are rectified and to safeguard my men as we depart the city. As for the unrest among the population, they are not stupid people. I'm sure they've reached the correct conclusions about our intentions from watching our actions. We could not expect that they would accept that fate without resistance."

Silence.

When Jodl spoke again, his words were clipped, his voice terse, projecting the force of his anger. "Regardless of the terrorists, the *führer* expects you to carry out the widest destruction possible in your command."

A sense of inevitability overtook Choltitz, bordering on dread.

Now, as von Unger left to direct restoration of telephone service, the general could not help reflecting on his meeting with Hitler at the *Wolfsschanze* just over two weeks ago. Decades seemed to have passed in the interim. Only five days ago, Hitler's deputy chief of staff for operations, General Warlimont, had sent a wire informing that the *führer* had ordered that "Karl" be transported for use in Paris. So far, it had not arrived, but Warlimont informed him that Hitler had ordered highest priority to its delivery and then its immediate use.

Choltitz had regarded the message with dismay, a sense that surprised himself—it was rare for him. "Karl" was a mortar, and the general knew it well. It was the most powerful artillery piece developed to date, anywhere in the world. Karl was nicknamed for its designer, General Karl Becker, and Choltitz had used it to destroy the defenses at Sevastopol. Other generals had deployed it with great effect against Brest-Litovsk and Stalingrad. Its rounds weighed two and a half tons and could be lobbed more than three miles to blast through eight feet of concrete and steel.

The general walked out onto his balcony and stared over the five-hundred-year-old Tuileries Garden, a favorite place of Parisians to stroll among well-tended flower beds. It had been originally cultivated for royalty in the 1500s, but after the French Revolution, it opened to the public. It was bounded at the east end by one of the most prominent custodians of French culture and history, the Louvre.

At the other end of the garden was the Place de la Concorde, a site that was at once a symbol of royal perfidy and mob vengeance. It was there that King Louis XVI, his wife, Marie Antoinette, and many other notables found themselves at the mercy of an enraged population and its guillotine.

With visions of bloody beheadings before his eyes, Choltitz rubbed his throat and turned to view the southeast. Over the roofs of countless lower buildings he observed the magnificent Gothic spires and tinted windows of Sainte-Chapelle, and beyond it, the twin towers and wondrous flying buttresses of Notre-Dame.

Grim-faced, he sighed. A single well-placed shot from Karl from three miles away would level any of those targets and anything standing within a block of them. The same was true for Sacré-Cœur, Montmartre, l'Arc de Triomphe, or even the Eiffel Tower. Combined with the demolitions that

Captain Ebernach had already placed around and beneath most of the city's monuments, he fully grasped that he, General Dietrich von Choltitz, could turn Paris into a pile of smoldering debris.

His mind went to his wife, Uberta, and his daughters, Maria and Anna. The edict rang in his ears regarding the fate of families of officers who failed, criminally, to do their duty. Certainly, if he did not carry out his directive, his family would suffer. Further, he was a professional soldier who had always obeyed his orders without question. The idea of willfully failing in his task was alien to him.

Von Unger knocked on his door and entered. "Sir, General Warlimont is on the radio for you. He's received reports of disturbances in Paris and wants to know the status of your preparations. He says the *führer* expects to be updated at the afternoon briefing and demands daily progress reports."

Choltitz sighed. "Tell him that I'll prepare one and send it."

Chantal heard the creaks and roar of a lumbering *panzer* before it came into view, and in a flash, the noise brought the horrors of Dunkirk. There, she and Amélie had been helpless girls, hunkering down inside their house with their father while explosions shook their home and gunfire sounded all around. In the aftermath, and although her own home was untouched, behind the rows of stores and shops along the beach was nothing but obliteration. Even the ancient cathedral had been razed.

For a fleeting second, she recalled that Dunkirk was where Amélie had rescued Jeremy and begun their romance too often interrupted by the war. But that was also where Chantal's near rape occurred, and the subsequent persecution of her, Amélie, and their father had commenced. She had felt helpless.

Not now. A few hours ago, the new Prefect Luizet had entered the office. Most of the telephone operators had fled. Luizet had attempted to place a call, but did not know how to operate the switchboard. In the process, he had inadvertently opened a line for an incoming call and heard a terrified voice screaming that a German *panzer* was attacking the town hall at Neuilly-sur-Seine, about five miles northwest. Almost immediately, they heard an explosion over the line and then it was silent. Then, just outside their own window, gunfire erupted.

A Resistance man at a window overlooking the main street gasped a short, guttural sound and fell to the floor holding his bloody neck. An operator screamed and went to him, but having no idea how to help him, she cradled his head and wept.

Chantal ran over and put pressure on the wounded man's neck, but very quickly saw that further aid was useless. His legs twitched and then fell still. She helped drag his body away and returned to find another operator helping Luizet place his call.

The dead man's rifle still leaned against the window. Chantal seized it.

All morning and into the early afternoon, reports flowed in of fighting all over the city. The Germans had seemed unable to stem the tide in the initial stages and had retreated to the safe environs of their garrisons. The action at Neuilly had been the first reported instance of offensive armor activity. And now, in mid-afternoon, she heard three tanks drawing near.

The lead *panzer* approached across the front square under fire, bullets pinging off its armor, its tracks clattering across the stone surface. It took aim at the main gate into the inner square, and fired from close range.

Watching from her window, Chantal saw a flash, and immediately felt the concussion. The shock wave lifted her and threw her several feet. The gate crashed open, half torn from its hinges.

Crawling back to the window and peering over the sill, Chantal watched the *panzers*, two Panthers and a Renault. They lined up facing a barricade of sandbags. Behind them civilian fighters armed with pistols and worn WWI rifles broke in fear as the turrets rotated to fix them in their sights. The Resistants ran to the prefecture and the safety of a tunnel that would take them to the bank of the Seine.

A French army sergeant ran to intercept them. Aiming his pistol at them, he bellowed, "I'll shoot the first man who tries to get by me. The only way we survive is by winning, and that means fighting."

Shamefacedly, the men turned back around. Meanwhile, the *panzers* started forward again. Behind them, the chiseled towers of Notre-Dame provided a dramatic backdrop. The armored behemoths closed on the building.

Three objects flew out of an upper window. The first two hit the side of the lead *panzer* and burst into flames from the impact of Curie's Molotov cocktails.

The unwary tank commander had left the hatch open. The third Molotov fell directly inside and exploded. Only the driver survived, screaming in pain as he clambered out, but gunshots ended his misery. The two remaining tanks retreated to a safe distance.

Chantal glanced at the switchboard. Lights blinked, but the control board was in the line of fire, so she wondered where she could be most valuable, taking critical messages or turning her rifle toward the enemy and pulling the trigger. During training in England, she had become an adept marksman.

The notion suddenly struck that she was outside of anyone's chain of command. She was known inside the prefect as a telephone operator only, another employee, nothing more. Now she was cut off from Chaban and in the midst of a deadly German siege. She was in charge of herself, and she had a rifle.

45

August 20, 1944

Swedish Consul General Raoul Nordling hurried up the stairs of the Meurice to General Choltitz' office. On reaching the landing, he took a deep breath to calm himself, and then walked deliberately the rest of the way. Von Unger met him in the outer office and escorted him in to see the general.

Choltitz stood outside admiring the view when Nordling entered. The consul joined him. Below them and across the street, Parisians, heedless of the events of the day before or perhaps disbelieving that they would continue, ambled along in the Tuileries Garden. Pretty girls and mischievous boys rode bicycles. Others floated sailboats on a pond. All enjoyed the warm sunshine.

"Ah, Consul Nordling," Choltitz greeted. He turned and gestured at the peaceful view. "It would be such a shame to kill all those people and destroy their fair city."

Nordling stared at him, aghast. The notion was unthinkable, and yet this short, stocky general commanded the power to do just that. "Sir, if you were to do so," he said quietly, "you would never be forgiven, not by those living now, nor throughout history."

Choltitz whirled on him. "I am a soldier," he snapped. He took a moment to calm himself, and then continued with a note of resolve. "I obey orders. And I don't like terrorists shooting at my troops. I will take that prefecture from them. I've already laid on a *Luftwaffe* air-bombing mission for tomorrow morning."

Horrorstruck, Nordling gasped, "General, your bombers are bound to have misses. The Notre-Dame is only two hundred meters away, and the Sainte-Chapelle is across the street."

"Did you not hear me when you came in?" Choltitz snapped again. "My orders include the possibility, now the probability, of destroying Paris. I'll remind you that Allied planes are destroying our cities all over Germany."

Nordling's mind flew, grasping for how to avert what appeared to be an unimaginable inevitability. At sixty-two, he was a big man with a round face, a slight mustache, and a high forehead with a shock of unruly white hair.

He had met Choltitz shortly after the general's arrival in Paris. The consul had come to plead with the general for the treatment of political prisoners being shipped to Germany. Nordling succeeded in transferring over three thousand of them to Swedish protection. It was he who had found Jeannie Rousseau's name on the list of women transferring to Ravensbruck, fifty miles north of Berlin, but she had already been moved.

Only minutes before arriving at the Meurice, Nordling had received a frantic phone call from the Prefecture of Police. "Can you do anything?" the caller had cried. "We are desperate here. We are almost out of ammunition." Nordling had been about to leave for Choltitz' office when the call came through. It had quickened his haste.

In his dealings with Choltitz thus far, Nordling had found the general to be cordial but strenuous in adherence to orders and military protocol. He perceived Choltitz as a man who was comfortable executing the orders of superiors but reluctant in making decisions. When the general had approved the transfer of political prisoners to Swedish control, for instance, he did so only after receiving recommendations from lower-level commanders.

"Sir, your soldiers have taken casualties. So have the Resistance fighters—"

"The terrorists," Choltitz retorted.

"As you will, sir. My point is that both sides could use a respite to collect their dead and tend to their wounded. What if you declared a truce for that purpose, one that could be extended if circumstances warranted?"

Choltitz studied Nordling and then turned to look out across the Tuileries once more while his mind worked. To go through with the bombing raid on the prefecture would be an irrevocable act of war against the city. Doing so would require a decision that only he could make. Nordling's proposition provided him time to consider other options or for more favorable circumstances to emerge. Nevertheless, the notion rankled him. At no time in his long career, in all the fighting he had done on the eastern front, had he ever sought a ceasefire.

He took a deep breath. "Your suggestion has merit," he said slowly. "I'll allow the following: if, within one hour, the prefecture demonstrates that it can control its terrorists, then I will consider a truce—with one other stipulation." He looked about and lowered his voice. "Do not associate my name with the ceasefire."

He walked Nordling to the door. "One hour," he reiterated as they parted.

On his way back into his office, the general called to von Unger, "Postpone tomorrow's air strike until I order otherwise."

Chantal looked along her rifle's barrel across the square outside the prefecture. Since firing had erupted that morning, she had exchanged shots intermittently with German soldiers in the courtyard. They had refrained from once again attacking with tanks.

Her face was smudged, her clothes wrinkled, and fatigue had set in. She heard a buzz emanating from the switchboard, saw a blinking red light, and recognized that a call was coming through from the Swedish consul's office. Scooting low across the floor, she connected the lines and called to one of Prefect Luizet's young assistants, "It's the Swedish consul's office."

She watched the young man's anxious face as he greeted the caller and listened. He leaned forward, holding the receiver tightly to his ear. Then his body went limp, he breathed a sigh, hung up, and fell back against the wall. "We have a truce," he murmured. "Paris is saved."

Not trusting that what she had heard was real, Chantal stayed low and moved back to the window. She sank down next to it with her back to the wall, reached over, and retrieved her rifle. "Let's hope," she breathed.

46

Same Day, August 19, 1944
South of Sisteron, France

Almost precisely at noon, Brigadier General Frederic Butler received the order he had been expecting from Major General Truscott. "Send a division north to Grenoble."

Having graduated from a Jesuit prep school and then West Point, Butler was an "all business" combat commander in whom Truscott placed much confidence. With his sharp mind, he organized quickly, led effectively, and met objectives efficiently, but he was not known for personal warmth.

Early on the previous morning, at Truscott's urging and with General Patch's endorsement, he had received the Scottish captain, Havard Gunn, who had patiently explained yet again the Napoleon Route, its history, the significance of the Vercors in separating the route from the Rhône Valley, and the advantages to be gained by pressing a force on to Grenoble.

After listening, Butler had conferred a short time with Truscott via radio and immediately sent an armed reconnaissance patrol up the road through Gap and La Mure. The report back had largely reflected Gunn's representation of the route, although the patrol had encountered elements of the 157th Reserve Division between Gap and La Mure. The general forwarded the information to Truscott's headquarters, resulting in the just-issued order with the information that the 143rd Regiment was on its way to join Butler to exploit that route.

Gunn remained long enough to answer questions. Having exhausted them, he had been rewarded for his efforts with six truckloads of American supplies and captured German equipment to be distributed to Resistance groups along the way on his return to his team, which, during his foray to gain Roger's freedom, had moved northwest to Thorenc in Andon.

Butler had been pleasantly surprised at the light opposition he had encountered thus far. The combat units of Task Force Butler had been assigned only the day before, forming a provisional armored group that included the Corps' 117th Cavalry Reconnaissance Squadron, an armored field artillery battalion, one light and one heavy tank company, a tank destroyer company, a motorized infantry battalion, an engineer battalion, and necessary service troops. It had already pressed fifty miles inland.

In selecting the units to be in this task force, Butler had sought out those with the most effective combat experience. All had been in at least two amphibious operations and had many veterans.

On the way north, his command had skirmished with defending *Wehrmacht* forces at Digne, but the enemy had quickly fallen back. While Butler was still in the town and preparing to press northward to Sisteron, his attached SOE liaison officer escorted a very tall man who identified himself as an SOE operative and went only by his codename, Roger.

Unaware of Roger's status or that of a small woman, Pauline, who accompanied him, Butler remained wary of them. Both were disheveled, looking more like country peasants than effective British spies.

With them was a Belgian, Max Waem, who, the purported SOE operatives said, had worked for the *Gestapo* and was now afforded British protection for services rendered to the Allies. They wished for the task force to take custody of Max and ensure that he arrived safely at Allied headquarters for proper handling.

"General," Roger said, "my government's word was given to protect Mr. Waem. Partisans seized and hung his colleague, Mr. Schenk, who also helped us and was promised Allied protection."

Butler grunted and turned to his adjutant. "Deal with it."

Pressed with the exigencies of a battle campaign in progress, Butler had little time to spend with Roger and Pauline. He was now intent on reaching Sisteron, and he dismissed them by turning back to his maps.

"Sir, we can help," Roger pressed.

"How?" Butler asked without turning.

"We have thousands of Resistance fighters in the area ready to do your bidding."

Butler half-turned and eyed Roger. "I don't have time to organize a private army," he said. Then he called to two sentries guarding his location, "Please show these two the road back to wherever they came from."

"Oh how the mighty have fallen," Roger growled as he and Pauline left General Butler

and set out in a small car back toward Seyne.

She glanced at him. He was seething. "Do you mean us?"

"General Butler sent us packing," Roger said, and took a deep breath.

"He was thoughtless and rude," Pauline exclaimed.

"He was too busy to spend a few minutes to learn how he might reach his objectives sooner and with perhaps fewer casualties."

Pauline scoffed. "He's a man with no vision or manners."

Roger recovered his composure and laughed softly. "He was busy, and I've had my dignity bruised."

Pauline sighed. "What now?"

"I overheard one of the chaps mention sending a division up the Napoleon Route to Grenoble. They'll be passing through Gap. A German unit is garrisoned there. Let's go see what mischief we can get into. We might be able to help this general in spite of himself." He stopped the car, consulted a map, and traced a new route with his finger. "We'll take this road north toward Sisteron. It goes through Gap."

As he drove off, Pauline grinned impishly and started humming the tune to "Frankie and Johnny."

Roger laughed. "When I heard that tune being hummed in the *gendarmerie* at Digne, I knew it was you."

She leaned across the car and kissed his cheek. "And I knew you were alive."

Roger reached over and squeezed her hand. Then he laughed again, and belted out in his sonorous voice, "Frankie and Johnny were sweethearts."

Pauline joined in.

The sun sank behind a mountain range as they entered Gap, casting golden fingers far over the horizon. The village, breathtakingly beautiful, was situated on a wide, low ridge surrounded by high mountains. "If not for the Germans," Roger murmured, "this place would be idyllic."

Then, as he steered through the streets, he and Pauline noticed that people smiled brightly and waved at them. "That's strange," he mused, puzzled. "I've been here several times. The secretary-general of the town's prefecture, Serge Barret, is a friend and a member of my Jockey network, but most people here wouldn't know me."

"I don't see any Germans," Pauline said. "Usually their sentries would be spaced along the street corners. Maybe they've retreated north. The people's friendliness is nice to see. They might be anticipating that the Americans will arrive soon."

When they pulled in front of Barret's home, he rushed out to greet them with arms wide open and a broad smile. "That's unusual too," Roger commented. "Usually, we'd low-key our greetings and watch over our shoulders."

Barret was an average-sized man, with dark, wavy hair. "My friends," he enthused warmly before either Roger or Pauline had a chance to speak. "I have wonderful news. We convinced the Germans here that the war is over for them. They surrendered to us."

"Are you serious?" Roger said, dumbfounded. "That's marvelous."

"Yes. We have them housed in the local theater. Our Boy Scouts are guarding them." He added, "Under supervision of the *Maquis*, of course."

Roger took a deep breath. Then he strode to the middle of the street and gazed all around, taking in the charm of the village and the magnificent view. "At last, a free French town."

Pauline ran to him and embraced him. "This is amazing," she exclaimed happily. "We really are winning."

Roger wound his long arms around her and swung her in a circle, around and around.

Barret watched the two, taking in the chemistry between them. "Is this your wife?" he asked finally when Roger had set Pauline down.

Roger turned to him, startled. Then he looked at Pauline and laughed. "Well, yes and no. I'll have to explain. It's a long story."

"Then come, come. We'll have dinner and you must stay the night. I want to hear your long story."

When Butler's tanks rolled into Gap at dawn the next morning, they found no resistance. Roger and Pauline joined the residents lining the main road to greet their liberators with jubilant cheers. The townspeople threw bouquets of flowers, and women hugged and kissed the soldiers tramping through.

A US Army captain approached Pauline. "Ma'am, I heard from Mr. Barret that you're Polish. I was hoping to find someone who speaks that language and asked him if he knew anyone. The tall man next to him overheard me." He pointed to Roger standing a few feet away. "He mentioned you. I have two thousand Polish POWs at a camp down the road a ways. Could you help me out with them?"

Surprised at the unexpected request, Pauline asked, "To do what?"

"I have to process them, but they don't speak English or German, and I don't speak Polish."

An idea flashed through Pauline's mind. "I can promise you they didn't fight for the Germans willingly," she told the captain. "Take me to them."

"The camp's not much of a place," he explained, "just a wide-open field. We put barbed wire all the way around it and we've got armed guards watching them, but they're not giving us any trouble."

Pauline scoffed. "Of course not. They must be thrilled to be released from the Germans. Let's go."

After saying their farewells to Barret, she and Roger followed the captain's jeep on the road back toward where they had encountered

General Butler. They rounded a curve, and there in a broad field stretching over several acres, they saw the prisoners.

The men looked haggard, worn, exhausted. Their uniforms hung on thin frames, their eyes sunk into deep sockets. They sat in clumps, milled about, or stood staring over the barbed wire strung chest-high on the field's perimeter.

Pauline caught her breath in shock. Then she composed herself, exited the car, and strode to the partition in the wire that served as an entrance. Two guards stood on either side, facing the enclosure.

Without waiting for permission, Pauline grabbed the pieces of wire holding the partition closed and parted them. Startled, the guards went to intervene but were stopped by the captain's command. "Halt! Let her go in."

An odor of dirty bodies stung Pauline's nostrils. She ignored it and called to her countrymen in their native language. "Hello, listen to me."

Several men had seen her enter, turned their attention to her, and nudged some of the others. "I am Polish," Pauline shouted. "I am one of you."

More men heard her voice and saw a cluster growing around her. "I am one of you," she repeated. "My name is Maria Krystyna Janina Skarbeck. I was born in Warsaw. I have worked with British Intelligence since the beginning of the war."

Some of the prisoners erupted into cheers. Others now crowded around, and as word spread across the field, they moved in, trying to hear Pauline. The men in front passed her words back to the others.

"The Germans took everything from us," Pauline shouted as loud as she could. "They stole our homes, killed our families, and robbed us of our country, our dignity." Emotion gripped her, and she paused for a deep breath. Then she continued, fury lacing her tone.

"They stole your liberty, your freedom of choice." She stood feet apart, her hands on her hips, determination on her face.

"I am Polish." She proclaimed each word distinctly, and paused, looking across the crowd now listening with rapt attention. "You didn't choose to fight for Germany. They forced you at gunpoint and they all but starved you. But we have a long war still ahead, and much fighting to do. The Americans and the British are now in France. And the French are fighting too, for their own country. The Allies are pushing the Germans out, and they need your help. Will you fight with them?"

The men in front stared at her, stunned. Then a roar went up and coursed through the throng as the POWs understood her proposal.

Pauline glanced about. Outside the wire, Roger watched. The captain, standing beside him, looked on, wondering. Neither had understood a word she said.

Pauline turned back to her countrymen. "Listen," she called. "You can't fight in those uniforms. You'll have to take them off."

A prisoner in the center leaped forward. His sunken eyes were suddenly bright, and his mouth broke into a yellowed, toothy grin. He tore at the buttons of his uniform blouse, ripped it off and, bare-chested, swung it wildly over his head, bellowing cheers all the while.

Before he had finished ripping off his jacket, men behind him followed suit, and their actions rippled across the field until, within moments, two thousand Polish prisoners shouted in celebration and waved their hated German tunics over their heads.

At the gate, Roger called to Pauline. "What's going on?"

As Pauline explained, the captain sidled up and listened. She turned to him. "Captain, you now have two thousand battle-hardened veterans ready to fight and awaiting your orders."

The captain stared in disbelief. Behind them, they heard the sound of a jeep, its tires scrunching in the gravel, and then the screech of brakes. As the captain turned, Pauline glanced over at the vehicle, noticing a red plaque with the single white star of a brigadier general. Inside the fence, the Polish prisoners continued cheering.

General Butler clambered out of the jeep. He stood for a moment observing the goings-on, and then beckoned the captain, who hurried to him. The two conversed for a minute, and then suddenly, the captain snapped to attention.

Butler stalked over to Roger and Pauline. "You're interfering with my prisoners," he stormed. "I want you out of my AO now."

Roger straightened to his full height. "General, you are speaking to a British officer, and we are both"—he indicated Pauline—"military intelligence operatives—"

"You told me that yesterday," Butler growled. "I've got a combat campaign to run. Get out now, or I'll arrest you."

Behind Roger and Pauline, the cheering abated, and a hush settled as the prisoners sensed the tension and watched, bewildered.

"Sir, if you'll let me explain—"

"The captain already explained." Butler turned to the two guards. "Escort these two to their vehicle. If they resist, arrest them. Use force if necessary."

Pauline turned to bid the prisoners farewell.

"Ma'am, step outside the wire. Now," Butler warned in a low, threatening tone. "I won't repeat myself."

Her cheeks hot, shaking with rage, Pauline complied. The guards, confused, trailed behind as she and Roger made their way back to their car.

As they drove away, Roger declared furiously, "We're going to see Patch."

Stone-faced, Pauline stared out the window at the prisoners. They stared back, some gripping the barbed wire, their eyes haunted with the realization that their moment of deliverance had passed.

Thick traffic slowed their progress as Roger and Pauline headed south. Most of it consisted of American combat and supply vehicles moving north in pursuit of the rapidly retreating German Nineteenth Army. Abandoned and burned-out *Wehrmacht panzers, kübelwagens,* artillery pieces, transport trucks, and stacks of destroyed or damaged war materiel lined the roadsides. Masses of people combed over them, scavenging for anything that might be valuable or useful. At intersections, military police guided the flow, halting civilian vehicles to allow army convoys to pass unimpeded.

Despite the resulting confusion, an air of gaiety permeated. Villagers poured out of their homes, stood in the streets conversing, laughing wildly, and jumping in excitement when long-lost friends joined them.

"The people are so happy," Pauline said quietly.

Roger glanced at her. She had a far-off look in her eye. "They deserve to be. They've been occupied for two years."

"And Poland for five years," Pauline murmured. "I wonder what will become of my country. The Soviet Union has Operation Bagration going on now, driving the Germans out of Eastern Europe. But once Stalin overruns Poland, he will never give it back." She sniffed. "I'll have no home."

Once more, Roger glanced at her and reached for her hand. He squeezed it, and held it until a turn in the road caused him to steady the steering wheel.

General Patch received the pair readily and extended courtesy that reduced some of the bad taste left from Butler's rudeness. "I heard what happened," he told them. "A combat reporter was there. He saw what took place and called me. Please accept my apologies. I've spoken with General Butler. He's a capable commander, but he acted inappropriately, and obviously he benefited in Gap from your work. He's been advised of who you are and what you've accomplished. He's currently working with the Resistance on that flank."

"What will happen to my countrymen now?" Pauline asked. "They deserve better than to be treated like POWs."

"Agreed," Patch said, "and I don't have a good answer. I'm looking into the matter, but I can make no promises. Those decisions will come from a higher headquarters. I'll do all in my power to ensure their good treatment. My guess is that they'll be held and repatriated after the war."

"To a Soviet-occupied Poland," Pauline breathed bitterly. "The spoils of war."

At a loss for words, Patch regarded her compassionately. "Perhaps," he said at last. "I won't lie to you."

The three sat quietly for a few moments, and then Patch turned to Roger. "I received word from General Fredericks about who you are. He was the first to meet with your Captain Gunn. The captain drove down here looking for an armed patrol to rescue you out of Digne. He's the reason we went up the Napoleon Route. We've gone farther in three days than we expected to do in several weeks."

"I wasn't aware of that," Roger said, surprised, and then added, "Gunn is a good man. I'm in his debt." He added ruefully, "It's good to know that my capture served some useful purpose." He then related Pauline's involvement.

Patch listened intently, and when Roger was finished, he said, "I've received more information about you from London through our intelligence channels." He reached for a file on his desk. "You, Roger, are the head of the Jockey network?"

"I'm the chief SOE liaison to the network, sir."

"Which you organized."

"With a lot of help. It's commanded by a Frenchman."

"Of course. I didn't mean to imply otherwise." Patch turned to Pauline with a slight smile. "And you, I understand, are Churchill's favorite spy, having operated in Poland, Egypt, Algeria, other places, and now here. You couldn't have come by that reputation easily."

"She is unsurpassed," Roger interjected.

Tears had formed in Pauline's eyes as she continued to contemplate the plight of Poland and her countrymen. She wiped them away and sniffed. "I do my job, sir."

Quiet reigned for a few moments, then Patch said, "I wonder if the two of you would consider liaising for me with the Resistance groups up the western side of the Rhône Valley? Our left flank will be moving north on that approach to link up with General Patton's 3rd Army moving east out of Normandy. We could use the help."

Roger and Pauline exchanged glances. She faced Patch with a steady gaze. "Of course. That's our job."

Roger stood and extended his hand to the general. "We'd be pleased to, sir."

47

August 20, 1944
Granville, France

General de Gaulle faced General Eisenhower across the operations section of an agglomeration of tents and trailers. The complex, located near the old seaside town on the west coast of the Cotentin Peninsula, housed Shellburst, the Supreme Headquarters of the Allied Expeditionary Force.

De Gaulle had flown into France that morning under withering and humiliating circumstances. First among the indignities he had borne was the requirement to request permission from the Allied command to enter his own country—despite landing a provisional government on French soil more than two months ago at Bayeux.

He and President Roosevelt held aversions to each other, goaded by conflicting objectives. The French general suspected that the American president intended to maintain France as an occupied protectorate after the war's end under a military governor, a proposition the French general would never accept. His stated objective had been to restore France to her historic place as a fully independent republic.

His next humiliation occurred when his Lodestar, low on fuel, had been forced to land on a tiny airfield at Maupertus-sur-Mer at the north end of the peninsula. The pilot had advised diverting to England, but de Gaulle refused, stating angrily that he would land nowhere except in France. When the aircraft taxied to a halt, a blinking red light on the Lodestar's instrument panel warned the pilot that only two minutes of fuel remained in the reserve tanks.

No reception party greeted the returning general. The airfield, situated at the edge of the town, had been battered by the Allied invasion and was vacant aside from a single barn that had been converted to a control tower. A lone FFI sergeant met the landing party with his submachine gun aimed at them, demanding to know who the men were and by what authority they had landed there.

At that moment, de Gaulle realized that he had been a virtual ghost to the Resistance. For four years, he had broadcast over the radio, and his countrymen had listened and heeded his call, but they had no idea what he looked like.

Taking the unintended slight in stride, he then shared the only razor that could be found in town with which he could clean up before setting about to conduct business. And his transportation had been a rumbling *gazogene*, a car modified to run on wood.

Arriving at his headquarters and while being briefed by General Koenig, he learned of the insurrection being fought in the streets of Paris. Furious because he had ordered that no such action should take place, his first thought was that the Communists were moving to seize power. His second was that he must see Eisenhower and plead for support to re-take Paris, preserve it from destruction, and prevent it from falling under Communist rule.

He met with Eisenhower that evening. As the two generals greeted each other, Eisenhower studied de Gaulle. Stooped and towering over the supreme commander, the Frenchman bore a grave expression that seemed to have been permanently locked onto his face.

Concerned about the Frenchman's motives, Eisenhower had granted him permission to enter the war zone on the condition that he would do nothing more than meet and encourage French soldiers fighting across Normandy. In authorizing Eisenhower to give such permission, US State Department officials weighed in with concerns similar to Ike's own, but they had not stood in the way, and neither had Roosevelt. All suspected, however, that once de Gaulle set foot on his native soil, he would have no intention of leaving. The instructions allowing the visit included the mandate that under no circumstances was Eisenhower to recognize de Gaulle as France's legitimate leader.

Eisenhower had only learned of the Paris insurrection a short time earlier and had been angered by it to a degree equaling de Gaulle's own. He was determined, however, not to change his plans. He saw the situation in Paris as one outside of Allied control that could force a change of plans before Allied forces were fully prepared.

Nevertheless, he welcomed the Free French leader cordially, acknowledging that de Gaulle had been the man who rallied France's Resistance in its darkest hours. He further recognized that three French divisions that had fought against the Allies in North Africa under Vichy French command now fought alongside the Allies in both the western and southern fronts. The troops in those divisions readily accepted de Gaulle as France's legitimate leader.

Eisenhower escorted the French general around the operations section, pointing out on maps the plans for liberating France and securing Paris. He left unmentioned that the *Wehrmacht* was reportedly withdrawing its forces from Denmark and the Nordic countries to protect its withdrawal from France and bolster its homeland defenses.

De Gaulle perceived quickly and accurately that Eisenhower's plans did not coincide with his own. The American anticipated a wide movement that avoided the capital city on its west side, consolidating to the north and then driving on to invade Germany. Plainly absent were any immediate plans to liberate Paris.

"Sir, I must ask you to reconsider your plans for Paris," de Gaulle said when Eisenhower had come to the end of his briefing. "You must have seen reports that the Germans will blow up the city and that street fighting has erupted. We face the real threat that, if the Allies do not immediately drive into Paris, the city will fall to the Communists, and if that happens, then so might France."

Stemming annoyance at de Gaulle's habit of attempting to change Allied plans, Eisenhower smiled patiently. "I understand, but let me advise you on the situation. If we go into Paris now, we will be in a street brawl that will occupy a quarter of the troops I have in France. We'll consume enough fuel that we won't be able to sustain a drive into Germany, which translates into not winning the rest of France or Europe. So, I must respond to your request with a firm, final no."

De Gaulle stared stoically at Eisenhower. Then, in a carefully modulated voice, he said, "General, I understand your position, but you must understand mine. Paris must be saved, and if that means that I need to withdraw my three divisions from your command for the purpose, then I must consider the option."

Caught off guard, Eisenhower had gazed blankly at the Frenchman. Then, in a tone as measured as de Gaulle's, he replied, "Certainly, you can do that, General, but you should consider how far you'll get without Allied fuel, food, or ammunition. From my view, you will not have improved your odds."

On leaving Eisenhower, and with his hands clasped tightly behind his back, de Gaulle had tromped stone-faced across the airfield to his Lodestar, mentally alone. His shoulders drooped below his normal posture, but his eyes stared straight ahead with unyielding resolve. His entourage trailed wordlessly behind him.

De Gaulle flew to Rennes in the middle of the Cotentin Peninsula's base. There he was greeted by General Alphonse Juin, who had triumphed at Monte Cassino and was one of his most trusted confidantes. Juin took him to a guest apartment at the town's prefecture.

Stating that he had urgent work to do, de Gaulle requested an office. There, alone, surrounded by magnificent Louis VI furnishings, he read through a slew of secret communications, received over the past twenty-four hours from General Chaban and Alexandre Parodi, describing the descent into chaos that now threatened Paris. One of the most urgent read, "The insurrection that was launched Saturday was held in check for two days by a truce. It cannot be contained beyond this evening. Battle looms tomorrow throughout Paris with a tragic imbalance of forces."

Without expression, de Gaulle composed a letter to General Eisenhower. So grave was the situation in Paris, he wrote, that he, General Charles de Gaulle, assumed the sovereignty of France and demanded immediate Allied entry into the capital, "even if it should produce fighting and damage in the interior of the city."

When he had finished, he summoned General Juin and directed him to hand-deliver the letter to Eisenhower immediately. Juin clicked his heels, saluted, and departed on his mission. De Gaulle then sat at the polished mahogany desk and wrote another letter, this one to General Leclerc.

When it was completed, he called for his aide. "Have this delivered by the most expeditious route." He handed over the missive and then pulled a piece of paper from his pocket. "And have this wired to London for immediate transmission on the BBC."

The aide took the paper and read, "*'As-tu bien déjeuné, Jacquot?'*" He chuckled. "Do you really care if Jacquot had a good lunch?"

De Gaulle was in no mood for humor. "See that it's done."

48

Saint-Nom-la-Bretéche, France

Major Roger Cocteau, codenamed Gallois, and Dr. Robert Monod sat on thin mattresses with only sheets to cover them in the dank foyer of an ancient villa eight miles east of the American lines. Outside, rain poured down.

Gallois was of average height, and his broad shoulders rested against the wall. He peered at his professorial companion, whose normally round face had grown thin from the stresses of war and minimal rations. Monod's shock of gray hair over a high forehead and mustache of the same color were all that were visible in the darkness.

The two men were old friends, but they had not seen much of each other during the war. Currently sixty years of age, Monod had treated wounded Resistance fighters since the German invasion without respect for political suasion. His own sentiments rested with the Gaullists.

Fifteen years younger than the doctor, Gallois had been a career cavalryman. Upon being deactivated per the armistice with Germany, he had joined the Communist faction of the Resistance.

Monod could not fathom why Gallois had attached to that side of the internecine struggle, but he suspected that the major had done so out of political ignorance. Gallois was for anyone who fought the Germans. Regardless, Monod knew Gallois to be a caring man of impeccable integrity whose mind was in the fight, not on the politics of the struggle. As opposed to Colonel Rol, who postured for post-war Communist power, Gallois only sought relief for his country.

As a medical professional, Monod enjoyed freedom of movement not allowed to regular citizens. He carried a stack of authorization certificates that permitted his travel with an assistant all the way to Berlin if needed, allowing him easy passage through German checkpoints. To protect his ability to gather information that was valuable to the Resistance, he had maintained a low profile, and to date he had not been compromised.

For this trip, Gallois would pose as his assistant.

Several weeks ago, Monod had discovered a gap in the American lines west of Bretèche, and an idea had formed. He took the information to Colonel Rol and suggested sending Major Gallois through the break to contact the Americans and plead for weapons.

Colonel Rol had listened closely, and then called for Gallois. He explained what the doctor had discovered, and told him, "Go with the doctor. This is the most important mission you've ever been assigned. You must convince the Americans to drop a major shipment of arms and ammunition over Paris."

Now, as the major and the doctor sat in darkness, Monod reasoned with Gallois as a professor would with a student. "Listen, Major. I've been thinking about what you should ask for when you meet with the Americans. I understand that Rol wants rifles and bullets, but I think you must consider that if they are dropped by parachute, they could fall into anyone's hands, including untrained civilians and criminals. If the wind blows the wrong way, the Germans could get them all. On top of that, the Allies can't drop a division's worth of weapons in one sortie, and that's roughly what the Germans still have in Paris. If we received that many weapons, the battle might last longer, but ultimately, it would be a slaughter, perhaps with even more casualties, particularly if the munitions were recovered mainly by untrained civilians."

Perplexed, Gallois had stared at Monod. "This trip was your idea. What do you suggest?"

Monod spoke with intensity. "You know that Alexandre Parodi received a message from London stating General Eisenhower's refusal to send more aid to Paris at the moment. The Allies intend to detour—"

"I understand," Gallois interrupted, "they'll come back when the rest of France is secure."

"But that will be too late." Monod's eyes were wide with passion. "Choltitz has explosives set all over the city. We know that. The people are already starving, and our Resistance fighters are running out of ammunition. They can't keep up the fight much more than a few days." He paused and tried to see Gallois through the darkness.

He resumed, "We need Allied soldiers. In Paris. As quickly as possible. Only they can stop what will otherwise be a calamity of monstrous proportions. Our people will die. Our beloved city will die. You must get to a senior commander, a field general, and convince him of that."

The doctor remained silent a few moments and then added, "At the very least, you must get to General Leclerc. Tell him how desperate the situation is."

With the rain beating a steady drum against the villa's windows, Major Gallois leaned his head back against the wall, his shoulders hunched. For a long time, he remained silent, listening to the wind and the downpour. Finally, he leaned forward and peered through the darkness toward his friend. "I think you are right."

August 21, 1944

After a sleepless night, Monod and Gallois resumed their journey as the first light of dawn illuminated a dark sky roiling with clouds. After being turned back at several German checkpoints and detouring over lesser-known backroads, the doctor had at last let the major out in a field with tall, round haystacks arranged in rows.

Monod pointed across the countryside to a line of foliage to their front. "Another field lies on the other side of those trees. The Americans are through there." He took a deep breath. "The Germans have a machine gun nest a hundred meters to our left."

As Gallois turned to look, Monod warned, "Don't stare. They have no one guarding this right flank. If you stay along the line of haystacks to the right, you'll limit your exposure. They probably won't fire on you—they can't afford to give away their position. Keep that in mind as you go, but don't doddle—I could be wrong."

He clapped Gallois on the shoulder. "*Bonne chance, mon ami.*"

With an uneasy glance to his left, Gallois started on his way. He hurried to the first tall haystack and rested against it, out of sight of the machine gunner. Then he started off again, walking straight, upright, and with a deliberate pace. On reaching the second haystack, he rested again, wiped sweat from his face, and calmed his breathing.

A burning sensation seemed to bore into his back as he walked to the third stack, but he realized that his direct-line exposure decreased the farther he went. At last, after five more iterations, he ducked into the safety of the trees with a sigh of relief. Then he stared across the expanse to his front.

Several hours later, Galois stood in a 3rd Army headquarters tent before General George Patton. "I'll answer your request with the respect of one soldier to another," Patton said. "I'm sorry. The Allies are here to destroy Germans, not save capital cities." Not known for sentimentality, Patton was nevertheless moved by the grim expression on Gallois' face.

The French major had been intercepted by forward sentries as he crossed no-man's land. "I am with the French Resistance," he had called out when challenged. "I have a message from the leaders in Paris for General Eisenhower."

After a two-hour jeep ride and successive interrogations, he found himself before Patton late in the day. The general listened attentively, but then delivered his disheartening assessment.

"We're strapped for gas," Patton said. "If we run out, the war's over and you can forget saving France, much less Paris. And at this stage, we cannot accept responsibility for feeding an entire city. We don't have the resources."

Gallois' demeanor captured Patton's attention. He studied the exhausted French major as the man accepted the verdict with steady eyes. The general left the tent where they had met, but he returned seconds later. "Are you up for a twelve-hour jeep ride? You'll get in late tonight and tell your story to another general at Laval. See what he says. I want to make sure you get a full hearing at the highest possible level."

Nearly physically and emotionally spent, Gallois only nodded.

49

Same Day, August 21, 1944
Écouché-les-Vallées, France

In the hours before dawn, Lieutenant Colonel Jacques de Guillebon ordered his driver to halt his command vehicle. General Leclerc emerged from the dark of night into the dim glow of blackout lights in front of his vehicle. He was recognizable at once by his cane as he sidled along the passenger door. Guillebon rolled down his window.

"You are lucky," Leclerc said softly. "You will represent the French army inside our nation's free capital." He inhaled deeply and grasped the windowsill. "Remember, avoid the Americans at all costs."

Guillebon nodded grimly. "Thank you for this honor, sir."

Leclerc slapped the side of the vehicle and stood back. "Now go."

Guillebon saluted, held it until Leclerc had returned it, and then nudged his driver.

Leclerc watched them disappear, and then sighed heavily. For the past four days, on his orders, his 2nd French Armored Division had drawn double its allotment of fuel, ammunition, and rations. It had also not reported battle losses such that the division drew allocations for those vehicles as well. To reach needed supply levels, Leclerc's soldiers had also conducted "midnight requisitions." As a result, Leclerc's division was fully provisioned to march on Paris independent of Allied support.

No one higher than he knew of his actions. He had hand-picked his men for Guillebon's mission, taking them by ones and twos from across his division such that their absence would not be widely noticed, and he had done the same with selected war machines. He had even sent Lieutenant Colonel Paul Littlefield and two American liaison officers assigned to his division on escorted tours of the 2nd Armored's positions so they would not observe the organization and departure of Guillebon's contingent.

He had misgivings about deceiving Paul, whom he now considered a friend. But he had no patience with the notion that now, only a hundred and thirty miles from Paris, the 2nd French Armored Division was ordered to remain in wait in the apple orchards around Écouché while American divisions drew near the capital. Yet he had heard of no plans for entering the city. Further, he had received intelligence reports from Resistance groups of street fighting in Paris between *Wehrmacht* troops and ordinary citizens. Clearly, his people needed military assistance.

His division had proven itself. On the same day that it had liberated Alençon, it had entered fierce combat south of Carrouges. The German 5th *Panzerarmee* under General Eberbach had mounted a counterattack to recapture Le Mans. Initially, it struck east from the Ecouves Forest against US XV Corps' flank.

Leaving the bulk of his division to block the escape route through Alençon, Leclerc deployed his 4th Squadron, 12th Cuirassiers Regiment to advance into Carrouges behind the German assault. After intense fighting lasting into mid-afternoon, and during which his forces destroyed several tanks belonging to the German 2nd *Panzer* Division, his 4th Squadron occupied a position a mile east of Carrouges. Light skirmishes followed during which ten German prisoners were taken, including a lieutenant colonel.

As night settled, the division had liberated Carrouges, the second city freed by French forces. It had maintained a blocking position against repeated German incursions.

Following those actions, and as the battle raged around Falaise, Leclerc's division had been relieved and ordered to retire for rest and recuperation in this apple orchard in which Leclerc currently found himself.

Quietly incensed, his instincts screamed that this was the time to head full-steam into Paris, now so close.

The encirclement at the Falaise Pocket was all but complete. He and Paul had toured the battlefield yesterday. It was unlike anything either of them had seen before and wished never to see again. The putrid stench of decaying corpses made breathing laborious, and the fumes did not arise only from dead soldiers. The roads and fields were littered with the cadavers of cattle, horses, dogs, cats, chickens, wild birds, rabbits, deer... Capsized horse-drawn German supply wagons clogged the roads along with destroyed tanks, jeeps, troop carriers, supply trucks...

Leclerc had kept an eye on battlefield reports, and they were ghastly. An estimated eighty to one-hundred thousand German troops were snared in the encirclement. Of those, forty to fifty thousand were captured, and ten to fifteen thousand were killed. An estimated additional twenty to fifty thousand escaped.

He and Paul had both gagged at the smell and the gruesome sights, and they did not linger. Both doubted the accuracy of the casualty and damage reports.

Leclerc had also monitored, distantly, a difference of opinion that had arisen between Generals Patton and Montgomery on one side of an issue and Generals Eisenhower and Bradley on the other. At the height of the battle, Patton had proposed, with Montgomery's support, to close the gap between Argentan and Falaise and trap the full Army Group B inside the pocket.

The decision would have been Montgomery's to make, but at Bradley's insistence, Eisenhower weighed in. Bradley's objection was that Patton blocked three principal escape routes through Alencon, Sées, and Argentan. To close the gap meant that Patton would have to stretch his line forty miles to Falaise. He stressed that nineteen *Wehrmacht* divisions clamoring to escape could have broken through and destroyed Patton's positions.

Eisenhower backed Bradley, and as a result, a sizable remnant of German Army Group B escaped through the gap and pushed east through Saint-Lambert, turned northwest of Paris, and then toward the Rhine River. Although Leclerc was dismayed, he could not overlook the Germans' tremendous losses: three hundred and forty-four *panzers*, anti-tank guns, and artillery pieces; over two thousand jeeps and trucks... The list went on in excruciating detail beyond the general's desire or need to read.

On Leclerc's mind now was that the enemy was routed, and the way to Paris lay open. For that reason, this morning, he had taken a monumental risk. On his own authority, he had deployed Lieutenant Colonel Guillebon and seventeen light tanks, ten armored cars, and two platoons of infantry to be a vanguard and enter the capital city. And the full 2nd French Armored Division was prepared to follow on Leclerc's order, irrespective of higher command. The general's immediate aim was to put the full division far enough on the road to Paris that his American superiors would be powerless to stop him.

He fully understood the consequences of failure.

His action could jeopardize France's standing with the Allies.

He could be court-martialed.

With that in mind, Leclerc crossed the road and mounted his command vehicle. He took a deep breath, exhaled, and nudged his driver to proceed. The vehicle's engine cranked and gears ground. It drove to a nearby airfield where a Piper Cub waited to fly Leclerc to US 12th Army Group headquarters to meet with General Bradley.

Riding along with the two American liaison officers the day before, Paul had wondered about the real reason why Leclerc had sent him on this tour. He had become accustomed to Leclerc's open manner, treating him more like a confidante than a liaison officer or an assistant. Paul was happy to accompany the general whenever so directed, but he had done very little liaison work. He was a bystander in most planning meetings, and he had seen very few occasions when his language abilities had been needed to sort out anything. Regardless, he was happy for the experience of spending time with the iconic general.

Then, several days earlier, he had noticed behavior on Leclerc's part that seemed circumspect. The general had sent Paul on several tasks that could neither be classified as missions nor were particularly important. This current trip with the Americans to tour the battlefield positions was a case in point. It was neither necessary nor enlightening, particularly given the combat Paul had participated in at the general's side over the past few days.

Paul did not see value in the tour or his other tasks. They seemed intended to take him away from headquarters, for each time he returned, Leclerc had adjourned a meeting of selected subordinate leaders. Paul had also noticed that fuel and supply trucks had been more active than after previous combat operations.

He finally concluded that his tasks had been make-work, intended to keep him away from the center of Leclerc's planning and operations. Considering the openness Paul had experienced up to then, he could only wonder why Leclerc was now keeping him at arm's length.

Paul dismissed the concerns, accepting instead the notion that perhaps Leclerc decided that Paul had been provided too much access. Given their differences in rank and responsibilities, that was not a far-fetched conclusion.

As the tour with the other liaison officers continued, Paul settled into his seat behind the jeep driver and took a letter from his jacket pocket. It was from his cousin, Josh, dated August 10. Paul skipped down below the salutations and read,

"Can you believe I'm sending this from Guam? The benefits of air superiority to a pilot are immense. Only a few weeks ago, we were dueling in the skies over Saipan against the full onslaught of the combined Imperial Japanese Navy. You've probably heard that we won that scuffle, and that their navy is pretty much restricted to defending its home islands, which are 900 miles west of here. We've taken the Marianas. The Pacific Ocean from here eastward is clear all the way to California.

"I'm standing near one of the westernmost points on Guam, and the skies are clear except for our own aircraft, which are still doing surveillance duty and practice runs. That's what I'm doing here now. I flew down with my squadron from Eniwetok this morning, and what a breeze, with one refueling stop at Saipan, and virtually no worries coming out of the west. If there had been a threat, our radar would have picked it up. What an incredible advance in technology from the beginning of this war. Someday, I'd like to compare notes with Jeremy about how things were when he flew in the Battle of Britain and during the *blitz*. Should be quite a contrast.

"I've followed the war in Europe, and I know it's pretty grim. I guess the world is wondering if the Allies will land in southern France. By the time you get this, we'll probably know.

It's not finished over here either, by a long shot. Between us and Japan are still the Palau Islands, the Philippines, and Okinawa—plenty of chances to get shot up. Guam still has a lot of Japanese soldiers who escaped into the jungle and they harass our soldiers and local farmers."

Josh went on to ask about the family and closed with normal niceties.

Paul sighed. He inferred that Josh was in a period of relative inactivity. *Not unlike my own. Oh well, it happens, even in war.*

He fixed a studiously interested look on his face as he toured the various sites with the two Americans. When he arrived back at his tent near the headquarters, night had fallen.

He had trouble sleeping, and early in the morning he went to visit the latrine. On the way back, he heard low voices and combat vehicles' idling engines. Thinking that having such vehicles this close to the headquarters was unusual, he looked about for security. Seeing none, he drew close. Then, in the dim glow of blackout lights, he made out Leclerc, leaning on his cane and speaking with someone on the passenger side of a half-track.

Having no reason to eavesdrop, Paul turned away, but as he did, he heard the general say, "Avoid the Americans at all costs."

50

Same Day, August 21, 1944
Fontainebleau, France

Paul Delouvrier, codename Fabri, listened to the crackle of the BBC over his radio. His concealed headquarters was nestled on a plateau in thick forest within the former hunting grounds of King Louis VII and near the famed Fontainebleau Palace. It was in the vicinity of where the historical figure, Thomas Becket, had once found shelter. Five thousand men of Fabri's commando group had entered the area by covert means over the course of two weeks and foraged in clusters in a wide area around the town.

This evening, Fabri, a gentle giant thirty years of age, had returned from a secret meeting with Chaban in Paris. There, Chaban provided the code phrase that would launch a most sensitive mission in which Fabri's men were key.

In preparation, Fabri had directed that the plateau be cleared sufficiently to allow an aircraft to land and that two Horch sedans be captured from the *Wehrmacht*. With that accomplished without complications, Fabri now listened for the critical phrase. The BBC broadcaster ran through a long list of short announcements, each seemingly innocuous, but each setting furtive Resistance activity in motion across France to subvert *Wehrmacht* operations and control.

"Susan says happy birthday to her grandmother," might signal to proceed with a raid on a munitions depot in Lyon.

"Charlie's dog recovered after a visit to the veterinarian," might order the detonation of a particular bridge in the north of France.

Fabri listened to them all, straining to hear above static interference so as not to miss or misconstrue the message he hoped for, and that had brought his large band of commandos to these woods. Finally, he heard, *"As-tu bien déjeuné, Jacquot?"*

Quelling an urge to yelp in celebration, he gathered his subordinate leaders. "At last, I can reveal our mission. It is to greet and secure our leader, General Charles de Gaulle, when he lands on our plateau. We will escort him into Paris." As his men stared in shock and began celebrating, he silenced them with a stern warning. Looking directly into the eyes of each one, he said, "Utter and complete secrecy is imperative. The Allies know nothing of this. President Roosevelt, in particular, would not approve."

The small group of men remained quiet, absorbing with bright, questioning eyes what they had just heard. "We will follow behind General Leclerc's 2nd Armored Division," Fabri continued. "That's our French division," he added with pride. "General de Gaulle is determined that our own countrymen will lead the liberation of our capital and fight with the Allies to free the rest of France. Our chosen leaders will govern our country as a fully independent and sovereign nation."

He smiled. "General de Gaulle is determined to go personally to Paris to restore our republic. The Allies might try to stop him. Our mission, gentlemen, is to secure the intersections and the major roads and bridges leading into Paris to make sure that General de Gaulle arrives there safely, regardless of Allied intentions."

Laval, France

US Army Colonel Albert Lebel watched as a jeep pulled up to Eagletac, General Bradley's 12th Army Group headquarters. Lebel was the Group's liaison to the FFI patriots who had so strenuously resisted German occupation that they had earned Lebel's deep affection and respect.

The night before, as midnight approached, he had typed out a note and slipped it among Bradley's briefing papers. The move was a risky one that could result in disciplinary action—a last-ditch effort to change the minds of his superiors. The note read, "If the American Army, seeing Paris in a state of insurrection, does not come to its aid, it will be an omission that the people of France will never be able to forget."

The jeep he saw arrive in the pre-dawn hours, covered in mud and dust, drove to the front of the intelligence section and halted. Lebel recognized that this must be the vehicle he had been advised by Patton's intelligence section to expect. The passenger door opened and a ghost of a man appeared. He was filthy, with deep sockets around his eyes, unkempt hair, and several days' worth of grizzly whiskers.

To Lebel, Gallois was a beautiful sight, a godsend. Seeing that the major was falling-down fatigued, he hurried over to steady him. "Get some water and food for this man," he ordered anyone within earshot as he led Gallois into the G-2 group of tents.

"*Merci*," Gallois murmured.

"Listen to me," Lebel said brusquely, "I know why you're here. Can you pull enough strength together for one more briefing? My boss is Major General Sibert. He is this army group's intelligence chief. He's flying out in a few minutes with General Bradley, our commanding general. Have you heard of him?"

Gallois nodded weakly.

"The two of them are going to meet with General Eisenhower," Lebel continued. "This is our last chance to change their minds regarding Paris. You won't have time to clean up. Can you do it?"

An orderly brought Gallois a canteen of water. He drank deeply and wiped his mouth while Lebel watched him anxiously. Finally, he nodded. "I didn't do a good job with General Patton last night," he rasped. "This time I'll do better."

When, minutes later, Gallois stood in front of General Sibert and a group of other officers, including Lebel, he reached deep into his being for poise, calm, and articulation. Manifesting sincerity, he explained the situation as it was when he had left Paris more than thirty-six hours earlier. "I was sent to beg for arms," he said, "but that is not our real need. Any weapons dropped could be picked up by anyone, friend or foe."

Sibert immediately held up a hand for a pause and turned to an aide. "There's a shipment already ordered and due to be dropped today by request of a Colonel Rol. Get it paused while we discuss, as well as any others that are planned." He reverted his attention to Gallois.

"We, the people of Paris," Gallois said, gesturing with his palms spread, "wanted to liberate our capital ourselves and present it to you, our Allies. But we cannot finish what we started. You must come to our aid"—he steadied himself and took a deep breath—"or we will see a terrible slaughter. Hundreds of thousands will die."

When Gallois had finished speaking, the group was silent. General Sibert had listened intently, but his expression remained non-committal. Then, as he started for the exit, he called over to Lebel. "Where is that impatient lion, General Leclerc?"

"He's due here this morning, sir."

"When you see him, tell him to stick around. We might have some good news for him." With that, the general walked out to the airfield. General Bradley joined him on the flightline, and the two climbed aboard separate Piper Cubs. Moments later, both aircraft took to the skies.

Grandchamp, France

General Eisenhower met with Generals Bradley and Sibert in his command caravan camouflaged within a line of trees near the battlefield at Falaise. "General de Gaulle doesn't let any grass grow under his feet." Eisenhower chuckled affably. "I met with him only two days ago and gave him a flat no about sending troops to Paris." He held out a sheet of paper. "Here's a letter he had General Juin hand-deliver to me yesterday, once more pleading his case for the Allies to make a beeline there. The guy never gives up. He had the brass to tell me that if I didn't send support, he'd pull his three divisions from the Allies and send them himself."

His face grew serious. "I'll admit the matter is grave. In his letter, de Gaulle took the step of assuming to act with the sovereignty of France, and he *demanded* action. He's never done that before. He says the insurgency is about to get out of hand. He believes the Germans have set charges all over the city and are about to blow them. And that's irrespective of a running street battle between the Resistance and the *Wehrmacht*."

He handed de Gaulle's letter over to Bradley, who scanned it and passed it on to Sibert. "He's sized it up succinctly," Bradley said, "and I think he's right." He gestured to Sibert. "Tell him about your Major Gallois."

Sibert related his conversation with the major. "I was impressed with him and his sincerity," Sibert began. "You could see that he wasn't making up anything. He was exhausted, he had his facts straight, and he spoke from the heart." He took a deep breath. "I believe that if we don't get at least a division in there, and soon, we will have an awful massacre."

"And if we do, we could have a major battle on our hands," Eisenhower muttered, "and a whole city to feed." He sat in quiet contemplation. Then he turned to Bradley. "Well, what the hell, Brad. I guess we'll have to go in."

Bradley's expression turned somber. "The president won't like it."

Eisenhower sighed. "I'll worry about that. He and de Gaulle never liked each other. Roosevelt sees de Gaulle as a narcissist seeking power and France as a conquered country that collaborated with the Nazis. His idea is to establish a military governorship over France when we've kicked the Germans out."

He grunted. "I see things differently. Nazi sympathizers exist in France just like they do in the US, but the country as a whole is a victim, just like Great Britain, Poland, and all the other countries Hitler's conquered. Once the war was on and we started winning, the Italians couldn't get rid of the Nazis and Fascists fast enough. Italy initially *fought* against us, but no one's talking about a military governorship in Rome."

The supreme commander stood and paced. "I was delegated authority by the heads of state of the three major powers to take whatever military steps are required to win this war in Europe and destroy the Nazi threat. That included the decision, that I took solely, to invade in southern France rather than go up through the Balkans.

"Paris now seems a test of our resolve. De Gaulle was on record warning about the Nazi threat before the war started. The French military brass ignored him—he was a lieutenant colonel at the time. But after the fall, he rallied his countrymen by radio from London. He's since set up a provisional government in Algiers, inspired the Resistance, and he took firm command of the French army in North Africa that's now fighting with us to liberate its own country. Regardless of all of that, if we don't act now, we might have a massacre of monumental proportions on our hands and the death of one of the world's great cities. And maybe we could stop it. I think we have to try."

"General, if I may," General Sibert interjected. "One point that Major Gallois was emphatic about was the desire of Parisians to liberate themselves. They had wanted to deliver Paris to us as a done deal."

Eisenhower smiled grimly. "But they can't finish the job."

"Send Leclerc and his 2nd Armored Division," Sibert suggested. "They've been stuck in an apple orchard waiting impatiently like racehorses at the gate."

"Hmm, it's a thought." Eisenhower turned to Bradley. "What do you say?"

"He's as fightin' a general as any you'll find, and his division is proven. Plus, his soldiers are fighting for their homes and to regain honor." He chuckled. "Hell, Leclerc'd give Patton a run for his money, but don't spread around I said that. I like my scalp."

Laval, France

General Leclerc and Major Gallois paced the airfield together. Shortly after Bradley and Sibert had flown out, Leclerc arrived. He and Gallois had not previously known each other, but after Lieutenant Colonel Lebel made introductions, they had walked up and down the airstrip becoming acquainted, talking about everything while awaiting the two generals' return.

An orderly had run out carrying a letter for Leclerc from de Gaulle. Dated two days earlier, it directed Leclerc to be prepared to move his division on Paris irrespective of orders received from any Allied command. Leclerc breathed a sigh of relief. His division was ready, and he had his national leader's support.

At midafternoon, just when Leclerc was approaching the time to leave for another commitment, he heard the buzz of a small airplane. Soon a Piper Cub appeared. It flew straight in, landed, and taxied to a halt. Sibert opened the door. Even before alighting, he called to Leclerc, "You win. We're sending you and your division to Paris."

Leclerc and Gallois stared at each other joyously, and then jumped around like schoolboys celebrating. So great was their excitement that they almost did not notice Bradley's Piper Cub landing and coasting to a halt a few yards behind Sibert's.

Bradley called Leclerc and Gallois over. "You're ordered to take your division and seize Paris," he told the French general. "One point of guidance I'll give is that there is to be no heavy fighting inside the city. We don't want bombs and artillery in there."

Then he looked back and forth between the two Frenchmen. "The three of us share responsibility for whatever happens in Paris. Me, because I'm giving the order. You, General Leclerc, because you'll execute it. And you, Major Gallois, because your information is largely what led to the decision."

Leclerc snapped a hasty salute. "Thank you, General," he called, already turning toward his plane. He paused and glanced at Gallois as well. "And thank you, Major. You've done your country a great service."

He snapped another salute to the major, and without waiting further, he limped to his Piper Cub as fast as his legs and his cane would carry him. Moments later, it lifted into the sky, banked left, and disappeared over nearby trees.

Gallois walked with Bradley and Sibert to the headquarters building. "You look like you could use some rest, Major," Bradley observed. He chuckled. "And a scrub."

"We'll take care of him," Sibert interjected.

51

Same Day, August 21, 1944
Paris, France

With his fiancée and secretary, Celeste, riding on his handlebars, Yvon Morandat pedaled hard through the streets toward Hôtel de Matignon, the stunning Baroque mansion where France's prime ministers had resided since the 1930s. The only exception had been the one installed by the German conquerors at the beginning of the war. He had since been succeeded by Pierre Laval, who then moved into the mansion.

As Morandat hurried on his task, he wondered if any of the gunfire he heard was from Communists shooting at Gaullists. He well recalled when, ten days earlier, a car almost ran him off the road. His firm conviction was that his near calamity had been an intentional act by Rol's Communists, initiated after Morandat refused to join them.

Alexandre Parodi, General de Gaulle's representative to the CNR, had assigned a mission to Morandat. Parodi realized that the insurrection he hoped would save Paris was slipping out of control. He knew that for every ministerial position of the former French government, de Gaulle had appointed a minister in the shadow government. They were patriots, experienced in their respective fields, who were prepared to begin their functions as soon as the capital was secured. And they were already in Paris.

Parodi was determined to seize the organs of government in the same way that Bayet and Luizet had taken control of the prefecture before Colonel Rol and his Communists could do so. To that end, he had sent Morandat to take possession of the prime minister's seat of authority at the Hôtel de Matignon. He had advised Morandat to take thirty men with him. Parodi had likewise sent Gaullists to take control of various other critical government offices.

Only one person was able to accompany Morandat, the pretty blonde girl he loved, who now rode on his handlebars. On some streets, gunfire was so thick that the couple dismounted and scurried from doorway to doorway of buildings along the way.

As they approached their destination, Morandat realized that he was unfamiliar with this section of the city, and he was unsure which turns he should take to reach the front entrance. Fortunately, he found another brave soul on the street to give him directions, a man calmly walking his poodle amid the strife. A short time later, Morandat and Celeste arrived at the main door of the mansion on Rue de Varenne.

With only Celeste to aid him, Morandat intended to run a huge bluff.

He hid his bicycle behind foliage against the mansion's stone wall. Then the couple climbed a wide, majestic set of low stairs to the massive arched door. Before knocking, he and Celeste stared wide-eyed at each other. "Are we really going to do this?" she asked incredulously.

He took a deep breath. "The Vichy prime minister fled. Now we're here."

With that, he turned and knocked loudly.

A Judas grille opened and a pair of eyes peered through.

"I'm here to see the commandant," Morandat announced firmly.

Moments later, the door opened. He stepped inside, followed by Celeste.

Morandat restrained himself from exhibiting severe shock at the sight that greeted him. Over one hundred men of fugitive Prime Minister Laval's personal bodyguard, in black uniforms, clustered about in a large courtyard. Judging from their arms stacked in rows, they were about to form up for administrative purposes.

Celeste tugged on Morandat's sleeve. "Put this on," she whispered, and handed him a tricolored FFI armband. While he did so, she slipped another one over her own sleeve to her upper arm.

A short officer marched across the gravel courtyard while the soldiers stared at Morandat in his shirtsleeves and Celeste in her summer dress. "What can I do for you?" the officer demanded. "I am the commander."

Morandat had entered the mansion not knowing what to expect or do once he was inside. He thought that he might run into trouble, and that it could be deadly.

He stared at the officer, his face becoming stern. Then he drew himself to his full height, pointed to his FFI armband, and proclaimed in a commanding voice, "I have come to occupy these premises in the name of the Provisional Government of the French Republic."

In a day full of shocks, Morandat was unprepared for what happened next. Just minutes before leaving his apartment on this mission, he had peered out his window in a practiced security measure. To his dismay, he had seen that the area was teeming with German soldiers. Perceiving with dread that the *Gestapo* was about to arrest him, he bemoaned that it was happening only days before the Allies would liberate Paris. Then he realized that the Germans were there to raid a brothel in the adjacent building.

Now, facing the commandant who had pledged allegiance to the German-installed Vichy government for four years, he was astounded to see the officer snap to attention. "I have always been a staunch republican," the little man said. He performed a military about-face and called the full guard contingent to attention. Facing about again, he snapped a salute. "I am at your orders."

Grasping a moment to think about what to do next, Morandat nodded and let out a deep breath. "First, no one other than the current staff and guard is allowed on the premises without my personal approval. Tell your men to use whatever force is required to prevent intrusions. I expect full compliance in that regard. No exceptions."

The commandant nodded grimly.

Morandat looked at the stacked arms. "Hostile activity could come this way over the next few days, but the Allies will arrive soon. Until then, the guards should never be out of arm's length from their weapons."

His face twitched involuntarily for a second. *I have no idea when the Allies will arrive.* He hoped his spike in anxiety was not readily apparent.

The commandant assented.

"Good. Take me to the official offices."

"I'll send a runner to inform the *maître d'hôtel* that you are here, and I'll escort you to him personally. He will see that your orders are carried out within the residence. My men will provide your protection."

With his jaw firmly set, Morandat consented. Minutes later, he and Celeste stood at the base of a magnificent marble staircase.

At the top, the *maître d'hôtel* waited, dressed formally in black tails and a white bow tie, a silver medal of his station hanging by a chain over his chest. He and the commandant made eye contact and nodded slightly.

"Welcome, sir," the *maître d'hôtel* pronounced when the couple had ascended to the landing. "I will show you to the Green Room, your quarters, formerly occupied by Monsieur Laval. I hope that it will be adequate."

"I'm sure it will be." Morandat gestured toward Celeste. "This is my personal secretary." He spun toward her to hide an irrepressible grin and saw that she stared in wonder at the circumstances, the finery, and the deference afforded them.

"Make note of where the Green Room is," he told her. Regaining his firm expression, he turned back to the *maître d'hôtel* and ordered, "Take me to my office."

"Sir, do you mean the prime minister's office?"

"I do. I assume the staff is still here?"

The *maître* bowed slightly. "Some members are absent, due to the difficulties on the streets."

"I wish to meet those who are here. Have them assemble in my office."

The *maître d'hôtel* gestured. "This way."

As the trio started off, Morandat said, "I'll hold a full meeting of the government there tomorrow. It must be fully prepared—"

"The *ministers*, sir?"

52

August 22, 1944
Paris, France

Chantal looked out the window of the switchboard room where she had stationed herself to help defend the prefecture for the past four days. Morale plummeted among her compatriots as food and ammunition supplies dwindled. Reports flowed in of high casualties around the city, more than five hundred Parisians killed and four times that number wounded, and still no sign of Allied support. Chantal wondered if she was the only person among those around her who knew that the Allies had no plan to liberate Paris immediately, intending instead to detour around it.

Water still ran to the prefecture's faucets, so Chantal had been able to keep herself relatively clean. Without soap, shampoo, or changes of clothes, however, she knew that her only saving grace from the way she must look and smell was that everyone around her was in the same dismal state.

The phone system worked erratically. Electricity had been cut to two hours per day. Chantal's nights had been spent on the same floor, by the same window, and without blankets. The fighting at the police headquarters itself was intermittent, but the cordon around it was tight. As both the Gaullists and Communists had expected, the Germans had concluded that the center of the Resistance and its control of the twenty-thousand *gendarmes* who policed Paris rested in that building.

General Choltitz was unwilling to cede it.

Chantal spent the many hours, day and night, sitting in her small corner of the war, thinking of those she loved. Horton, where was he? Was he even alive? Tears formed in her eyes as the thought overtook her that their love story might already have ended—that she might learn months from now that he had never made it past the beach at Normandy. *If I make it out of* here *alive.*

And Amélie. Was she still in Paris? Was she safe? A prohibition against attempting personal calls in favor of keeping lines open for crucial reports was enforced. Understanding the circumstances, no one in the prefecture complained much, but that did not lessen worry about family and friends who might have been caught up in the city-fighting.

When such thoughts plagued her, Chantal took a deep breath and shrugged them off. Reports of stiff fighting by the Resistance continued to flow into the prefecture. Women and children had joined the fight, building massive barricades at intersections with whatever materials they could gather. Men and boys blocked some streets by chopping down large trees, and they made other streets impassible by unearthing bricks and stones from the pavement. Women and girls had formed lines to carry the paving materials to the street barriers.

The continued resistance of Parisian patriots reassured those inside the prefecture that all was not yet lost. Individual stories brought hope: at a stockyard across town, a small group of FFI fighters held out against attacks by two platoons of German soldiers.

A mile away on Rue de Jessaint, as was done at many junctions across Paris, fighters had used a huge barricade of burned-out vehicles, car and truck tires, furniture, or any other object or material that could provide cover from which to shoot and slow enemy progress. On a street near Montmartre, determined railway employees had stopped four German squads.

While the reports of Parisian heroism imparted a sense of hope, they could not quell a more immediate sensation: hunger. As the hours passed, thoughts faded of Horton, Amélie, Fourcade, Jeremy, Chaban, or any of the other people who occupied large spaces in Chantal's life. They were overtaken by fast-looming starvation.

In the early afternoon, Choltitz greeted Nordling in his office with the first semblance of a smile that the Swede had seen the general display. After they had taken their seats, the German reached behind his desk and brought out a bottle of whiskey. "Please don't tell the British," he said with a slight grin.

Nordling winced inwardly at the awkward attempt at humor and wondered about its relevance. The terrace door was open, and even now, he heard shooting. However, he made no remark concerning the incongruity.

"Your ceasefire doesn't seem to be working very well," Choltitz observed as he poured two glasses of the liquor and handed one to Nordling. He added with a bite to his tone, "I released three high-level prisoners yesterday as a goodwill gesture, for which I seem to have received no appreciation."

"General, if I may," Nordling interjected, "the people know what you intend. They've deduced it. Any gesture pales compared to the horror facing them of being blown up along with their beautiful city."

Choltitz grimaced only slightly.

"As for the Resistance fighters—"

"Terrorists."

"Have it your way. Regardless, there is only one man who commands the entire FFI, be they Communists, Gaullists, or whatever, and that is General de Gaulle himself. You'll recall that British Prime Minister Churchill recognized him as the legitimate leader of the FFI four years ago—"

"The Americans haven't," Choltitz growled. "And neither have we."

Nordling conceded the point with a solemn nod. "In any event, General de Gaulle is probably in Normandy with the Allies. He's not here."

Choltitz held up his glass and watched while he swirled the clear liquid. Then he looked directly at Nordling. "Why doesn't someone go speak with him?"

The Swedish diplomat coughed in astonishment. He leaned forward, set his drink on the desk, and took a moment to gauge the general's seriousness. At last he asked, "Would you authorize someone to pass through your lines for the purpose?"

"Why not?"

Hesitantly, Nordling said, "If you were to do that, then I would go myself on such a mission."

The general flipped his hand indifferently. Then he drew from his tunic several sheets of blue paper. "These are orders received over the past few days from German High Command directing me to commence what would be the methodical destruction of the city. I've been pressured to begin from every quarter, including by Adolf Hitler himself. Every day he asks, 'Is Paris burning?'" He lifted his eyebrows in a matter-of-fact expression. "Instead, I've tried your truce." He gestured toward the terrace and the sound of gunfire. "As you can hear, it has not worked."

He sighed, stood, and crossed to a map. "*Generalfeldmarschall* Model is supposed to be sending reinforcements. They're coming south out of Denmark. If they arrive, my hand will be forced. Come, let me show you."

Puzzled, Nordling left his seat and joined Choltitz. The general ran his finger along a line south of Paris.

"I have two divisions placed along here to defend Paris, which is my first mandate. I have them placed here and here." He indicated the general locations of the units. "As you can see, there is a wide gap between them. When the divisions arrive from Denmark, they will naturally fill that gap." He lowered his voice and looked directly into Nordling's eyes. "Very soon, I will have to give the order to execute."

Realization dawned on Nordling that Choltitz had consciously revealed the status of Paris' defenses, including a vulnerability that was probably within the general's power to close. He had further disclosed that reinforcements were on the way and how they were to be used. The diplomat could only conclude that the weakness had been purposely created and revealed. His brows furrowed as he concentrated on what he had heard and seen. The inescapable conclusion was that this commanding general of

Gross Paris had provided an avenue for Allied forces to enter the city.

Choltitz continued, "If you haven't already, you'll soon conclude that what I have told you could be construed as treason."

Mouth agape in wonder, Nordling asked, "Would you provide a document for me to take to the Allies?"

Choltitz tossed his head. "I'm not volunteering for the slaughter. Essentially, through you, I am asking the Allies for their help to save Paris. But what I've told you cannot be put in a document. My name cannot be associated with this effort."

He crossed to his desk and wrote out a note on his letterhead. "Here," he said, handing it to Nordling, "this should provide safe passage."

The consul took it and read, "The Commanding General of Paris authorizes the Consul General of Sweden, R. Nordling, to leave Paris and its line of defense." He gazed up, almost disbelieving. "What else can you do for safe passage?"

Choltitz' expression indicated that he had anticipated the question. "Take Bobby Bender with you."

Nordling stared and then nodded his comprehension. When he was first assigned to Paris, a friend had introduced him to Bobby and later told the consul in a hushed voice, "If you need doors opened in Paris, see Bobby Bender." Through Bobby, Nordling had first been introduced to Choltitz.

That had occurred when Nordling had worked strenuously to transfer the three thousand political prisoners to Swedish protection. Without the former World War I German fighter pilot's help, the effort would have been stymied. The worst outcome would have undoubtedly happened as it already had in Rennes and Caen. At the prisons in those two cities, *SS* troops evacuating ahead of the Allied advance had slaughtered the inmates.

Nordling had sought out Emil "Bobby" Bender and found him just as the German was about to abscond to Switzerland. With the personality and flair of a playboy who represented a Swiss paper pulp manufacturer, Bender had a new assignment at Sainte-Menehould, two hours east and close to the German border. He preferred to join his mistress in Switzerland and forget the war; and with an *Abwehr* pass, he had the ability to do just that. Only Nordling's entreaties on behalf of the political prisoners had interrupted his plans.

As they had worked together, Nordling gradually discerned Bobby's real role in Paris. He was an undercover operator with the *Abwehr* and involved with a secret network that opposed Hitler situated within the intelligence agency. Now, the Swedish consul wondered if General Choltitz knew of the covert agent's political leanings.

Nordling did not dwell on the issue. He recognized that Bobby had the ability and authority to escort him through the checkpoints along the way to and at the front.

"If he has any trouble at all," Choltitz told Nordling, "Bobby can call me and I will reiterate over the telephone what is written on that authorization." With that, the general escorted Nordling to the door. "Twenty-four to forty-eight hours," he said, grasping Nordling's elbow in a friendly gesture. "That's all the time we have. Remember, Model is sending a division or two of reinforcements. If they arrive first..." He shook his head.

Nordling hurried to prepare for his trip. He estimated that the drive through the German and American checkpoints and then to General Eisenhower's headquarters would take twelve hours. Once inside American defenses, his party would need to be vetted and then escorted—if the Americans would listen, and Nordling was believed.

Within two hours, the car was ready with sufficient fuel, and Bobby had joined Nordling. The consul rose from his desk, picked up his suitcase, and crossed to the door. As he turned the knob, he collapsed with a heart attack.

53

August 22, 1944
Saint-Nizier, France

"Let's go," Huet called to Jeremy. "It's time to meet the Americans. They're holding at Le Pont-de-Claix on the east side of the Vercors. That's a mistake." He paused and a rare grin spread across his face. "General Pflaumm vacated Grenoble and took all his *boche* soldiers with him."

Thoughts flew through Jeremy's mind of the events that had transpired since the massacre at the Grotte de la Luire. Then, the Vercors' deliverance had seemed an utter impossibility. In the week immediately following, conditions had worsened across the plateau as the Germans continued to pillage the villages. Reports of atrocities piled up on Huet's field desk.

Then the very next week, the number and scale diminished, and the decline repeated in the following week. By the third week after la Luire, Huet and the *Maquis* forces camped around the rim of the Vercors had ventured back onto the floor of the plateau and began offensive operations against the remaining *Wehrmacht* elements.

Despite still reeling from six weeks of deprivation and the huge loss of family and friends and the horror of their tortured deaths, the Resistance members set out to harass the enemy as it departed the plateau. With ammunition still in short supply, they understood that the best they could do was to execute hit-and-run raids to sting *les boches*. A chief objective, however, was to restore confidence and inform the *Wehrmacht* that, against overwhelming odds and Germany's greatest effort, a disciplined, capable fighting force remained on the Vercors.

Four Weeks Earlier

Jeremy arrived back at Huet's camp from Grotte de la Luire, the cave hospital, exhausted, famished, and dispirited. The commander had let him rest for two days, and then sent him south to link up with Captain Geyer. "He can be difficult," Huet said, "but Geyer is a fighter."

Jeremy noted the respect and admiration Huet now held for the willful captain.

"He's become more cautious, more judicious in his attacks," Huet said. "The Germans fear him. He hides in the deep forest on the mountains with his *cuirassiers*, but he's never stopped striking the enemy at every chance. The Germans have to fight British and Americans on the European continent now, and the Soviets have unleashed hell with their Operation Bagration in the east.

"The Allied southern invasion into France must happen soon. That's a necessity, to drive the German Nineteenth Army north. Meanwhile, Geyer could use your help."

Jeremy had scoffed. "He needs my help? I don't see that he'd think he needs anyone's help. Even if he did, he'd never admit it."

"Then go learn something from him."

Jeremy realized that Huet's order was a kindly attempt to raise his spirits. "You saw terrible things," Huet said. "You'll never forget them. But you need to install new memories, successful ones, to lessen the images of la Luire." He eyed Jeremy and added, "I have good and bad news. Which would you like first?"

Jeremy looked at him glumly. "Give me the bad news."

Huet nodded and let out his breath. "We lost Captain Tournissa."

"And his assistant," Jeremy breathed, "the one with the broken shoulder." An image of the engineer's corpse at la Luire flitted across his mind.

He remembered Tournissa well. The captain's dedication and hard work to build the runway capable of handling Allied bombers at Vassieux in six days had been remarkable, and he had succeeded.

He recalled Tournissa's frustration, after it was completed, on being told that it had to be extended another fifty meters and widened by ten meters before Allied aircraft could use it. Before the expansion could be completed, however, the Germans began their attack on the Vercors, and the *Luftwaffe's* fighters and bombers had no difficulty landing at the airfield.

Jeremy sighed. "What's the good news?"

Huet smiled. "Dr. Ganimède and his family escaped."

Surprised, Jeremy exclaimed, "All three of them? How?"

"They were taken back to Saint-Martin on that truck you saw. The American, Lieutenant Chester, was also on it. When it arrived at headquarters, Chester was the first American the Germans had ever seen, and they were so intrigued with him that they let security lapse. Mrs. Ganimède and her son simply walked away. The doctor asked to use the restroom, and while in there, he realized that no one was paying any attention to him. He crawled out through a window."

"What about the nurses?"

Huet shook his head. "They were sent to Ravensbrück, near Berlin." He paused. "Not all the men were executed at the cave. They brought some back to headquarters for unknown reasons." He frowned. "They executed them the next day. All but Chester. He was sent to a POW camp in Germany."

He sighed. "But there is one last piece of good news."

Jeremy regarded him expectantly.

"When Mrs. Ganimède and her son walked away, they had one other person with them. Lilette Lesage."

Jeremy's body went limp with relief. He had not been prepared for the news or how it would affect him. He had met Lilette on a few occasions, but they had not interacted much beyond their brief exchange at la Luire.

Lilette was so young, so brave, and had taken such chances to try to save the five *maquisards* who had been subsequently executed by the same soldiers who shot and left her for dead. She had shown equal courage at la Luire.

And she was alive.

Huet noticed Jeremy's shocked reaction. "She's in a safe place. Now it appears that most of the people left on the Vercors will survive, Lilette among them."

Despite the harsh conditions, Jeremy's time with Captain Geyer was unexpectedly thrilling. The captain and his *cuirassiers* had made a rough home in the *Forêt de Lente,* France's largest virginal forest located on the southwest quadrant of the Vercors. His cavalrymen had learned the game trails, the hidden streams, and where caves provided shelter, where friendly farms were located, and where lightly wooded areas allowed their horses to gallop full out.

"We don't attack for the moment," Geyer told Jeremy. "Our mission now is to collect information. We have observers out and a steady stream of intelligence coming in so we can develop a map of German camps and their strengths. When the time comes to strike, we'll be ready."

During Jeremy's first night at Geyer's headquarters, he heard aircraft engines and then heavy explosions reverberating over the mountain ridges from the outer slopes. Hurrying out of his tent, he found Geyer and his adjutant looking up into the western sky. Flashes illuminated the high ridges, and vestiges of gun smoke soared high and floated into the valley, bringing with it an acrid albeit welcome scent.

"The Allies are finally bombing Chabeuil," Geyer enthused. "We're getting reports of heavy bombers striking the control towers, runways, and aircraft on the ground."

Behind him, his troops whooped in celebration, but he cautioned them to observe noise discipline. "The *Luftwaffe* over the Vercors is finished," he muttered to Jeremy. "We won't be seeing any more reconnaissance flights or fighters gunning down civilians." Later reports established that Allied Halifax bombers had destroyed thirty enemy aircraft.

Jeremy could not help wondering how many lives that had become important to him could have been spared had the bombing come sooner. "Count your blessings," he breathed, thinking of Dr. Ganimède's family, Lieutenant Chester, and Lilette Lesage.

At Jeremy's insistence, Geyer sent him on mounted patrols. Despite the danger, Jeremy found them to be exhilarating. The awesome strength of his horse, its responsiveness to the nudge of Jeremy's heel or his light pull on the reins was as thrilling as flying a Spitfire or rounding a tight curve on a motorcycle, the difference being that the animal was a living, breathing creature that returned his affection. He found himself reveling again in the beauty of the Vercors mountains and plateau, although sobered by its enormous losses.

Veteran soldiers and *maquisards* who had been separated from their units or had moved south from the vicinity of the Gorges de la Bourne after the defeat at Valchevrière found their way to Geyer's camp to a warm welcome, including the Senegalese bodyguards. Then, during the second half of Jeremy's week with Geyer, reports filtered in that *Wehrmacht* units were moving off the plateau and back onto the plains. The frequency and severity of atrocities waned. Word reached Geyer that Huet was preparing to go on the offensive. The message included instructions for Jeremy to transfer to Captain Beauregard's group south of the Gorges de la Bourne.

Jeremy and Geyer sat atop their horses. Jeremy was about to dismount to take the car sent for him. "I've enjoyed my time with you, Captain," he told Geyer. "I've learned from you."

Geyer grinned. "Who would have thought that possible?" He leaned forward in his saddle as he scanned the landscape, now beginning to show the russet colors of autumn. "I made mistakes. I freely admit it," he said. "But I love my country and the Vercors, and I love the people here. Everything I did was in hopes of ridding ourselves of the German blight as soon as possible. Lieutenant Colonel Huet and I still don't agree on strategy and tactics, but he's a good man, a good officer—"

"And you always obeyed his orders," Jeremy interjected, "even when you strongly objected to them and could have ignored them. He appreciates that."

"Farewell, my friend. I hope to see you again when this is all over."

Jeremy joined Captain Beauregard's group at Plénouze, a forested crest near the north point of the arrow-shaped Vercors' mountain mass. It occupied terrain that overlooked approaches into the mountains northwest of Grenoble. Barren slopes surrounded much of the area. The men were physically weakened for lack of adequate sustenance, their conditions strikingly worse than those of Geyer's *cuirassiers*. Without the speed and range of horses, Beauregard's *maquisards* foraged a much smaller area, and without the deep forest to protect them and obscure their movements, they were restricted to maintaining security. They survived on reduced rations, and when Jeremy joined them, they were haggard shadows of the men who had fought at Saint-Nizier.

Despite the conditions, Beauregard maintained stiff resolve among his men, and as the *Wehrmacht* receded from the plateau. Upon Huet's guidance to undertake offensive operations, he set up a string of ambushes at Col de la Croix-Perrin near Saint-Nizier and along Gorges de la Bourne.

Fierce fighting over several days left twenty German soldiers dead and fifty more severely wounded. Then, a week after Jeremy joined Beauregard, they received the long-awaited news that the Allies had invaded southern France.

Two days later, Lieutenant Colonel Huet summoned Jeremy and Beauregard to meet him at Saint-Nizier. When they arrived, the emaciated condition of both men did not escape him.

"You've done well," he told Beauregard. "By this time tomorrow, the last of the Germans will be out of the Vercors."

"I'll go after the ones that are still here," Beauregard said. "Not one of them should be left alive."

"You can't," Huet replied.

"Why not? They're on the run. We can make sure they don't pillage anyone else on their way back to Germany."

Huet regarded him thoughtfully. "They've burned down more farms to retaliate for your ambushes, and Geyer's." Seeing Beauregard grimace, he added, "They've killed eight hundred people on the Vercors since Bastille Day."

While Jeremy looked on, Beauregard stood ashen-faced. "I didn't know the numbers," he gasped. "That many?"

Huet nodded. "And many more on the plains. They're leaving, and I'm sure they'll continue killing. Let's not poke the wolf as it slinks away." He placed a hand on Beauregard's shoulder. "I wanted to tell you that personally. I ordered you to take the offensive. You needed to understand this change."

Beauregard nodded morosely. "Thank you, sir."

"Go back to your men and take them down onto the plateau. The people are traumatized. Help them start rebuilding." Huet turned to Jeremy. "An American brigade under General Fredericks reached Sisteron, south of the Vercors, three days ago. Another unit, Task Force Butler, is moving through there and pushing a division north toward Grenoble. I'm going to meet them. I'll need you there to interpret."

Jeremy relived those four weeks as he and Huet swept downhill from Saint-Nizier to Grenoble on bicycles, moisture streaming from the corners of their eyes from the rush of wind. They had no gas for motorcycles or any other vehicle.

Despite the steep inclines, they pumped their legs hard, driving to high speeds, even passing normal traffic and swerving to avoid oncoming vehicles. They passed large boulders and tall firs lining the road, sweeping by them so fast that they appeared as nothing more than blurs. Cold wind blew down from the mountain peaks surrounding them, stinging their faces, but they paid it no heed.

As the crow flies, Pont-de-Claix, the forward edge of the American advance, was little more than five miles away, but the road's circuitous route around hairpin turns and over long straightaways in the opposite direction stretched the distance to nearly twenty miles. However, after several hair-raising near-calamities, the pair reached level ground on Grenoble's north-western outskirts and turned south onto the Napoleon Route. Still they pedaled hard, the muscles in Jeremy's legs screaming and his lungs gasping despite his months of trekking the Vercors' mountains and plateau.

Huet had received word early in the morning that the Americans had reached Pont-de-Claix, apparently intent on halting there and preparing for a battle with General Pflaumm's 157th Reserve Division. The French officer had been aghast. Staring at a map, he jabbed a forefinger at it and snapped, "They're only six miles from Grenoble. They must not know that the Germans have abandoned the city."

That conclusion had sparked his resolve. He and Jeremy had seized the first two bicycles they saw outside the burnt-out villa he had used for his headquarters before the German attack only a month ago.

Now cycling furiously south on the road that Napoleon had used for his surprise attack on Paris, Huet and Jeremy maneuvered around jubilant crowds celebrating the departure of the hated *Wehrmacht*. The populace milled on the sidewalks and spilled onto the streets, hugging each other and shouting with joy that, for the first time in four years, they woke up as free people.

Huet bellowed at them to move aside, and Jeremy joined in yelling loud warnings to part the crowds ahead of them. Some turned toward them in annoyance, but on seeing Huet's French Army uniform, they cheered him, moved out of the way, and called ahead to warn the crowds.

Soon Huet and Jeremy were outside the Grenoble city limits and riding through wide fields. As they raced across the countryside, thrill replaced dread as what had seemed impossible morphed into the probable—the mighty *Wehrmacht* was on its way to defeat.

The snow-covered mountain peaks fell away behind them, and ahead of them the road wound around low hills. Along the way, streams of people shouted and waved in celebration. In the distance, the first buildings of Pont-de-Claix appeared, and as they came near, the crowds grew again proportional to the size of the small village.

The two men rounded a curve at the base of a rise, and there, in the middle of the road, was a Sherman tank, glistening in the sun despite its dark color. Villagers grouped on either side of it, staring in wonder at this monster of war that had arrived to deliver them. Among them, American soldiers gladly accepted the affections and thanks of a grateful population. Behind the tank, a column of war machines extended between two- and three-story homes and shops lining the main street.

Huet slowed his pace, glancing about for someone in authority. Jeremy watched him, marveling at the lieutenant colonel's straight back, astuteness, and physical toughness. *If it's possible to be dignified on a bicycle, Huet does it best.*

This was the man who had advised strenuously against activating Operation Montagnard. When he was overruled, he threw all his effort into defending the Vercors until the last possible moment, resisting calls for guerrilla action in favor of maintaining military cohesion until he had no other option. He had arrived at Autrans-en-Vercors on a broken-down bus to assume his command; he had hiked into the mountains to contact his subordinate commanders, toured the mountain defenses tirelessly on a motorcycle until Pflaumm's forces invaded the plateau. He had executed a plan for survival against *Wehrmacht* atrocities, taken the offensive at the first opportunity, and now rode a bicycle on a wild ride down a treacherous mountain road to urge the Americans forward.

Mindboggling audacity and judgment.

Huet rode up to the first tank and halted. Still breathing hard, he called to the first soldier who made eye contact, one still sitting atop the tank. The soldier stared at him, not comprehending.

"This is Lieutenant Colonel Huet," Jeremy shouted. "I am British Army Major Littlefield. We need to see your commander immediately."

The soldier's uniform was dirty and his eyes sunk in sockets from fatigue. His M1 rifle rested across his legs. He peered at Jeremy with obvious curiosity and then regarded Huet with uncertainty. Then he called down into the tank, "Hey, Sarge, there's two guys here sayin' they need to see the ol' man. One of 'em's wearin' a frog uniform."

Seconds later, another soldier's bare head appeared, looking equally disheveled and fatigued. On seeing Huet's uniform, he chided the first soldier. "Show some respect, Smitty." The sergeant clambered out of the tank commander's cupola and jumped to the ground. Then he saluted Huet. "Sorry for his bad manners," he drawled. "We've been on the go for several days."

"That's neither here nor there at the moment," Jeremy cut in. "We need to see your commander. It's urgent."

The sergeant eyed him. "A Brit, huh? And who are you?"

"Major Littlefield of the British army."

The sergeant snapped to attention and saluted. "Are you one of those secret squirrel guys, sir?"

"I am," Jeremy replied, and showed the ID disk hanging around his neck on a leather cord. "We don't have a lot of time. The jerries are on the run. We must speak with your commander."

The sergeant now moved with alacrity. "Smitty, take these guys to the ol' man's HQ. I'll let the LT know and call ahead to company headquarters."

Jeremy assumed that the "LT" was the platoon leader. In any event, the sergeant had taken the initiative to move him and Huet on to the company commander. A short conversation there resulted in an expedited audience with the battalion commander, Lieutenant Colonel Philip Johnson.

"There are no Germans in Grenoble," Huet reported through Jeremy. "I am the commander of the Free French Forces on the Vercors, the mountain region on your immediate left flank. We just rode down from Saint-Nizier, which overlooks Grenoble, and as you can see, I wore my full uniform. We were unmolested the entire way. We have operatives in Grenoble. They are reliable, and I can tell you with certainty that there are no Germans in the town."

He paused and grasped Johnson's arm. "Colonel, you can push into the city. Now. We want to see American uniforms in Grenoble today, and you'll be positioned to block the German retreat up the Rhône Valley from the west side of these mountains."

Johnson regarded Huet cautiously. "I'll need to check higher. I only have a tank squadron, an artillery battery, and a company of infantry."

"Then let's go. We have no time to waste. You'll go in unopposed, but the *boche* could regroup and counterattack."

"I'll see what I can do."

54

While they waited, Jeremy and Huet rested in the shade of a tree against a parked jeep. "Do you think they'll do it?" Huet asked.

"You mean enter Grenoble today?" Jeremy shrugged. "They should. Then again, the Allies should have launched the invasion back when they said they would—or they should not have activated us."

Huet tossed his head. "We French would say, 'Life is a tree whose fruit is often bitter.' In this case, we would add, 'Who does not advance, retreats.'"

Jeremy chuckled. "On the British side of the Channel we might say, 'That's water under a bridge,' and 'No use crying over spilled milk.'"

"They fit," Huet mused, "but the spilled milk is a lot of innocent lives."

"Agreed—"

Before he could say more, a voice called from behind them. "Jeremy? Jeremy Littlefield?"

Surprised, they both turned. A young second lieutenant stood before them. He was bigger than Jeremy, his thin figure reflecting the gaunt conditions of all the soldiers milling about.

"Do I know you, Lieutenant?" Jeremy said, dismissing the familiar way in which the officer had addressed him while reminding himself that he was not in uniform. The man greeting him might not know his rank.

"Jeremy, it's me, Zack. Your cousin."

Amazed, for an instant, Jeremy could only gaze. Then he whooped in astonishment and lunged forward to throw his arms around Zack. "What a surprise. How did you know I was here?"

"A soldier told me. Smitty. He said he'd just escorted a British major named Littlefield. He said you'd identified yourself that way. It seemed too much of a coincidence—"

"And it is. I'll have to thank Smitty."

He was about to introduce Huet when a runner arrived seeking Huet and Jeremy. "The colonel wants to see you asap."

Jeremy turned to Zack. "How great to see you. I'll look you up later."

Disappointed at having to leave Zack so soon, Jeremy followed Huet and the runner into a hastily set-up operations tent.

Johnson met them inside. "You're on," he said. "I'm cleared to take my battalion into the city today." He glanced around the interior of the tent. "My ops guys are groaning about taking this down. They just put it up. Before they start, let me show you what's going on."

He guided them to a map hanging on one of the canvas walls. "Here's where we are at Pont-de-Claix, and here's Grenoble to the north." He pointed them out. "This large mass is the mountain range Colonel Huet mentioned earlier. Down here to the south is Gap, and going up the far side of the Vercors is the Rhône Valley. There's a town, about midway down, Montélimar." He pointed it out.

"Right now, the Nineteenth Army is in full retreat up that valley. General Dahlquist, the VI Corps commander, has his forces gathering at Gap. The main body of the corps will press north from there up the valley past Montélimar and establish the main blocking position in the high ground north of the town.

"While they're maneuvering into place, this division, the one I'm with, will liberate Grenoble. Then we'll send units south on the west side of the Vercors to reinforce the blocking position at Montélimar."

He turned to face Jeremy and Huet. "Your intel just saved us days and soldiers' lives. There was a man and a lady who came through our unit a few days ago. They met with General Butler and then General Patch. They gave us the low-down on the *Wehrmacht's* 157th Division being in Grenoble. We didn't know the Germans had vacated the premises. That's new information." He chuckled. "Maybe the whole German army will keep runnin' on up past the Rhine."

While he spoke, members of his staff began breaking down equipment for transport. Jeremy glanced at Huet, who affirmed a shared thought. The "man and a lady" had to be Roger and Pauline. *They're safe and operating.*

The procession into Grenoble was as ebullient as Huet had predicted. Huge crowds numbering in the tens of thousands poured onto the streets. The squeak and squeal of tracked vehicles rumbling through the city were drowned by the roar of a jubilant crowd. Gone were the scarlet banners emblazoned with black swastikas, replaced by French and American flags adorning many buildings and many smaller banners waved by thousands of men, women, and children.

"They're so happy," Jeremy observed.

"They have a right to be," Huet replied. Then he grimaced. "We still have a long war ahead of us."

"But the Vercors is saved."

Huet nodded with a set jaw. "The Vercors is saved," he repeated solemnly. "I would like to know how our friend, Eugène Chavant, is doing. I haven't seen him since the night I ordered dispersion. He established the first *Maquis* there. He championed Operation Montagnard, which would have saved many French lives if the Allies had done their part on time. Chavant inspired our people. I fear he'll never receive acknowledgment for the many great things he did."

He took a long, measured look at Jeremy. "What will you do now?"

Jeremy grunted. "I don't know. My job on the Vercors seems to be finished. I'll stay a day or two to see if I'm needed here, and if not, I'll make my way over to Lyon—"

Huet cast one of his rare grins. "To see your fiancée? What's her name?"

"Amélie." Jeremy reddened slightly. "She'll probably be out on a mission somewhere." He pursed his lips. "I tried to see my cousin, Zack, again this afternoon, but his unit is being sent forward to reinforce at Montélimar." He blew out a breath. "I hope he makes it.

"In any event, I'll contact London from Lyon to see what's in store for me."

"You might want to stay with one of these American units," Huet commented. "Once the Allies destroy the Nineteenth Army at Montélimar, the next major objective will be Lyon. That's obvious. You'd be invaluable on one of their liaison teams."

"The Jockey network—"

"Did its job, Jeremy. Roger created independent cells capable of carrying out their missions. That's what all the networks did. His main function, and yours, was to help organize, arm, train, and supply them. That's been done. We're all joined in the battle now. I doubt that SOE will send you to an area to perform the same function. With no orders, you're in the unique position of choosing your own next assignment. If your heart's set on Lyon, entering there with the US army seems to make sense."

Jeremy mulled Huet's words. "That's a lot to think about," he said noncommittally. "What's next for you?"

Huet pursed his lips while weighing his response. "I'll move my headquarters to Grenoble. It's on the German escape route to the northeast, so it's still vulnerable. Despite the last six weeks on the plateau, the casualties among our fighting forces were relatively light. They're trained, blooded, and the Americans can arm and feed us. That's at least five thousand more men we can throw into the fight here.

"The Vercors will start rebuilding immediately. I'll leave Captain Beauregard in overall charge of seeing to that."

Jeremy smiled. "Not Captain Geyer?"

Huet sighed. "He's a good man and he learns from his mistakes, but he's still too impetuous and he doesn't get along so well with civilians. He's an excellent combat leader and we'll need him in future battles. Of the two, Beauregard is better suited for higher command. As a combat leader, he's as good as Geyer, and he can also take on the challenges needed to help the people on the plateau recover. He likes them and they like him."

The next day, as 88 mm rounds dropped and exploded with shattering concussions near their position in General Pflaumm's former headquarters, Huet told Jeremy, "Beauregard's reconstruction work will have to wait." The barrage had begun during the night and continued into daylight. They originated nearly four miles east at Murianette, a small town in the foothills overlooking Grenoble.

As Huet had predicted, the *Wehrmacht* was obviously attempting to keep an escape route open to the northeast. Lieutenant Colonel Johnson called upon Huet for support, and within hours, Beauregard's unit had descended into the valley and linked up with Johnson's infantry for the attack. US spotter planes orbiting overhead directed artillery fire onto German positions with increasing volume and accuracy.

Jeremy watched Huet. The French officer had taken up an observation post on the third floor of the headquarters building where he could see the exchanges of artillery and monitor the progress of the battle.

German spotters were nowhere to be seen. However, American planes flew well above the action and called in adjustments to fire without fear of antiaircraft guns.

Jeremy had to chuckle. Huet's expression remained impassive except that his eyes squinted with intensity as the small planes circled, American artillery adjusted, and explosive rounds rained down yet another salvo on Pflaumm's troops.

Huet knew the helplessness that the German general must now feel.

Jeremy wondered whether the French officer reveled in Pflaumm's discomfort.

Later that afternoon, a guard detail escorted a German lieutenant into Johnson's office, the one previously occupied by General Pflaumm. Present with Johnson were Lieutenant Colonel Huet and Jeremy.

The German lieutenant carried a white flag. Visibly nervous, he glanced around the room. Then he clicked his heels, came to attention, and saluted Johnson. "Sir, may I speak with you privately?" he asked in heavily accented English.

Johnson looked puzzled. "Why?"

The lieutenant glanced at Huet and returned his attention to Johnson.

"Sir, I was sent to surrender the *Wehrmacht* forces at Murianette, but only to an American officer."

Johnson eyed the lieutenant with a hard expression. Then it softened into one of amusement. He crossed the room and stood next to Huet. "This officer," he said, "commanded the forces opposing you during the *Wehrmacht's* entire campaign against the Vercors. You threw everything you had against his military forces, his *Maquis*, and against the civilians. They held against you. Not once did they surrender a unit."

He turned to regard Huet and clapped an arm around his shoulders. Then he grinned and turned back to the German officer. "My comrade and I belong to the same liberation army. We will accept your surrender together."

The lieutenant nodded disconsolately.

Johnson turned back to Huet. "Colonel, would you like to do the honors and accept the lieutenant's pistol?"

Jeremy barely suppressed a grin as he translated.

Huet straightened his back and squared his shoulders. With a stern light in his eyes over a constrained smile, he stepped forward. "*Avec plaisir.*"

55

August 23, 1944
Écouché, France

Under the apple trees surrounding Écouché, spirits soared as word spread that, at last, after four long years of exile and fighting in distant lands for the dream of liberating their own country, the men of the 2nd French Armored Division received orders to move on Paris. Late that night, General Leclerc had issued a fourteen-point operations order, including a letter to be read to the soldiers.

The men he commanded were an assortment of soldiers drawn from France and its colonial empire. Many had never been to Paris. Others, born in Paris or elsewhere in Continental France, remembered the humiliation of fleeing from the *Wehrmacht* onslaught of 1940. To them, Paris had become the new Jerusalem of a modern crusade. They had dreamed and talked about it as they fought in far-off Chad, Morocco, Algeria, Tunisia, Egypt, Libya, and Italy.

The division consisted of French citizens, some of whom spoke little to no

French for being born in the jungles of Cameroon, in the Moroccan Atlas mountains or in the sands of the Sahara, or in other places remote from France. Twenty-two colonies in all. They included veterans of loyalist Spanish armies, fighting in solidarity with Frenchmen who had fought alongside them during the Spanish Civil War.

The air was electric as the soldiers worked through the night. Gone were strict security measures to reduce light and sound. In their place were shouted commands, engines firing up or idling, and the clatter of tank treads. Soldiers cleaned weapons, drew rations and water, or studied their individual missions with fervor, and wherever they went, they walked with alacrity.

Always before when facing battle, a sense of dread had pervaded in the final minutes before launch. The loss of friends and ghastly wounds experienced by many reminded them of their mortality but could not override shared excitement, as dawn approached, of traveling the last one hundred and thirty miles, fighting the final battles, and entering the city that had for so long been a wish too far.

On the previous evening, the sun had dipped below the horizon when Leclerc's plane had landed on his return flight from seeing General Bradley. His operations chief, Major Gribius, had waited at the airstrip with a command car to meet him.

Leclerc bounded onto the ground and hurried toward him. "Gribius," he shouted with unbridled enthusiasm. "*Mouvement immédiat*. We are going to Paris."

A few minutes past midnight, his soldiers had listened with rapt attention as the general's letter was read to them, ending with, "I demand, for this movement which will lead the Division to the capital of France, a supreme effort, which I am sure to see from all of you."

That night, despite soldiers' abilities to slumber under almost any conditions, many under the French general's command found sleeping impossible. Their excitement was too great.

At 06:30 hours, Leclerc gave the order and the 2nd French Armored Division commenced its last march to Paris.

Paul had watched the preparations with mounting interest. Then, as he clambered into his customary position on Leclerc's command vehicle, he caught the ebullient spirit. As he settled into his seat, he called to the general, "No need to avoid the Americans now!"

Leclerc gave him a long, searching look. "You caught me." His face broke into a grin as he leaned toward Paul. "We're not going to avoid anybody."

All day they drove through heavy rain, slipping and sliding over muddy roads. The French division's lines stretched back thirteen miles. The heavy tanks, trucks, and other war machines shook the ground, vibrated windows, and rattled rafters of homes in the towns they passed through.

Wide-eyed villagers, at first timid, peered out windows at the clanking procession passing by their doors. Initially fearful, they soon perceived that the war materiel looked and sounded different than the *Wehrmacht* equipment they were accustomed to seeing, that the shape of the tanks was unfamiliar to them, and that the soldiers called friendly greetings to them in their own language.

"The Americans have come," people shouted in glee.

"No. They are French," others yelled. "They are French. Our own army has come home to save us."

Uproarious celebration followed the division, and then preceded it as word spread ahead of the combat parade. Vehicle drivers took great care as thousands of residents crowded the streets. People climbed on the vehicles, offered food and drink, and slowed the division's forward movement.

Paris, France

Chantal rubbed her eyes. They stung from acrid air caused by huge black smoke clouds that rose over the city and hung there, the result of a massive fire at the Grand Palais on the south side of the Champs-Elysées. Word reached the prefecture of a horrific confrontation there between German forces and the FFI.

Confronted by a German officer demanding entry to investigate "terrorist" activity in the basement of the magnificent classical theater with its vaulted glass roof, a young Resistant retorted, "Colonel, you don't give orders here anymore."

Two hours later, the colonel's *panzers* approached the theater. Strapped on the turret of each tank were two Parisian human shields. However, the tanks merely acted as security for an even more inconceivable weapon.

As residents gaped, a small radio-controlled tank left the armored formation, advanced on the Palais, and systematically fired incendiary rounds across the front of the domed classical structure until an explosion in its basement rocked the city. While the towering flames devoured the structure, German soldiers shot holes through firemen's hoses, frustrating attempts to quell the fire. The still smoldering building served as grim confirmation of what most Parisians had concluded: the *Wehrmacht* possessed the power to annihilate the city.

At the prefecture's telephone exchange, a young law student screamed into the telephone. Chantal had no idea who was at the other end of the call, but the law student's message was clear, confirmed by three *panzers* approaching from the opposite end of the square. "We are almost out of bullets," he shouted. "The Germans are preparing another assault on us."

Suddenly, he was silent and listening. His back straightened, he whirled around with wide eyes, and then he started jumping up and down, shouting ecstatically. "They're here," he yelled as he hung up the phone. "Our French army is here, just south of the city, at Rambouillet. I heard them. My friend held up the phone so I could hear their tanks going by. He said they would be here soon."

Everyone in the room cheered, Chantal with them. But when she sat down, she stared across the square at the three *panzers*, their main guns pointed at the prefecture, and their engines rumbling. And black smoke from the Palais still rolled across the sky.

Across town, General Choltitz spoke by telephone with *Generalleutnant* Hans Speidel, *Generalfeldmarschall* Model's chief of staff. "You'll be happy to know that the Grand Palais is in flames." Choltitz then proceeded to inform Speidel of other steps completed to fulfill Hitler's order to level the city. "I'll be able to blow up the Madeleine and the Opéra with a single detonation. We'll explode the Arc de Triomphe next, to clear fields of fire down the Champs-Elysées—the Allies will want to use that thoroughfare. And when we topple the Eiffel Tower, it will block access to several bridges. The prefecture is still occupied, so we won't be able to line it with dynamite, but on our way out of the city, we'll blow it the same way we did the Grand Palais—with incendiaries. It won't be left standing, nor will anyone left inside it."

Speidel had listened quietly. At the end of the call, he responded, "I'll pass along your report. I'm sure the *führer* will be pleased."

Choltitz hung up, puzzled. Speidel's tone had been so tepid that Choltitz wondered if the chief of staff agreed with the intent to destroy Paris. He lit a cigarette, poured a glass of schnapps, and went out onto the terrace to ponder.

Laval, France

General Bradley conversed from his Eagletac headquarters with General Eisenhower over a phone while eyeing a big man standing across the tent. "I know the story sounds implausible at first blush," Bradley said into the phone, "but it was easy to check out. The man with me now is Rolf Nordling, the brother of Raoul Nordling, the Swedish consul in Paris. The permit allowing safe passage through German lines was signed by General Choltitz, the *Wehrmacht's* commanding general in Paris. Raoul had a heart attack. The travel permit was made out for R. Nordling, so Rolf took his place."

Bradley listened and responded to a question. "Yes. The details he relates about the current state of affairs in Paris line up exactly with what was reported by General de Gaulle and Major Gallois."

He listened again, and when he replied, Bradley's voice became grave. "The new information is that Field Marshal Model is transferring reinforcements to Paris. They're coming out of Denmark. The rest of what I have to report is incredible. Choltitz sent a request via Nordling for our help to save Paris. He's left a corridor open south of Paris between two of his divisions. He says that if Model's reinforcements get there first, his hand will be forced. You know what that means. He'll detonate."

Listening to Bradley's side of the conversation, Rolf swayed with fatigue. He glanced at the general's aide and indicated a vacant folding chair along the tent's wall. The aide nodded, brought it to him, and held it while Rolf seated himself.

The ordeal of the past twelve to fourteen hours had been surreal. Like everyone in Paris, Rolf had heard the gunfire, listened to the radio, and was concerned that the city was in great peril. However, as opposed to his brother Raoul, Rolf had been a

peripheral figure, not of great consequence to the outcome of earth-shattering events.

Bobby Bender had informed Rolf that his brother was resting from a heart attack. Then, Raoul Nordling's mission was explained to him, including the horrifying prospect of Paris' destruction, the annihilation of her residents, and Choltitz' attempt to enlist Allied help to save the city ahead of *Wehrmacht* reinforcements.

Bobby wore a uniform of the *Sicherheitsdienst* or SD, the internal intelligence agency of the Nazi party. Rolf found that disconcerting, particularly since the safe-passage document with the initial he shared with his brother was to be used to certify Rolf, falsely, as the person authorized to make his harried way through German lines in the middle of the night. His anxiety rose on learning that a man attached to his group was an Allied covert operator being sought by the SD. Rolf had wiped sweat from his own large face with a handkerchief as he consented to the trip.

Bobby had performed marvelously, and the group moved easily through successive German checkpoints. At the last one, as dusk settled, the group passed into no-man's land between German and American lines. Then Bobby, the one man in the group who knew exactly what he was doing but not wishing to become a POW, said his goodbyes.

The remaining group passed through another set of checkpoints, American this time, showing the letter, and explaining that Rolf wanted to speak with either Charles de Gaulle or General Eisenhower. The enlisted men they encountered had at first been incredulous, even mocking, but Rolf was insistent. Eventually, he was escorted through successive levels of command until he found himself in the tent of the commanding general of the American 12th Army Group, General Bradley.

The general needed little convincing. He immediately placed a call to Eisenhower. "Our 4th Infantry Division is a hundred and twenty miles southwest of Paris," Bradley said. "I'll have it maneuver behind Leclerc's in case he needs support. His division is already on the move."

Bradley listened as Eisenhower spoke.

"Roger, sir," he replied. "I'll put the order out as soon as I hang up."

Rolf watched, tired but fascinated. Both Eisenhower and Bradley were now well-known names across France in the battle for its liberation. Rolf was accustomed to seeing German military men, but here he sat among Americans, one level removed from the pinnacle of Allied authority in Europe. And he had just listened to a conversation between a man who moved armies speaking to a man who commanded a whole theater of armies.

Bradley turned to his aide. "Get the ops chief. Tell him to alert the 4th Infantry's ops section that an immediate order is coming down to divert in support of Leclerc. Then he needs to get over here asap. I'll call the division's CG now."

As the aide went to comply, Bradley turned to Rolf. "You'll be with us for a while. We can't send you back to Paris now." He smiled at the bemused expression on Rolf's face. "We'll make you as comfortable as we can."

Rolf replied, "How exciting. Please, point me to a corner where I will be out of the way. I don't want to be a bother."

"Then have a seat and excuse me. I have several more calls to make." He paused as a thought flashed through his mind. "We'll put you with Major Gallois. Do you know him?"

"I'm afraid I don't."

Bradley smiled. "By the time you two get back to Paris, you'll have had plenty to talk about."

General Patton listened to his logistics officer with anger that rose to fury. He had just been informed that his fuel supplies were running low. Deliveries required for planned operations to close on the Rhine River and enter Germany, now less than one hundred miles away, would not arrive until late September. His current shipments had been diverted to support the immediate liberation of Paris.

Patton did a quick mental calculation. His troops would stall while the *Wehrmacht* continued its wholesale flight back to Germany's borders without obstruction and would reinforce defenses. At new projected fuel levels, he could not resume aggressive offensive operations until around the beginning of October. Then the weather would turn wet and cold and head into the winter months. *Casualties will be a lot higher.*

For a moment, he thought about the young French officer, Major Gallois, whom he had listened to just two days earlier and sent on to General Bradley. *Maybe I shouldn't have done that?* Dismissing the thought, he set about revising his plans.

Rambouillet, France

Lieutenant Colonel Guillebon groaned in dismay. Forty-eight hours ago, he had led his mixed contingent of armor and infantry on a foray to Paris' edge, intending to enter. He had halted less than forty miles from the capital's center only because Leclerc's orders had been explicit: he was to go no farther without express orders from Leclerc himself.

Guillebon had reached his position without being detected by either friendly or enemy forces. Throughout the night, he had repeatedly requested permission to advance. A response had not been received, and now the lead elements of Leclerc's full 2nd Armored Division entered Rambouillet at the western end.

Unbeknownst to Guillebon, his entreaties to allow his advance had been received late at night at 2nd Armored headquarters while the division was preparing to move and during the few hours that Leclerc slept after issuing his operations order. Fearful of waking the general, his aide had not delivered the messages.

Heavy rain had deluged Rambouillet and the deep forests around it. Over the mud-soaked roads, Guillebon heard elements of the division catching up to him. He had been alerted that such might be the case by people pouring into the streets ahead of the columns. Exuberant villagers along the route had telephoned ahead to share the news that French forces were now—at this very moment—on the way to move the boundaries of free France closer and closer to Paris.

Reluctantly, Guillebon returned his handpicked men and their equipment to their units and rejoined his own. He still aspired to be the first man of the 2nd French Armored Division to enter Paris, but he felt the chance slipping away. Resigning himself, he settled in for the night with the division's exhausted soldiers.

56

Same Day, August 23, 1944
Paris, France

Loud banging on Georges Lamarque's apartment door caused Amélie to jerk her head around. She reached inside a pocket of her dress and grasped her pistol. She had been staying there with Chantal after Fourcade's departure for southern France. Chantal had left for work four days ago and had not returned, leaving her sister in a dreadful state of worry while gunfights erupted all around Paris.

"I'm sorry," a woman's voice called out, "Hérisson sent me. She couldn't reach you by telephone. So many of the lines are down. I don't know the sequence to knock on your door. There are no Germans anywhere around out here."

Amélie thought rapidly. The woman's use of Fourcade's codename, "Hérisson," gave Amélie some measure of relief, but Alliance had been infiltrated and nearly obliterated twice. The woman at the door could be part of the *Milice*, the parapolice force formed of Nazi sympathizers by the Vichy government to seek out Resistance members. Because French was their native language and they knew the local populace, they were more feared and hated than even the *Gestapo*. In fact, several of them had been spotted on the rooftops among snipers firing into the crowds.

Amélie recalled viscerally her arrest at Valence two years ago, her discovery by a *Gestapo* agent on a train last year, and her close scrapes while being a courier for Jeannie Rousseau here in Paris. Amélie had then carried some of the most sensitive pieces of intelligence of the war. And Jeannie had been captured through betrayal.

"Are you alone?" she called.

"I have three men with me. We have an urgent mission and need your help. Hérisson said to tell you that Labrador is well and safe."

Amélie's breath caught. *Jeremy!*

Experience had taught her to maintain caution. "Did she say anything else?"

"Yes. She said she hopes you are able to rescue Amniarix."

Once again, Amélie caught her breath. "Amniarix" was Jeannie Rousseau's codename. Fourcade would not share it or Jeremy's codename with just anyone.

"She also said to tell you that she hopes Papillon is staying out of trouble."

Tears welled in Amélie's eyes. "Papillon" was her little sister, Chantal.

"Please," the woman pleaded. "My real name is Madeleine Riffaud and my codename is 'Rainer.' I am from Arvillers in Somme. I wouldn't tell you that through the door if this were not urgent."

Amélie took a breath.

"*Eh bien*," she called. "Are you armed?"

"No."

Amélie thought rapidly. "Stand back from the door."

She turned the deadbolt quickly and with an audible click, and pressed herself against the wall to one side of the portal, pistol ready. "Open the door and step inside."

The door creaked open, and Rainer entered cautiously. "I understand why Hérisson recommended you," she said, eyeing Amélie's pistol as one of the men closed the door behind the group. Petite and perhaps around Chantal's age, she had very light skin, thick, shoulder-length brown hair, and large, dark eyes. She wore short culottes and a flowered blouse that appeared to have been worn for several days. "I'm sorry to approach this way. We just came from fighting in Chartres. We supported the American, General Patton, to liberate the city. We don't have much time. We need help to get to the park at Buttes-Chaumont. None of us are from Paris."

Uncomprehending, Amélie stared. She glanced at the three men. They were roughly the same height, thin, unshaven but competent-looking, and their clothing was as disheveled as Rainer's. All four looked exhausted. She regarded them quizzically. "Who's in charge?"

"I am," Rainer replied sharply, "and my comrades are fine with that." She gestured at them individually. "This is Marcel, Bernard, and Alain."

"Rainer knows what she's doing," Alain cut in. "She's proven herself."

"We're running out of time," Rainer admonished. "We have a car and will fill you in on the way."

"I haven't said I'd go," Amélie exclaimed, startled. "Can you at least tell me what we're supposed to do?"

Rainer exhaled impatiently. "Most of the Germans in Paris are pushed into their strongholds, and they're mostly low-quality fighters anyway. But the ones at Prince Eugénie Barracks are a sizable force. They could attack our fighters in the city center from the rear. That would be a massacre. There's a train on its way to bring arms, ammunition, and reinforcements to the barracks. We've been ordered to stop it."

She paused while Amélie absorbed the information, and then continued without slowing down. "We have a map, but so many of the streets are blocked—"

Amélie cut in, glancing toward the door. "Do you have more fighters outside?"

Rainer shook her head impatiently. "Just us. But we have explosives. Hérisson said you know how to use them and that you were trained at the spy school in England. Now, can we go?" She strode to the door.

Amélie stared in amazement. "I—I suppose so," she stammered. "I'm not really familiar with that part of the city. But—"

"Hérisson said that you'd either know the way or someone who does." Rainer gestured with her chin to her three companions. "Let's go." She looked back at Amélie. "Are you coming?"

Resolve crossed Amélie's face. She nodded and followed the group out the door. In the car, she took the front seat between Rainer and the driver while the other two men crowded into the back among bags of loose explosives and grenades.

"Where is the train coming from?" Amélie asked as the small sedan started off.

"It left Gare de Lyon this morning," Rainer replied. "It took the small ring railway on the east side of Paris. It's reached Ménilmontant on the way to Gare de l'Est. It must go through a tunnel in the Buttes-Chaumont park. That's where we'll hit. It has fourteen cars carrying a ton of ammunition, many rifles, and a hundred soldiers."

Amélie took a deep breath and exclaimed, "*Vous êtes fous!*" Then, puzzled, she observed, "If the train left Gare de Lyon this morning, it should have reached Gare de l'Est already. It must be traveling very slowly."

"The Germans are taking no chances," Rainer replied, nodding. "They have soldiers out front checking the tracks, intersections, and bridges along the way."

"Let me see your map."

Rainer handed it to Amélie, who spread it out and studied it. After a few moments, Amélie pointed a finger at three main thoroughfares. "These streets are closed off. We'll need to stay south of them and go east to get outside of conflict areas."

She had remained close to the apartment for most of the past few days while the insurgency raged, but she had been out enough to see the roadblocks that Parisians had thrown up. They were impressive, some many feet thick with sandbags and destroyed vehicles—they had been effective enough to hold back German forces despite heavy machine gun and sniper fire.

Driving through the streets with Rainer's small group, Amélie realized the scale of the civilian effort. Her chest welled with pride for her countrymen. "When we get outside this area"—she indicated on the map—"we'll turn north for a few miles and then come in to the target from the west."

They were stopped at several Resistance checkpoints along the way, but Rainer's group had painted "FFI" in large white characters on the car's roof, sides, and trunk. With the armbands they wore and Rainer's authoritative manner, they were allowed through. Finally, the way was clear.

Amélie continued consulting the map. "We can get close to the northern mouth of the tunnel along Rue de Crimée," she said as she pointed out the location.

The closer they came to the target, the stronger her heart beat. Not having anticipated such a venture, she chastised herself for the way she was dressed. She wore a light dress, slip-on shoes, and a white blouse—not the best uniform for hiding from sharpshooters, and she expected that her group might encounter some. However, she still knew little of Rainer's plan and doubted that one existed.

"We have reconnaissance reports that the tunnel is in a low area, with high ground on both sides of its mouth," Rainer told her as they drew near. "All we have to do is block the train from exiting. If we can—"

"That's all?" Amélie said with a touch of irony.

Rainer ignored the tone. "If we can stop a counterattack long enough, the Allies will have time to get into the city and force a surrender."

"And we might all be dead," Amélie said on impulse, surprising herself.

Rainer nodded matter-of-factly. "If we don't, we might all be dead anyway, along with the rest of Paris."

They turned and traveled north along Rue de Crimée and parked the car among thick trees lining the left side of the road. "The mouth of the tunnel should be back there to the south about a hundred meters," Amélie said.

"Let's go see." Rainer instructed Alain to come with her and Amélie, and left the remaining two to watch the car. The trio set out and soon encountered a trail through the underbrush and followed it.

Ahead, they heard voices speaking in German.

Staying low within the foliage, they crept forward. Then, peering through the leaves, they beheld a sight they had not expected. They were at the top of a nearly vertical stone retaining wall. It overlooked a man-made gorge with a flat bottom and an almost identical wall on the opposite side, also covered with thick foliage. Two parallel railroad tracks ran down the center of the gorge's floor, and at its north end, the mouth of the tunnel appeared, clearly visible.

Several soldiers had emerged from the tunnel's recesses. More startling, the train's black locomotive sat just inside the shaft, its engine idling low and threatening. Its buffers barely protruded out the front.

Rainer whirled. "Come on," she whispered, and the three rushed back to the car.

"Amélie and I will bring as many grenades as we can," she said. She pointed to her male companions. "Grab all the explosives you can carry and follow us. We'll all throw five grenades each, very rapidly. Then the three of you will run to the car and bring back more demolitions. Amélie and I will keep lobbing grenades, and you three keep hauling demolitions until everything is down there. The *boches* will retreat into the tunnel. Then we'll throw smoke grenades to keep them there.

"While they're in the shaft, we'll throw all the explosives onto the locomotive, ignite them with a grenade, and then throw in more smoke grenades. Any questions?"

She saw only glinting eyes and quick nods. "Let's go."

Spurred by adrenaline, Amélie hurried with the others to drag the bags of grenades and explosives out of the car and back down the trail.

The locomotive remained stationary.

Fifteen to twenty German soldiers probed the tracks.

Rainer's group gathered around her. "Spread out and get set. As soon as I throw, pull your pins and let fly."

The group exchanged grim expressions, grabbed their grenades, and dispersed. Amélie ran a few yards along the trail above the retaining wall, getting closer to the tunnel. She found a good position and laid five grenades out in front of her. Then, holding one chest high with her right palm pressed against the safety lever, she looped the index finger of her other hand through the metal ring connected to the retaining pin, and waited.

Her chest heaved. Sweat trickled from her temples. Exhaust from the locomotive rode the air and stung her nostrils. Her eyes watered and stung.

Below her, only yards away, the Germans stepped carefully over the ground by the tracks. They probed under the rails and the wooden ties, examining each of them, searching for anything that would indicate sabotage. Fortunately, that meant that their eyes and attention were focused on the ground.

Amélie heard the telltale slight ringing of a grenade dropping its safety lever as it sailed through the air. Without waiting for an explosion, she pulled the pin on her own, chose a target area, extended her left arm high to her front, and brought her right hand over her shoulder in a swift motion, lobbing the small pineapple-shaped device well out over the gorge among the unsuspecting soldiers.

Rainer's grenade exploded. Then four more detonated in quick succession.

Soldiers dropped where they were. Others cried out in pain. More ran or limped into the safety of the tunnel.

Amélie took no time to observe the damage. Furiously, she prepared and launched her second grenade, and then her third, fourth, and fifth.

To her right, Rainer, Alain, Marcel, and Bernard did the same. Twenty-five grenades struck within a matter of seconds.

Then, Amélie looked over the gorge. Dead bodies lay about in pools of blood and dismembered limbs. No one posed an immediate threat.

The barrel of a rifle protruded out of the tunnel's mouth. Amélie lobbed another grenade. The rifle disappeared.

Rainer threw a smoke grenade. Amélie followed suit.

Alain and the other two men arrived with the second load of demolitions and then went back for more. As the smoke cleared, the two women on the lip of the gorge threw another round of grenades to discourage enemy probing.

When the third trip from the car was completed, all the demolitions had been delivered. Rainer clustered her group again, and pointed to the steep hillside above the tunnel and a ledge over the entrance. "Look. We can throw the explosives directly onto the locomotive from there."

Rainer's team lugged the lethal material to the ledge while keeping the enemy penned in with more grenades and smoke. Within minutes, they were atop the ledge, tossing packets of dynamite down onto the locomotive. Then Rainer tossed in a grenade and retreated to the safety of the hillside.

With terrifying thunder, massive flames shot out from the tunnel. The ground trembled. Large chunks and tiny slivers of iron and steel flew out of the entrance. They smacked the gulch's earthen floor and the retaining walls in a deluge. The steel rails rang under the heavy torrent.

Rainer raised her head. "*Sacré bleu*! That was bigger than I expected." She sprang to her feet and peered over the edge of the ledge. The curling smoke wafted into the mouth. "The tunnel acts like a chimney," she shouted. "It's sucking in the smoke. Throw down more smoke grenades, and keep doing it. We'll suffocate *les boches*."

Furiously, the group lobbed smoke grenade after smoke grenade. The small cannisters spewed out ascending layers of thick white smoke that was impenetrable to their sight. It spread into the tunnel, filling every void.

Amélie heard coughing. A soldier staggered into the open with his hands held high over his head, followed by another soldier, and then another. Soon a group of them stood in the middle of the tracks, coughing vigorously, their hands held high.

"I speak German," Amélie volunteered.

"Take Alain and go down there," Rainer said. "Grab weapons from the dead soldiers. Find out who is authorized to surrender the whole command." In a low voice, she added, "We have no small arms. We'll need theirs to guard them."

Amélie smiled steadily. "I have my pistol. That'll serve until we have their rifles."

"Bernard and Marcel will gather up more rifles and cover you. We'll have help here soon."

Three hours later, after the surrender had been effected, the weapons secured, and the Germans moved to an FFI holding facility, Amélie turned to Rainer. "What will you do for an encore?"

Rainer grimaced tiredly. "I don't know. We captured eighty Germans, all their rifles, a carload of ammunition, and we stopped the counterattack. The arms and ammo will be distributed across Paris—"

Alain laughed. "We're taking Rainer to celebrate," he told Amélie. "She turned twenty today. You're welcome to come along."

Rainer whirled on him. "*Mon Dieu!* My birthday. I had forgotten."

57

Same Day, August 23, 1944
Valence, France

Lieutenant Zack Littlefield swore under his breath. He shared his men's frustration.

Only eight days ago, they had come ashore near Saint-Raphaël. Resistance had been light, but then the 36th Division had pushed north as part of VI Corp's intended foray up the Rhône Valley, west of the Vercors. But the objective changed before the unit even started moving, and suddenly the division was headed toward Castellane instead of toward towns farther west at the south end of the Rhône Valley. That was fine, but then the entire division turned north in seeming fits and starts, preparing to move on one objective and then switching to another.

Another division from VI Corps, the 141st, had been attached to a task force under the command of General Butler to thrust northwest and set up a blocking position across the German Nineteenth Army's most likely avenue for withdrawal at a place that the Corp had not expected to reach for ninety days. That was beyond Zack's immediate concerns. As part of the Corp's remaining two divisions, his company and platoon had marched past Castellane, through Digne, and had held up at Sisteron pending further orders.

Despite light enemy resistance, the going had been far from smooth. People on the roads and streets were wonderful to see, but the imperative was to keep moving, and civilian traffic impeded progress. The truck transports that carried his platoon followed others in a convoy, rumbling past piles of abandoned German war equipment and the rubble of bombed-out villages, and over rough, pockmarked roads. They all but outran their supply lines, crucial to bringing forward four imperatives for combat: gas, bullets, food, and water.

At Sisteron, his battalion had refilled their fuel tanks, but Zack was shocked to learn the way gas re-supply had been orchestrated. Company-sized convoys had run shuttles back and forth between the coast and the lead units. He questioned how long that could occur as the front continued north. Infantry units could forage and march forward on foot, but when tanks and artillery ran out of fuel, they were useless.

Even infantry is limited without bullets.

Over the course of a single evening at Sisteron, he had received a string of warning orders. The first was to prepare to move northwest to a town called Montélimar in support of Task Force Butler's planned blocking operation. The second warning order, which superseded the first, was to prepare to move northeast to a town called Gap. Almost before Zack had pulled out his map to trace the route, new orders changed the destination back to Montélimar. Finally, the last set of orders required his platoon to proceed to Gap to confront a German presence.

Zack's platoon had arrived there two days ago with other lead elements and found that most of the German troops had vacated and moved north toward Grenoble. The secretary-general of the town's prefecture, a Monsieur Barret, had accepted the surrender of the German 157th Reserve Division's rear guard. Its soldiers were in the town's theater under the watchful eyes of Gap's Boy Scouts. This pleasant surprise was magnified by the townspeople's exuberant welcome of their American liberators.

Zack had wondered why such swings in directives had occurred, and now he thought he understood. The *Wehrmacht* was withdrawing faster than anticipated. He recalled from pre-operation briefs that General Patch's

7th Army, VI Corp's higher echelon, had expected to push up the Rhône Valley for three months after landing on the coast.

However, not even a week had gone by before the 143rd arrived at Gap, more than one hundred and twenty miles into enemy territory. Now, General Patch faced the question of how to support his entire right flank.

Hardly a shot had been fired as the soldiers plowed north, and the *Wehrmacht's* panicked flight was manifest in piles of discarded equipment along the roads. But almost before Zack's soldiers could take a collective breath, they had been ordered to continue north toward Grenoble.

Zack had wondered about that last directive. Previously, he had been briefed to expect contact with Germany's 157th Reserve Division that included crack mountain troops. He had studied a terrain map, particularly the steep mountain range of *le* Dévoluy, which appeared immediately to the left of the road he was to traverse.

The rocky peaks were magnificent, towering thousands of feet above a breathtaking valley turning to autumns colors. Recalling the misery of crossing similar ranges in Italy during winter, Zack was glad he did not have to navigate through these, but for a moment, he thought that he might return someday and explore them.

Battle-hardened and inured to accept sudden and frequent change, he returned his mind to the present, accepting that part of his job was to minimize risk for his men. He believed that such responsibility ran through the chain of command to the highest levels. Recalling the heavy casualties from American assaults at the Garigliano and Rapido rivers of southern Italy, he wondered if his higher commanders were making prudent decisions that would avoid unnecessary casualties in the current fight.

As a squad leader at the Garigliano, he had led his men at the front of a division-wide assault across a fast-moving river. The Germans, entrenched behind formidable defenses, easily defeated the attack with overwhelming fire. In the process, the 36th Division suffered thousands of dead and wounded.

The 5th Army's Commanding General Mark Clark had ordered the attack. Even before the operation was executed, his judgment had been questioned from the lowliest private to high echelons of command. His justification had been that his maneuvers there had drawn German divisions away from the amphibious assault on Anzio.

Zack put the matter out of his head. *Ours is but to do...*

Once again, his men were at the front. After leaving Gap, the battalion drove north to Pont-de-Claix. Arriving early in the evening, the men rested overnight, and the next morning, Zack's company commander briefed them to prepare for house-to-house fighting in Grenoble.

Then, wonder of wonders, a tank driver, Smitty, in one of the battalion's light armored companies, informed Zack that a French officer had approached Smitty's tank and demanded to speak to the battalion commander. A British man in civilian clothes had accompanied the Frenchman and identified himself as Major Littlefield.

"Did he mention his first name?"

"No, sir. But Littlefield's not a common name. I thought you might be interested."

Zack had hurried to the battalion commander's headquarters and was overjoyed to find Jeremy waiting to see Lieutenant Colonel Johnson and conversing with the French officer outside the battalion operations tent. Then, with barely enough time to greet each other or make introductions, Jeremy and the Frenchman had been whisked away to see Johnson.

Shortly thereafter, Zack's company commander summoned the platoon leaders for a briefing. Higher command, they were told, had received intelligence that the road to Grenoble was clear and that the Germans had left the city. Residents begged to see soldiers in American uniforms there that same day.

Disappointed that he would have no further chance to visit with Jeremy, and his body aching with fatigue from days on the trek, Zack ordered his equally exhausted platoon back on the road.

No one had anticipated the huge reception awaiting the liberating force as the units rolled into Grenoble. It was beyond any of the jubilant welcomes received from the numerous villages along the way to the city. Horns blew, and people poured onto the streets, cheering, shouting, and waving French and American flags. They climbed onto the war machines rumbling through, their relief from oppression and hopes for bright futures expressed on their happy faces.

The soldiers, too, forgot their woes of the past few days and their weariness. They reveled in the triumphant celebration, eagerly falling into the arms of pretty girls to be showered with kisses and accepting food and drink from the townspeople.

The next day proved relatively pleasant, despite artillery exchanges and the sounds of infantry skirmishes to the northeast accompanied by friendly spotter planes circling over the battle area. Looking at his map, Zack saw that the fighting took place in the vicinity of a village called Murianette. It soon quieted as the enemy disengaged and continued its withdrawal toward Germany. Otherwise, the Americans mixed with Grenoble's rejoicing residents and enjoyed their status as liberating heroes until being ordered by their leaders to refit, re-supply, pull maintenance, and catch up on much-needed sleep.

Then, late that evening, a warning order came down. The company commander, Captain Bellamy, issued it to his platoon leaders gathered around the front of his jeep.

Zack liked Bellamy. The dark-complected captain was of average build and a few years older than he, perhaps in his mid-twenties. He had joined the 36th Infantry as a replacement officer during the Italian campaign and had fought most of the way up the country's mountainous spine. He knew his business.

"The 179th trailed behind us on the way up. It'll take over our security mission here," he said. "We're headed to Valence. Tonight. When we arrive, we'll re-group and march south toward Montélimar." He grimaced. "General Truscott's order to General Dahlquist was 'to get those men there if they have to walk.'"

He pointed out the town on a map. "We'll skirt the northern end of this mass of mountains labeled the Vercors, and then head southwest to Valence. It's roughly sixty miles by road. Then it's about a thirty-mile straight shot down to Montélimar."

By car during normal times, the route was easy. For a combined-arms battalion traversing mountainous terrain in ponderous military vehicles with weary men, the challenge was enormous, compounded by low fuel supplies.

The fuel scarcity had been a major concern on reaching Grenoble.

Fortunately, 7th Army headquarters rushed in a special convoy of fuel, and Pflaumm's troops, in their haste to vacate the city, had left stocks of it behind. The combined volume was enough to meet immediate needs but insufficient for sustained operations.

Zack walked back to his area. His platoon sergeant, Tech Sergeant Wilbur, stood against a tree at the edge of the road happily surrounded by several young women vying with each other to draw his attention. They kissed his cheeks and offered bunches of grapes, sacks of apples, French pastries, and other delicacies.

Zack watched in amusement. He and Wilbur had first met when Zack transferred into the regiment. The two were roughly the same age, and Zack found the sergeant to be highly competent. On more than one occasion, Zack wondered why he had been promoted instead of Wilbur, but the sergeant accepted the situation without protest. His skill and good humor had lightened the burden of many dark moments.

Wishing he did not have to break up Wilbur's party, Zack reached past the girls and grabbed the sergeant by the shoulder. "Round up the men. We're moving."

"Geez, sir. Now?" But Wilbur detached himself, leaving behind disappointed *mademoiselles*.

Minutes later, coffee in hand and with a map laid out on a flat rock, Zack briefed his squad leaders. "VI Corp set a trap for the kraut Nineteenth Army. We're currently north of them, and the main body of the 36th Division is driving them toward us from the south." He gestured toward the Vercors' rim south of Grenoble. "While we went north on the east side of these mountains, the other two divisions pursued the krauts up the west side.

"The Nineteenth is boxed in over there. The Drôme River is to their north. The Vercors is on their east flank, and the Rhône River is to their west.

"The 3rd Infantry Division is moving north to destroy whatever enemy elements are still in its path. It'll screen on the far side of the Rhône on our western flank.

"General Butler's task force already occupies the key terrain at Hill 300 north of Montélimar. The Nineteenth will be channeled through a narrow passage there on the main road. It's the Germans' only way out, and it's just a thousand yards wide, with high ground on both sides—and they've got to put that whole army through there.

"Our battalion's mission is to reinforce Butler's blocking position across that escape route. The 45th Division coming up from Nyons will reinforce in the south."

Zack paused to sip his coffee, taking a moment to scan his squad leaders' faces. He trusted these battle-tested veterans who had fought up Italy's boot, but he was concerned about the inexperienced soldiers whose only exposure to war had been the tromp up from Saint-Raphaël to Grenoble. His instincts told him that the coming battle would shock those fresh troops despite all the battle stories they must have heard.

He resumed his briefing, indicated the company's objective and that of his platoon, and then identified the specific mission for each squad. When he was finished and all questions had been answered, he said, "General Truscott wants every soldier to understand this part of his order." He took a breath. "Not a single German vehicle gets past Montélimar."

He let the order sink in and added, "When we're done, the 7th Army heads north to link up with General Patton's 3rd Army. It's fighting toward us from Normandy."

His comment was met with only hard-nosed stares. Zack grunted. "Get ready to move."

58

Same Day, August 24, 1944
Lyon, France

Jeremy Littlefield's back ached from hunching in the long overcoat he wore to disguise himself as an old man. Forcing himself to walk with slow, halting steps tried his patience. Most troublesome was keeping his brown beret pulled low enough to hide his face but high enough so that he could see while averting suspicion. The role was one he had developed with Amélie's and Chantal's help the first time he had come to Lyon. It had served him well on several occasions when he needed to enter the city.

His train ride from Grenoble had been interrupted sporadically as it departed from a station now controlled by the Allies and entered areas still under Nazi control. Gone were the despised and arrogant soldiers and officers who had ridden the train and taken the best seats. Also absent were the guards along the platforms of villages the train passed through. However, as it entered German-controlled territory, the *Wehrmacht's* and *Gestapo's* unseen presence was palpable. Friendly chatter dissipated.

As the locomotive chugged into the Lyon station, the passengers, Jeremy included, searched for changes in routine. The sentries were still there, perhaps in greater numbers, but some red swastika-bearing flags were askew and left that way. *Gestapo* officials demanded travel papers, but their actions were furtive, as though they were more concerned with who might be watching them than with the real identifications of those travelers they screened. They barely paid Jeremy any attention.

Despite its desolate condition under Nazi dominance, Jeremy liked Lyon with its broad avenues, magnificently laid-out gardens, now overgrown, and centuries-old buildings. Situated at the confluence of the Rhône and Saône Rivers, it had been the capital of the Gauls during Roman times.

It was now a city of spies due to its position at an intersection of highways and railroads brimming with warehouse-lined back streets and boasting a historically independent spirit that flouted authority. As a hub of Resistance operations, it had also attracted a strong *Gestapo* presence, but Jeremy noticed that fewer *Wehrmacht* patrols roamed the streets than previously, although they did so in larger groups. They seemed to stop people less frequently and took strong measures to protect themselves rather than rely on arrogance to intimidate their "suspects." Many signs had been removed from German-occupied office buildings, and soldiers helped secretaries load trucks parked at their entrances.

Most telling was the sparse number of German officers at sidewalk cafés that had formerly catered to *Wehrmacht* officialdom. A pall hung over these few patrons. Their expressions were long, their boasting less loud, their laughter less frequent, and they had ceased glaring at passing French pedestrians.

Meanwhile, out of sight of their seemingly fading oppressors, Lyon's residents had more spring in their steps. They walked more upright, made eye contact with each other more frequently, and repressed smiles only with difficulty.

As Jeremy ambled along, he heard wisps of conversations, furtively exchanged news—news about Paris. News that the American—no, the French army—had arrived

outside Paris, poised to enter. Also relayed was gossip that Paris had been wired with demolitions and that the Germans intended to destroy it before leaving. They noted grimly that the German commander in Paris, General Choltitz, had already done much the same at Sevastopol.

Jeremy wondered how much of the chatter was true. *The people's hopes are the German's fears. They wonder about how far north the Allies will push and how soon.*

The notion sparked a momentary thrill as he continued his slow walk through city streets and up a steep hill toward a tall apartment building. Therein lived Madame Marguerite Berne-Churchill, no relation to the British prime minister.

The physician and former model lived high above the city with a spectacular view near the junction of the two great rivers. She had made her abode the operations headquarters for Madame Fourcade's Alliance network, which had arranged for Jeremy to be seconded to SOE, the Jockey network, and Roger. To aid in Marguerite's work for the Resistance, she had even enlisted her teenage son and daughter as couriers.

Marguerite, codenamed Ladybird, worked in Alliance as Fourcade's personal secretary. She greeted Jeremy with open arms, albeit quietly and with a furtive look over his shoulder and down the hall before closing the door. As always, her exquisite beauty and lithe figure took Jeremy's breath away.

"How wonderful to see you," she enthused. She stood back to observe him while he removed his disguise. "You're thin," she said mournfully, "and you look exhausted."

"I've been busy," he said as she led him into the sitting room.

"How exciting to hear about Allied progress toward Paris. Our couriers bring us news. We hardly dare to listen to the radio at the moment. That's the quickest way to get yourself arrested. These days, the *Gestapo* will shoot you as easily as detain you. They're in a vengeful mood, the lot of them. Anyway, there's fierce fighting at Montélimar now—and that's only ninety miles south of here."

"What have you heard about Paris?" Jeremy asked anxiously.

"General Leclerc is supposedly approaching the city, but that's not been confirmed. Accurate information is still hard to get."

"I overhead people say that he's just outside the city. They say that his armored division is preparing to enter there now."

Surprised, Ladybird brought her hands to her mouth. "So fast? The

Americans landed in Provence only ten days ago and there's that fighting at Montélimar."

"I've had no confirmation. A BBC reporter broadcast several days ago that Paris had been liberated, but that turned out to be false. He jumped the gun."

"I'll call around to find out what's happening," Ladybird said, "and we'll turn on the radio later when it's safe. Maybe we can find out for sure." She took Jeremy's arm and led him into the sitting room. As they took seats opposite one another, she chuckled. "I'm prattling on, and I know the question at the top of your head—how's Amélie?"

Jeremy smiled sheepishly. "Guilty."

Ladybird frowned. "I'm sure she's all right, or I'd have heard, but she's not here in Lyon." Seeing a look of alarm on Jeremy's face, she raised both hands in a placating gesture. "I'm sure she's safe. She hasn't been involved in Resistance efforts since you left for the Vercors back in January. She felt terribly guilty that the *Gestapo* had captured her friend, Jeannie Rousseau. She feels like that was her fault. It wasn't, but Amélie is determined to find Jeannie. She spent most of her time trying to track down where the Germans are holding female prisoners, and she believes her friend might be in Fresnes, near Paris. She's gone there—"

"Paris?" Jeremy blurted. "That's the most dangerous place she could be."

"It's dangerous anywhere in France, except perhaps along the Riviera, and there only for the last ten days."

Still alarmed, Jeremy pressed. "You have no idea where she is?"

"She was staying at Georges Lamarque's apartment with Fourcade. He's working with the Resistance farther north. Amélie was set on staying away from Resistance activities in favor of finding Jeannie." She rose to her feet. "I'm being terribly rude. I should bring you a drink and some food." She laughed. "I can offer you only water at the moment. Hopefully that will change soon."

Jeremy smiled bleakly. "Water's fine."

He mulled while Ladybird went to the kitchen. When she returned with a tray laden with bread, cold cuts, and a pitcher of water, he asked, "What about Chantal and Madame Fourcade? Where are they now?"

Ladybird took a breath and arched her brows as she sat down. "Chantal was on Normandy's coast when the invasion took place, and I understand from Dragon—you might recall that he was the head of her Resistance cell there—that she was determined to join in liberating Paris. Last I heard, she was making her way there."

Jeremy closed his eyes and shook his head as he absorbed the news. "What an awful world we live in," he said. "Everyone I love is in mortal danger all the time."

"And you too—"

"I can gauge my own risk and take action. I'm helpless to do anything for my loved ones. My mother on Sark, occupied by the Germans; my father and one brother in separate prisons somewhere in Germany. My sister, thank God, is safe in London. I saw my cousin briefly south of Grenoble, but he was headed into battle at Montélimar, and his brother is fighting in the Pacific. I have no clue where Paul is. The last I knew, he was in combat somewhere in Italy, and now my fiancée and her sister—" He stood and paced. "It's maddening. Worrying about them is almost the hardest part of the war."

"Almost?"

Jeremy exhaled sharply. "I've seen atrocities up close."

Ladybird stood, crossed the room to stand in front of him, placed a hand on each of his shoulders, and looked steadily into his eyes. "Jeremy, listen to me. I'm in contact with Fourcade almost daily—"

"Where is she?"

"In Marseille. She was in Paris but returned south near Saint-Raphaël for the invasion. She was detained there by the *Gestapo*, but they didn't know her real identity and got careless." Ladybird chuckled. "Fourcade got away the same way Chantal did back in May—by stripping down and squeezing through the bars.

"Anyway, as of today, Marseille is liberated—by our own French army under General de Lattre. Toulouse too. And that news is confirmed. So Fourcade is definitely safe. She keeps tabs on all her agents. If anything had happened to either of the Boulier sisters, I would have learned about it. I've heard nothing of the sort."

She suddenly stopped talking and peered at him questioningly. "What are you *doing* here? Why did you come to Lyon at this time."

Jeremy looked at her, flummoxed. He gestured for her to sit down and took his own seat. "I'm here to scout for the Americans. They'll push this way after Montélimar." He took a deep breath. "The Vercors is just as beautiful as you told me it would be. I fell in love with the place and the people." He related in detail the events that had transpired there, of Huet, Roger, Pauline, Chavant, Abel, Geyer, Beauregard, Lilette Lesage, Captain Tournissa and his airfield, the Ganimède family, and many others.

"Strangely," he said when he had finished, "the one who affected me the most was Lilette Lesage. I think because the rest of us had reached full adulthood and were fighters. But Lilette was only twenty, and she was shot mercilessly while she tried to save others. I will never forget her. The Germans murdered a lot of children."

He wiped tears from his eyes and added, "The loss that hurt the worst was Abel Chabal. He knew when we went to defend at Valchevrière that he probably would not return alive." Suddenly overcome with grief, his body shook and he fought back emotion. "They are all absolute heroes," he rasped.

Ladybird crossed the room, leaned over, and kissed his cheek. "Oh, Jeremy, you've witnessed true heroism, and you've seen such awful things."

He regained control of his composure. "I had to put everyone I love out of my mind and concentrate on the job."

"Ah, then you must do it again until our part of the war is over. Have you collected the information you need for the Americans?"

He nodded. "I'll take it back to them tomorrow."

Ladybird regarded him quietly for several moments. "I suggest you leave immediately, give them your information, and then go to Paris. The people there will fight. They won't sit and wait to see if they'll be blown up. Go to Lamarque's apartment. If Amélie is still in Paris, you'll find her there. You've been there."

As if a light had been turned on, Jeremy's face lit up. "Of course, what a grand idea. Thank you, thank you. I'll go right now." He broke a wide smile, leaned over, and kissed Ladybird's cheek.

She grinned. "That's the most genuinely happy smile I've seen during this whole war. Rest. I'll find out more about Paris and arrange for our Resistance group to take you straight back to the Americans, and then on to Paris."

59

August 24, 1944
Rambouillet, France

At dawn, General Leclerc watched from a hilltop as his division formed up for the attack to liberate Paris. Among their four thousand war machines were Sherman tanks, Stuart light tanks, anti-tank guns, half-tracks, field guns, and armored scouts. Manning those deadly weapons systems were sixteen thousand well trained, battle-hardened French veterans.

Leclerc had organized his division to attack in three columns along his seventeen-mile-wide corridor. Cloaked against the rain in an overcoat borrowed from a captain, he watched impassively by his half-track near a hunting lodge used through the centuries by French royalty. Dismissing the thrill of being received as a liberating hero, the general stoked steely resolve for the certain lethal battle ahead.

He inhaled deeply. *Can we prevent the detonations?*

Against the backdrop of a jubilant population, Leclerc had pushed a hundred and twenty miles east to Rambouillet. He then wheeled his columns northwest to face the city. He had ordered Colonel Pierre Billotte to conduct the main attack on the right by thrusting his element northward along the main artery, passing through the industrial suburbs of Longjumeau and Antony, to enter Paris via the gateway at Porte d'Orléans.

Lieutenant Colonel Paul de Langlade would simultaneously push his forces in the center up through the scenic Vallée de Chevreuse. They would pass through Toussus-le-Noble and Vélizy-Villacoublay and enter the capital through the Porte de Vanves.

On the left flank, the general ordered Major François Morel-Deville's units, the lightest of the three columns, to conduct lightning strikes along US V Corps' original axis of advance as a diversion to convince the German defenders that his was the main attack. They were to navigate through Trappes, bypass Versailles and Saint-Cyr, and enter the city through Porte de Sèvres.

While formulating his plan, Leclerc had received fresh intelligence from famed novelist and war correspondent Ernest Hemingway, who ran his own private intelligence network. The information he provided was corroborated by several FFI agents who had slipped in and out of the city. They reported that the *Wehrmacht* had seeded the area across Leclerc's intended path with minefields and backed them up with sixty *panzers*. To avoid them, the general had shifted his advance seventeen miles to the east to attack northward through Arpajon and Longjumeau.

As the sun broke over the horizon, Leclerc received word that the entire division was ready. He keyed his radio and called his three subordinate commanders. "My friends, take us home."

Paris, France

On being advised that he had an incoming call from the *Luftwaffe*, Choltitz picked up the receiver to be greeted by Major Hahn, a ruddy-faced *Luftwaffe* officer whom Choltitz detested for being unctuous and a shallow thinker. The major commanded the *Luftwaffe* assets remaining in the area.

Choltitz had been expecting the call. It came by direct order of Adolf Hitler. "You were supposed to have provided me with your aerial bombing plan two days ago," he growled at Hahn.

"The airfield at Le Bourget has become too dangerous for our bombers," the major explained. "I had to move them. That took time. Unfortunately, the new airfield is too far away to do shuttle-bombing as I originally planned, so now I aim to do an all-out, large-scale terror sweep."

Choltitz frowned. "Would you conduct the mission in daylight or at night?"

Hahn replied with a tone of incredulity. "At nighttime, of course. We can't expose the bombers remaining in France to attack by the Allies."

Choltitz grimaced. "Let me remind you that I still have twenty thousand men in Paris, and *Generalfeldmarschall* Model informs me that thousands more are enroute—perhaps as many as two divisions." His voice turned to acid. "If you bomb blindly in the dark, you'll kill as many Germans as you will Parisians."

A long silence ensued. Hahn sighed audibly. "I have no choice in the matter. We must carry out the bombing, but it must be done at night. I'm sure you understand that presently, the loss of a single aircraft is more catastrophic to the *Reich* than the loss of a few men."

Stifling his fury at the comment with great difficulty, Choltitz queried with forced calm, "Can you tell me the day and time that you intend to execute? Then I can evacuate my men from the target areas where they might be hit." He paused, picked up a document from his desk, and scanned it. "Your orders say, and I'm looking at them now"—Choltitz glanced down at the document in his hand—"that you are to bomb all areas of significant insurrectionist activity. At this point, that is the entire city."

He listened to Hahn breathing hard on the other end of the line.

"*Herr* General," the major said, his voice strained, "the entire city?"

"Precisely. And then you can explain to High Command why you wiped out three divisions' worth of German combat-experienced soldiers and equipment."

Hahn stuttered while muttering that he needed to consult with his superiors. Disgusted, Choltitz hung up, rose from his chair, and walked out onto the terrace to gaze across the city. He could hear the noise of battle coming from the south now, with smoke rising from that direction in greater intensity than that hovering over the city from gunfights with the

Resistance. The dull thuds from the impact of large guns told him that the Allies were at the edge of Paris and drawing closer.

Chantal had become inured to gunfire crackling and heavier weapons booming. Since early morning, however, those sounds had become louder and more frequent, and she found them strangely welcome. That was particularly so when the three tanks in front of the prefecture suddenly departed, leaving behind only foot soldiers with light weapons.

Ravenous hunger, worsened by lack of sleep, dulled her senses and sapped her strength. Resistance fighters outside the prefecture had braved the gauntlet to get food into the building, but it was not nearly enough, and once inside, they could not leave because the enemy maintained a tight cordon around the prefecture.

News seeping into the building told of widespread battle in all parts of the city, including reports of *Gestapo* and *Milice* snipers on rooftops who targeted random civilians on the streets. Whole German garrisons forayed against civilian barriers and then retreated as they encountered volleys of returned fire and thrown Molotovs.

A new sound coming from the sky caught Chantal's attention. She lifted her head wearily and glanced cautiously out her window.

A small, single-engine plane circled above. It was painted green, and appeared to have white stars on the underside of each wing. She could not be sure because her vision had become blurred.

Across the square, the Germans fired at it, confirming her growing sense that the plane was American, or at least belonged to one of the Allies. As she watched, its engine coughed, its nose dipped, and it began a spiraling descent toward the ground.

As it reached low altitude, something dropped from the aircraft and landed a few feet from the front entrance. Then the plane's engine kicked in, and the aircraft straightened out and flew away over rooftops.

Almost as suddenly, someone ran out the front door, grabbed the object, and scampered back inside the prefecture. Hunger forgotten, Chantal joined everyone in the room with curiosity about the object. Soon, a muted roar of excitement rippled through the gathering—the dropped object had been a weighted burlap bag. Inside was a scrap of paper with a handwritten four-word message. "Hold tight. We're coming."

Chantal returned to her position and stared at the point where she had seen the small plane disappear over the rooftops. Her chest swelled with gratitude for the unknown pilot who had risked his life to bring hope to the besieged fighters in the prefecture.

Laval, France

General Bradley paced as he spoke on the phone with Major General Gerow, Commanding General of V Corp and General Leclerc's immediate superior. "Where is Leclerc?" Bradley demanded. "We expected that he'd be in the city center by noon." He glanced at his watch. "He's late. I'm worried about Rolf Nordling's report. General Choltitz opened the door for us. We need to get in there before he changes his mind."

"I don't know where Leclerc is," Gerow growled. "I've been out of radio contact with him for hours, and he shifted his forces west without my approval and without advising me. He moved his division right into the planned path of my Corps, and specifically the 4th Division." His anger grew. "Frankly—" Gerow caught himself. He was about to say that he was seriously considering relieving Leclerc of command.

Bradley responded slowly. "All right. If he can't get the job done, we'll do it. Send in the 4th Infantry without regard to where Leclerc's division is right now, and get it done quickly. If you make contact with that impatient lion, tell him to hurry himself up."

60

La Croix de Berny, France

In late afternoon, General Leclerc stood near a major intersection half a mile north of Antony and only ten miles south of Paris. To the west, he heard constant explosions as his tanks battered against stiff *Wehrmacht* resistance. Progress had been slower than he had hoped, and his radios had broken down, so he had been out of communication with his higher command for several hours.

At the outset of its advance, the 2nd Armored Division had covered ground quickly. Unfortunately, joyous residents crowded the streets, surrounded his convoys, and slowed progress. They had scattered with the first blast from enemy tanks. The people had taken shelter, and the battle was joined.

One of Leclerc's armored platoons, while crossing a field line-abreast over a slight rise, had suffered nearly one hundred percent casualties in the first engagement. As they had reached the crest, a line of German 88 mm anti-tank guns had let loose a salvo that turned the tanks into flaming hulks in a matter of seconds.

Leclerc's three columns had deployed exactly as planned, and he still had confidence that his plan would work, but opposing forces had been stronger than expected. He finally accepted that he was looking at an estimated twelve-hour battle before entering the city.

Bearing on his mind was the need for speed. *We must prevent the detonations.*

Red-bearded Captain Raymond Dronne, a native of French-colonial Chad, had promised himself that he would be the first liberator into Paris. Like so many other French soldiers, he had dreamed of carrying the French blue, white, and red banner streaming in the wind as he careened down the Champs-Élysées and past l'Arc de Triomphe while guns blazed and pretty *Parisiennes* cheered. Only yesterday, for that vision and on receipt of orders for the division to advance on the capital, he had trimmed his beard.

Big and normally soft-spoken, he was infuriated at the moment. His unit had been in the thick of fighting at an intersection ten miles from Paris. Twice in the last hour, he had perceived an open avenue into the city and taken it. Twice, his commander had ordered his unit back into battle.

As Dronne retraced his path south to Berny, he spotted Leclerc standing by the intersection in front of his half-track, unmistakable for the cane the general tapped on the road's surface. "Halt!" Dronne shouted to his driver. He had served with Leclerc for four years. The general knew him, liked him, and respected him.

Brakes squealed and tires screeched as the jeep staggered to a forced halt. Behind it the drivers of the following combat vehicles jammed on their brakes and scrunched to a stop.

Dronne vaulted out of his seat, ran across the road, and reported at attention. Startled, Leclerc stared at him and then up the road in the direction the captain had been traveling toward the battle. "What are you doing here?"

Dronne explained what had happened.

"Don't you know to disobey stupid orders?" Leclerc grasped Dronne's shoulder. "Go straight into Paris. Take whatever you've got and go! Don't stop! Forget about fighting Germans. Just get into the center of Paris. Tell the people to hold on. We'll be there tomorrow."

Moments later, cheering erupted across the road as Dronne briefed his men on their mission. Within twenty minutes, Dronne's unit—three Shermans, six half-tracks, and his own jeep—had reversed direction and were heading full speed toward Paris.

Now he was grimy and sleepless for forty-eight hours, but no less determined, and his wish appeared to be coming true. He would lead the first French army element—the first Allied unit—to liberate the capital of France.

On his map, he judged the distance to his destination, the Hôtel-de-Ville—the city hall—to be five miles in straight-line distance. The actual distance, however, was twice that because of the layout of the thoroughfares into Paris. A few hours later, he turned onto Route Napoleon, awed by the notion that he traveled the same route as the great French conqueror for the same purpose, to take Paris.

The landscape whooshed by as Dronne pushed on and night brought darkness. As he entered the suburbs, people poured into the streets. They had heard the sounds of battle to the west all day, and at first they thought the Americans had come to free them. On finding that French soldiers were headed into Paris, the residents cheered louder, some of them bursting into tears. They clamored around the combat vehicles. Young women climbed aboard to hug and kiss their saviors while the populace, including children, showered them with food and wine.

Dronne stopped only long enough to ask, "Is this the road to Porte d'Italie?" He referred to the famous landmark where Napoleon had entered the city. When villagers argued about the best way to go, he shouted, "We'll find it," and kept going.

Finally, his vehicles swept past the famous landmark on Napoleon's route, one of the main historic portals into Paris, and Dronne's men, packed tightly into their war machines, let out a loud cheer. Finally, after fighting across continents and oceans, they had entered their capital city. They thrust their arms in the air and clapped each other's shoulders for being the first of the French army—of the Allies—to come home to Paris.

Thus far, they had encountered no Germans. Guessing that *Wehrmacht* troops would have blocked the main thoroughfares, the unit turned onto side streets that paralleled the Seine River and roared past intersections without slowing down.

German soldiers at one checkpoint saw them from a block away and fired, but the unit kept going without returning fire. They reached Pont d'Austerlitz, turned a hard right onto the bridge, and careened across the river. Arriving safely on the other side, they turned left sharply and curved along the Quai des Célestins.

Only now did Dronne dare to take a long breath and contemplate what he and his men had just done. A waxing crescent moon behind thin, intermittent clouds reflected off the surface of the Seine River flowing to his left. Ahead and across the waterway, the majestic spires of Notre-Dame rose into the sky.

Dronne suddenly found himself overwhelmed with exhaustion and emotion. He had studied maps of Paris over the course of four years as he had dreamed of such a mad dash. He knew that nearby was the Louvre, Sainte-Chapelle, and other Parisian wonders, and that the mighty Eiffel Tower reached into the heavens just over two miles to the west.

Only one turn remained, and it came quickly as their destination appeared on the right. They drove the width of pale, high, architecturally fine walls and dormer windows that appeared ghostly on the right.

His jeep, the tanks, and the half-tracks reached the front of the edifice, jerked right, jumped a curb, and amid sparks, the clatter of tracks, and the creaks and groans of war machines, Dronne brought the formation to a halt, line-abreast, at the bottom of wide marble stairs. Before them stood the seat of the Parisian municipal government, the magnificent Hôtel-de-Ville.

For several moments, he and his men just stared, hardly daring to breathe. Then they spilled out of their vehicles and jumped around, cheering and hollering. Above them, from high in the building, they heard loud celebrations, and looking up, they saw windows thrown open. Clanging metal sounded against anything that would make loud noise, and then men sang "*La Marseillaise*." Moments later, the main doors flew wide, and a crowd, led by Georges Bidault, president of the CNR, rushed down to the exhausted soldiers.

"You're here," Bidault exclaimed, breathless, pumping Dronne's hand. "Our French army is home."

Bleary-eyed, Dronne grinned as he and his men were surrounded and lifted onto the shoulders of the exultant throng to celebrate their arrival. A few feet away, a radio newsman made the first public, independent announcement to his eager audience. "Our army has arrived. It is now at Hôtel-de-Ville."

Minutes later, the bells of Notre-Dame rang, and as word spread by word of mouth and then by radio announcements, church bells all over Paris joined in. Families across the city threw open their windows and turned up the volume on their forbidden radios as the stirring strains and lyrics of their national anthem played over and over.

Electricians at power plants called each other and soon adjusted their equipment for maximum output, so that radios could be turned to full volume to repeat "*La Marseillaise*" and the news that deliverance was at hand.

General Choltitz sat at a formal dinner in an upstairs dining room at the Meurice. He had dressed in his full formal dining uniform, anticipating that this might be his last meal as commanding general of Paris.

A woman at the table, one of the few German female staff members remaining in the city, suddenly paused mid-bite and cocked her ear. "The church bells are ringing," she said. "Why are they ringing?"

Choltitz blew out a breath. "They're ringing for us," he said. "That's the people of Paris telling us that the 2nd French Armored Division has arrived, and the full might of the Allies will follow."

He turned to his adjutant sitting at his left. "Please place a call to *Generalleutnant* Speidel and bring the telephone so that I can speak to him from here."

When the adjutant had complied, and after greetings, Choltitz said, "Tell me, Speidel, what do you hear?" He held the receiver in the air a few moments and then returned it to his ear.

"I'm not sure," came the reply. "Maybe bells."

"They *are* bells, my friend. The Allies are here. Do you have any orders for me?"

Speidel was quiet a moment. "I have no new orders for you."

"Will *Herr* Model's reinforcements arrive?"

After a brief pause, Speidel replied, "They're on their way. I cannot say if they will arrive in time."

"What about the bombing run?"

"None is ordered."

Choltitz grunted. "And if I carry out my current orders to detonate, can you evacuate my staff and my command?"

Again, Speidel was quiet. "I cannot promise that."

"Then there is nothing left to say other than farewell. Please ensure that my wife and daughters are safe."

"I will," Speidel replied. "That, I promise."

Choltitz hung up and looked somberly at the anxious faces lining both sides of the long table. "Ladies, I'm sure the Red Cross will be here soon to provide safe conduct for your repatriation.

"Gentlemen, it's time to destroy what documents you have remaining and pack your important personal items in luggage you can carry. In a few hours, we will be prisoners of war. Prepare yourselves for profound humiliation."

He rose from the table and left for his room. On the way, Captain Ebernach met him in the hall. "The demolitions are set."

Choltitz nodded.

"We only need to leave a small contingent of men to ignite them," Ebernach said. Anxiety rose in his voice. "May I evacuate the rest of my men?"

Choltitz regarded him with glassy eyes. "I suppose you'll leave someone in charge who is capable of carrying out the task?"

"Of course, *Herr* General. I wouldn't delegate such a task to just anyone."

Choltitz glared at him. "Leave," he said. "Take all your men with you. But go."

"The detonations, sir. Shall I—"

"I ordered you to leave Paris. Go! Now!"

Back in his office, Choltitz poured a glass of schnapps and walked out onto the balcony. Machine guns thundered just blocks away, and tracers lit up the sky, crisscrossing over Paris' architectural treasures. *The insurrection continues, and the Allies appear not to be taking the avenue I opened for them. If Model's reinforcements arrive...*

He sighed. The heavy German guns would remind Parisians that a small contingent at the Hôtel-de-Ville did not constitute Allied control of Paris.

61

August 25, 1944
Paris, France

General Choltitz walked in the early morning sunshine through the Tuileries Garden opposite his Meurice Hotel balcony. He knew from reports from across the city that his men had been driven into their strongholds by the FFI and the FTP with the enthusiastic assistance of regular Parisian residents.

Cut off from normal living conditions by the threat of Resistance attacks, his immediate staff and security troops had moved to hidden positions in the gardens. To carry out their morning ablutions, they had spread their toiletries and towels along the cement shelf at the edge of a pond where only days before, children had floated sailboats and skipped among the flowers.

Choltitz greeted his soldiers and staff with perfunctory cordiality, telling a *panzer* crew, "Watch yourselves. Today, the Americans will surely come."

On returning to the hotel, von Unger followed him into his office. "General, I've received a note to you passed from a French commander through Consul Nordling and the *Abwehr* agent, Bobby Bender."

"Is Nordling feeling better? I'd heard he had a heart attack."

"I assume so, sir, since the message came from him, but I didn't inquire."

"And what about the message. Is it from General Leclerc?"

"No, sir. It's from one of his subordinate commanders."

Choltitz tossed his head. "What does he want?"

"It's an ultimatum."

Choltitz whirled around. "I don't accept ultimatums," he replied tersely. "Send it back."

Von Unger nodded. "I also received a message from high command. They didn't bother to code it."

"Let me see it."

Von Unger handed him a two-word message. "Demolitions started?"

62

Same Day, August 25, 1944
La Croix de Berny

In front of his half-track on the last bridge before entry into Paris, General Leclerc reviewed final plans. Morning had dawned to a beautiful day with mild weather, blue skies, and an air of expectation. FFI intelligence had informed that German troops defending against his advance had withdrawn to strongholds within the city. He could expect minimal opposition on entry.

Nevertheless, he had reformed his division into four columns to push through the final miles to the Paris city limits. His soldiers in Fresnes and surrounding villages prepared to cross the Seine on the Pont de Sèvres.

Anticipating that this would be the day of their long-awaited liberation, the people south of the Seine watched from a distance. They recognized that the climactic moment was upon them and the best they could do for their liberators was to stay out of the way. Seeing that north of the Seine the streets were empty, the windows shuttered, the doors closed, they held in check their desires to overwhelm their champions with gratitude.

Leclerc ordered his advance. The city held its collective breath, joined by the anxious countrymen on the river's southern shore.

The tanks of the lead elements of the 2nd French Armored Division creaked over the Pont de Sèvres. They reached the other side and continued up the empty street.

A window creaked. A tank commander in a turret whirled his machine gun around and took aim.

A woman's head poked out, and she screamed in excitement, "*Les Américain! Ils sont Américain!* "

More windows flew open, and then doors, and people streamed onto the street, shouting, waving the French tricolor and the American Stars and Stripes. They were met with thrilled greetings in their own language, and soon word rippled through that these soldiers were their own sons, husbands, and fathers, returned to deliver them.

The people sensed that this was the day. Women pulled from hiding places the special dresses they had pieced together years earlier for this day. Children waved French and American flags they had made from scraps and memory, as they had been encouraged to do by independent radio stations after Dronne's war machines careened to the front of the Hôtel de Ville.

Men and women grabbed rifles and pistols and poured into the streets. They also brought bottles of wine out of hiding to offer to their 2nd Armored champions as they joined in the final battle to rid Paris of the Nazi scourge.

South of Fresnes, at Nozay, the American thrust into Paris commenced. At the vanguard, Technical Sergeant Milt Shenton drew the dubious honor of being point man for the 4th Infantry Division. It was not one he sought or cherished, having occupied the same position for the division on plunging into the roiling surf of Utah Beach at Normandy only eighty days ago. *But who's counting?*

Although he had survived the landing intact, he figured that a man was allotted only so much luck, and his was bound to run out soon. In an attempt to beat the odds, he loaded extra ammunition into his jeep. Recalling with irony that at the outset of this war he had dreamed of liberating Paris, now he wished he had never heard the name.

The division took to the road, rolling toward the city at top speed. Unfortunately, the fluidity of the situation meant that lower-level units had no maps to help them navigate the distance between them and Paris.

By stopping to query villagers along the route, using the few words of French the Americans knew joined with equally sparse English among the Frenchmen, and combined with comical hand and arm gestures, the 4th Division made its way north. It entered Paris with all the verve and enthusiasm of their French counterparts, finding to their surprise, and Shenton's relief, that they were celebrated by overjoyed Parisians.

Paris, France

Bobby Bender received Choltitz' reply to the ultimatum with dismay but not surprise. He went immediately to Nordling's residence where the two had met earlier when the consul had received it. "Choltitz is a proud man," Bender said after relating the general's response. "He'll order a general surrender of the Paris garrison, but only after a show of force in which he is taken prisoner."

Nordling sighed deeply. "In other words, more people must die."

Bender affirmed with a grim nod. "He's a soldier. He can't abandon his sense of duty. The pressure is enormous. While I was at his headquarters, I saw piles of communiques from German High Command screaming at him to fulfill his orders. If he doesn't start soon, he could be arrested and his family executed.

"He knows that two Allied divisions are heading this way, the 2nd French Armored and the American 4th Infantry. One of them must arrive within hours. If that happens, he'll know that surrender is inevitable. He has too few forces to mount an aggressive defense. However, if *Generalfeldmarschall* Model's reinforcements arrive before the Allies do, he'll fight."

Nordling drew a long breath and exhaled. "And the city?"

Bender shrugged. "The explosives are in place. He's dismissed the demolitions unit, which demonstrates his reluctance to detonate, but that could be reversed. At the very least, he could destroy the most important buildings. Paris would be left in flames."

Chaban's aide, Lorrain Cruse, arrived and greeted Bender and Nordling. The Swede related the situation just discussed.

Cruse listened intently. When Nordling finished, Cruse leaped to his feet. "I must get word to Leclerc."

Minutes later, he pedaled his bicycle furiously through the streets on his way through Paris to find the French army. He hoped to deliver a warning in time.

General Leclerc—bareheaded, dressed informally in khakis soiled from days on the campaign, and wearing muddy combat boots—stood in his half-track as he rode into the city, grasping the side to steady himself.

Paul stood near him, out of the limelight, enjoying the experience of watching this general interact with his adoring populace. Obvious to him was that Paris was ready for this glorious day of bright sunshine and blue skies. Equally apparent was that the people wished to celebrate their deliverance.

Ahead, Leclerc's war machines proceeded with caution. The clatter of their tracks, the roar of their engines, and the squeal of rubber tires on cobblestone streets created a loud cacophony. Infantrymen, their rifles and machine guns held at the ready, patrolled on either side. From adjacent streets and far-off neighborhoods, the sounds of gunfights added to the hubbub, with the smell of munitions heavy in the air.

As the advance elements passed by dwellings and continued forward, windows flew open with people of all ages waving the French and American flags. Others poured into the streets alongside the soldiers, cheering wildly. As had happened all along the way from Normandy, the jubilant crowds celebrated their saviors unreservedly. Women wore their special dresses and showered the soldiers with warm welcomes. Children with shy smiles or beaming faces approached the rugged combatants in awe, taking in their long rifles, the grenades hanging on utility belts, the helmets gleaming under camouflage netting, and the weathered but happy faces.

Men, too, hugged their compatriot-soldiers, thanking them over and over for the long fight that had brought them, at last, to Paris.

Unlike the towns and villages along the way as Leclerc's forces maneuvered toward the city center, the crowds behind them followed, growing larger with every increment of advance. Men appeared carrying rifles and pistols. At the front of the crowds, some women, with determination gleaming in their eyes, grasped firearms and moved ahead to engage the enemy with their own French soldiers.

Radioing to his subordinate commanders, Leclerc learned that the situation was similar wherever his division had entered the city. His heart thumped with pride on seeing these long-suffering Parisians throw themselves into the fight. Any doubt he might have had about routing the *Wehrmacht* today dissipated. *By nightfall, Paris will be ours once again.*

Amazingly, he found the going much easier than expected. Over five days of hard fighting, the Parisian FFI and FTP had herded the remnants of the erstwhile one-hundred-thousand-strong occupation army, now reduced to fewer than twenty thousand of questionable skill and motivation, into the *Wehrmacht's* remaining strongholds. The bulk of the force that had been in Paris was sent west to reinforce in Normandy or back to Germany to prepare defenses for the battles that were sure to come.

Tall buildings barred a long view, but the general knew the city and his current position. In his mind's eye, he saw the monuments and historical buildings that would soon come into clear view. Momentarily, he would see the majestic spire of the Eiffel Tower rising into the sky, and beyond it, l'Arc de Triomphe. On the right would be Notre-Dame, the Louvres, Les Invalides—all the wondrous gardens, parks, memorials, and stately edifices he had longed to see over four years of combat.

He caught Paul's eye and raised a triumphant fist.

A disturbance among the crowd caught the general's attention and he recognized Chaban's aide, Lorrain Cruse, struggling past annoyed onlookers to reach him. Leclerc stopped his vehicle and beckoned to Cruse. The people fell away and let the aide through.

"I've just come from Consul Nordling," Cruse cried, panting heavily as he clambered aboard the vehicle. Between gasps for air, he reported what

Bobby Bender had related about Model's reinforcements and the still impending demolitions.

Leclerc's jaw tightened as he listened. He motioned to his driver to proceed, and then stood straight with narrowed eyes.

A hush had fallen over the crowd. Perceiving the change in atmosphere, he stood straight, forced a smile, and turned all around, waving.

The people thundered, "Leclerc! Leclerc! Leclerc! *Vive la France!*"

His throat constricted from the attention of the adoring crowd. He leaned down, bracing himself against the vehicle's frame as he reached out to touch the people and grasp their hands as they continued to call out his name.

Fireman Captain Lucien Sarniguet heard rifle shots aimed at him and his five other firefighters and the bullets pinging from the Eiffel Tower's steel trusses. The men continued to climb. For the captain, this was a necessary mission to expiate the shame he had carried for four years. In June of 1940, he had been the man ordered to ascend the seventeen hundred steps of France's greatest icon to lower the French flag and raise the Nazis' scarlet banner with the black swastika.

Across the city, he saw clouds of smoke rising from the various gunfights and heard the sounds of street fights. Closer to the tower, a battle raged between German forces entrenched at a military school near Champ-de-Mars and a French force of Leclerc's soldiers and FFI volunteers.

Sarniguet and his men paid the gunfire no heed. Despite the large, diamond-shaped spaces between the trusses, the mammoth main structure and its supporting beams provided cover to the extent that only the most practiced snipers with exceeding luck could hope to hit targets that diminished in relative size as the men climbed ever higher. Nevertheless, close-in strikes against the hard metal rang loud, causing the firemen's hearts to pound harder. Their faces and bodies streamed sweat.

The climb became a race, each man hoping to best the others in reaching the top. However, they all knew that the final honor would rightly go to their captain.

Days earlier, Sarniguet pieced together a huge banner from scraps. The colors were faded, but they were the blue, white, and red of the French flag. He carried it in a bundle under his arm.

The wind moaned, the sound of battle faded, and still he climbed. His legs ached, his lungs heaved, but he continued on until he reached the zenith. There, exhausted, he watched as his men ripped down the detested Nazi flag. Then they helped as he hooked his banner to the mast.

At noon, as the battle raged far below, Sarniguet hoisted the French flag to once more fly from the Eiffel Tower over Paris.

Lieutenant Henri Karcher of the 2nd French Armored Division could not help himself. As his platoon pushed through the crowds, he searched the faces for his wife's or that of his four-year-old son, the latter known only from a photograph.

Since before the boy was born, Karcher, a thirty-six-year-old surgeon who had lost his father in World War I, had fought as an infantryman across North Africa and Italy. Dark-haired, lean, and gregarious, he sported a small mustache over a ready smile.

Resigned to the improbability of spotting his wife and son, he turned his troops west off of Avenue du Général Lemonnier at the Place de Pyramides, gazing appreciatively as he passed by the golden statue of Jean d'Arc. He was now on Rue de Rivoli, a long commercial street that paralleled the Seine on the north side.

Between the river on his left and his current position was Tuileries Garden. On his right, five-story buildings rose as far as he could see, their bases lined with elegant stone arcades that stretched over the street's shops and cafés. Now the establishments stood forlorn, their meager wares displayed in glass windows, their interiors empty of customers.

Before completing the turn from Lemonnier onto Rivoli, Karcher stopped in the intersection to take in the contrast between the opposite ends of the street. On the west end, the street was empty. Nothing moved.

The noise of celebrating Parisians on the east end was thunderous, and as Karcher scanned in that direction, he saw waving and cheering crowds, so thick that they were held back by police. They were joined in their festivities by residents in every window all the way to the fifth-floor rooftops, as far back as Karcher could see. They shouted their joy and flourished their French and American flags. Two hours earlier, the celebration had reached new heights as news passed, first by word of mouth, and then announced over the radio, that the French flag once again flew over the Eiffel Tower.

As Karcher's unit had traversed the city, throngs had followed and grown to stupendous masses. They were peppered along the way by German and *Milice* snipers shooting at random civilians. With each resounding shot, the people scattered or huddled in place, but they also returned fire with their hunting rifles and pistols, joined by the French army's heavy machine guns and small arms. Each time, the snipers were subdued, and as the army progressed to the heart of Paris, so did its people.

Karcher spun around from the crowd east of Lemonnier and stared once again down Rivoli to the west, the section he was about to navigate. Along its second floors, scarlet Nazi banners with their ominous black swastikas still swayed in a slight breeze. And there, three blocks down, across from the Tuileries, was his objective: the Meurice, the luxury hotel and headquarters of the commander of *Gross* Paris, General Dietrich von Choltitz.

Karcher's company commander quickly dispatched the platoons to their objectives. The first would enter the Tuileries on the left flank and proceed among the foliage of its gardens to provide covering fire on the front of the hotel. The second would head north to Rue Saint-Honoré, a block away. There it would maneuver left, traverse northwest among the erstwhile fashionable boutiques along the street to Place Vendome, and then cut south to approach the objective from the rear. Determined to enter the Meurice through the front door, the company commander accompanied Karcher's platoon, traveling directly along Rue de Rivoli.

General Choltitz' orderly, a corporal, stood at the door to the balcony in the general's office, alternately staring over the gardens across the street and then up and down the avenue. Suddenly, he called out in alarm, "*Herr*

General, you ordered me to inform you if I saw enemy troops. A company of infantry is deploying to the east near Jean d'Arc's statue. I see men entering the Tuileries there, and others heading into the arcades along Rivoli."

Choltitz looked up distantly, and then called through his open door to Colonel von Unger. The chief of staff appeared immediately.

"Please make final preparations and alert the staff."

Von Unger nodded disconsolately.

Choltitz grunted. "Still nothing from Model? What about Karl, the mortar?"

Von Unger shook his head again. "Nothing encouraging. Seidel says the *generalfeldmarschall* ordered every remnant of any viable organization to come to our aid, but"—he took a deep breath and exhaled—"all over France, the Resistance is blowing up trains, railroad tracks, bridges." He sighed. "Our reinforcements can't get through, including Karl."

Choltitz grunted and tossed his head impatiently. "Then we wait." He jerked open his desk drawer and reached inside. "Shall we have an English whiskey?"

Before the colonel could respond, the corporal called from the window. "Sir, an enemy tank approaches from the east."

Choltitz grunted and glanced around at the room's fine furnishings. "This once elegant hotel is about to become a battleground."

Karcher's men darted between the arcades' pillars as they advanced under its ceiling. Across the street, First Platoon had disappeared behind trees and shrubbery.

A hailstorm of shooting rang out from inside the gardens farther down the street. Bullets smacked into the arcades' stone walls and columns. One of Karcher's men cried out in pain. A medic scurried to the wounded man's aid.

Karcher's squads responded with full volleys and then scampered to new positions. The stone pillars provided good cover, particularly at the slanted angle of the line of enemy fire, but within the arcades themselves, cover was sparse. Sandbags had been stacked high, but they mainly protected the businesses that occupied them. Repositioning them during a running battle was a deadly proposition. The soldiers scrunched together and peered around the columns' bases.

Karcher exhaled and took stock of his situation. Inside the elegant garden and along the now-pockmarked fence lining it, the flanking platoon was fully engaged. Vision became impeded by smoke. Behind him, he heard the clatter of a Sherman tank heading down the center of Rivoli. When he turned to see its position, its 75 mm cannon

spewed flame. At the opposite end of the street, a *panzer* blew up, its ammunition erupting and sending its turret skyward. Nearby glass windows on the Meurice shattered, sending shards of glass flying over onto the boulevard.

Karcher seized the moment to push his men farther down the street under the sheltering arcades toward the Meurice. The rat-tat-tat of machine guns joined with the irregular cracks of M1s and Mausers, criss-crossing tracers, and flying shrapnel and fragments of rubble, to create close-combat bedlam, broken only by the cries of the wounded. The cheers of happy Parisians had faded to the rear.

Karcher's men were stalled. Gunfire continued unabated for a seemingly endless time. Across Rivoli, the fighting inside the gardens gained in ferocity, the center of it moving steadily west toward the Meurice.

More Shermans roared up from behind, blasting away at caving German defenses. Karcher rallied his men and pressed forward. Then, from the western side of the Meurice, behind the enemy positions on Rivoli, more gunfire erupted. Second platoon had arrived from their trek along Saint-Honoré and Place Vendome.

Karcher turned to shout an order. A tracer hissed by, singeing his eyebrow. He wheeled, stunned, but with no time to contemplate his close brush with eternity, he swung back around to his front. Hanging from the ceiling of an arcade ahead of him was a sign, in gilded letters, announcing the entrance to Hôtel Meurice.

Calling three men to follow him, Karcher plunged through the door. Straight ahead on a wall over a glass display case of jewelry, a large portrait of Adolf Hitler stared down at him. He dispatched it with his carbine.

An enemy machine gun fired down at him from atop a grand staircase leading to the second floor. Karcher ducked behind a marble counter, grasped a grenade from his belt, pulled the pin, and hurled it. Seconds later, it exploded on target.

Rushing up the stairs, he saw the German machine gunner lying sprawled atop his weapon behind a bank of sandbags. Karcher was saddened by the sight—an old soldier, probably in his late fifties, with sagging skin and gray hair.

The lieutenant, followed by his three men, rushed on through billows of smoke and dust. A German officer appeared, arms raised.

Karcher jabbed the barrel of his weapon into the officer's belly. The German yelled out a command, and firing ceased.

"Herreman, get over here," Karcher called to one of his privates, who spoke German. "Tell them to come out, one by one, hands raised. Tell them to stack their weapons inside the door before they come out."

Karcher stood by as the Germans, with dour, downcast expressions, filed by. They glanced at him furtively but did not hold eye contact. Dust-covered, they formed a dejected line down the stairs and into the lobby, where Karcher's platoon sergeant organized a security team to watch over them. They sat cross-legged on the luxurious, debris-laden carpet, a forlorn group, with their hands clasped behind their heads. Cautiously, they eyed their captors.

When they were assembled, Karcher scanned them. Spotting a tall officer with a red seam on his trousers, he recognized the symbol of a German general-staff member and called to Herreman. "Ask him where his general is."

Minutes later, Karcher entered a small room on the second floor. General Choltitz sat with his head in his hands at a table. Colonel von Unger sat next to him. They were flanked by two more German officers. All four men had laid pistols in their service caps on the table in front of them. Choltitz, who did not own a sidearm, had borrowed one.

With an air of resignation, Choltitz raised his head. *My men are fighting to their last bullets. I did my duty.* He took a moment to observe the lieutenant in front of him, and then rose to his feet.

Karcher snapped to attention. His temples throbbed. Visions passed before his eyes of battles in Africa's Saharan deserts; of mind-numbing cold and burned-out villages along Italy's mountainous crests; of blood sprayed across his face from comrades shot next to him; of half-starved countrymen cheering him and his platoon on as they tramped across France; of the bullet that had singed his brow and nearly taken his life only moments ago; of the wife he had been absent from for four years; of the young son he had never seen. This moment, representing victory over the Nazis for all his countrymen, vindicated his personal odyssey.

He stood tall and took a deep breath. "Lieutenant Henri Karcher of the Army of General de Gaulle."

Choltitz stood silently, studying the infantryman before him. The lieutenant was dirty, his face darkened with the smoke of battle, his combat uniform rumpled, still wearing his helmet, but now allowing his carbine to hang loosely at his side. Unmistakably, Karcher bore a sense of pride.

The German squared his shoulders. "General von Choltitz, commander of *Gross* Paris."

Karcher took a moment to size up the general before him. Garbed in a formal uniform, Choltitz stood shorter than his staff, yet he carried himself with quiet dignity despite his obvious humiliation.

"Do you surrender?"

Choltitz nodded. "*Ja.*" Careful to indicate no hostility and in a ceremonial gesture, he picked up his borrowed pistol by its barrel and proffered it to the lieutenant. His fellow officers followed suit.

Lieutenant Karcher—son, husband, father, surgeon, and infantryman—stepped forward and accepted the general's weapon. "Then you are my prisoner."

63

General Leclerc glared at Colonel Rol. Moments earlier, he and Choltitz had signed a surrender document. In accepting the capitulation, Leclerc had signed in the name of the Provisional Government of the French Republic rather than in the name of the Allied Command, a distinct departure from Allied practice.

As the informal ceremony ended, Colonel Rol had pushed into the room inside the train station at Gare Montparnasse where Leclerc had established his headquarters. "Why was I not invited to watch the surrender," Rol demanded angrily. "I command the Paris contingent of the FTP, which is the largest Resistance group in the country. For six days, we've fought the *boches* in this city"—he glared contemptuously at Choltitz—"and we've fought as hard as anyone."

After Lieutenant Karcher had accepted Choltitz' personal surrender at the Meurice, a French major entered the room. He ordered the general to command an immediate cessation of fighting outside the hotel, and then escorted him out. By then, news of his and his staff's capture had reached the crowds of celebrating Parisians. They had rushed *en masse* to watch the transfer of the hated prisoners.

A near riot erupted when the major emerged with Choltitz through the hotel's front entrance. People attempted to charge through the armed escorts with flailing fists. They shouted insults and hurled trash, seeking to heap four years of pent-up anger for German brutality on this last commanding general of *Gross* Paris who had arrived in their midst sixteen days earlier.

Choltitz braced his shoulders against the assaults and walked briskly to the back of a panel truck in which he was spirited to Leclerc's new headquarters at Gare Montparnasse. There, the two opposing generals signed a document surrendering all *Wehrmacht* forces in Paris. Immediately thereafter, they dispatched trios of French, German, and American officers to order the remaining German strongholds to concede.

A group of officers had gathered to watch the signing. Arriving after it had ended, Rol roared his fury at not having been invited to the ceremony. Now, as he glowered at Leclerc, one of Rol's supporters shouted, "The colonel's signature should be on that surrender document."

Exasperated and impatient, Leclerc thrust the document at Rol. "Sign it."

Fabri, the leader of de Gaulle's five-thousand-man commando security group, escorted General Charles de Gaulle to Paris. They secured the country roads and bridges along the way, the same ones the general had taken to escape the German juggernaut four years earlier. For this occasion and at the general's insistence, Fabri requisitioned an automobile of French manufacture, an open-topped Hotchkiss luxury sedan.

De Gaulle breathed in the late summer-afternoon air and let his eyes roam over the landscape with its fields and villages. Ahead of him, his entourage rode in the two German Horch sedans Fabri had expropriated from the *Wehrmacht*. They transported officials whom de Gaulle had appointed to his provisional government.

The Eiffel Tower gleamed in the distance and, drawing nearer, de Gaulle saw the national banner waving proudly in the wind. As the motorcade approached the Porte d'Orléans, one of Leclerc's armored cars pulled in ahead to lead it into the city.

A crowd had gathered on each side of the route. Although not immediately recognizing the general in the French automobile, they sensed from the dignity of three black open sedans led by a 2nd Division armored car that they witnessed the arrival of some French personage of momentous stature in their city, and they let out a mighty roar. As word spread by proud members of the general's escort of exactly who they were seeing, they chanted, "De Gaulle, de Gaulle, de Gaulle..."

The general glanced at his watch and registered in his mind the time he passed through the portal. Four-thirty. *At long last, I am home.* Maintaining serene dignity, he waved at the crowd.

De Gaulle and Leclerc met and saluted each other on the platform of Track 21 at Gare Montparnasse. His figure slightly bent as always, de Gaulle took and scanned the surrender document that Leclerc handed him. As he read, his face grew taut.

"Why is Colonel Rol's signature on here? He's not my subordinate. He had no business signing this."

Leclerc explained what had happened.

De Gaulle did not hide his anger. "The Communists will try to use this to claim credit for Paris' liberation and to gain legitimacy in governing France." He glared at Leclerc. "You should not have acquiesced."

He inhaled and looked about before returning his attention to Leclerc. "Georges Bidault and the CNR issued a proclamation this morning. They hailed Paris' liberation, but nowhere did they mention our provisional government, and they presumed to speak 'in the name of the French nation.'"

Leclerc listened at attention and without expression.

"They are waiting now to receive me at the Hôtel de Ville," de Gaulle went on. "Do you understand the ramifications?" His anger grew, expressed in the low, steely quality of his voice. "We have two factions seeking power, the Communists and this Committee for National Resistance. If our republic is to be restored, neither can be allowed to dominate. Civil war will break out."

He was silent for a moment. When he spoke again, his tone had softened. "I'll tell you bluntly, Leclerc, this document challenges my authority and consigns me at best to a consultative role and more probably to oblivion." He inhaled sharply. "We fought hard for a free France. I won't tolerate petty ambitions. Cancel the visit to the CNR. That committee cannot be seen to lead our movement. The committee must come to me."

"Consider it done, sir," Leclerc replied. "You know my loyalties lie with France," he continued. "When all seemed lost, you led us. You inspired our people with your radio messages, you won the support of our army in North Africa, you raised Allied backing for our Resistance, you organized a government in absentia—you brought us back from shameful defeat to the brink of victory. What are your orders?"

De Gaulle quickly laid out a plan. They hashed out the details, and then he said, "Get me to a place where I can speak securely with General Eisenhower."

64

Same Day, August 25, 1944
Montélimar, France

Zack Littlefield crept through the shadow of Hill 300 cast by a three-quarters waxing moon that glinted off the rifles of his men moving stealthily through trees to his left and right. Their prior day had been long, extending into these early hours after midnight, and they knew the inevitable: after days of maneuvering to outflank each other, the Germans and Americans were about to clash head-on. And Zack's platoon was prowling at the left flank of the German behemoth.

Early the previous morning, the 143rd Division's elements still in the north had been ordered west across N7, the main north-south highway. They were to seize and hold fording points across the Rhône at Loriol and Livron, two neighboring villages along the river roughly twenty miles north of Montélimar. The N7 paralleled the river and was the Nineteenth Army's obvious escape route to Germany. Hill 300 commanded the terrain, the river on one side of it, and the highway on the other.

A week ago, upon leaving Grenoble, the 143rd had marched through the night and paused at a position north of Valence. Then, on order, it captured the town and proceeded south into what had become known as "the Box," the area that began just south of Montélimar and was bounded in the east by the Vercors rim, in the west by the Rhône, and in the north by the Drôme River.

Skirting below the south end of the Vercors rim, General Butler had deployed his task force on the eastern side of the Box and onto the high ground at Hill 430, above the expected enemy path. As part of Butler's maneuvers, Lieutenant Colonel Johnson maneuvered his battalion from Valence to protect the right flank on the ridge of Hill 300.

Although Zack did not know the precise movements taking place, he could read the topographical features that constrained the opposing forces to an area of only two hundred and fifty square miles. Much of it was in view. From those landmarks, he discerned the probable moves and countermoves of both sides.

Those thoughts rendered a sobering reality: the Nineteenth Army dwarfed the combined Task Force Butler even with the 36th Division units deployed in support and the other units of General Patch's 7th Army road-marching from the south to reinforce.

Zack realized with dismay that his platoon would be at the focal point of the impending battle. To his right below Hill 300 was the narrow passage that his company commander, Captain Bellamy, had pointed out. The main highway, N7, sliced the valley floor between his position above La Coucourde and Hill 430 overlooking Condillac. Both knolls were forested, offering plenty of cover and concealment, but the distance from Zack's post to the crest of the opposite hilltop could not be more than twelve hundred yards.

Gazing over the small valley and focusing on the highway less than half a kilometer below him, and mindful of General Truscott's order that no enemy vehicle could be allowed to pass by Montélimar, Zack sucked in his breath. *The whole German Nineteenth Army will try to thread the needle right in front of us.*

Only hours ago, when Zack and his platoon arrived on Hill 300, they received joyful news that Paris was on the verge of being liberated. Then they heard more good news. The French general, de Lattre, who commanded the French 1st Armored and the 9th Infantry Divisions, the Algerian 3rd Infantry Division, and the bulk of the VI Corp's assets, had liberated both Toulon and Marseille. At the battles' end, de Lattre's forces had snared fifteen thousand POWs from a demoralized fighting force. After initial fierce combat, the German defenders, having been left with orders to fight to the last man, had been abandoned by their army retreating north. They were all too ready to capitulate.

The ports in Toulon and Marseille were taken intact, and the mooring facilities needed little repair. With Allied cargo ships already docked there, timelier resupply to forward units was expected. Similarly, attacking units would receive better combat support once VI Corps assets that had been detached to support the campaigns to liberate Marseille and Toulon returned to Truscott's direct command.

Zack had no time to reflect on these developments, and the news did little to assuage his concerns. The German Nineteenth Army, with elements already firmly ensconced in the town of Montélimar, was consolidating for its withdrawal north. It continued to bear down on the relatively small task force barring its way to Germany. Intelligence reports indicated that the 11th *Panzer* and the 198th Infantry Divisions, supported by the 63rd *Luftwaffe* Training Regiment, approached Nyons south of the Box with orders to clear the Rhône Valley of Allied forces.

Zack shook his head. *Cornered wolves sink their fangs deep.*

Meanwhile, Butler's task force had grown from its initial configuration to two divisions, and possibly three, depending on whether the 45th Division reached him in time. Regardless, the German forces he faced were many times larger.

Zack breathed in deeply. *And my men are in the killing field.*

Although the news of German surrenders in Toulon and Marseille reduced the specter of an impregnable Teutonic army in the minds of those soldiers new to combat, Zack had no need to prod his men to keep their attention glued to the threat to their front. They had spent most of the day overwatching as a battalion of the 141st Infantry Regiment, still attached to Butler's task force, pushed up N7 below them, captured Condillac below Hill 430, and proceeded to take La Coucourde. By early evening, two US rifle companies, four tanks, and seven tank destroyers blocked the highway and protected Zack's left flank.

That night, sounds of German preparations for a counterattack at the checkpoint between La Coucourde and Condillac stretched nerves, particularly when measured against difficulties in re-supply and the limited ability to reinforce. On Zack's mind was Truscott's mandate that no German vehicles should pass that blocking position. *Obviously, that's not happening.*

However, engine rumblings and the sounds of tracked vehicles in the east suggested that US forces were also on the move. Zack learned at his commander's pre-dawn brief that General Dahlquist, Butler's immediate boss, had maneuvered units on a line between Crest and Valence to protect the northern end of the blocking position. He had also established positions at Marsanne in the middle of the Box to buttress the eastern flank. Word was that General Truscott was receiving reinforcements from the south and had sent the remaining elements of the 45th Division, the 157th Regimental Combat Team, and the 191st Tank Battalion to further reinforce the blocking position.

The next night, Zack and his platoon watched flashes of tank and small-arms gunfire below them, and they heard the hiss of artillery rounds overhead. From what they could see and hear, they sensed the battle going against friendly forces.

When dawn broke, the German tanks stood at the checkpoint between La Coucourde and Condillac where the American tanks had been the previous dusk.

Almost immediately, friendlies counterattacked, pouring fire from Condillac and re-taking the roadblock. Helpless to participate aside from standing ready to interdict enemy probes, Zack's men stayed close to their positions, straining to see the ebb and flow of battle. Then German artillery rained down, so they hunkered in their foxholes.

Around them, explosions rocked the ground. Expecting return salvos from the friendly side, Zack was surprised when they came in short, intermittent barrages.

Realization dawned. The supply problem had caught up with Butler's task force and with the 143rd Regiment. Friendly forces were running out of ammunition.

In the eerie light before the sun emerged and during an interval when enemy fire abated, Zack dared to raise his head above ground level. He peered down his line and dropped his head in anguish.

A foxhole two down from his own had taken a direct hit.

Luke and Nathan. Gone.

Zack took a deep breath. Luke was one of his veterans, a squad leader who had fought up the length of Italy from Salerno and had taken pains to train his squad. Nathan had been new to combat with the landing at Saint-Raphaël, but he had been steady and reliable. Zack would miss them both as valuable platoon assets, and Luke, as a friend.

The ghostly quiet roused an instinct developed in three years of combat. The interval since the last enemy salvo had been too long. Zack ducked back into his foxhole. "I'm going to check the line," he told his radioman. "Call company headquarters and the adjacent platoons. Ask if they see infantry movement out front."

With that and another wary look over the lower terrain, he vaulted up and over the top. Keeping low, he scurried to the next position to find Sergeant Wilbur already there checking the left flank. Zack hurried to the next position, which had been where Luke and Nathan had sheltered.

The foxhole had been demolished, its sides caved in and blackened. Smoke still rose out of it. Bits and pieces of uniforms, some coated with blood and raw flesh, were scattered over the ground, but he saw no body parts of any size.

Wilbur edged up to him. "Too bad about those two. I'll put Luke's assistant in charge of the squad." He gestured the way he had come. "I've checked this end. Enemy artillery stopped firing. Our guys are awake and prepared for an assault."

The other two squad leaders emerged from the trees. They stared into the dark remains of the foxhole and turned to Zack. "I've got a couple of wounded guys," one of them said. "Nothing serious. The medic is tending to them."

"I've got one dead," the other squad leader, Sergeant Thackrey, reported. Quiet, likable, and steady, Thackrey was the last of the company's original cadre to have deployed from Texas with the 36th Division. He had seen action in North Africa, Sicily, Italy, and now France. "We pulled him behind some rocks down the backside of this hill. We can get him later. No one else is seriously hurt, but their bells are rung. They're watching downhill."

Zack scanned through the trees in the early morning light. "Yeah. Without this ground, the Germans won't get their army through that valley. They're comin'."

The words had hardly left his lips when he heard hollow thumps of mortar rounds leaving their tubes. Even before the projectiles burst behind them, machine guns opened fire, and rapid volleys from rifles spewed clouds of smoke. Hot steel smacked into the trees. Small limbs and chunks of wood dropped to the ground, and leaves floated down in clusters.

Zack and his cadre ducked below the crest. "Get back to your squads," Zack hissed. "Return fire. They're here in force."

Barely fifteen minutes later, amid fierce fighting, Captain Bellamy ordered all three of his platoons to pull back. "They're coming through," he hollered.

Zack attempted an orderly withdrawal to his fallback position in an outcrop of rocks near the hill's summit, but as the Germans pressed forward, some of Zack's men broke and ran. Fortunately, Thackrey's squad arrived intact and provided covering fire while the remainder picked their way through the trees and underbrush.

The new position was not ideal, but ringed by rocks, it provided hard cover with good observation over approaches. The main situational weakness lay in the problems that had plagued US forces in this area since landing at Saint-Raphaël: too few combat assets, separation from support, and not enough ammo.

Zack peered through a chink between two small boulders toward the German position. It was obscured by thick woods. "Relief had better come soon."

Surprisingly, the enemy did not press its assault. Nor did it leave. A small German force stationed itself beyond range of Zack's rifles. Obviously, its mission was to keep Zack's platoon pinned down.

Wilbur crawled up next to Zack. "The krauts don't want to get killed on their way home," he muttered. "That's why they're holdin' back."

Zack nodded. "If they move on us, we'd better know it quick. Set out observation posts on a rotating schedule and keep everyone alert. If they come..." He shook his head.

All that day, Zack and his men listened to the German convoys rolling by on the road below while US artillery rained down on them. The salvos were insufficient to halt the procession.

Zack had studied the Nineteenth Army's makeup and knew that it included the 11th Reconnaissance Battalion, the 119th Replacement Battalion, most of the 119th *Panzer* Artillery Regiment, and part of the 15th *Panzer* Regiment. He had also heard of a Groupe Wilde that was expected to move north on N7, but he did not know its configuration. Units of the 305th Grenadiers would pass by, and Groupe Hax, also of unknown composition. Included as well were the armed masses of the 198th Division, the 338th Division, the 63rd Luftwaffe Training Regiment, and other units that trailed through Montélimar and the erstwhile blocking position that the Germans had once again forced their way through in the narrow passage between Hills 300 and 430.

"Out of curiosity," Wilbur asked, "what's the deal with that *Luftwaffe* unit? I thought they flew airplanes."

Zack chuckled. "It's a manpower issue. The *Wehrmacht* is running short of troops. Two years ago, Hitler ordered Göring to organize his excess *Luftwaffe* units into infantry divisions. The *Luftwaffe* was already losing the air war and had a lot of ground and support crews sitting around twiddling their thumbs. Göring complied, but he kept those units under his own command.

"I don't know how good they are at fighting, and the one trailing along this morning is a training regiment." He laughed. "Maybe they'll throw wrenches at us."

Wilbur laughed and then glanced at Zack. "How come you know so much about the enemy, sir? It's not like you can find it in the *Stars and Stripes* or hear it on the BBC."

"I want to know my enemies," Zack replied. "I spend time in the regiment's ops and intel tents and learn as much as I can. Higher headquarters gets the info and passes it down." From downhill to their right came sounds of fierce battle. "General Truscott won't be happy that the krauts are getting through Montélimar," he muttered. "Let's check the men again."

He knew that the 3rd Infantry Division was supposed to enter the Box and screen to the west along the opposite side of the Rhône. The river meandered in clear view along flat ground below Hill 300 on the opposite side from N7. Thus far, Zack had seen no sign of the 3rd ID. On the contrary, looking through his binoculars, he observed enemy soldiers skulking north, out of range, in twos, threes, and larger groups, presumably to ford the river at points north.

65

Same Day, August 25, 1944
Paris, France

Someone knocking on Georges Lamarque's apartment door once again startled Amélie, this time with the correct sequence of one long rap, four quick ones, a pause, and two more long ones. Nevertheless, from habit, she grasped her pistol as she approached the entrance.

"Who's there?"

"Papillon." Recognizing Chantal's voice, Amélie threw open the door, embraced her sister, and all but dragged her into the sitting room. "I've been so worried about you. Where've you been?"

Still hugging Chantal, she sensed her sister's emaciated form and intense fatigue, and noticed the rifle strapped over her shoulder. Standing back, Amélie looked her over. "You're pale, and you look like you haven't slept in a week."

Chantal smiled wanly. "I'll be fine," she said as her sister closed the door and led her to the sofa. "Just a little tired."

"I'll get some food." When Amélie returned from the kitchen a few minutes later with bread and cheese, she found Chantal stretched out, asleep. She started to tiptoe out, but Chantal stirred and pulled herself to a sitting position. "I'm awake. Please stay. I need to talk."

"I'm so relieved to see you." Amélie sat down next to her and grasped her hand. "I'm sorry, there's not much food in the house."

"There's not much food anywhere in Paris," Chantal said sardonically. Then she forced a smile. "Today is the day. I feel it. By tonight, Paris will be free of *les boches*."

"Tell me what you've been doing."

"I'm not sure how much I can say."

Amélie lifted a brow. "If Paris is to be free today, we can tell each other anything. Besides, sisters in our circumstances don't need secrets between them."

Chantal nodded with a mischievous grin reminiscent of her days before her SOE training in London. "All right, but then you've got to tell me what you've been up to."

As Amélie listened, Chantal related all that had transpired since her first meeting with Chaban. She told of her job at the prefecture, of having followed Colonel Rol and almost being caught. "I really wanted that rabbit," she said, laughing.

She told of her days during the siege and the brave pilot who had flown down to deliver his message of hope. "We thought we'd lost until he came. Then this morning, the Germans suddenly vacated, and we could leave. Other Resistants came to relieve us and secure the building."

Amélie's eyes widened in amazement. "You kicked off this insurgency," she said. "You delivered the warning that the Communists were about to act."

Chantal shook her head. "If I hadn't, someone else would have, and for all I know, someone else did. De Gaulle had all the pieces in place." She leaned toward Amélie. "Tell me what you've been doing. Do we have any good news about Jeannie or Fourcade?"

Amélie frowned. "I'm afraid not. I last saw Jeannie loading onto the train to Ravensbrück." She sniffed. "That was heartbreaking." She related all she had seen to a horrified Chantal. "Fourcade flew back to London and then to the south of France for the invasion. Georges Lamarque is still in the north. I've been here alone except—" Her eyes brightened. "I met another incredible woman two days ago, Madeleine Riffaud. Her codename is Rainer. I celebrated her twentieth birthday with her."

Amélie related all that had happened during the attack on the train at Buttes-Chaumont. When she had finished, Chantal exclaimed, "*Ma sœur!* You helped save Paris."

"I can't take credit. Everyone played a part, and on that mission, Rainer was superb. She had no time to plan and only as many explosives as she could load into her car. She took them and her comrades to an unfamiliar place and thought fast on her feet. And Alain, Marcel, and Bernard never let ego get in the way. We just did our jobs."

They talked for hours, with Chantal dozing off occasionally but refusing to sleep. Then she asked, "What's next for us, Amélie? Will Jeremy and Horton return to our lives, or will those dreams fade with the end of the war." A sob escaped and she sniffed it away. "Rainer told you that Fourcade had been in touch with Jeremy, but I've had no word about Horton. Is he even alive?" Her chest jerked in a spasm as her lower lip quivered.

Amélie moved closer to comfort her. "I'm sure he'll be all right." She was quiet a moment. "To answer your question, I won't rest until I find Jeannie. I won't be able to live with myself if I learn that I could have done something to save her and didn't. In that case, I won't be good for Jeremy or anyone else. I know that Fourcade feels the same about finding Henri La Faye."

They remained quiet for a time, comforted by each other's company and a relished sense that danger did not lurk immediately outside their door. At last, the Nazi wolves were truly on the run.

"I want to see Paris," Chantal said after a while.

"And so you shall, as soon as things settle down."

"No. Now. This evening. I want to go to Montmartre. Surely you can find a way to get us there."

"Whatever for?"

Chantal smiled mysteriously. "I think it will be a lovely place to spend the first evening of our liberated Paris. A friend from the prefecture invited us to stay the night."

As dusk settled over the city, Amélie and Chantal climbed a set of steep stairs between two apartment buildings on the side of the famed Montmartre hill leading up to the equally renowned white domes of the Basilica du Sacré-Cœur. On the way up, they passed artists already perched on stairs, sidewalks, terraces, and balconies, dipping their brushes into thick, variously colored oils and transferring them to canvases, the first time in four years they could do so without fear of harassment.

The sisters reached the crest where the magisterial architectural wonder rose high above them, and they stood on a terrace overlooking the city. From that vantage, they viewed the Eiffel Tower with its flag still waving in a stiff wind. L'Arc de Triomphe was easy to spot at the opposite end of the Champs-Elysées from the Place de la Concorde, as was the Louvre, Les Invalides, Notre-Dame, the Tuileries Garden, and the other wonders of Paris that had enchanted friend and foe alike over centuries.

Amélie and Chantal stood side by side wordlessly, taking in the sights. After a while, Chantal murmured, "It's really done, isn't it? The Germans surrendered the city. Most of southern and western France are in Allied hands."

Amélie smiled and wrapped her arm around Chantal's shoulders. "The whole of France will be a free country again." She sniffed. "I wish Father could have seen it."

Chantal choked back a sob but said nothing. She turned as she heard her name called out.

A woman approached them. "Ah, I'm so glad I found you. This was a good place to rendezvous. I live just a short distance from here."

Chantal made introductions. "This is Angelique," she told Amélie. "She worked with me at the prefecture. She was with us the whole time through the siege."

While the sun sank on the horizon, the three walked together to Angelique's apartment, comparing notes and making small talk along the way. They reached her sixth-floor flat, which looked out over the city. "I have a bottle of wine," she said. "I've saved it for this day."

Angelique brought the wine onto her balcony and poured three glasses. The sun was barely a sliver above the landscape, and then it disappeared below the horizon, leaving brilliant scarlet fingers reaching into the sky before fading into twilight.

A moment later, the sky suddenly brightened with a million lights. The Eiffel Tower once again reveled in its magnificence, the Notre-Dame in its splendor, l'Arc de Triomphe in its victory, the Tomb of the Unknown Soldier in its serenity—and the people of Paris let out a joyous roar in a united voice of millions-as-one in celebration for their city reclaiming its title of the City of Lights—*la Ville Lumiére.*

Amélie spun and locked eyes with Chantal. "You knew about this."

Chantal smiled and acknowledged with twinkling eyes. "The electricians at the power stations told us. They've been working feverishly since Lieutenant Dronne's arrival in front of Hôtel de Ville—first to let everyone play their radios at full volume, and since then for this." She swept her palm across the brilliance of Paris.

Angelique lifted her wine. "May I offer a toast? To Paris."

The three women clinked their glasses. "To Paris. *Vive la France.*"

The balcony door was open, and in the living room, Angelique's radio played "*La Marseillaise,*" as it had intermittently done all day long. When the anthem finished, a broadcaster announced that he was transmitting from the Hôtel de Ville. Then, in an astonishing announcement, he introduced General de Gaulle as the President of the Provisional Government of the Republic of France.

The three women glanced at each other in disbelief. "De Gaulle is here, in Paris, at the Hôtel de Ville," Chantal exclaimed. "He's going to speak."

As they had done so many times before in clandestine places, they sat in front of the radio, listening to the high-pitched voice. The general spoke of the struggle to free France, of the justifiable outpouring of emotion at Paris' victory. Then his voice rose, and he declared,

"Paris! Paris outraged! Paris broken! Paris martyred! But Paris liberated! Liberated by itself, liberated by its people with the help of the French armies, with the support and the help of all France, of the France that fights, of the only France, of the real France, of the eternal France!"

He continued, speaking of the struggle ahead to free all of France, of the gratitude owed to the Allies, and of the intent to pursue the war into Germany. Amélie, Chantal, and Angelique listened, enthralled. When he had finished, they sat in reverential silence. Then Chantal lifted her wine glass. "I propose another toast, to General Charles de Gaulle."

They clinked their glasses.

66

August 26, 1944
Montélimar, France

The next day was a repeat for Zack. He watched through binoculars as American units, presumably of the 3rd ID, pushed northward on the opposite side of the Rhône. The enemy soldiers on the Highway N7 side of Hill 300 fired shots to keep his platoon pinned down, and Bellamy radioed guidance to stay put pending new orders.

Those new orders came in the middle of the next night. The German unit guarding Zack's platoon had stopped firing. He sent scouts out who reported that the enemy had vacated the area. Zack informed his higher of the new situation.

"Get to my CP," Bellamy ordered. There, by flashlight shined onto a map on the front of a jeep, he reviewed the current situation. "Butler's reinforced task force didn't stop the Nineteenth from getting past Montélimar," he began, "but he's going to make it run a gauntlet from hell."

Bellamy then assigned each of his platoons a new mission. "The 198th Division will be the last major German unit heading north on N7. Its CG split the formation into three columns. They're navigating abreast of each other."

He pointed to Zack. "Your target is the one moving up the middle on N7. It'll pass between Hills 300 and 430. Maneuver your platoon down to the highway, and head south toward Montélimar." He indicated a point on the map. "TF Butler is setting up a seventeen-mile-long ambush from here to the Drôme. You'll anchor it on the south flank. Your position is here. Let the convoy go through until it's all the way past your right squad, then strike from the rear. Destroy everything you can. Our re-supply has gotten better, so ammo won't be an issue. Pick up extra loads of whatever you can carry. Re-supply will get more to you by back roads."

"We're hitting from the rear of our ambush position? Why?"

"That will become clear."

Zack nodded. "What friendly forces will be south of us?"

"The 141st Regiment. It'll maneuver around you and go into Montélimar. It'll clean up whatever enemy elements are still there after the main body goes through."

"How will I know the last enemy unit is coming by? There could be gaps between large formations."

"I'll hear from higher and radio down a single word. 'Scorpion.'"

"Scorpion," Zack repeated. "Got it."

On this, the fourth night of battle and eight days after General Butler's task force entered the Box, Zack crept downhill through trees with his platoon to attack the flank and rear of a full third of a German division—essentially, a brigade-sized unit roughly thirty-six times larger than his platoon.

The mission further sobered him. He had lost three men to artillery on the first night of real fighting, and he had not received replacements. Two men were superficially wounded, but they were still deemed combat ready. Zack knew them. They were not slackers, so he hoped their injuries did not interfere with their ability to fight.

On arriving back at his position, he sent a detail with Wilbur to the company supply truck to see what was available. The group came back with three extra Browning Automatic Rifles. The men commonly called them "BARs." They also brought back five bazookas, full loads of ammunition for the entire platoon, and C-Rations.

Zack gathered Wilbur and his squad leaders and explained the mission. "We'll be covering a line about three hundred yards long. When we arrive at our objective, spread out, line abreast, inside the wood line. We won't have time to dig defensive positions, so make sure your men are behind thick trees. Remind them that M1 bullets go through medium-sized trunks. In the heat of battle, they'll forget."

He turned to Thackrey. "3rd Squad will be on the right flank at the south end. I'll get word to you when the last of the 198th formations is going by. Don't start firing until its rear has gone past. We've got eight bazookas. You'll have four of them with plenty of extra projectiles."

"Sir, the bazookas don't work so well."

Zack grimaced and nodded. "I know. But sometimes they knock out vehicles, and they make plenty of noise when they do. If you keep firing them as fast as you can and aim at specific targets, we might get some lucky hits, and they'll add to the confusion. Make sure your men watch out for backblast. We don't want to kill our own guys."

He sipped his coffee. "You'll also get two of the extra BARs. The 198th is bound to have infantry pulling rear security. You'll need the extra firepower. Guard your flank."

Zack turned to the 1st Squad leader. "You'll be at the north end, supported on our left by our adjacent unit. We're ambushing an infantry division, but if they have any armor, it'll be at the front."

Zack saw the sergeant's skeptical look. "You'll have an extra bazooka and an extra machine gun. Fire as soon as you hear 3rd Squad shooting."

He turned to the remaining squad leader. "2nd Squad, you're at center section. You'll also have an extra bazooka. Same thing. Take out the heavies as soon as 3rd Squad starts shooting."

Zack caught Wilbur's eye. "We'll have a total of seven machine guns. Station along the line so that we have interlocking fire across the road for the entire engagement. If we find ourselves attacked in strength, the final protective line will be across our front toward the lead enemy elements. Tell everyone to watch for enemy soldiers breaking to our side of the road. If the krauts train the way we do, they'll attack into the ambush. If some get too close, use your hand grenades.

"Any vehicles that make it past our ambush, let 'em go. They've got seventeen miles of pure hell to get through. Our actions will be the signal up the line." Zack turned back to Thackrey. "That's you, Sergeant."

Thackrey nodded grimly.

"Keep this in mind," Zack went on. "The best German troops were sent to Normandy. A lot of the ones coming this way are conscripts, and some are POWs from the eastern countries who are forced to fight. They're not well motivated, but don't underestimate them. Their bullets kill like any others.

"These guys are as scared as we are, and they don't want to die either, so they'll fight for their lives and to get home. They won't take unnecessary risks. Take advantage of that. Keep firing, and keep 'em confused."

The ponderous armored column creaked along the road mere yards from where Zack and his men lay in wait. The convoy had been unceasing even as his platoon crept its way down the backside of Hill 300 and maneuvered around the south end. As they approached their ambush position, 1st and 2nd Squads maneuvered to the left. When the full platoon was positioned in the trees parallel to N7, the men stole forward until they were within fifty yards of the enemy procession.

Zack maneuvered along the entire line, checking the position of each man. A supply of additional ammo and bazooka rounds arrived, carried forward by company supply men in jeeps and trailers stationed behind the hill.

Zack took up his position near the middle of his stretched-out squads. From behind underbrush, he saw the road. As thousands of vehicles lumbered by, warm air generated by the convoy's engines and exhaust mixed with road dust to create thick clouds with suffocating fumes.

Clearly, the vaunted German army was in disarray. *Panzers*, troop trucks, *kübelwagens*, immense six-wheeled staff cars, maintenance lorries, towed field artillery, tank destroyers, and myriad other types of military vehicles staggered by in stops and starts. Soldiers holding submachine guns with barrels pointed loosely toward the woods trudged by, their bent backs, drooping shoulders, and plodding footfalls bearing witness to their physical exhaustion and defeated spirits. Zack could only imagine their fear and sense of abandonment associated with their frantic withdrawal northward.

Most astonishing, as dawn's first light revealed, were piles of discarded military equipment sprawled chaotically along both sides of the road, including tracked and wheeled vehicles, personal items, bedding, blankets, uniforms, satchels, shattered small arms, destroyed binoculars, emptied first aid kits... The sheer number and type of battle refuse was indescribable. Smaller items had been ground into the road's surface, and large ones had been shoved to the side of the road by heavy vehicles following behind. With the battle ongoing, the local population so far had no opportunity to pick over the spoils.

At last, after an excruciatingly extended time of pulsing hearts, needle-pricked nerves, and deliberately measured breath, Zack heard the radio message from Bellamy. "Scorpion."

Adrenalin coursing, Zack belly-crawled backward from his position, moved into a thick stand of brush, and rose to his knees. "It's on," he hissed to Wilbur a few yards away. "Alert the center and left flank. I'll position with 3rd Squad for kickoff."

"Roger," the platoon sergeant whispered back.

Keeping an eye toward the road, Zack used low ridges, trees and their shadows, and underbrush to slide, crawl, and run to the far end of Thackrey's position. He arrived sweating, his chest heaving. "That's the last of the 198th's formation," he rasped hoarsely. "You'll hear shooting to the south. That's our 141st. It'll take care of German stragglers. Alert your squad."

"Roger. I checked the line a few minutes ago. We're ready."

"Let's go see 'em anyway. We can offer encouragement." Zack clapped the sergeant on the shoulder. "Yours is the most crucial part of this operation."

The squad leader held Zack's steady gaze. "We'll deliver, sir."

True to the sergeant's word, his men were alert, leaning forward in their positions, and concentrating on the funereal procession of a defeated army slinking home. Its war machines' discordant roar constituted an inharmonious dirge.

Moments ticked by. Then, in the morning light, amidst the veil of dust and exhaust, the tail end of the convoy came into view.

Zack watched Thackrey. The sergeant had his eyes on the road, scanning every vehicle and infantryman who passed to his front.

The last vehicles trailed by. Behind them straggled a company-sized formation of infantrymen spread single-file along each side of the road.

The sergeant's eyes met Zack's.

Zack nodded.

Thackrey took aim at the nearest enemy foot soldier and fired.

The soldier dropped in the road.

Immediately, the backblast of three bazookas broke above the din of the creaking, groaning convoy and its roaring engines. Then, the machine guns opened up. Two mowed down the nearest German infantry troops behind the convoy. The third delivered fire on soldiers along the enemy flank, while riflemen picked off individuals.

The bazooka rockets landed. One bounced off the door of a truck dragging a field artillery piece. However, one of the remaining two landed in a troop carrier and exploded. The flanking machine gun put burst after burst into the canvas-covered rear. Agonized shrieks punctuated the explosions and gunfire.

The third bazooka rocket struck an ammunition truck. The shattering blast shook the ground and sent towering flames into the sky followed by thick black smoke. Behind the conflagration, vehicles ground to a halt to be caught by 3rd Squad's withering fire.

A second round of bazooka backblasts erupted. More vehicles went up in flames. Enemy soldiers ran looking for shelter. Thackrey's unrelenting machine guns and his riflemen's pinpointed shooting cut them down unmercifully, leaving them sprawled and lifeless on the road's hard surface.

A few German soldiers managed to return fire. Bullets whizzed by the length of the 3rd Squad's position. Vehicles to its front were in flames. The engines of those not disabled rose in tenor as they accelerated northward to escape the cauldron, creating a gap between them and the rear security company. Lacking protection, enemy infantrymen were quickly cut down.

Vehicles blocked by those already hit became stationary targets without protection.

Behind the convoy, two of Thackrey's BARs swept both sides of the road. The gap widened between the convoy and its trailing protection.

To the north, the firefight spread the length of the platoon's position and continued up the seventeen-mile-long line as Butler's full task force launched the scorching gauntlet. From farther south came the sounds of more fierce fighting.

Thackrey glanced at Zack.

"That should be the 141st heading into Montélimar. Watch your flank." He gestured toward the enemy's rear-security company. "Concentrate on those guys. They're the biggest threat to your squad now."

Thackrey shifted a machine gun and three riflemen to cover his right flank and increase the rate of fire on the hapless enemy soldiers caught on the open road to the south. Dead bodies lined both sides in streams of blood.

Then, from among the straggling German infantry, a white cloth rose into the air on a stick. Enemy fire from the rear abated into sporadic shots. More elevated white flags appeared.

Zack turned to observe events beyond the squad's left flank. The sounds of battle had not diminished, but the fight had clearly moved on, perhaps even north of 2nd Squad's position.

"Tell your men to cease fire," he ordered.

Thackrey gave Zack a hard, questioning look, and then called out, "Cease fire, cease fire!"

Following more cease-fire calls, 3rd Squad's firing ebbed and halted.

Sergeant Wilbur arrived at Zack's side. "The battle's moved past us. The krauts aren't stopping. They keep heading north as fast as possible. We're taking prisoners."

"Keep 1st Squad in place until the shooting stops north of us. Then put them in charge of securing the prisoners. Get 2nd Squad to round them up between here and the platoon's northern boundary. 3rd Squad will gather the ones from here to our southern boundary. Find a clearing behind the hill where we can bring them."

As Wilbur went to comply, Zack turned to Thackrey.

"Get Stalbach over here. Time for him to earn his keep."

Wilbur nodded and called out for the soldier. Moments later, Stalbach appeared, gaunt and out of breath. His family had immigrated to Texas from Germany in 1939, shortly before the war started. His father had urged him to return to fight for the Motherland. Instead, he joined the US Army. Initially having to overcome suspicions of his motivations, he had proven an able soldier with the willing ability to interpret at the front between German and English.

Zack pointed out the white flags. "Those guys are ready to surrender. Tell them to lay their weapons down, stand up, and put their hands over their heads. If they don't comply, we'll open fire again."

Grimly and with a worried look, Stalbach nodded. He took a position behind a tree and faced down the road. From both north and south, the sounds of thick battle continued, but it was farther away now, and joined by salvo after salvo of artillery and air-dropped bombs on German fixed positions.

"*Legt eure Waffen nieder*," Stalbach shouted. "*Steh auf. Hände hoch. Wenn du dich nicht daran hältst, wirst du erschossen.*"

General Truscott received General Patch at his temporary field headquarters in the badly mauled Montélimar. Together they walked through its streets to observe the damage, followed closely by a security detail. Beleaguered residents, suffering from shock, regarded them with curiosity but kept their distance, more intent on learning of the damage to their homes.

"Sir, I failed to destroy the Nineteenth Army," Truscott said while looking over the rubble. He grunted. "A lot of *Wehrmacht* vehicles got past Montélimar."

"A lot did," Patch said. "And you were rather hard on General Dahlquist for it."

"I'm not sure how I feel about that yet. I took over from General Lucas at Anzio. I saw what happened because he didn't push inland to meet the enemy coming from Italy's south. Thousands of lives were lost for his decision to stay put on the beach for so long.

"Here, I thought Dahlquist was too slow coming down out of Grenoble and Valence to support Butler. I came very close to relieving him."

"I'm glad you didn't. This is his first major command. He was thrown into one of the most complicated battles I've seen. He was short-handed, under-supplied, had commo problems, and fought against an overwhelming force. He held his own."

Truscott started to interrupt.

"Hear me out," Patch said. "This operation was a gamble from the start. We anticipated taking six months to get where we are now. If we hadn't learned about the Napoleon Route and exploited it, we would have had no force to bring down from the north to support Butler's blocking position. You forced the Nineteenth to use its most lethal element, the 11th *Panzers*, to blast through at the front rather than as a rear guard. Your gauntlet wouldn't have worked otherwise.

"Butler did a terrific job, but at the outset, he made a significant error in the way he handled the Resistance fighters. Fortunately, we were able to turn that around before too much damage was done, and he corrected himself.

"Word going around is that if we had followed your advice at the landing at Saint-Raphaël, we might have given the farm away. Who knows? For that matter, who knows what would have happened to Lucas' VI Corps if he had gone inland more quickly at Anzio? The Germans assembled a massive force against him within a day. He could have had armies striking his flanks or rear from the north and south. That could have been a worse fiasco.

"You know that some people questioned the wisdom of doing Operation Dragoon at all. They say that the troops coming across from Normandy were sufficient to liberate France, and that if we had gone up through the Balkans and hit Germany from the east, we could have added the Slavic countries and its manpower to our strength. What they neglect to consider is that this Nineteenth Army was poised in the south and could have struck at our forces coming out of Normandy from the flank or rear.

"It was our landing on the French Riviera that prompted Berlin to yank the Nineteenth Army back to Germany. Ike wanted to do the southern invasion simultaneous with Normandy, but we just didn't have the resources to pull it off that way, or we would have.

"His mandate was to liberate Europe most expeditiously. He believes going through the Balkans would have scattered our forces. Going through France consolidated them for a hard thrust toward Berlin.

"We're not gods, Lucian. We're fighting men in lethal circumstances. We do the best we can. So let's look at what was accomplished.

"We entered France fourteen days ago. We've captured Marseille and Toulon, and we're two hundred miles into France. The rest of our army is following up the Rhône Valley with ease, and any day we'll link up with Patton's 3rd Army. Hell, Normandy happened less than three months ago, and Paris is liberated."

Truscott interjected, "But the Nineteenth Army, sir—"

"Let's look at some numbers," Patch interrupted. He reached into his shirt pocket and pulled out a slip of paper. "Casualties always hurt, but ours were five percent compared to an estimated twenty percent for the Germans of a much larger force. That translates into a hundred and eighty-seven of our men killed, a thousand and twenty-three wounded, and three hundred and sixty-five missing.

"On the German side, we estimate that in the last ten days, they've lost nearly six thousand men. We don't have the breakdown, but those were front-line combat soldiers. In addition, they lost over two thousand vehicles, fifteen hundred horses, all the artillery in two divisions, and six of their long-range railroad guns—the 'Anzio Annies.' You know about those."

Truscott pursed his lips. "Yes, sir, I do. They harassed the hell out of us at Anzio."

"My point is that you, Butler, and Dahlquist did your jobs. You depleted the Nineteenth Army's ability to fight, and we're still biting at its heels. When it gets back to Germany, it'll have us and the Russians to fight with whatever it has left.

"On balance, I'd say we won."

67

Same Day, August 26, 1944
Paris, France

Prompted by radio announcements that had repeated throughout the previous night, more than a million Parisians congregated to welcome General de Gaulle at a parade that was to begin at two o'clock in the afternoon. Parisians waited at the southwest end of the Champs-Elysées for a glimpse of the man now acclaimed as the savior and leader of France.

The Boulier sisters stood together at the front of the crowd at Place de La Concorde, jockeying good-naturedly with other eager citizens. They understood that they had slight chance of seeing the general up close; they had arrived too late for a favorable place near l'Arc de Triomphe at the opposite end of the boulevard where he would first appear. However, if he were to travel down the center of the avenue, they might be able to see him for most of his procession.

While they waited, Amélie recalled the days of fear when, as Jeannie's courier, she had avoided German soldiers patrolling this same boulevard. She pointed out to Chantal the vicinity of a café on the other side of the boulevard at the opposite end, closer to the arch. "Right there is where Jeannie was sitting surrounded by senior officers of the German High

Command when she communicated to me an urgent message. It was the one that led to the bombing of Peenemünde where the V-1 and V-2 rockets were developed and assembled.

"I didn't know that's what it was at the time, but I was carrying that information when a *Gestapo* officer discovered me. I was so scared." She let out a long breath. "But Jeremy stepped in and rescued me. He had set up a security team around me, and he was disguised in a *Gestapo* uniform. He killed that officer. At first I didn't recognize him,

and I was terrified of him too." She sighed. "Paris was such a different place then."

"It was still that very different place just yesterday morning," Chantal exclaimed. "It seems like a century already, but only twenty-four hours have gone by since the *panzers* left the Hôtel de Ville."

Standing tall and straight at the other end of the boulevard, General Charles de Gaulle stepped forward to lay a wreath and re-light the eternal flame at the Tomb of the Unknown Soldier under the massive, stately arches of l'Arc de Triomphe. The throng crowding the streets surrounding the legendary monument observed the moment in profound silence. Then, as de Gaulle turned and the people saw the serene face of the general whose voice they had heard over the radio delivering hope for over four interminable years, they went wild, roaring out his name.

He first inspected units of the 2nd Armored Division spaced around the Place de l'Étoile. Then he returned to the base of the arch and faced southwest, where joyous Parisians lined both sides of the Champs-Elysées leading to the ancient Egyptian Obelisk in the Place de la Concord. A coterie of CNR officials, including Georges Bidault, followed as he began striding down the center of the long, wide, tree-lined boulevard. The citizens recognized the courage and defiance in de Gaulle's undertaking this mile-long trek, walking openly, protected on the ground by 2nd Division units but completely vulnerable to rooftop snipers. Their cheers thundered.

All night, the city's presses had run full tilt, printing out and distributing thousands of banners reading, "VIVE DE GAULLE." The people waved them furiously as the general proceeded at a measured pace. They crowded in and were held back by *gendarmes* and soldiers aided by Boy Scouts who locked arms and leaned their backs against the multitude.

De Gaulle continued his unhurried gait. The CNR cadre followed close behind, smiling and waving. He maintained an impassive countenance, gazing about and lifting his arm to wave periodically. Unknown was whether he was moved by the outpouring of affection, by the smiles of boys and girls, the tears of mothers and grandmothers, or the approbations of fathers and grandfathers. He continued undeterred toward the Place de la Concorde.

Along with the other Parisians at the southeast end of the Champs-Elysées, Amélie and Chantal watched as General de Gaulle continued his walk. They listened to the murmurs among the crowd as their regard for him grew beyond bounds.

He reached the Place de la Concorde and stood near the obelisk, acknowledging the throngs with waves. He did not smile, but his expression softened to one of deep serenity as he gazed across his fellow French citizens. His open-topped French Hotchkiss sedan waited for him, the back door open, with an attendant standing by.

Led by Chantal, the sisters nudged their way through the crowd until they suddenly found themselves within a few yards of him. They exchanged glances of disbelief that they had come so near. Chantal grabbed Amélie's arm. "He's going from here to Notre-Dame. If we hurry, we can watch the ceremony there."

"It's a mile away," Amélie protested. "We'll never make it in time. Not through all these people." To emphasize her point, she swept her hand in a wide gesture over the throngs.

With an impish expression reminiscent of her adolescent days, Chantal persisted. "We can try. He'll be here for a while, and his car will have to go slow, or he'll hit someone." She tugged at Amélie, who, with a sigh of resignation, followed her.

Barely had they started when a shot rang out, followed by another and another. The cheering was immediately quelled. The sisters hunched down and whirled. Across the Place and as far up the boulevard as they could see, most of the people had done the same or sought cover wherever they could find it, including behind the 2nd Armored Division vehicles. The soldiers and policemen too had ducked and were gazing around,

searching for the source of gunfire. People near its origin pointed, gunmen on rooftops scurried, and in an instant, the army's heavy guns blasted, aimed at the retreating figures and joined by rifle and pistol fire from FFI members and regular citizens.

Amélie and Chantal diverted their attention to de Gaulle. He appeared unperturbed, proceeding calmly toward his car with his same measured pace.

"Let's go," Chantal said. "We can make it."

The crowds were equally large in front of the grand cathedral. The sisters arrived out of breath, but well ahead of de Gaulle's motorcade. By darting through gaps and pulling Amélie along with her, Chantal led the way to the entrance.

Word had spread about the shootings, so the celebration had become muted as people exchanged looks of concern. Within minutes, however, the jubilation reignited as de Gaulle's car drove into view. It steered to the main entrance, the Portal of the Last Judgment. He stepped out of the sedan, smiled slightly, and bent down to accept bouquets of yellow flowers from two small girls.

As he straightened, more gunfire resounded across the square, apparently coming from the cathedral's towers. People hunched in place or scurried for shelter. The 2nd Division and armed citizens returned fire, chipping the gargoyles and sending bits of granite flying. General Leclerc, having joined the procession at the church, admonished his officers with his cane to restore order.

De Gaulle ignored the disturbance and continued into the interior.

Amélie and Chantal exchanged thrilled glances as, once again, he passed within yards of them. As he made his way toward the aisle engulfed by his entourage, Amélie took in the magnificent artistry of the arched stonework high over her head. As she did, more shots rang out, this time inside the cathedral. They came from somewhere high above the floor within the shadows of the vaulted ceiling.

With no place to go, the congregation crouched as one, seeking whatever shelter was offered by the prayer benches. De Gaulle continued down the left aisle, turned at the head of the nave, and took his place of honor before the transept.

A voice boomed, echoing from the stone walls, "Have you no dignity? Stand up!"

Amélie raised her head and glanced across the hunkering congregation. Another tall general stood behind de Gaulle. He faced the people angrily. "This is our moment," he shouted. "We will not let terrorists steal it."

"Who is that?" Chantal asked.

Amélie shrugged, but she stared in awe at the general's courage.

Hearing Chantal's question as the congregation took to its feet, a nearby man said, "That's General Koenig, the commander of the FFI."

The firing continued sporadically, apparently intended to intimidate, as it traced across the ceiling but was not aimed into the crowd. The officiating priest appeared and took his position to lead in reciting the Magnificat. At the end of each section, when he paused for the congregation's repetition of verses he had just read, de Gaulle's voice resounded above the others. When the recitation was finished, as if perceiving that with the intermittent gunfire continuing the service was pointless, the general made his exit with the same measured pace.

The people followed, Amélie and Chantal included. "Do you believe it?" Chantal enthused. "Not once did he lose composure. Not once did he flinch."

Suddenly, she gasped. When Amélie turned to her, Chantal had flushed red. She stared, and then pointed. General Leclerc was nearing the exit with his retinue of officers. Among them was an officer in British uniform. His hair was dirty-blond.

Amélie inhaled sharply. Her breath came in short bursts and blood drained from her face. For a moment she felt glued to the floor.

Chantal grabbed her hand. "It's him, it's Jeremy," she shouted. "Let's go." She yanked Amélie back to awareness and pushed through the crowds, reaching the massive doors.

Outside, de Gaulle had continued his deliberate walk to his waiting car, stopping to accept flowers from little girls, return the salutes of little boys, comfort black-garbed widows, and bestow his appreciation on the people. General Leclerc and his staff followed behind a few feet, including the British officer.

De Gaulle climbed into his car while Leclerc continued on to his half-track. His staff waited while he clambered aboard.

Chantal shoved her way through the tight throng, pulling Amélie along and disregarding annoyed bystanders. When they were a few feet from the vehicle, the officer started to board its rear.

"Jeremy," Chantal shouted with all her strength, "Jeremy Littlefield!"

The officer halted and turned.

"Jeremy," Chantal shouted again, "Jeremy Littlefield. It's Chantal and Amélie."

He turned full about, facing them, and they were both brought up short. He looked enough like Jeremy, but he appeared older, even accounting for war's stresses. Seeing him up close, Amélie's face dropped in disappointment. His eyes were brown. Jeremy's were green.

He peered at them curiously. "Which one of you is Amélie?"

Dismayed and embarrassed, Amélie lifted a hand. "I am," she said meekly. "I'm sorry, we thought you—"

The officer's face broke into a full smile and he threw his arms around her. "Amélie! I've never had the pleasure, but I know all about you"—he turned to Chantal—"and your sister. I'm Paul, Jeremy's brother."

Amélie and Chantal ambled through the crowds along the Champs-Élysées back toward Georges Lamarque's apartment. Thrilling as the day had been, made even better by encountering Paul, the disappointment on finding that he was not Jeremy and had no news of his brother clouded the celebration with personal disappointment.

Amélie tried to join in the festivities and not nurse her aching heart. After all, Chantal was in the same state, knowing nothing about Horton's whereabouts, and others across Paris grieved the loss of loved ones killed as recently as yesterday in the fighting. Even this morning, vile snipers on the rooftops brought anguish to a glorious day.

Paul had been extremely happy to meet the Boulier sisters and had taken their contact information with a promise to see them that same evening. For her part, Chantal maintained high energy for the few minutes they spent with Paul, but she also fell into glum silence as they meandered along.

Memories surfaced for Amélie as they strolled the streets. She walked Chantal by the café where Jeannie had signaled the urgent need for a meeting and past the outdoor market where she had sold flowers on her first foray to Paris as Jeannie's courier. "That was painful," she said. "That was where Jeremy first came to watch out for me, but we couldn't talk to each other or indicate that we even knew each other."

They passed the butcher shop where Amélie had worked on her second foray to Paris for the same purpose. "I lived with that family. They were very nice."

"Do you want to stop and say hello?"

"Not now. I will another time. I owe them a great deal of thanks."

They crossed a bridge over the Seine where, so many times before, Amélie had stood in line at a checkpoint, terrified that she would be found out as German guards inspected her papers. She shuddered, but then forced a smile. "It feels so good to cross here without fear."

They turned onto their street. Ahead of them on the left was a park that spanned several blocks, and across from its center was the entrance to Georges Lamarque's apartment. Amélie observed it, glad to see it full of people on this beautiful day, but she felt a sense of melancholy over the mini-dramas that had played out there.

Several benches were spaced around the park in front of small gardens. Happy Parisians occupied every seat, enjoying freely the pleasure of each other's company. "This park was always so empty," Amélie told Chantal. "People would stroll through, but they wouldn't linger." She pointed out a particular park bench. "I've sat on that one many times with Georges, and with Madame Fourcade and Jeannie. We'd sit there to observe if we were being watched before entering the apartment."

They went on and mounted the low stairs to the apartment entrance.

While Amélie fumbled with the keys, Chantal continued absently observing the park, the benches, and the one that Amélie had pointed out.

It was occupied by several people. Chantal tried to imagine dark nights with her sister sitting there either alone or with one of her Resistance comrades, watching this door before finally deciding that entry was a safe proposition.

As she watched, a man stood up from the bench and started toward the street. He was thin and his clothes hung on him. His hair was grown out though not long, and his face was covered with several days of stubble.

Chantal had watched him only because he made his way through the crowd in their direction, but when he reached the street, he crossed and walked straight toward them. Chantal's breath caught. His hair was dirty-blond.

Chantal nudged her sister. "Amélie, turn around."

"What? I'm having trouble with this key."

"Turn around, sister."

An urgent note in Chantal's voice caught Amélie's ear. She turned rapidly, and then brought her hands to her face as tears poured from her eyes. Dropping the keys and her handbag, she ran down the two stairs, along the short walkway, and leaped into Jeremy's arms.

68

August 27, 1944

"General, Paris is not secure."

General Eisenhower heard de Gaulle's statement in disbelief. "I don't understand. You're here. Your government is here. Your 2nd Armored Division forced the German surrender. After the parade and the events at Notre-Dame yesterday, you have your people in the palm of your hand. The details were widely reported. I came to congratulate you."

Despite his generous approbation, Eisenhower remained somewhat rankled. He had been unaware of de Gaulle's plans for his entry into Paris and ceremonious seizure of French national authority. Before those events, Eisenhower had ordered his staff to search far and wide across the front to determine the French general's whereabouts.

The two men now met in the War Ministry offices with only their interpreters joining them in case they were needed. Though de Gaulle always preferred speaking in French, which he touted as the most beautiful language in the world, he spoke English now with a heavy accent. He knew that Eisenhower had studied French but had gained no conversational ability with it.

"Civil order is not firmly restored," de Gaulle said. "I am sure that the shootings at the Place de la Concorde were done by German and Vichy *Milice* snipers still in the city. But the firing over the people's heads at Notre-Dame had to be the Communists, intending to intimidate. We are still investigating.

"Our people celebrate, but the war is not over. The hard part of liberating all of France and bringing peace to our country still lies ahead. Political parties on the left and right intend to seize power, and both will resort to violence to achieve their objectives. The Communists are the strongest of the major factions. If we don't defeat the left, this country will fall to communism, but if we don't curtail the right, France will fall to the ambitions of bureaucrats. Neither is good for France or western civilization."

Eisenhower remained silent as he contemplated de Gaulle's assertion. At last he said, "How can I help?" Without waiting for a response, he added, "You know, two of my commanders, Bradley and Gerow, are not particularly happy with your General Leclerc. Gerow caught wind of yesterday's parade and ordered Leclerc not to participate without his direct approval. Leclerc did it anyway."

De Gaulle waved away the comment. "Leclerc operated under my orders. I loaned the 2nd Armored Division to the Allies. I could certainly borrow it back for a few days to re-capture our own capital and restore order. Besides, the Germans threatened a counterattack northeast of Paris, and we dispatched a combat task force to stop that."

Recognizing that the Allied effort in Europe was a collective effort of many nations, Eisenhower contained his irritation. "How can we help?"

"We must re-establish civil authority," de Gaulle replied without hesitation. "The Communists are attempting to assert their control over policing. Meanwhile, the CNR has grand designs on becoming a permanent force in the government with its own palace and expansion of its own volunteer police organization."

"How are you going to control that?"

"Send me military and police uniforms. I will formally absorb the FFI into the army and bring all the parapolice organizations into the lawfully constituted *gendarme*. Law enforcement will be the sole responsibility of officers duly appointed by this government.

"Members of the FTP will be invited to join, but if they refuse, their organization will be declared an illegal insurgency and its members arrested. Most are patriots and care nothing for leftist ideology. They will gladly cross over.

"Regardless, we must cease the vigilantism rampant in the streets now, with women's heads being shaved on the mere accusation of having slept or collaborated with the Nazis. Citizens are conducting their own open courts and trials. And as the food situation worsens, crime will rise. We have to manage all of that."

Eisenhower contemplated the request and the thought process behind it. "All right. We can supply the uniforms. Those are good steps. What else?"

"We need a show of force. Our people need and want the rule of law, but our government is not yet strong enough to enforce it alone. You have the 4th Division camped at Vincennes Forest. Would you please send a regiment to march down the Champs-Elysées just like we did yesterday? The gesture will signify that the Allies are behind my government."

Eisenhower drew back in hesitation. "You want me to buttress the authority of your provisional government with the full force of the United States and the Allies?"

"That is correct."

The American general took a long, deep breath. "I can order the march, and people can draw their own conclusions, but you know our president has consistently refused to recognize your government. Besides that, we need those soldiers for operations north of Paris. They'll march through and continue on into combat."

"The show of force is necessary," de Gaulle countered. "Please relay to President Roosevelt my respectful request that he reconsider his opposition and recognize the provisional government of France as legitimate.

"As you said, I have the people. I can promise that, with Allied support, our country will go forward as a democratic republic." He paused and took another breath. "I can also say, with equal assurance, that any attempt to govern France as a military protectorate will lead to greater violence."

Silence. Then Eisenhower said, "I'll take that under advisement. Anything else?"

De Gaulle nodded and sighed. "We must have food," he said solemnly.

"The Germans stripped our supplies, which were already sparse. The Paris food stores are near starvation levels. Everyone knows it. Fulfilling that request will do as much to build confidence in the new government—"

"Consider that request done. We'll have it here within two days." Eisenhower stood and paced across the floor, deep in thought. After a long interval, he said, "General de Gaulle, I can commit to a major US unit, at least a division, marching down the Champs-Elysées, and to delivering tons of food, probably both by the day after tomorrow. We can work on plans for longer-term supplies. I also promise to broach the subject of recognizing your government with the president. However, I can provide no confidence regarding how he will respond."

De Gaulle bowed his head slightly. "I understand, General. You've always been considerate of our people and courteous to me personally. That is much appreciated. Thank you also for coming."

EPILOGUE

Same Day, August 27, 1944
Sark, Guernsey Bailiwick, Channel Islands

Dame Marian Littlefield sat alone on a trunk in the storage room at the back of her house. A single bulb cast dim light over a stack of luggage to her front, the vestiges of valued personal possessions belonging to friends who had left them in her care for the duration of their absence from Sark. Most of those friends had been deported to German internment camps, and the same fate had befallen her husband Stephen. When entering this room, Marian always wondered how many would return to reclaim their suitcases and trunks. *How many are still alive?*

Having stationed her two emaciated poodles to sound the alarm while she listened to the BBC, she was reasonably confident that she would be unmolested and have time to hide the radio in its regular place should someone approach the house. Her diminutive frame was as withered as those of her poodles.

Still, today's news had given reason to smile. Paris was liberated, and the Allies pressed on toward Germany. "We're looking to have our troops home by Christmas," the announcer said.

"By Christmas," Marian murmured. She hugged her arms to her chest. "Maybe I'll live to see Stephen and my children again." Picturing each one of them, she whispered their names in the order of their births. "Paul, Claire, Lance, and little Jeremy." She smiled. "I'll see you soon."

August 28, 1944
Stony Stratford, England

Claire hung up the phone with a sigh of relief but with mixed emotions. She had just spoken with Paul, who was with Jeremy, Amélie, and Chantal in an apartment in Paris. All were well, he said, including Lance, although Paul did not know his whereabouts. He had been assured by SOE HQ of Lance's good health.

Despite the good news, Claire continued to worry about the conditions on Sark Island in general and the welfare of her parents in particular. Making matters worse, with the Germans blocking all Red Cross messaging, Claire had no way of communicating with her mother. She sighed and went to find Timmy playing in the back garden. He came running to her, and she crouched next to him. "I just spoke with your Uncle Paul," she said. "Do you remember him?"

Timmy stared back with uncertain eyes and shook his head.

She laughed, suddenly wondering when she had last seen her older brother. "I don't suppose you would." She tousled his hair. "What about those two nice sisters, Amélie and Chantal. Do you remember them? They were with us last Christmas."

Timmy nodded. "I 'member they spoke in Fwench," he said with wide, serious eyes.

"You are right," Claire said, amused at his childish mispronunciation. "Your Uncle Paul is in Paris there with guess who?"

Timmy thought for a moment. Then his eyes opened wide and he yelled, "Jermy!"

Elsie joined them. "He's awfully excited."

Claire stood up straight. "Yes. I just spoke with Paul. We talked about the BBC broadcast reporting that our troops might be home for Christmas. Paul said it's possible but unlikely. We still have the rest of France to cross and then Germany. He said the most optimism he would give it at present was to keep our fingers crossed."

"Then we should do just that."

Timmy tugged at Claire's skirt. "Gigi, when is Jermy coming home?"

Claire smiled down at him. "Soon."

"Yay!" Timmy celebrated, jumping up and down.

Claire gazed at Timmy and sighed. *Who gets to keep you when he does?*

Massif Central, France

Roger and Pauline walked together through a high meadow overlooking a placid lake in the mountains southeast of Paris where they had worked together over so many weeks. Pauline paused on a promontory to take in the view over the wide valley. She breathed in deeply. "Everything is still so green, but autumn approaches. Leaves are starting to fall. And the countryside is so peaceful." She sighed. "Breathing without looking in every direction for lurking danger feels strange, and yet so pleasant." She faced Roger. "Paris is free."

"Paris is free," Roger repeated. "Only days ago, that seemed impossible."

"And it would have been without you."

"Oh, I tried to do my part, as did you, and so many other good people."

"What's ahead for us now, Roger? What's next? Our jobs here are pretty much wrapped up. We'll never hike these mountains together again. The people we grew so close to, who we fought with, will now live in our memories. We're unlikely to see most of them again. Huet, Chavant, Jeremy—"

Melancholy engulfed Pauline. She sniffed. "I'm getting emotional. I don't mean to." She stood silently, a slight breeze blowing through her short hair.

Suddenly she turned, threw her arms around Roger's neck, and buried her head in his chest. "I love you, Roger. I always will. You've been my rock these past weeks, and I'll never forget you."

Roger caressed her arms and kissed her forehead. "I love you too, in a way that I can never love anyone else."

Pauline stepped back and tilted her face to look into his eyes. "You have your wife and son to go back to. You should do that as soon as possible—"

Roger chuckled. "As soon as SOE releases me."

"Me too."

"And then what will you do?"

Pauline exhaled a deep, anguished sigh. "I don't know. I think Poland will be gone—under Soviet dictatorship. I won't be able to go back. But—" She caught herself and forced a smile. "I'll land on my feet. For the time being, I'll wait to see what SOE wants me to do next."

They lingered a while, soaking in the peace and tranquility, and then they ambled slowly down the mountain.

August 29, 1944
Paris, France

"That was a tremendous parade," Jeremy said as he dropped onto the sofa in Lamarque's apartment. "General Eisenhower was very gracious to have the American 28th Infantry Division march through Paris, though I hate to think that those soldiers went straight to another battle.

"Regardless, between Leclerc's division on parade three days ago and the one today representing the US Army, those were the most powerful symbols anyone could hope for to establish who's in charge in France with full Allied backing. De Gaulle must have been pleased. And now that President Roosevelt recognizes his government as legitimate, the country can start its reconstruction. I think civil war in France is averted."

Amélie nestled contentedly next to Jeremy. Watching her from a chair across the sitting room, Chantal smiled but then looked away distantly.

"I see your point, Jeremy," Paul interjected, "but I think the internal problems of the country are far from over. A power vacuum still exists, and it'll be filled by criminals until de Gaulle gets the police back up and running. The black market flourishes. His move to bring the vigilante groups into the police and the Resistance groups into the army was smart. They'll be paid employees of disciplined organizations with real jobs to do, and they'll help restore order to the rest of the country."

"That overflight with tons of food cannisters parachuting in was a welcome sight," Amélie chimed in. "People see that they're being supported by our government and our Allies. Our prospects for a bright national future are real."

"So, what are your plans now, Paul?" Jeremy asked. "You seem to get along awfully well with General Leclerc."

"Yes, well, he requested that I remain with him as a liaison and that's been approved. The war's still on, and he intends to be in the thick of fighting all the way to Berlin. Oh, and I inquired about Lance through MI-9. He escaped from Colditz again shortly before the invasion—"

Jeremy sat straight up with a start. "That's thrilling to hear. Where is he? What's he doing?"

Paul chuckled. "Yes, it's good to know he's still with us and apparently in one piece. He fought with a Resistance group in Brittany. He's since been seconded to the Jedburghs, but I haven't a clue who they are or what they do. I'm sure, though, that he'll see all the action he could hope for. I do hope he quenches his thirst for adventure. What about you? Where do you go from here?"

"I've been granted a few days' leave," Jeremy replied. He put his arm around Amélie. "And I intend to make the most of it right here in Paris. I'm still assigned to SOE, so after my leave is up, I'm at their disposal."

"Well I'm joining the Rochambelles," Amélie declared.

"The what?" Jeremy asked. Chantal returned her attention to the discussion with a puzzled look.

"I know of them," Paul interjected. "They're a group of nurses in Leclerc's command. He thinks very highly of them, I can tell you that."

"The Rochambelles," Amélie repeated, nodding. "I noticed them the other day among Leclerc's troops during the parade. They were women in French army uniforms. I inquired about them. They're highly trained ambulance drivers and nurses, and they've been everywhere with the 2nd Division since North Africa. They'll continue with the division through northern France and then into Germany. I've been in touch with Raoul Nordling, the Swedish consul. With his help, I hope to get more information on Jeannie. We know she's in Ravensbrück. I think that if Leclerc's division is near Berlin, I might have a chance to rescue her."

Jeremy took his arm from around Amélie, leaned forward with his elbows resting on his knees, and exhaled in obvious frustration. "I'll be glad when this war is over and our worries about each other are just the normal ones." He raised his eyes to gaze around at the other three. "We're always wondering if one of us has been killed in combat, or worse, taken by the *Gestapo*."

"Your point is well taken," Paul interjected, "but I think that the *Gestapo* is less of a threat now, even in northern France. Germany's main concern is getting its army back within its own borders." While he spoke, he noticed Chantal's withdrawn appearance. He shifted his attention to her. "I've also inquired about your Sergeant Horton, Chantal," he said kindly. "I'll let you know the instant I hear anything."

She glanced at him bleakly, wiped her eyes, and nodded quickly by way of thanks. "I'll keep on fighting in the Alliance," she murmured numbly. "As long as Horton's in the fight, I will be too."

A hush fell over the group. Jeremy broke it. "I saw our cousin Zack a few weeks ago. He was field-promoted to second lieutenant. I worry about him, though. Right after I saw him, he was on his way to Montélimar, and that's still a mess down there."

"I heard that it's pretty much over," Paul said. "Some of the Nineteenth got through, but they're heading back to Germany as fast as they can, and they've been reduced tremendously.

"I got a letter from Josh a while back. The US had just recaptured Guam and was preparing for a campaign against the Japanese home islands. That will be one fierce fight." He shook his head. "When I spoke with Claire, she mentioned a visit from Sherry. She said that Sherry looked worn but healthy." Leaning back with an admiring expression, he added, "Treating the worst of the wounded on aircraft flying from combat zones would wear anyone down. She has my utmost respect."

A knock on the door interrupted the conversation. It was soft and rapped out in the recognition pattern of days gone by. Amélie and Chantal sat bolt upright and spun around to face the door. Amélie reached for her pistol and then laughed nervously. "Force of habit," she said. "I felt my heart stop again. I suppose that reaction will take years to go away."

The knocking sounded again, and she went to answer the door. "It's Hérisson," a woman's voice said quietly.

Amélie turned the knob and jerked the door open, beaming in surprise. There stood Madame Fourcade. Wordlessly, the two women stared at each other for a moment, and then embraced. Then Amélie stepped through the doorframe to glance about in the hall. "Isn't Georges Lamarque with you."

Fourcade shook her head. "The action in northern France and Belgium is heating up," she said. "Georges is kept quite busy. I won't be here long myself."

As Amélie stepped back inside and closed the door, Fourcade glanced across the room at Chantal's mournful face. Greeting the others as she crossed the floor, she took Chantal in her arms. "I have something for you," she said, and then rummaged in her handbag. "I heard through SOE that Jeremy and Amélie had found each other and that you were here, but I had no word about Horton. So I did some inquiries, and then I sent some Alliance members to find him. Here."

She handed Chantal a brown envelope. "This came by wireless through official SOE channels. It's short, but it came from him."

Chantal gazed at her with wondering eyes. Then she took the envelope and opened it with shaking fingers.

"By the way," Fourcade added, "your Horton's been credited with taking down a German tanker legend, one Michael Wittman." Seeing that Chantal's eyes were studiously on the message and paid her no mind, she chuckled. "I'll tell you about that later."

As Chantal read, her eyes brimmed with tears and then widened, bright with joy.

"Dearest Chantal," the note read, "I landed in Normandy at Arromanches—"

Chantal sighed as she recalled, vividly, searching among the British soldiers landing there and wondering if Horton was among them. *We were so close.*

She continued reading. "—but I'm alive and well, perhaps a little worse for wear. I love you dearly, and I think of you night and day. When this war is over, if you'll have me, I intend to marry you. Don't worry, I'll get down on one knee and ask you proper. All my love, Horton."

STORMING THE REICH
Book #8 in the After Dunkirk Series

As winter casts its long shadow across Europe, the pulse of battle beats louder, drawing the Littlefield family into the fray of the Siegfried Line and beyond.

Jeremy Littlefield stands at a crossroads, his loyalties torn between two continents. On the verge of departing for Burma, he faces a crucial decision: heed the urgent call of the Pacific Theater, or remain in France to support the Resistance alongside his beloved Amélie. Each choice carries the weight of survival, not just for himself, but for those he might leave behind.

Meanwhile, in the secretive confines of Bletchley Park, Claire's world of codes and ciphers exposes a desperate German ploy to turn the tide of the war. The success of the Allied forces hangs on her ability to crack these messages; failure could spell disaster.

In the thick of the action, Paul, with the 2nd French Armored Division, orchestrates and leads daring assaults deep into enemy territory. His tactical prowess is crucial as the Allies push through the Siegfried Line toward the German heartland.

At the same time, Lance, embodying undaunted resilience, escapes captivity once again. His return to the Resistance fuels a series of perilous sabotage missions designed to dismantle the enemy's operations from within.

AUTHOR'S NOTE

Picking names for characters can sometimes become tricky, particularly when writing historical fiction and using the real names of real people. For instance, when writing about the events in the Vercors, I had the similarly sounding names of Eugène Chavant and Abel Chabal. That was easily resolved by referring to the two men as Chavant and Abel respectively. Still, with the occasional reference to Chantal Boulier in that sequence of events and whom I had consistently referred to by her first name throughout the series, I had to take extra care to be clear for readers about the person I intended to mention on any particular occasion.

That dilemma popped up when writing about the intrepid Yvon Morandat and his fiancée, Celeste, as the two set out on his bicycle to take possession of the Hôtel de Ville, the Paris city hall. As much as possible, I attribute real actions to the actual persons. In this case, the fiancée's real name was Claire, and of course, that is the first name of our heroine at Bletchley Park, Claire Littlefield. So as not to cause confusion, I changed the real Claire's name to Celeste. However, in the interest of giving proper credit for courage where it is due, this is to inform that the young lady who rode on Yvon's handlebars through the running Parisian gunfights to assist in taking over city hall was Claire, whose last name, subsequent to the couple's wedding, became Morandat. To Claire Morandat go our thanks for her part in securing the freedoms we all enjoy.

ABOUT THE AUTHOR

Lee Jackson is the *Wall Street Journal* bestselling author of The Reluctant Assassin series and the After Dunkirk series. He graduated from West Point and is a former Infantry Officer of the US Army. Lee deployed to Iraq and Afghanistan, splitting 38 months between them as a senior intelligence supervisor for the Department of the Army. Lee lives and works with his wife in Texas, and his novels are enjoyed by readers around the world.

Sign up for Lee Jackson's newsletter at
severnriverbooks.com
LeeJackson@SevernRiverBooks.com